THE LION IS HUMBLED

THE LION IS HUMBLED

WHAT IF GERMANY DEFEATED BRITAIN IN 1940?

BOOK ONE OF THE THOUSAND YEAR REICH

BY
ROBERT BLUMETTI

iUniverse, Inc.
New York Lincoln Shanghai

THE LION IS HUMBLED
WHAT IF GERMANY DEFEATED BRITAIN IN 1940?

All Rights Reserved © 2004 by Robert Blumetti

No part of this book may be reproduced or transmitted in any form or by any means, graphic, electronic, or mechanical, including photocopying, recording, taping, or by any information storage retrieval system, without the written permission of the publisher.

iUniverse, Inc.

For information address:
iUniverse, Inc.
2021 Pine Lake Road, Suite 100
Lincoln, NE 68512
www.iuniverse.com

ISBN: 0-595-32651-X

Printed in the United States of America

Contents

Chapter 1:	STACKING THE DECK	1
Chapter 2:	THE SCRAMBLE FOR PEACE	20
Chapter 3:	ONE HAND WASHES THE OTHER	50
Chapter 4:	TOTAL WAR	74
Chapter 5:	NORTHERN LIGHTS GO OUT	94
Chapter 6:	THE LOW LANDS LAID LOW	117
Chapter 7:	DISASTER AT DUNKIRK	140
Chapter 8:	THE FALL OF FRANCE	154
Chapter 9:	IL NOSTRA MARE	171
Chapter 10:	RED STAR-BLACK SWASTIKA	187
Chapter 11:	PANZER ROLLEN IN AFRIKA VOR!	208
Chapter 12:	THE SUN NEVER SETS ON THE BRITISH EMPIRE?	225
Chapter 13:	VICTORY!	237

Chapter 1

▼

STACKING THE DECK

Movement in the bedroom woke him from a sound sleep. His eyes opened but he didn't move. The room was dark, with only the star light through the window to temper it. He was sleeping on his left side, with his left arm tucked under two large pillows. A blanket and down comforter pulled up and over his head. He listened and heard the sound again. "Blondi? Is that you, girl?" He called to his German Shepard bitch, who always slept in the corner of the room where her own bed was located. "Is that you, Blondi?" he repeated, but he heard nothing. He listened for a couple of seconds, and was about to close his eyes and go back to sleep, when he heard his dog whimper.

"Blondi, what is it?" He pulled the covers off him and was about to investigate what was troubling his dog, when the darkness of the room disappeared in a flashing white light.

"My God in heaven!" He raised his arms to cover his eyes from the blinding light that flickered, as he struggled to make out what was causing the illumination. He feared a fire had started, but he felt no heat. The light was intense and pure white. He noticed there was no smoke. His eyes quickly adjusted to the brightness and saw what looked like a human form. It was clad in a silver suit of some kind. Where its face was suppose to be, there was a large, black shiny visor. It seemed as if it was struggling with a black device that it held in its hand. He wanted to shout for help, but couldn't find his voice. The light continued to flicker, but there didn't seem to be any source for the light. It just seemed to appear and disappear, encasing the silvery figure in a phosphorescence halo. This was followed by an electrical discharge that seemed to race about the figure's silver suit. He finally discovered his voice and began shouting for help.

"Guards! Guards! Someone is in my room!"

The figure backed up a few steps, as it continued to fumble with the black box it was holding.

"Who are you? What are you doing here?" he shouted at the top of his lungs.

The double doors to his bedroom burst open and two armed guard jumped into the room, as the mysterious figure disappeared in a final burst of light. The light in the outer hallway invaded the room until one of the guards flicked on the light switch on the wall, next to the door. The other guard moved further into the room and began searching for the intruder.

"There! There! Check in the corner! Check behind the cupboard!" he began ordering to the guard.

Footsteps could be heard racing down the hallway, as the house came alive in the commotion.

"What is it?" a beautiful young woman asked, as she entered the room through a side door that led to another bedroom.

"Adi. Dear Adi. What is it? Who is there?" she tried to calm him down, as she joined him on the bed and cuddled him in her arms.

"I saw someone. Someone was in the room, I tell you," he kept repeating.

"Search the entire room!" shouted an officer dressed in a black uniform.

"We should get out, Adi," the young girl insisted. "Let the guards search the room."

She helped him get out of bed as the officer held up his silk bathrobe. He put it on, but before he left, he stopped and turned around. "Where is Blondi?" he asked. The dog wasn't in her bed.

"I found her!" one of the guards announced.

The dog was cowering in the corner. She was terrified and wet herself.

"Good Lord! What happened in here, my Fuehrer?" the SS officer asked Adolf Hitler.

The large, deep blue Mercedes rolled down the mountain road, noiselessly and effortlessly. The auto-hydrogen burning engine was almost soundless. The huge vehicle represented the height of Western technology. Only the wealthiest people possessed anything like it. They were monuments to the European civilization that long ago collapsed under the weight of two billion people that now populated the continent. The high quality automobile included all the comforts a man of vast wealth and power, as Heinz Kruger could afford. Herr Kruger never concerned himself about money. He belonged to an exclusive circle of some three thousand families that dominated Europe. In the last one hundred and fifty years they engineered European unification, and transformed the European Union into the number one superpower in the world. This was accomplished in the Twentieth-first Century, after the Russian Federation joined the EU in 2056. This unification came about ten years before the United States dissolved into a dozen, warring ethnic enclaves.

Herr Kruger often thought how easily and rapidly the United States degenerated, from the only superpower at the beginning of the Twentieth-first Century, into a balkanized expanse of ethnic and racial conflicts. The population of the United States exploded in the Twentieth-first Century. After the last restrictions on immigration were removed, and the United States borders were thrown open, the multitudes of the Third World poured in. By 2060 there were over six hundred million people in the United States, and the European-Americans were reduced to only a fifth of the population. When the Chinese challenged the US over control of the Panama Canal, six southwestern states all voted to succeed from the United States and formed the Aztland Republic. The Mexican majorities in these states expelled or killed all non-Hispanics. The new Aztland government declared the crisis with China an "Anglo" problem. The United States government was too weak from internal divisions, due to its ethnic diversity, to oppose the succession of the Southwest. Within the next thirty years other ethnic enclaves declared their independence until finally, the United States disintegrated into several dozen warring states. Canada soon suffered the same fate. Race wars among competing groups were on such a scale that the atrocities of Rwanda, Bosnia, and Cambodia of the Twentieth Century paled in comparison.

The thought of what happened to the United States and Canada terrified the ruling families of Europe in the late Twentieth-first Century. Third World immigrants flooded into Europe during the Twentieth and the early Twentieth-first centuries. Unlike America, Europe never possessed a immigration "heritage." Europeans at first resisted the arrival of Third World peoples. But, an alliance of socialists with dreams of an egalitarian paradise, and trans-nationalist corporations, seeking cheap labor, eliminated all restrictions on immigration, permitting the entry of millions of Third World immigrants into Europe to replace the dwindling European nationalities, due to low birth rates. The European superstate lacked a constitution, or a Bill of Rights, similar to the United States. There was nothing to hinder the ruling establishment from creating a totalitarian state to maintain order. As racial and ethnic conflicts increased in Europe, an oligarchy of about three thousand European families soon controlled this totalitarian super state.

The large Mercedes passed into a suburb of Bern. Herr Kruger looked out of the tinted window. The scene of his thousand acres estate still populated by Europeans who maintained the Kruger estate, disappeared. The Swiss landscape soon changed into a sprawl of poverty-stricken villages, filled with dark faces of different hues belonging to East Asians, Africans, Moslems, Hindus and limitless, nondescript mixtures, resulting from intermarriages over the last one hundred years. The once perfectly manicured fields and columns of trees that lined the well-kept avenues of Europe were replaced by tumbledown homes, pocked with decaying walls and broken windows, shutters hanging askew, with goats and chicken running loose among the debris and endless numbers of vagabond children with dirty faces, eating whatever garbage they could find.

Hardly any white faces could be seen. The European population was restricted to small pockets in such places as northern Scotland, the forests of Scandinavia, the mountainous regions of the Balkans and in the northern areas of Russia. The only Europeans that could be found throughout the rest of Europe were on the estates of the wealthy families that still ran the continent.

Herr Kruger looked away. His face froze, steel-like in hatred for the reality of the Twentieth-second Century. He hated his class for permitting this to happen to Europe. He had warned the others of the impending danger that Europe faced, but they didn't listen. He was a young man back then, and the leaders of United Europe laughed at him when he talked about blood, heritage and family. All they care about was wealth—the almighty Euro. He thought to himself how wrong the old saying was. Power doesn't corrupt, and absolute power doesn't corrupt absolutely. Oh no. It was not power, but wealth that corrupts, and overwhelming wealth corrupts overwhelmingly. It especially corrupts power and those who weld it, just as it corrupted the ruling classes of Europe. Herr Kruger continued to think back when he was a young man. He thought of his wife and children, and the prospect for a better future he once hoped for them. Oh yes. He had dreamed, but all his dreams had turned into one terrible nightmare. A nightmare from which he could not wake—the nightmare of the Europe of 2123. All he wanted now was to put a stake through the heart of this nightmare world. He dreamed of putting an end to this horrible reality created by greed and stupidly, once and for all. To undo everything that had happened. He sought to ease the burning pain. It especially hurt when his only daughter ran off with a Nigerian doctor, and later, when she was beaten to death by her African husband in a fit of rage. It was as if someone had thrust white-hot irons into his heart. He refused to recognize the five mixed-blood grandchildren that she brought into the world. Just as he refused to remember the death of his only son, who was pulled from his automobile in the race riots of 2061, beaten senseless, and burnt to death because of the color of his skin. Someone had to pay for the alleged crimes of the White race, and his son was unfortunate enough to be in the wrong place at the wrong time. It mattered not to his murderers that has son had devoted his life to assisting immigrants entering Europe. The only thing that mattered to the mob, when they put the burning auto tire around his neck, was the color of his skin.

Herr Kruger did not cry. He had no more tears to shed. He used them all up when his wife died from a broken heart. That was fifty-five years ago. A long time ago. A life time ago. Herr Kruger never remarried. He was wealthy and powerful, and soon discovered he was not alone. There were others who belonged to the ruling class of wealthy Europeans, who felt like him. They too had loved their families, and hated to see their heritage, history and culture dry up and evaporate like water in a desert. And like him, they had grown hard and cold with hate. Hatred for everything around them. Hatred for the world that was slowly sinking into the swamp of barbarism. Hatred for those who came before him and built this Hellish world. Hatred for an Europe dying with a whimper, like a beaten dog. He would make them pay. Even though they were all dead, he would reach back through time and erase them from the chronicles of history.

Despite the lost and pain, Herr Kruger went on living well into old age. He would be one hundred years old later this year. He had been the product of Twentieth-first Century technology—a technology that had mastered aging through genetic engineering. It was now common for people, at least for those who could afford it, to live well pass one hundred years of age. How ironic, he thought that the Western science had developed the means for Western man to live on within the Hell that Western man had created for himself. But the small group of people he belonged to within the ruling oligarchy of wealthy families were now determined to use this science to rectify the mistakes of the past. Europe's religion, culture and heritage were all dead concepts now. The only thing left of European man was his science. And they saw it as their only salvation. This small band of men and women had pooled together all their wealth for one purpose—to develop the means of undoing the present. They lived in a world where there was no future for them. So they decided to use their wealth and resources to end the nightmare that imprisoned them and tormented their souls.

The Mercedes now turned onto a highway. Herr Kruger was glad. The transformation of his Switzerland into a poverty-ridden, filth-spewed approximation of the Third World sickened him. He could no longer stand to visit larger cities like Zurich and Bern. They were transformed into overcrowded, broken down slums that seemed more like the squalor of Calcutta, Cairo, or Capetown. And it was even worst in the once beautiful cities of Paris, Rome, London and Vienna. The highway was elevated. Its raised height shielded him from the squalor of the Bern suburbs below. His vehicle raced over one hundred miles an hour. Soon it reached the exist, and made its way through the rolling hills to the "Colony." It was a subterranean compound built within the security of the Alps, hidden away from prying eyes. It housed the most advance scientific equipment, and administered by the most brilliant scientists in the world.

This region of the Alps was classified top secret and off limits to all but specially select personnel. Private troops patrolled the region. Herr Kruger's car came to a guarded gate, which opened automatically. The car passed through the gate and proceeded along a heavily wooded road. It led to a huge steel door build directly into the side of a mountain. The door opened and the car disappeared down a tunnel. Kruger's vehicle finally came to a stop in a subterranean chamber far beneath the mountain. An uniformed orderly dashed to the car and opened the door.

"Good morning, Herr Kruger," he said, as the old man stepped out. He looked at the orderly and thought how beautiful a specimen of European manhood he was. What a lose, he thought to himself. What Europe must have been like three hundred years ago?

"Good morning," he said, maintaining a formal demeanor. The orderly closed the door and the car spun away. Herr Kruger walked energetically to a well-lit entrance that led to an elevator. Two heavily armed guards snapped to attention as he disappeared into the elevator.

In seconds, Herr Kruger was descending three hundred feet straight down, until the elevator finally came to a halt. The doors opened and he stepped out into the Colony's main complex. He stood on a raised platform. Below him he could see people in grey lab coats, busy about their assigned tasks. Rows of computer consoles filled the huge chamber, and were manned by an army of technicians and scientists. Voices blared orders over an intercom system. The constant humming of powerful engines could be heard. The entire complex was a great hive of activity.

A tall grey-haired man, well over seventy years old, but possessing a youthful appearance of a man closer to forty, noticed Herr Kruger. Doctor Ziegler immediately discontinued his conversation with several technicians and greeted him.

"Good morning, Herr Kruger."

Kruger did not return the greeting. "I hope there will be no more unforeseen misfortunes, Herr Doctor. I trust today will not be a rerun of yesterday?"

Kruger's remark didn't phase Ziegler. The Doctor began walking along side Kruger.

"I'm sure it will not only be a better day, but perhaps the last day."

The Doctor's dry wit was not lost on Kruger.

"Does that mean you don't expect any problems?"

"Everything has been tripled checked this time, Herr Kruger. We can't afford any further mistakes or our entire project will fail."

Kruger stopped and faced the Doctor. "Good. And the coordinates have also been tripled checked?"

"Yes. We are confident that we can retrieve Herr Hitler from the coordinates that we have. Our teams have researched the coordinates very carefully. The next possible time for a successful retrieval is during the last week of September, 1939. Of course, even the most reliable historical records can't be 100 percent certain. But we are sure that Herr Hitler was alone on the designated point in time. If there should be another person with him, it most likely will be Fraulein Braun. We'll be able to render her unconscious as well."

"Is there no earlier date that we can retrieve Herr Hitler from?"

"You mean, before the start of the Second World War?"

"Yes."

"Unfortunately, no," the Doctor said. "Not if we want to maintain the maximum possibility of success."

"Too bad. It would be better if we could avoid the start of the Second World War, all together."

"But our program for this eventually is well thought out," the Doctor said. "In fact, it should have a better probability of success than if we prevented the start of the war, the course of events that will follow will be less certain."

"If we fail, when is the next possible date of retrieval?"

"In December of 1939—still within the window of greatest possible chance of changing history according to our desired goal."

"Make sure we are successful this time, Herr Doctor."

"Yes, Mein Herr."

Just then, another elderly man with straight, white hair approached. He was slightly older than Kruger, but just as vigorous.

"Good morning, Heinz," Jean Le Beau smiled.

"Good morning, Jean."

"Has Dr. Zeigler filled you in on the progress we've made?" Le Beau patted Dr. Zeigler on his back and smiled.

"Yes, he has."

Le Beau could see the apprehension on Kruger's lean face. "Don't worry, Heinz. The Brotherhood has complete confidence in this project." Le Beau laughed softly. The three men began walking down the corridor. "The mishap was due to the effect of time travel on the equipment. The temporal distortion disrupted the immobilizer. It malfunctioned when our tempornaut tried to use it on Herr Hitler. He was forced to abort the mission when Hitler began calling for help. But he's sure no one but Hitler saw him before he disappeared. It was our first attempt, and we had no way of knowing what effect the temporal field would have on our equipment. The Brotherhood expressed their apprehension about such matters. It was to be expected. There are bound to be mishaps."

Kruger's blue eyes glared at Monsieur Le Beau. "We can't afford too many such mishaps."

Le Beau ignored Kruger's glare and continued to speak smoothly. "We have taken additional precautions to prevent them from happening again."

"I'm sure you have, but I wish we could retrieve Herr Hitler from an earlier date, before the war broke out," Kruger shook his head. "It would give us more options."

"It can't be helped," Le Beau said. "The date of September 26, 1939 was chosen as the earliest one in which we can be sure with any certainty that Herr Hitler was alone in the Chancellory, in Berlin. He had just returned from touring the battlefield in Poland. It's just four weeks after the beginning of the war, and we can at least direct the entire course of the war from this date. On September 27, Hitler will make a major speech to his General Staff on the future course of the war. We have downloaded every possibility, known and speculated. Her Hitler will be programed to make all the right decisions necessary to ensure a German victory, early in the war."

Kruger's eyebrows rose high and his head nodded in approval. "I suppose you're right. When can we begin?"

"We will be ready in slightly less than three hours," Le Beau smiled. "The time machine has been powered up. Our technicians have been checking everything all night. Nothing will go wrong this time. Isn't that right, Dr. Zeigler?"

"That's correct, Monsieur Le Beau."

Everything was prepared for a second try. The time machine was once again at full power. The technicians were busy at their stations, double checking the coordinates. The tempornaut was suited up and standing by. Power relays were humming. The time machine began to cut a tunnel through time and space, reaching back to September 26, 1939. It did this by forming a quantum singularity within an electromagnetic containment field. The computers had to pinpoint the exact location and time in the past. Then the temporal tunnel had to be kept open and the tempornaut sent through. The amount of power necessary to perform these tasks was enormous. Herr Kruger and the Brotherhood were powerful enough to requisition the energy needed from very part of Europe and Russia.

"Are we ready, Dr. Zeigler?" Kruger asked. He stood with hands clasped behind his back. Even at his advanced age, he refused to sit. His icy blue eyes stared straight ahead. His face was frozen and motionless with cold indifference.

"The final countdown has begun, Herr Kruger," Dr. Zeigler reported.

"Counting—fifty-nine, fifty-eight, fifty-seven..." the voice over the intercom announced.

The tempornaut was now in place within the time chamber, and the technicians were quickly making last minute adjustments to his equipment. Loud speakers blared orders, over the countdown. "Thirty-eight, thirty-seven, thirty-six..." The power relays began to glow with a buildup of energy. The technicians finished and left the time chamber. The glass doors closed and the tempornaut was locked in place.

"All hands, prepare for send off," the voice over the intercom announced "Eleven, ten, nine, eight..." The countdown continued without problems. The send off chamber began to fill with engulfing light and consuming the tempornaut.

"Ready for send off," the voice announced. "Three, two, one, send off!"

The light within the chamber flashed nova-bright and then instantly faded into nothing. The chamber was now empty.

"The tempornaut has been successfully sent to the past," the intercom announced.

"We have a stable temporal tunnel," a technician reported. "Temporal gate holding nicely."

A few minutes later the intercom announced the tempornaut's progress. "Subject has been sedated and ready for retrieval in three, two, one."

The chamber once again flashed with an intense light that instantly disappeared. In the chamber was the tempornaut in his silver suit. Lying on the floor of the chamber before him was Adolf Hitler. He was sedated and still dressed in his pajamas. The tempornaut removed his helmet and took a deep breath.

Technicians raced to the chamber as the glass doors opened. The sedated figure of Adolf Hitler was lifted onto a dingy and immediately removed. His life signs were monitored by medical personnel.

"Success!" Monsieur Le Beau was visibly pleased. The entire crew of the control room was shaking hands and congratulating each other.

Herr Kruger remained stone-like and outwardly unmoved by the successful spiriting away of the Fuehrer of the German Reich. He was not prone to pre congratulation. There would be time enough for that after Hitler was returned to the past, but then it wouldn't matter. Would he even exist? Kruger wondered if his time line would continue, or would they simply cease to exist? The thought of nonexistence didn't frighten him. His heart long ago had turned to cold, hard steel. It had become a burden, weighing heavy in his chest and crushing his soul. He longed for release from the pain he suffered. That could easily be achieved through death. No! He thought. That would be too easy. He didn't want release, but revenge—revenge against the universe. Revenge on those who caused the death of his family, his heritage, his race, and their future. He would welcome nonexistence, like the Gods in Wagner's *Gotterdammerung*. Better to bring an end to this nightmare and then hopefully his children, if they are ever born in the new time line, will be born into a nobler and better reality. A reality where there is still hope for his race, his people, and for a glorious future. And for the rest? Damn them all! Damn them for what they did to Mother Europe. Damn them for how they defiled her, raped her and poisoned her. If life could not be noble—then it was not worth living.

Adolf Hitler was rushed into surgery. All his life signs were monitored and maintained on life support. Every precaution was taken to make sure nothing would go wrong. They couldn't afford to let anything happen to the German Fuehrer. If he should die, all their plans would come crushing down on their heads. Hitler was kept under sedation and would remember nothing of what was being done to him. Surgeons rushed to prep him. He was placed on a specially designed table that held him in place. His head was locked, motionless. Restrains were used over his entire body to immobilize him. There was no fear of him waking, but every precaution was taken to prevent his head from moving.

The table Hitler was on slowly moved into a horizontal position. His head was actually held back so that his nostrils were facing straight up. A small laser from above was beamed directly into the left nostril. This was merely to make sure it alined a probe suspended from above. A team of several surgeons were in the operation room with Hitler.

"Alinement is set," a surgeon said.

"Prepare to insert," another surgeon said.

"Probe is ready."

The leader of the team of surgeons checked the coordinates.

"Begin the descent."

The probe slowly and silently began to move toward Hitler's face. It looked like a mechanical arm, long, silvery and metallic. At the tip of the probe was a needle-like appendage. It continued to descend until it was right above the left nostril and stopped. Then, a long and very thin protrusion extended from the needle probe into the nostril. It was snake-like and could easily and effortlessly moved through the nasal passage without causing any damage internally.

"The probe has reached the cribriform plate."

"Activate the laser."

The plate was porous. A tiny laser in the probe was able to cut a pin-size hole in it, and then passed through, reaching the frontal lobe of Hitler's brain.

"The probe has entered the frontal lobe."

A surgeon watched the computer-guided probe's progress into the frontal lobe on the monitor. If he had too, he could alter the passage of the probe, but the coordinates programed into the computer were perfect.

"The probe has reached the lateral prefrontal cortex."

"Proceed with the insertion."

The probe instantly inserted a computer chip, smaller than a grain of sand.

"Insertion has been successful."

"Begin the withdrawal."

Once it achieved its task, the probe retreated through the cribriform plate, and sealing it. The probe quickly passed out of the nasal passage and the procedure was complete.

Herr Kruger watched the entire procedure from the observation room with other members of the Brotherhood. They stood before a large window. They could hear and see everything that took place. Everyone listened carefully. No one spoke until the operation was complete. A collective sigh of relief was heard.

"Now that the computer chip is in place, in the lateral prefrontal cortex within the subject's frontal lobes, it has already established links with Herr Hitler's brain," Dr. Zeigler explained. "The brain has billions of neurons that interact. It establishes links to the neurons in the frontal lobe and acts like a somatic marker, establishing a positive responds to certain ideas, words, names and theories that we have programed into the lateral prefrontal cortex in each hemisphere of Hitler's brain. This region of the brain deals with solving novel tasks, keeping many things in the minds at once, and screening out irrelevant information. It is crucial to high-level thinking. In this way, we can literally program the proper response by Herr Hitler to different military strategies, weapons' development programs, or make him more willing to listen to the advice of certain individuals. We have also downloaded certain information, such as atomic theory that would convince Herr Hitler to develop the atomic bomb, and recognize which theories and scientists to listen to, and know who is lying or telling the true."

"It sounds very simple," Le Beau said.

"Actually, the program is extremely complex. There are literally billions of bits of information contained within the chip. It will respond by detecting not just one word or name, but a combination of factors. Each combination will initiate the proper response causing Herr Hitler to make the correct decision."

"What about detection?" A young Italian gentleman asked.

"There is no possibility of detection while Herr Hitler lives," Dr. Zeigler said. "The chip is so small that it is undetectable by mid-Twentieth Century medical technology. Her Hitler won't feel anything and will never know that he has been altered. Only after his death, will there be a possibility of detection, and we have prepared for that eventuality."

"What about x-rays that were in use during Herr Hitler's lifetime?" Kruger asked.

"If the subject should be examined by x-rays, the chip will show up as a spec so small that no one will give it much thought. There is a possibility that someone might think it a cancerous growth, but after time, they will see that it has not grown and will most likely explain it away as an anomaly, or a harmless growth.

"Don't worry, gentlemen. The technology we used is the most advanced. Not even the Chinese or the Japanese have anything even close to what we have achieved."

"How can we be sure it will have the desired affect?" a general with a distinctive Russian accent, asked.

"As I explained before, the chip has already established links with the neurons in the frontal lobes. The chip is programmed to change certain ideas in Hitler's philosophy. Through the rest of his life, the subject will receive ideas from the chip whenever he is confronted by a certain situation. He will not realize that his decision-making process is being influenced, and will think they are his own ideas. After he is returned, he will immediately begin to change the course of the war, and the history of the world. The first year after he returns will be the most crucial, because once Herr Hitler makes decisions that changes the course of history, the probability of knowing the outcome will decrease. As the years progress his changes will become more profound. This is why we have tried to include every possible scenario that could arise from each alternative."

"This must work," Herr Kruger said.

"We all share your desire, Herr Kruger," Monsieur Le Beau said. "We have scoured the world for the highest caliber scientists and doctors for this project. Never before has such a team of skillful and brilliant men and women been collected in one place. If what we plan can succeed, this facility can do it."

"I don't doubt that," Herr Kruger said. "But everything depends on the most meticulous attention to detail. Even the slightest miscalculation can result in disaster. We can't afford even the most minute mistake."

"We are well aware of what is at stake," Le Beau said. The others nodded in agreement. Kruger remained unmoved. His voice dropped several dozen degrees. "There will be no more mistakes. Once Herr Hitler is returned to his time, there is no way we can make any alternations."

"The subject is being prepared for his return to 1939," Dr. Zeigler reported. "Return is schedule for thirty minutes."

"Proceed as planned," Kruger said.

Dr. Zeigler spoke into his intercom and ordered the technicians to prepare the German Fuehrer for the return trip back in time.

"This is it, gentlemen," Kruger said with hands clasped behind his back. He turned and looked at his colleagues and raised his eyebrows. "I must look into the face of the devil before he is returned to 1939." He then turned and left the observation room.

His voice sent chills through the others. The entire Brotherhood was driven by the same desire to change the course of history as Kruger, but they did not share his fanaticism.

The technicians were busy preparing the sedated Hitler for the return trip. The control room was bustling with heightened expectation. Everything they had planned and worked for during the last twenty years was about to come true.

"All systems are go," the voice boomed through the intercom. "Time and location are confirmed."

"Ready the chamber."

Hitler was rushed to the time-chamber. Once within it, he was lift off the dingy and placed on the floor in the same position he was in when he was apprehended. Before the doors to the chamber was closed Herr Kruger appeared and entered the chamber. He stood over the comatose body of Adolf Hitler. Dropping to one knee he examined the face of the most hated man in history. Kruger was taught from early childhood that Hitler was the personification of all that was evil in the world—the devil incarnated. He believed it all his life, and now this most detested man was lying before him, helpless and unconscious. His face looked ordinary and uninspiring. There was nothing about it to reveal anything out of the ordinary. If he had passed by him on the street, he would probably not have taken notice of him. It was his eyes, cold and blue that were reputed to posses hypnotic, Svengali-like qualities. But his eyes were closed and he was sure they would not radiate anything unusual in his state of unconsciousness. He wondered what Hitler's reaction would be if he woke him now? He was curious about what it would be like to speak with him. But that was out of the question. It would undo all his work. Herr Kruger could hear the countdown.

"One hundred and twenty-three, one hundred and twenty-two, one hundred and twenty-one, two minutes, one hundred and nineteen…"

Kruger stood up and marched out of the chamber and made his way back to the observation room. Once there he rejoined the others. He could hear the countdown.

"Eleven, ten, nine…"

Kruger turned to the others. "Well, gentlemen, prepare to meet oblivion." His cold, hard white face stretched into a devilish smile that caught everyone off guard. They never saw him smile before and now wished they never did.

The time-chamber began to fill with light. It grew in intensity.

"Three, two, one, send off."

The white light continued to grow brighter. It soon spread out of the time-chamber and filled the entire control room, but it did not recede. It continued to expand until everyone was blinded by its brightness. Hitler disappeared, and instantly, so did the reality of 2123.

Adolf Hitler walked into the conference room where his supreme commanders of the German Armed Forces were waiting on September 27. He had no memory of what had transpired the night before.

"Attention!" The command caused everyone present to stand at attention. Hitler raised his right hand to the level of his face in a modified Nazi salute.

"Gentlemen. Please be seated," Hitler said. He took a seat in the center of the conference table and placed his notes on the table before him. Generals, admirals and field marshals shifted in their chairs, waiting for their Fuehrer to begin. Finally, Hitler looked around the conference table. His blue eyes searched from face to face. Finally, he coughed and then began the conference.

"This morning Warsaw has surrendered. The Campaign in Poland is over. All there is left to be done, is round up of the last remnants of the Polish army." Hitler was interrupted by applause. He raised his hand to continue. "But the war is not over. I've decided that Great Britain and France will never accept any peace proposals that we might offer. They will never agree to the rectification that the German Reich has made in the East. Therefore, we have no choice but to pursue this war to a victorious conclusion in the shortest possible time."

"My Fuehrer, if I may?" General von Brauchitsch interrupted. Hitler nodded for him to continue. "With General Halder assistance the Army has investigated the possibility of an offensive against Britain and France. Our force can nip in the bud any attempt by the enemy to invade German territory, but we will need time to prepare for an attack. Half of our tanks had broken down or were disabled in the assault on Poland. Even if they were in good shape, they could not stand up to the French tanks. We will need to wait until our new Mk. III and Mk. IV tanks have been repaired. They might have a chance of standing up to the enemy tanks and anti-tank guns. But we won't have enough of them until October of next year. If we conduct a defensive strategy, motorize some infantry divisions, demobilize some units to permit skill workers to return to their factories and plan for long-term recruiting, training and equipping our forces we should be able to attack in the West sometime in the Spring of 1941."

Brauchitsch leaned back, confident of his argument. General Franz Halder nodded his agreement with Brauchitsch.

Hitler stared at the two generals. He let the silence linger a while. Leaning forward he stared at the two generals. The generals began to shift uncomfortably in their chairs. Hitler's icy blue eyes could cause the most steel-hearted men to squirm. "We achieved a great victory in Poland because we applied revolutionary tactics with National Socialist fanaticism. But great victories have little enduring luster. We must ready out forces for a quick and decisive victory in the West. That's why I am issuing Directive # 6, putting the German Reich on a total war footing. The entire economy will be converted to a war economy. Our workers will have to work increased hours, and though I'm not yet ready to begin draconian rationing, we will have to ask out people to make sacrifices. I will need someone of exceptional qualities—someone who can mobilize our industries with the utmost efficiency. That's why I asked you to attend this meeting, Dr. Speer."

Albert Speer's eyes opened wide. He was sitting at one end of the table and had felt out of place sitting there with so many of Germany's highest ranking officers. He thought Hitler called him to the meeting because he wanted him to take over the construction of the fortifications of the West Wall. After all, he was an engineer and architect. "Me, my Fuehrer?" was all he could think of saying.

"Yes, Dr. Speer, you," Hitler said. "I know you will do an excellent job."

Before Speer could say another word, Hitler returned to his monologue.

"I am determined to triple U-boat, panzer, and aircraft production in the next nine months. Development of new and advanced panzers, aircrafts and U-boats will be accelerated. I want a three hundred U-boat fleet ready by the full of 1940."

Hitler stopped and fixed his gaze on Admiral Raeder who favored the production of large surface ships. Admiral Doenitz, who sat next to Raeder, smiled. He had disagreed with his superior and believed Germany could knock Britain out of any way a submarine fleet of three hundred.

Hitler continued. "We'll continue with our plans to build the *Bismarck* and the *Tirpitz* battleships, but if the war is drawn out into 1941, the only way to take down the obstinate British will be through economic strangulation. This can be only be accomplished with our U-boats.

"There will be no invasion of the West before May 1940." Eyebrows rose on the faces of the other officers. They had been trying to convince Hitler that any invasion of the West should wait until the next spring. Hitler had disagreed with them. He had wanted to invade the West in November 1939. His sudden reversal surprised them.

"I'm convinced that the British and French won't attempt a direct attack on our Western Wall. But any invasion of the West will have to include the occupation of Belgium, Luxemburg and the Netherlands. It has come to my attention that General von Manstein has proposed a new and radical plan for the invasion of the West. It involves penetrating the Ardennes Forest with a strong panzer force. It sounds bold and innovative, just what we need to win this war quickly and decisively."

Hitler looked at General von Manstein. "I want a complete proposal of your plan before me within one month, Herr General."

"Yes, my Fuehrer," the General said.

Manstein's superiors were not pleased. They were of an older generation and didn't understand the new panzer weapon. The plan they thought of was a variation of the von Schlieffen Plan. Hitler had just made a loyal supporter of General von Manstein.

"I'm also convinced that the British might try a diversionary maneuver. In the Great War, the British were obsessed with assaults on secondary fronts. They attacked Gallipoli, Palestine, Greece and Mesopotamia. They most likely will try this again by attacking Scandinavia. Our Reich receives vital supplies of iron ore from Sweden. The British might try to invade Norway and halt the ore from reaching Germany. If they do, we must be ready to move first. I want a plan drawn-up for just such an eventuality. For this to succeed, our intelligence must not be compromised."

As Hitler spoke these words, hatred swelled up from deep within him. It was a black, hard hate fed by thoughts that coursed through his mind. Canaris! The name shouted within his mind. Traitor! Hitler locked his eyes on the Admiral sitting at the end of the table. The hard, blue gaze pierced Canaris' heart, turning him ice cold with fright. He shifted in his chair. Hitler continued to stare without saying a word. Canaris was overcome with a terrible anxiety. His stomach knotted up and felt green around the gills.

"Excuse me, my Fuehrer. I think I'm ill." Canaris rose and rushed out the door. Everyone watched with shock and horror the way Canaris retreated. When he had disappeared, everyone looked at Hitler.

"I fear the Admiral's health has taken a turn for the worst." No one said anything as they exchanged looks and wondered what the Fuehrer meant.

"That brings us to the Mediterranean," Hitler continued. "On second thought, I'm now glad Il Duce decided to keep Italy neutral. The Italian armed forces are exhausted from the wars in Ethiopia and Spain. It's better Italy and Spain remain neutral. If they were to enter the war on our side, they might suffer defeats by the British and French in the Mediterranean, and we would be forced to divert badly needed forces in Europe to assist them. No! Let them remain neutral."

The General Staff nodded in approval. The German officers didn't have much faith in their Latin friends.

"I'll eventually communicate with Il Duce and General Franco and assure them of certain territorial rewards for their friendship and neutrality. If we overrun France next spring, and Britain refuses to surrender, then we can bring Italy into the war and strike from Libya through Egypt and into the Middle East. By taking the oil-rich Middle East, Britain will be dealt a blow from which she will never recover.

"This brings me to the matter of weapons' development." Hitler pushed back from the table and slumped into his chair. He brushed back the lock of hair that swept down across his forehead. "I estimate this war will last about a year to eighteen months. We might suffer a million deaths. That's why I've decided to go over to a total war footing. We'll increase production of tanks and fighters, as well as every class of weapons necessary to knock out France first, and then Britain within one year. That is why I'm issuing Directive # 7, which calls for the speedy development of new weapons."

"What type of weapons, my Fuehrer?" Brauchitsch asked.

"Last month the Heinkel Company successfully test flew a jet powered aircraft named the He178. It is the first jet-powered aircraft. I want it developed and massed produced by next summer."

"But, my Fuehrer," Brauchitsch interrupted Hitler. "You decided that it was not necessary to develop the jet aircraft. That we would have to divert valuable resources needed for production of the Stuka aircraft, which you felt was sufficient for our purposes."

Hitler raised his hand. "Enough! I'm looking beyond 1940, Herr General. After Britain and France are subdued, the German Reich will still be faced with a much greater menace in the East. I'm speaking, of course of the Soviet Union. God knows I never wanted war with the West. I've always believed that Germany's destiny laid in the East. But the Jew-ridden Western powers were bent on war. I thought the West would not go to war without the support of the Soviet Union. That's why I was forced to make a deal with Stalin. I had to choose between Jew-capitalists and Jew-communists.

"Stalin made a pact with us, not because he sympathizes with our cause. No! He wants time. He hopes Germany, France and Britain will destroy each other in a long and bloody war of attrition. When we are exhausted, Stalin will not hesitate to launch an attack against the German Reich from the East. Perhaps in the summer of 1941. That's why we must develop new weapons.

"Along with jet fighters, we need to resurrect the development of the Ural-bomber. Our two-engine bombers will be useless in a war with the Soviet Union. Research will be conducted on the possible construction of a jet-powered bomber that will have the capacity to bomb Soviet industrial centers in the Ural Mountains. Another weapon that we should seek to develop was proposed by the scientist Werner von Braun. He has been conducting experiments with rockets in Peenemunde. We should give the Doctor and his rocket some consideration.

"I'm also concern about the shortage of trucks. We need to build a truck hardy enough to keep up with our panzers, and easy enough to build in mass quantities. These trucks will be invaluable in any future war with the Soviet Union. I don't want to rely on horse-drawn carts to supply our troops. Our panzers can't be held back because of a poorly developed supply system. We might get by in any invasion of France, but in any future war with the Soviet Union, it will slow down our panzers, and that could cause us a victorious conclusion to this war. That's why I'm ordering Directive # 8, the development of a more efficient supply system.

"I'm also issuing Directive # 9, the enlargement of our airborne troops. We need to have a force of two hundred thousand such airborne troops by the summer of 1940. If Britain does not sue for peace, we might have to land troops in England by air, or on Gibralter and Malta in the Mediterranean Sea. It will be essential to knock Britain out of the war if she proves stubborn.

"Gentlemen, I did not plan a major war, but it looks like we have one on our hands. I'm determined to win it as soon as possible. Britain and France must be brought to their knees no later than the end of 1940."

Hitler stood up. Everyone else did the same. This was the single that the meeting was over. As everyone filed out of the room, Hitler asked his Foreign Minister, Joachim Ribbentrop to remain.

"Herr Minister, there is an airplane at the Berlin airfield," Hitler said, as he asked Ribbentrop to sit. "It'll take you to Moscow. Stalin is waiting for you. You'll settle the details of the final partition of Poland."

"But my Fuehrer, I..."

Hitler raised his hand and Ribbentrop shut up.

"It is imperative that you meet with the Soviets tomorrow. I do not want any revision of the agreed borders. Our troops had to pull back from the Bug River to the Vistula, and I don't intend to send them back. Stalin wants Lithuania in return for extending our frontier to the Bug River, but I will not give him Lithuania. It will be a strategic jumping off point when the time comes for our invasion of the Soviet Union."

Hitler began to laugh.

"My Fuehrer?" Ribbentrop asked.

"I was just recalling how Goring suggested we demand to include the Bialystok region within our zone of occupation. He is after all a member of the 'the green freemasonry of men' and is interested only in the forests of Bialystok. All he cares about is hunting the stags that live there. He talks of woods, but he really means stags! Let the Soviets have Bialystok."

"I understand, My Fuehrer," Ribbentrop laughed with his Fuehrer at Goring's expense.

"Good! Remember, you will be laying down the definitive frontiers between Asia and Europe. Your's is a task worthy of the foreign minister of the Greater German Reich!"

Chapter 2

▼

THE SCRAMBLE FOR PEACE

In October 1939, events unfolded within unofficial channels between Berlin and the Western capitals, including Washington. Hopes for peace were lifted by the unexpected intervention of the influential American oilman, William Rhodes Davis. He arrived in Berlin with an offer directly from President Roosevelt. Davis met with Field Marshal Herman Goering and informed him of a ninety-minute conversation he had with FDR. The meeting was arranged by John L. Lewis, the powerful leader of the labor union, the CIO. Lewis was neither pro-Fascist nor pro-Communist, but after visiting Nazi Germany, he came away impressed with the rise in living standards of the German workers. He feared that a long war in Europe could adversely affect the U.S. economy. To prevent this from happening, he convinced Roosevelt to agree to an unofficial peace mission led by Davis. Davis had his own concerns. He feared the war between Germany and the Western Allies would disrupt his oil business with Germany. After meeting with FDR, he immediately left for Berlin.

Davis presented Goering with a peace proposal from President Roosevelt. He told Goering that Roosevelt sought to exploit the situation, and to break Britain's monopoly on the global markets. FDR opposed Britain's declaration of war against Germany, and suspected Britain was never truly concerned about Poland's sovereignty, but sought to enforce the *"Dictat"* of Versailles and keep

Germany weak. Davis told Goering that FDR assured him that he supported Germany's claims on the city of Danzig, the territories Germany ceded to Poland after the First World War, the return of all former German colonies in Africa, and financial assistance.

Goering was surprised at FDR's favorable proposals. He especially was amazed when Davis conveyed to him Roosevelt's assurance that the U.S. would supply Germany with goods and supplies, convoyed to Germany under the protection of American armed forces, if Britain and France refused to comply with the peace proposals. Goering was also told that the CIO leader, Lewis, had threatened to prevent the manufacture of war supplies for Britain and France if they refused FDR's peace proposal. When Goering asked Davis what FDR expected from Germany, he was pleased at what Davis told him. Roosevelt asked for an independent Poland and some form of a self-government for the purely Czech areas to be arranged at some unspecified future date.

After the meeting with Davis, Goering went straight to Hitler and presented him with Davis' message. On October 3, Goering informed Davis that Hitler agreed to the proposal, including a new Polish state and an independent Czech government. He said that Hitler would present a peace proposal in his speech before the Reichstag on October 6 that would include all of FDR's points.

Davis immediately left Berlin and returned to Washington with Hitler's reply, but when he reached the U.S. capital, he was not admitted to the President. When he tried to find out why, he was rebuffed without an explanation. Davis never was able to meet with FDR again, and the proposals came to nothing.

On November 3, Goering met with Adolf Hitler at the Chancellory. He was wearing his sky-blue Luftwaffe uniform, decorated with an assortment of medals and gold braid, and he carrying his field marshals' baton. His jolly smile radiated confidence, though behind it he contained his anxiety over his failure to open peace negotiations with the Western Democracies. He appeared like a Germanic Falstaff, overweight, glamorous, magnetic and charming to the point that he was very unlike most of the other Nazi leaders. While Goebbels could be charming, he was always conspiring to assassinate the reputation of anyone who got in his way with his sharp wit and cunning mind. Himmler, completely lacked Goering's disarming personality and maintained a stoic persona. Rosenberg was a brewing intellectual, and Hess was a faithful follower who worshiped "his" Fuhrer. None of them possessed Goering's social contacts with the upper classes, both within Germany and in other countries. His connections, combined with his impeccable manners, plus his massive figure of vitality endeared him to the German public, and made him the most popular figure within the German

Reich, second only to Hitler. These qualities gave him an advantage in his quest to try and open a channel with the governments of Britain and France, in an attempt to end the war. "Canaris sang like a canary," Goering laughed as he reported to Hitler, of the incarceration of the former head of the German intelligence service.

"I don't know how you knew of his treason," Goering said, "but when you stared at him and all but accused him of treason, his backbone melted like ice under a hot light. My police arrested him trying to escape across the border to Switzerland. Once in custody, he broke down and spilled his guts, implicating General Hans Oster, General Georg Thomas, and General Ludwig Beck. We are investigating everyone associated with the Abwehr. It turns out that it was a nest of traitors, but we'll weed out every last one of them." Hitler's icy-blue eyes stared at his number two man. His face seemed fixed, revealing no emotions as he listened. He didn't say anything. "Canaris was spinning a web of sedation that led to the Foreign Ministry. The Gestapo has arrested Ernst von Weizsaeche and Albrecht Houshofer. Carl Goerdeler, the former mayor of Leipzig and Ulrich von Hassell, the former ambassador to Rome was also in on Canaris' treason. We are combing the ministry for their accomplices. Canaris was even drawing into it members of the General Staff."

"Who?" Hitler asked. Hitler's features now turned hard with hate. Names began racing through his mind. "Did he enlist Brauchitsch and Halder? What evidence did you discover?"

"Nothing that can tie either of them directly to the conspiracy," Goering said. He sat back into his chair. His blue eyes sparkled with delight. "Canaris and his cronies approached many Generals, as well as lesser officers in the military. Most turned him down, some feign interest but would not commit. Canaris did approach both Brauchitsch and Halder, but we haven't found anything incriminating. My Fuhrer, get rid of these birds of an ill omen. They can't be trusted. Neither are reliable, and both seek to undermine your plans for an offensive in the west. You saw their delight when you announced that you were postponing the attack against the west until next spring. Hell, they want to postpone the attack for two years. They have no interest in defeating our enemies and might even betray Germany to Britain and France. They are hoping for a defeat, as a pretext to moving against you."

Hitler waved his hand and his mouth contorted in a tight smile. "No, not yet," Hitler finally said. "Brauchitsch and Halder don't have the steel in them to move against me. You are right about one thing, they are hoping for a defeat. It would give them a justification to turn against us, but that won't happen. I assure you, we'll be victorious against France next spring. And in twelve months from now, Britain will sue for peace."

Goering was captivated by Hitler confidence. The Fuhrer never failed to lift his spirits. He seemed to possess some hypnotic power that made the listener see clearly what he wanted him to see. "You said you have some plan that will assure victory."

"Yes," Hitler said and smiled again. "But I can't tell you what it is, yet."

"Then you've rejected the modified von Schlieffen plan Brauchitsch and Halder came up with?"

"Yes. Yes. And let them go on thinking their plan is the plan we will use. Hopefully they'll betray us to the British and French. I can't remove them without evidence. Not yet."

"Yes, my Fuehrer," Goering said. His face flushed red as he rubbed his hands together. "But I must report that Mr. Davis has informed me that he has been unable to convey our willingness to accept President Roosevelt's proposals. He's tried to meet with the President, but has been denied access to the White House. I fear the proposals have been a subterfuge. For what end? I cannot say. But I believe Mr. Davis was sincere."

Hitler was listening carefully. He rubbed his chin. "I had hoped for a reply from the American President. I thought it was a long shoot from the beginning, but it would have been a cruel blow for London to be urgently advised by Washington to sue for peace." Hitler pushed his forelock of hair from his forehead. "But it doesn't surprise me. We've received dispatches from the Polish government's archives that clearly show that Roosevelt was goading Britain and France into war with Germany. He seeks time to rearm the United States and psychologically prepare the American people for war with us. One report recites a conversation by the American ambassador to Paris, William C. Bullitt, speaking of the President's desire for a war between Germany and the Soviet Union, whereupon the Western Democracies could attack Germany in the west while our armies are tied down in the east. Another report from spring, 1939, Bullitt quotes Roosevelt as saying that the United States would not participate in the war from the start, but would be in it at the finish. Roosevelt's apparently pushing Britain and France into war with promises of eventual American intervention. The Warsaw documents leave little doubt in my mind that the Poles refused our generous proposal for border adjustments and a German-Polish alliance against the Soviet Union because of assurance from Washington."

Goering was aghast at Hitler's revelations. "When do you think this could happen?" he asked."

Probably not until sometime in 1941," Hitler said as his hand cut through the air. He was clearly becoming agitated. "Roosevelt can't make any noises about going to war until after the election next year. The American people would never reelect him if he began pushing for war with us. The Americans are soft. They don't have the stomach for war. No! Roosevelt will talk of peace for the next year, while he secretly prepares for war. After he is reelected, he will try to bring the United States into the war. He is a puppet of the Jews that fill his cabinet. They are itching to bring the United States into this war. But they won't succeed. We will put an end to this war before the end of 1940.

"I'm also convinced that Britain wants war and will not agree to any proposals we submit, no matter how generous," Hitler said. "I've repeatedly extended the hand of peace and friendship to the British, only to have them try and bit it off. I wrote in Mein Kampf, fifteen years ago, that friendship with Great Britain was to be the cornerstone of my foreign policy. It has always been in the interests of Germany to ensure the survival of the British Empire. We have nothing to gain if Britain loses this war. The only ones who gain by Britain's demise will be the Americans, the Soviets and the Japanese. That's why I was so disappointed by Chamberlain's speech last month. He condemned our war with Poland and yet, have I demanded the British right the wrongs done to Egypt, India and Palestine? Britain could have peace with Germany at any time. Daherlus' attempt to broker peace has failed. London is in the grip of a Jewish-controlled, lunatic minority, centered around Churchill. He has been an agent of Jewish capitalists and journalists' agencies for the last ten years. Chamberlain is an impotent old man who has collapsed under the Jewish war party. I know. I remember what a spineless worm he was in Munich. There will be no peace with Britain until after she has been defeated. We have to prepare for an extensive campaign against Britain for the next year. But first we must break France. Once France is defeated, our forces will have to sweep Britain out of the Mediterranean and the Middle East. This will threaten the survival of her Empire. Only then will she sue for peace, but it will leave the British Empire in ruins, and that is not in our interests."

"What about the British Isles?" Goering asked. "We will invade England?"

Hitler stared off into the room, as if he was watching some scene unseen by Goering being played out before him. He shook his head. "No. Our navy is not up to it. We don't have the landing equipment needed to transport our armies across the English Channel. And even if we could secure air superiority, the British navy could still wreck havoc with any force we send against them."

"I'm sure my Luftwaffe could sweep the British RAF from the skies over the channel," Goering insisted. "I've already seen to the production of the Heinkel jet fighters, just as you ordered. We should have the first jets in operation by next September, and a Messerschmitt jet fighter by the spring of 1941."

"By then it will be too late for any invasion attempt," Hitler said as he shook his head. "The weather will not be right for an invasion, and I can't permit this war with Britain to drag into 1941. The danger of the United States entering the war is too great. It will upset my plans for a war against the Soviet Union. Stalin did not sign the non-aggression pact with us because he hopes we will win. He wants Germany and the Western Democracies to destroy each other in a war of attrition, just as it happened in the Great War. When he thinks the time is right, he will attack Germany. The jet fighters and the Ural-bomber will be needed for the future war with the Soviet Union. What I need from your Luftwaffe is a stronger airborne corp. We will need them in the Mediterranean."

"We'll have one hundred and fifty thousand airborne troops ready for the invasion of the West in May, and another one hundred and fifty thousand by August of 1940," Goering said.

"Very good," Hitler said. "It's imperative that our forces are up to strength by next spring. That's why I ordered the Reich to go on a total economic war footing. I know it will be hard on the population, and I fear a repetition of what happened during the Great War. Our armies were undefeated, but the suffering by the civilian population due to economic hardships snapped the national will to continue fighting. The only way to prevent that from happening again is to put an end to this war in twelve months."

"One last item, my Fuehrer," Goering said.

"What is it?" Hitler said.

"The matter of your security," Goering said. "With the arrest of Canaris' people there is fear that some conspirators who might have escape our net might try to assassinate you. Police reports fear that the greatest danger for an attempt on your life is between now and November 10. I suggest you tighten security and take extra measures to ensure your safety."

Hitler's piercing blue eyes seem to flash with an inner intuition. "A man must have faith in Providence," Hitler said as he slapped his knee. He put his hand over his heart. "One must listen to an inner voice and believe in one's fate. And I believe very deeply that destiny has selected me to make Germany great. I walk with all the confidence of a sleepwalker, sure that Providence will not take me away until I have fulfilled my destiny."

Both the Dutch and Belgium monarchs appealed to both sides in an attempt to end the war in early November. They feared that history would repeat itself, and their countries would once again become the battlefield for the conflict that was to come between Germany, and Britain and France. Their good intentions were met with rejection by Lord Halifax in a public speech that he made and outraged Germany's leaders. On October 6, Hitler made a speech before the Reichstag, calling for an end to the war. He did not make any public statement about the Low Countries' peace proposals. Hitler referred to the leaders of Britain and France as liars, murderers and hypocrites. He claimed that Britain and France wanted war and were being pushed into continuing this unjust war against Germany by International Jewry. He swore Germany would be victorious even if it meant destroying both the British and French empires. Hitler was convinced that the peace party in London had lost. British Fascist Leader, Sir Oswald Mosley had tried to intervene on the side of peace, but was imprisoned for his efforts, even though he swore that he would fight to defend Britain if Germany invaded the British Isles. Hitler was now convinced that Britain was determined to fight.

The British Secret Intelligence Service had been conducting secret rendezvouses with members of the German military, who claimed they were part of a conspiracy to remove Hitler from power, eliminate Nazism and put an end to the war. The meetings took place in the Netherlands, just across the German border. The British were meeting with a Major Schaemmel, a man close to the center of the German High Command, and someone on whom the British possessed a dossier. What the British didn't know was the real Schaemmel was sent to serve in Poland, and his identity was assumed by a young SS officer by the name of Walter Schellenberg.

Schellenberg was a brilliant, hard-drinking twenty-nine-year-old chief of SS Counterintelligence. He was handsome, dashing and full of confidence of the righteousness of National Socialism. He was in on the arrest of Canaris and sympathizers, and now was given this mission by Hitler himself. During October 1939 he met with British agents of the SIS and told them he sought their support in removing Hitler. The British told him they wanted the German military to remove Hitler from power, as well as his closest assistants, then peace would be concluded between Germany and the Western Powers. The terms were to be the restoration of Austria, Czechoslovakia and Poland to their former status.

When Schellenberg informed Hitler of the British proposals, Hitler didn't react. He listened carefully and thanked Schellenberg and promised not to forget his service to the Reich and to him personally.

It was raining in London on November 3, 1939 when Prime Minister Neville Chamberlain was holding a meeting of the British war cabinet. He wore his high collar as a badge of his loyalty to a past age when Great Britain was the singular super power in the world. His paler seemed pail the last few months, and he appeared tired. When questioned about it, he would say it was from the pressures of the last few years, actually, he was suffering from cancer.

"We have received offers from the governments of Holland, Belgium, Spain, Norway, Finland and others to help mediate a settlement between Germany and ourselves," Chamberlain said. He cleared his throat. His eyes flashed about the room. No one reacted. "Mr. Birger Daherlus told Halifax here that he met with Hitler on September 26. He said Hitler was prepared to guarantee the status quo of the rest of Europe. He was prepared to end the war and guarantee some form of independent Polish state, shrunken in size, surely, if we agree to end hostilities. He needed peace in order to cultivate his newly acquired eastern territories. He wanted to restore them to the German cultural sphere, and that would take fifty years. Even President Roosevelt has offered to act as an intermediary between us and Germany. I understand that President Roosevelt had been pressured by the head of the American labor union, the CIO, to send Mr. William Rhodes Davis to Hitler with a similar proposal. I believe Hitler told Mr. Davis that he would accept the President's proposals. The question I ask you, gentlemen, is, can we trust Herr Hitler? I have my doubts."

Winston Churchill, the newly appointed First Lord of the Admiralty rolled his cigar in his mouth and then removed it. He was dressed in a black jacket and stripped pants. His stocky body was slumped in his chair as if melted to conform to the chair's shape. He thought about Roosevelt's offer and was tempted to laugh. He was in constant communication with FDR ever since hostilities began two months ago. His communications with the President were secret, so he didn't tell the Prime Minister that Roosevelt had no intention of mediating. He knew that Davis would never get to see the President again. He was the only one present that knew the truth—that he and the President were in agreement that Great Britain and France should pursue the war to a victorious conclusion.

"I would not accept as truth anything Herr Hitler says," Churchill said. He took a gulp of whisky and continued. "He has proven himself duplicitous and untrustworthy in the past, and has not shown himself to have reformed his conniving nature. He has made promises of guaranteeing the integrity of other states before, only to break his word and seek additional territories. And what of the peoples that have fallen under the darkness of Hitlerism? What fate awaits the Jews during those fifty years?"

Chamberlain swallowed. "I understand from Dahlerus that Hitler proposes the creation of a reservation in the east, in which he intends to settle the Jewish population within those territories under German control."

"If that truly is his intent? But I would not trust the fate of those Jews under his control to his good intentions," Churchill said.

"You are probably right, Winston," Chamberlain said. The tone of the Prime Minister's voice was agreeable, but the expression on his face revealed his annoyance with Churchill for bringing up the Jewish question. Churchill never made it a secret that he supported the Zionist cause in creating a Jewish state in British-controlled Palestine. Successive British governments had wrestled with the question of the future of Palestine. Pro-Arab elements within the British establishment opposed additional Jewish settlements in Palestine, for fear of alienation of the Arabic populations under British controlled territories. Churchill had been a champion of the Zionist cause, and it contributed to his political exile in the years leading up to the outbreak of this war.

"I say we make it clear that it is the policy of Great Britain, to let it be known that if Germany wants peace, then Herr Hitler must step down," Churchill said. "Tell the Germans they must get rid of Hitler. Hitler's elimination! That must be our war aim."

"But if the Germans removed Hitler that could plunge Germany into civil war," Edward Halifax, the Foreign Secretary, said. "Frankly, I doubt the Germans would remove Hitler, even if they wanted to. He's to popular with the people. He just defeated the Poles and now sits on his conquest, ending the possibilities of a two-front war. I believe we have the next move, and have to decide what that is."

Churchill pressed down on the handles of his chair to help himself lean forward. His pink face was fixed in a bulldog expression of tenacity. "If the next move is our's to make, then we should do something decisive. I suggest we send a foray of battleships with fifteen inch guns into the Baltic Sea. This will confound that paperhanger in Berlin. His links with Scandinavia will be severed, and the flow of precious Swedish iron ore through Norway will cease. Our ships can continue to patrol the Baltic with the support of oil tankers to keep them fueled."

"Winston," Halifax said with a note of exasperation. "Any fleet we send into the Baltic will be under the umbrella of German fighters and outside our fighters' range. Besides, how can we keep the German U-boats from sinking our tankers? This is a foolhardy notion."

Churchill grunted, but did not argue. "If we are too squeamish," he raised his eyebrows and glanced at Halifax as he said the word, "then at the least, we can mine the waters off the coast of Norway to prevent the ships hauling the Swedish iron ore from Norwegian port of Narvik to Germany."

"Won't that mean violating Norway's neutrality?" Chamberlain asked. "How moral is that?"

Churchill leaned back in his chair once more. "It's absurd to consider morality. Morality is simply a question of fashion changing, as she does between long and short skirts for women." Chamberlain was about to respond, Churchill ignored him and continued.

"We're fighting to reestablish the reign of law and to protect the liberties of small countries. Our defeat would mean an age of barbaric violence, and would be fatal not only to ourselves but to international life of every small country in Europe. The struggle we find ourselves in, with that stinker in Berlin, gives us the right, and indeed the duty to abrogate the very laws we seek to reaffirm."

Chamberlain stared with disbelief. Shaking his head and taking a deep breath, he finally spoke, "Really, Winston, you can't expect us to crawl in the muck with Hitler? We would be no better then him if we should begin violating the neutrality of other countries. But I do agree that the offer of peace that Hitler presented in his speech on October 6 before the Reichstag has less substance then the smoke from your cigar." Everyone chuckled, including Churchill, who began puffing harder to generate more smoke. "We must insist that any proposal for peace must be backed up with acts, and not words alone. We need convincing proof. It was Hitler who fired the first shoots of this war when he violated Poland's sovereignty. He must now take the first steps toward peace."

Everyone in the room approved and began knocking their knuckles on the table.

Halifax proceeded to describe to the War Cabinet the progress of the SIS meetings with the German military in the Netherlands. He proposed they continue the meetings in hope of convincing the German military to remove Hitler and the Nazis from power, Britain could then make peace with a new German government on terms that would undo all territorial acquisitions made under the Nazis. As soon as he stopped talking, Churchill exploded.

"I must say," Churchill said. His pinkish face turned deep red. "I found these conversations distorting, at the least. I would rather we conduct negotiations with old Beelzebub himself then try and make a deal with the Hun, even if it did result in the removal of Hitler. What business do we have with them? I say to you all, Germany must be defeated and a peace imposed on her of our choosing."

Chamberlain and Halifax were dumbfounded. For years Churchill had condemned them as appeasers. Here they were trying to remove Hitler, but

Churchill was pushing them toward what could turn out to be a long and costly war. They could not understand Churchill's objectives, but they feared being labeled with the old stain of appeasers, once more.

"The Germans must be told they must remove Hitler first, and then, and only then will we entertain any political discussions," Churchill said. "There must be no preconditions."

Chamberlain and Halifax acquiesced Churchill's proposal. The others in the War Cabinet, sensing that Churchill had the upper hand, also agreed.

Churchill studied the Prime Minister's face with acute interest. He was pleased at his new found resolve. Chamberlain was no coward. He truly sought a peaceful revision of the territorial settlement that was dictated at Versailles, with Germany. His policy before the 1939 was incorrectly referred to as appeasement. Many in England felt that Germany was ill-treated after the First World War. They feared the Soviet Union to be the greater threat to the civilization of Europe, and hoped to harness Germany, as a bulwark against the spread of Communism in Europe. What Chamberlain hoped to accomplish was the gradual economic and political expansion of German influence in central Europe, as a barrier between the democratic-capitalist West and the Communist East. But Hitler acted too rashly for their liking. Expansion of German influence in central Europe was acceptable to Chamberlain and his supporters in the English establishment, but German violation of the borders, conquest and occupation of non-German territories were unacceptable. Churchill never supported Chamberlain. He had called for war against Germany and Hitler, and now he felt that events had proved him right. He was the prophet and his star was rising. He planned to convince Chamberlain to create a new post of Minister of War for himself, and hoped to even replace Chamberlain as Prime Minister. He could plainly see that Chamberlain was in ill health. It was only a matter of time before he had to step down. Churchill knocked on the table with everyone else, but he contemptuously watched Chamberlain like a predator buying his time for the right moment to pounce.

Franklin Delano Roosevelt was sitting in his wheelchair, behind his desk in the oval office of the White House. His mood was upbeat, and his indomitable self-confidence was contagious. It had never failed him, even when he was struck down with polio that left him paralyzed from the waist down. Despite his handicap, he was able to get the Democratic Party to nominate him as their candidate for President in 1932, and beat President Hoover. He was reelection in 1936. His optimistic personality could charm most individuals as well as the masses. He used it just as effectively as a fine-tuned instrument in his political career. Only Hitler excelled his charismatic powers with the masses.

With FDR was his Secretary of State, Cordell Hull. Hull was older than Roosevelt, tall and balding. He was a fierce defender of free trade and a lifelong enemy of tariffs. Roosevelt appointed him as point man for his New Deal policies. Hull also engineered opening diplomatic relations with the Soviet Union. He was a true believer in America's destiny to lead the world into a new globalist order.

Also present was Sumner Welles, under Secretary of State. He was tall and handsome and though most people who knew him found him abrasive and arrogant, he and the President were good friends. Roosevelt felt comfortable around him because they shared a powerful sense of pride in their class. They both attended Groton and Harvard, and despite Roosevelt's populist persona with the American people, the President preferred the company of America's Anglo-Saxon gentry.

Though Roosevelt's partiality for his class manifested itself in a crude anti-Semitism, and he would often make vulgar remarks about his many Jewish associates, he never let it interfere with his rise to power. He had appointed many Jews to his cabinet, more than all the presidents before him. They numbered among his many advisors, but must were wellborn and wealthy. One such appointment was Henry Morgenthau as Secretary of the Treasury. Morgenthau possessed a wizardly demeanor and brilliant mind for financial matters. His father was a diplomat and banker, and a supporter of President Wilson and his dream of world government. Morgenthau had supported collective action against Germany as far back as 1935, and now advocated aid for Britain and France against Germany.

The only remaining person in the room was Joseph P. Kennedy, the US ambassador to Great Britain. Unlike the others, Kennedy was not a supporter of FDR's New Deal. He was an ardent isolationist and believed Hitler would win the war. He thought FDR's desire to enter the war was wrong, and he was critical of Roosevelt's foreign policy. Why then was he appointed as ambassador to court of Saint James by Roosevelt? Kennedy had amassed a fortune through banking, investing in the Stock Market, and some claim through bootlegging in the 1920s. He was very ambitious and possessed a controlled competitiveness and determination to succeed at anything he did. His highest ambition was to run for President, and had begun to make plans to run in 1940. Despite his Catholicism he massed a great deal of support among the right-wing in the Democratic Party, especially among the South White Bourdons, who liked his conservatism. But

Kennedy was no fool. In 1932 he had generously contributed to Roosevelt's campaign. For his generosity, he was rewarded with the appointment as ambassador. Roosevelt did it as much to get rid of Kennedy as to reward him. The New Dealers were horrified by Kennedy's conservativism, especially Hull, Welles and Morgenthau.

"I want to welcome back our dear Ambassador," Roosevelt said as he beamed one of his famous smiles at Kennedy. "How long can we enjoy you company?"

Kennedy smiled back, revealing his equally famous toothy, Kennedy smile. "Only a week or two," Kennedy said. "Things are heating up in Europe, but I felt it was important to report to you first hand on what is happening across the Atlantic."

"Good fellow," Roosevelt said, but he didn't believe Kennedy. He suspected Kennedy was in the US to further his own political ambitions, but he was too shrewd to say anything. The President noticed Hull making a face like he just tasted something unpleasant. Hull never liked Kennedy and never tried to hide it. Morgenthau didn't like Kennedy either. He hated him especially for Kennedy's pro-German sympathies, but he was too cunning to make a display of it. Welles also hid dislike for Kennedy. He kept his feelings hidden from Kennedy because he was too high breed to reveal them. That is why Roosevelt appointed Welles. He liked men of good breeding, and who possessed the tact not the reveal what they really felt.

"Please, Joe, do enlighten us," Roosevelt said.

Kennedy looked more like a clerk than a ruthless businessman. "London is determined to fight." Roosevelt continued to smile without making a comment as he listened. "The war party, led by Churchill, is firmly in control within the British government. All of Hitler's peace proposals have been tuned down. I doubt if there is anything that Hitler can offer short of resigning as head of the German government that would satisfy Churchill and his supporters. The war will go on, but London has no idea on how to proceed with the execution of the war. The British are expecting the Germans to attack in the west, but there is no sign of an immediate German offensive against France or the Low Lands. From what I can tell, London is desperately seeking to reflect the expected offensive by initiating hostilities on the periphery, possibly Scandinavia."

"Churchill was always one for assaulting the periphery," the President said. "Remember Gallipoli in the last war? That was Churchill's idea. The British are always sending their army anywhere but on target, while the French prefer to remain hidden behind their Maginot Line. It's a pity we failed to convince the

Soviet Union to side with Britain and France and defend Poland against the Germans. Lord knows, I tried to persuade Stalin to stand with them."

"Hitler was able to make Stalin a better offer," Welles said. "He could offer them half of Eastern Europe."

"If only we were as successful with the Soviets as we were with the Poles," Roosevelt said. "They jumped at the chance of standing up to the Germans. Brave souls they were."

"Fools," Kennedy said. "Where did it get them? They're languishing under the heels of the Nazis and the Soviets."

"It's not what I wanted," Roosevelt said. "Bill Bullitt informed the Poles that what we sought was to pit Germany and the Soviets against each other. Then the British and French would have time to build up their forces until they are ready to attack Germany in the west. But now they must face the threat of a German attack without a hostile Russia in her rear." Roosevelt looked at Hull. "We have got to assure our British and French friends to hang in there and not to give up. They must be convinced to resist the Germans until I have time to psychologically prepare the American people for war. And I won't be able to do this until after the elections, next year. If I begin advocating our entry into this war at this time, I'll lose any chance of getting reelected President next year."

Roosevelt cocked his head and glanced at Kennedy to see his reaction to his intention to run for a third term. The President knew that Kennedy had aspirations of his own for the Presidency. Kennedy's cheeks flushed red, but revealed no other reaction. He knew the President made the remark for his discomfort and he refused to give him the satisfaction of enjoying his annoyance.

"I don't think you will have the opportunity, Mr. President," Kennedy said. The smile of Roosevelt's face disappeared as his eyes locked on Kennedy's.

"Please, explain why not?" FDR asked.

"Because I believe Germany will bring this war to a victorious conclusion before the end of 1940." Roosevelt didn't speak, but Hull did. "How in the name of all that is righteous and good in heaven did you come to that conclusion?" Hull was not pleased with Kennedy's prediction and made no attempt to hide his displeasure.

"Because the British have no army to speak of," Kennedy said. "And their air force is no match for the Luftwaffe. All they have is their navy, and while it will prevent any attempt by the Germans to invade the British Isles, all they can do is blockade Germany. And this won't work because of Hitler's non-aggression pact with the Soviet Union. I understand tons of goods needed by the German economy to wage this war is flooding across the new Russo-German border. The amount of supplies will only increase in the next year."

"Aren't you forgetting France?" Hull interrupted. "The French army is still the best in the world, or haven't you noticed?" Hull sniffed, raised an eyebrow and sat back, satisfied with his point of fact.

"Frankly, the French are suffering from defeatism," Kennedy said. He fought to remain calm and in control. "Their political leadership is busying themselves drafting terms of surrender they plan to present to the Germans. While France's political leaders are planning on how to surrender, the French generals are preoccupied with digging deeper holes to hide in when the Germans finally do attack."

"You've been taking to Bill Bullitt again, Joe. Haven't you?" the President laughed. "Poor Bill. The trouble with him is in the morning he will send me a telegram, 'Everything is lovely,' and then he will go out to have lunch with some French official and I get a telegram that everything is going to Hell." Everyone laughed. Kennedy just smiled.

"But Bill is right, and so are you, Joe," Roosevelt continued. "The French do suffer from a black mood. They feel they are living in the last days of Pompeii. I know no informed Frenchman who does not feel that he is living in the last days of his civilization."

"That's why we must do whatever is in our power to give support, both morally and materially to the Western Democracies," Morgenthau said. "I cannot begin to express the urgent need to reinforce their resolution to stand fast and confront the Nazi threat. We must make sure they have the means to stand up to the Nazis until we can enter this war. They have to know that we need time before we can enter this war 'on their side'. They must give us the time we need. We must find ways to give them whatever assistance necessary to hold out until we can enter the war."

Roosevelt smiled broadly and toothy. He loved the way Morgenthau put so much emotion into his forewarning of the Nazi threat.

"We must do as Henry says," Roosevelt said. "Joe, you must do whatever is in your power to assure London that we are behind them 100 percent."

"I will do as you say, Mr. President," Kennedy said. "But I still believe this war is wrong. France and Britain should have never lived up to the guarantee they gave to Poland. It was made in haste, and was a false promise they could never keep. If it had not been for us, they would have never given Poland that guarantee. Poland would have been forced to make some kind of accommodation with Germany. Afterwards, Germany would have eventually invaded the Soviet Union, while the rest of the world would have been left in peace. Hitler would never have declared war on the Western Democracies. His aim is expansion in the East."

Morgenthau shot Kennedy a hateful glare, but before he could speak, Welles spoke first.

"I do believe you really don't understand just what is at stake here. The fate of the entire future development of our humanist civilization is at stake. Nazism represents everything that is abhorrent to our civilization. It is the quest of the United States to see that a new world order, built upon the principles of international trade and commerce and economic and political interdependence becomes a reality in the next century—the American century. We cannot sit by and permit the cancer that is Nazism to grow and spread in Europe. Fascism in Spain and Italy is harmless, but a Germany armed with such an ideology is a threat too great to ignore and permit to continue. There is simply no way that our two philosophical imperatives can coexist."

Kennedy sat motionlessly and listened until Welles was finished. "I'm sorry, but I still believe we should stay out of this war," Kennedy said. "The real danger to our civilization is Communism and the Soviet Union, not Germany."

"My dear Joe," Roosevelt said. "The truth is we have more in common with the Communists then we do with the Nazis. Both capitalism and communism are, after all, economic interpretations of the human condition, or so I'm told by my dear wife, Eleanor." Roosevelt laughed as he flicked the ashes from his cigaret into an ashtray. "Eleanor has always possessed enough political cognition for both of us. I've always been just a good politician. She has the brains in the family. Lord knows I didn't marry her for any other qualities."

The others laughed along with the President as he winked. "I believe that in time, after Fascism has been eradicated from the face of the world, the Soviet Union and the Western Democracies, including the United States, will move closer together. But there is no way this can be done with Nazism. You do understand? Don't you, Joe?"

"Yes, Mr. President."

Roosevelt smiled at Kennedy, once more. He noticed Kennedy's expression never changed, but his stony facade did not fool him. Roosevelt knew his words did not penetrate. Kennedy still believed Britain and France would be defeated and the United States should not enter the war. Kennedy did not share the vision that Roosevelt's class did for the future of the United States and the world. He shrugged it off as Kennedy's anti-British bias. He was, after all, a product of his Irish-Catholic upbringing. But he was sure of one thing, he would have to find a way of replacing Kennedy as ambassador to the Court of Saint James, before the Presidential elections next year.

Berlin was overcast on November 5, 1939, and the German people are being introduced to the new lists of war rationing that the government's total war economy was putting into place. Announcements that the production of certain domestic goods will be discontinued or reduced were being circulated. Most industries would undergo a transformation as the Reich government instituted a war time synchronization of the German economy. All national resources would be diverted into the production of weapons and armaments needed for the rapid expansion of the armed forces in the next year. The number of men who were called up to serve in the armed forces was increased. Berlin was a city at war.

Several large, five-liter, black Hoch and Mercedes limousines proceeded down the *Whilhelmstrasse*. Miniature red, white and black swastika flags fluttered on the black fenders. Once the vehicles reached the new Reich Chancellory building, they turned into the courtyard and came to a halt. The new building was built from white granite. It towered over the old limestone Reich Chancellory building next door.

Orderlies in smart uniforms quickly rushed to the stopped vehicles and opened the doors. The passengers stepped out, ignoring the orderlies in the class-ridden Prussian tradition. The passengers included the highest ranking officers of the different branches of the German armed forces; army generals in field grey uniforms and high, black leather boots, naval officers in blue-black uniforms, air force officers wearing pale blue uniforms, all of them spangled with Germany's highest and most prestigious medals and decorations. They quickly passed through the high bronze doors situated between massive Corinthian columns. On either side were SS guards in black uniforms, standing as immobile as the two huge statues glorifying the ideal Aryan racial type that towered over them. The officers marched down the five-hundred-foot-long entry hall. Their steppes resonating on the polished marble floor. At the far end another pair of huge doors seemed to grow as they approached. They passed through this doorway into an oversized reception area. Beyond it was Hitler's four-thousand-square-foot study.

Two SS troopers, like the two that stood guard outside, were standing guard outside of Hitler's study. On the left sleeve each wore a braided band with Hitler's name. Silver daggers hung from their belts and black helmets donned their heads with swastika insignia and SS runes. They opened the doors as the officers reached the doorway, permitting them to pass inside. The study was huge and spacious, not cluttered with too much furniture. When the officers entered the room, they could see the sunlight streaming through the large windows. To their right, at the far end of the room was a large fireplace with a sofa and several chairs gathered in front of it. Over the fireplace was an oil portrait of Otto von Bismarck. At the other end of the room was Hitler's desk, made of find wood. It was situated under one of Hitler's favorite mural depicting the Virtues—Wisdom, Prudence, Fortitude and Justice.

Hitler was sitting behind his desk. With him was Reich Marshal Goering, Albert Speer, who Hitler appointed to lead up the total mobilization of Germany's economy for the war, and Field Marshal Keitel. They turned in the direction of the doors when the officers entered the study. Brauchitsch and Halder were leading the way. Hitler stood up. Before moving, he spoke in a low voice, "Here comes my Coward Number One," referring to Brauchitsch, the army commander in chief, "and Number Two," referring to Halder, the army's chief of staff.

Goering fought the urge to laugh. Speer and Keitel just exchanged glances. Hitler stepped forward and walked to greet his officers. With a disarming smile he marched up to them. The officers gave the Nazi salute as they clicked their heels. Hitler returned the salute with his own modified version of it, his right arm bent at the elbow and right palm opened, and over his right shoulder, close to his ear.

At fifty, Hitler was still in good health, standing five-foot, nine inches tall and showed no signs of greying. He had discarded his brown party uniform for a new one. It included straight black trousers, simple dress shoes instead of his black ridding boots, and he wore a, double-breasted jacket in the traditional field grey color of the army. As usual, he wore no decorations on his jacket other than his party pin and the Iron Cross first class that was awarded him during the First World War. Right behind Hitler was Goering, Speer and Keitel.

"Welcome, gentlemen," Hitler said. He waved toward the chairs located before the fireplace. "Why don't we make ourselves comfortable by the fireplace and get to work?"

The others all nodded and followed Hitler.

Everyone was soon seated and waited for their Fuehrer to open the meeting. Hitler cleared his throat and began speaking softly, which was his custom. As he continued to speak his words gradually became more forceful and emotional. He started the meeting by talking about the rejection of his offers of peace by the British and French.

Goering sat on one side of Hitler. His huge bulk was fitted into a white, gold-trimmed uniform of his own design which included a Crusader's sword suspended on his belt. His pale blue eyes flashed with attentiveness, and his dimpled face was beaming with admiration for Hitler, and approval for everything he said. General Walter von Brauchitsch sat erect and silently without reaction to Hitler's words. He was slight in built. His face, which was still handsome, was locked in a typical expression of Prussian self-discipline. Admiral Raeder did not look typically Prussian, but more like a businessman. Serious and even tempered, he sat and listened without expression. Keitel sat to the other side of Hitler and would occasionally glance about, watching the reactions of all those present as Hitler spoke. General Franz Halder was taking notes. He looked more like a schoolteacher, then general. He wore his hair closed cropped and wore rimless spectacles. He seemed to vibrate with nervousness that never showed itself, but lurked beneath the surface.

Halder had reason to be nervous. Ever since Admiral Canaris, General Oster and a long list of people, both civilians and officers, were arrested, Halder's thoughts were preoccupied with the fear of being arrested, himself. The conspiracy to overthrow Hitler and remove the Nazis from power was crushed ruthlessly by the Gestapo. Long lists of conspirators were discovered in the Abwher files. Halder expected to receive a call from the Gestapo, but so far nothing happened. He was approached on more than one occasion by General Oster, in the last couple of years with plans to topple Hitler and National Socialism from power. He had always refused to join the conspirators, but never turned them in. But after the war began in September, he finally agreed to support the conspirators. He even spoke to Brauchitsch about the conspiracy. Brauchitsch was also approached but refused to give his support. He was Prussian through and through, and a Prussian officer did not break his oath. Brauchitsch also believed Hitler had the confidence of the German people. But Halder really wasn't much different from Brauchitsch. Every time he went to see Hitler, he took a pistol with him and thought about shooting Hitler. But each time he lacked the courage to do it. He had no troops directly under his command. He knew he needed Brauchitsch's support, but Brauchitsch repeatedly refused.

Halder believed that Germany could not stand up to Britain and France. He pinned his hopes on Hitler insisting on an early attack in the west. If the invasion failed, he believed the German Military would rebel and set up a military dictatorship. But things had radically changed. Hitler somehow got wind of Canaris's plans. Canaris realized he had been discovered on September 27. The way Hitler stared at Canaris with a black look that could kill. Made Canaris flee, but not fast enough. Once Canaris left Berlin, the Gestapo set to work, confiscating Canaris's files. The whole damn conspiracy network was laid bare and hundreds of arrests were made. Halder continued to wonder if he was going to be arrested. Maybe his conversations with Oster were never recorded? He struggled to put the thoughts out of his mind and concentrate on what Hitler was saying.

"I made a sincere peace proposal in my speech on October 6," Hitler said. He had been speaking for several minutes and the words were now flowing from him. "I made it clear that there was no reason France and Britain could not retract their declaration of war on us. There are no direct issues between us. Germany has no designs on France and Britain. I've renounced all claims on Alsace-Lorraine. I want not one square mile of territory in Western Europe. All I ask is for a free hand in Central and Eastern Europe.

"Our goal was to secure our eastern boundaries with the Soviet Union. I offered the Poles an alliance against the Soviets. All I asked in return was the annexation of the city of Danzig. Danzig was 100 percent German and had a Nationalist Socialist government. Other than Danzig, I asked for the right to build an autobahn and railroad across the Polish Corridor. In return I promised to compensate Poland with Soviet territory. But did the Poles accept my generous offer? No! And why not? Because the British gave a carte blanche guarantee of defending Poland's boundaries—a guarantee that they could not live up too. And now we find out that FDR and his Jew-infested government was behind the Polish refusal to cooperate with us, and they have been goading the British and French into going to war against us. They expected the Poles to hold out against us, but they didn't expect us to outmaneuver them with our treaty with the Soviets.

"The Poland created by the Dictate of Versailles has now disappeared. I promised to create a shrunken Polish state on October 6, and I will live up to my word. Those sections under our control have been divided into two sections. Germany will annex the first section directly and begin too fully Germanize these new territories. I will divide this section into three parts. Two new districts will be created as 'West Prussia' and 'Posen' and Albert Forster and Artur Greiser will be appointed as district leaders. The third section will be annexed by East Prussia. This will be accomplished by the removal of most Poles into the new shrunken Polish sate under our control, which is now known as the General Government of Poland, with its center in Cracow.

"I've put Reichfuehrer Himmler in charge of the Germanization program. We will start with the schools. All Polish children will be taught to speak German and think as Germans. Any children who lost their parents will be sent to Germany and raised as Germans. As many Poles as possible will be Germanized. Any Pole deemed worthy of being Germanized will be treated equally as a German. He will not be defamed or harassed and will quickly obtain citizenship for himself and their family, if he is willing to serve as a soldier and fight alongside our German troops. Those Poles who resist Germanization as are considered unsuitable in the annexed territories will be resettled in the General Government territory."

The Generals listened with approval. They had heard Hitler talk of reducing the Poles to slavery in the past, and felt it was beneath their Prussian sensibilities as gentlemen to treat conquered peoples so horribly. Hitler's last minute change of mind regarding the treatment of the Poles was a relief. Hitler's plans to deal with the Poles were similar to Germany's policy during World War One. Hitler appointed General Hans Frank, a Party lawyer whose sole ambition was to carry out the will of his Fuehrer by creating a new Polish state. Hitler gave him orders to organize what was left of the Polish elite for the purpose of eventually reestablishing the Polish state farther to the east. Those who accepted would be treated as allies, but those who refused will be killed. The Generals were amazed by Hitler's generosity, considering that they discovered that the Polish military had killed over five thousand German civilians in Poland in September. Hitler was outraged by the atrocities when he first learned of them, but he now seemed willing to overlook them. This puzzled everyone who listened to him. Hitler even offered the Poles the opportunity to join a newly established Polish Waffen SS unit. This would be the first of many non-German Waffen SS units that would be created in the next few years.

If the generals were pleased with Hitler's plans for the Poles, they were revolted by Hitler's plans for the Jews of Poland. "I've ordered that all Jews in the East must wear an armband on their right arm with a yellow Star of David. I have given orders to Gruppenfuehrer Heydrich to begin the removal of all Jews to concentration centers where they will preform manual labor. Eventually, we will set up reservations, territories further to the east in what is now the Soviet Union where they can be relocated and placed under control. There they will not be able to spread their poison and infect Europe. They're eventual fate will be determined later. It will all depend on the success of our eventual conquest of the Soviet Union."

Most of the generals shifted in their seats, trying not to display their avulsion for Hitler's anti-Semitism. It was not that they really cared about the fate of the Jews—they approved of their segregation from German society but they preferred a more subtle measure.

"Do you still intend to postpone the attack in the West?" Brauchitsch asked.

"Yes," Hitler said. "With the programs for increased war production and economic mobilization, we should have superior numbers and quality in tanks and planes by May 1940. Then we can launch an attack and sweep across the Low Countries, knock France out of the war, and expel Britain from the continent."

Hitler began to describe his plans for the execution of the war in the next year. "We will occupy Holland and Belgium with lightning speed and secure an early defeat of France. France will be knocked out of this war by the end of the June 1940. Once France is defeated, we can then turn our attention to forcing Britain to her knees. This can't be done by invading Britain across the English Channel. No, I want to strangle the British Isles with our submarines. That's why I agreed to the Navy's request for increased submarine production. Currently we have fifty-seven submarines, but we will need at least three hundred to deal with Britain. We are aiming for this number by September 1940."

Hitler turned to Grand Admiral Raeder for a second and then continued. "I want the naval air force increased."

He now looked at Goering. The Reich Marshall nodded his approval, but secretly he was displeased. He had no desire to share air power with the navy. He was jealous of his control of all air forces.

"We must strangle Britain economically with bases in Northern France and possibly in Norway, if it becomes necessary to occupy that country," Hitler said. "If the British should make any moves in Scandinavia, we must be ready to act first."

Hitler turned to Goering once more. "We must proceed with an air assault on Britain and assemble a phoney armada that will make them think we intend to chance an invasion. We must make the English believe we are planning to cross the Channel. And while the British prepare to defend their island, we will strike in the Mediterranean."

Admiral Raeder nodded his approval. He was advocating a Mediterranean strategy.

"What about Italy?" Raeder asked. "Will the Duce bring Italy into the war?"

"He will," Hitler said. "Once France is defeated, the Duce will bring Italy into the war. I will promise the Duce Corsica, Savoy and Nice, in return for the creation of a joint Italo-German command, with our Generals in charge, of course." Everyone chuckled. They knew the Italian officers were defeatists and worthless.

"All I have to do is promise the Duce that he will get to ride into Cairo on his white horse and he will gladly place all of Italy's armed forces under our command."

Everyone now laughed out loud at Hitler's joke, at Mussolini's expense.

"We'll first take Malta with our airborne troopers," Hitler said. "This is why I've ordered their rapid expansion. It will be imperative that Malta falls early in the next Summer. Four panzer divisions will be sent to Libya. With the three hundred thousand Italian infantry troops, we will invade Egypt, take the Suez Canal and then sweep through Palestine and the Middle East. I want the oil fields of the Persian Gulf securely in our hands by the end of next Fall. Britain will have to sue for peace or see her Empire crushed.

"Once the Middle East and North Africa are under our control Britain won't be able to stand against us. They are dreamers, still living in the Victorian era, when all they had to do was send out cruisers to restore order in the world. Now, America is the bigger factor, as is Japan, Soviet Union and Germany. All are stronger than England. Can't the British see that the world has changed?"

Hitler turned to Goering. "Have you begun to implement the increase in fighter production?"

Goering beamed with excitement as he shifted in his chair. "Yes, my Fuehrer," he said. "Production of all types of fighters will increase by 25 percent per month beginning in January 1940. We're giving special attention to our dive bombers, the Junker 87. We will have more fighters than the combined forces of Britain and France by May 1940. I have also resurrected plans for the production of both four engine bombers, the Ju89 and the Do19. It seems at this moment that the Ju89 is the better of the two planes. Production for both types will begin in July 1940. We will have a large fleet of bombers for any future war with the Soviet Union. We should be producing five hundred a month by May 1941. We will have a sufficient force of long range bombers that will have the capacity to reach Soviet industrial sites in the Ural mountains."

Hitler now turned to Albert Speer. "What about the development of jet fighters? When will production start?"

"I have reviewed the suggested projects by both Willie Messerschmitt and Ernst Heinkel. Messerschmitt's jet fighter will not be ready for production until the Summer of 1941. Ernst Heinkel's design for a jet fighter is simpler and easier to build, even with the modifications that he has made in his new design. His latest design has twin engines, which has made the aircraft more stable in flight. He's designated it He280. I've met with Herr Heinkel and I'm convinced that we can begin production of his jet fighter in nine months."

Goering stared at Speer with jealousy. He didn't like sharing the planning and production of the jet fighter project with him, but Hitler insisted that Speer head-up the project.

"Herr Heinkel assured me that he will set his men to work, around the clock, to make sure that the He280 will be ready for a test flight by April 1940," Speer said. "I have reviewed his estimation and believe we should have the first fifty He280 ready for operation by the end of August 1940. From September on we can cease production of propeller fighters and convert all production facilities over to jet production. If my estimations are correct, we can produce another two hundred in September, five hundred in October and begin producing one thousand a month beginning in November 1940."

Hitler nodded his approval as he listened.

"Since Messerschmitt's jet fighter is more complicated and won't be ready until 1941," Speer continued. "I recommend we immediately begin production of the He280, and permit Messerschmitt to continue the perfection of his jet fighter so that it will be ready for production the following year."

Hitler approved. He leaned back in his chair and wiped his hair back over his forehead. "Once the war with France is concluded, we'll need the jet fighter for the further prosecution of the war against England. But everything will depend on knocking France out of the war as swiftly as possible."

Brauchitsch and Halder had agreed before arriving, to discourage any plans to attack France, and try and convince Hitler that any attack would have to wait until the Spring of 1941. They hoped for a war of attrition, similar to World War One, in which Germany would be worn down, causing unrest among the military as well as among the civilian population. Dissension and rebellion would create a climate of unrest that would offer Brauchitsch and Halder the opportunity to topple Hitler and the National Socialists from power.

"My Fuehrer, the army staff has examined the possibility of an offensive in the West in the Spring and I'm afraid it is out of the question. I doubt the army will be up to strength for an attack before the Spring of 1941," Brauchitsch said. Halder nodded his approval. The General Staff had compiled reports on the need for further recruitment and training for a future attack. "Our forces need additional equipment, especially tanks, artillery and planes to counter the superior numbers by the joint forces of Britain and France. Even with total economic mobilization, the army won't be ready for an attack until 1941."

Brauchitsch looked at Hitler, who was now sitting silently and erect in his chair. He listened to Brauchitsch without interrupting.

"The industries of the Ruhr Basin are vulnerable to attack by British strategic bombing," Brauchitsch said. "We need to conserve our fighters for the defense of the Ruhr. This means there will be fewer fighters to support any attack against France and the Low Countries. The number of fighters required for an attack will not be replaced until 1941, even with increased production and the new jet fighters. Then there is the problem of our tanks.

"During the invasion of Poland, about half of our tanks, Mark Is and IIs, broke down and are in need of repair. If we face the French and the British with these models, they will be demolished by the French and British antitank guns, which the Poles lacked. It would be advisable to waited until our newer models, the Mark IIIs and Mark IVs, begin arriving in large numbers before we attack. We won't have such numbers, by our estimation, until the beginning of 1941."

Brauchitsch continued to elaborate on the main arguments against an invasion, in 1940. He was reading from a report he had written himself in longhand. He tried to explain that the landscape in the Low Countries and in Northern France were too moist from deliberate flooding by the governments of Belgium and the Netherlands. He also explained that this problem would be made worse by the Spring rains that would prevent a rapid movement by armor divisions.

"It rains on the enemy too," replied Hitler curtly.

Brauchitsch stopped speaking. Hitler's sharp words stopped him cold. He looked into Hitler's piercing blue eyes that were now riveted on him. When Hitler didn't say anything else, he glanced at Halder and then continued with his report. He began describing how the fighting spirit of the German infantry during the Polish campaign was far below what it was during the Great War. He then reported on signs of insubordination among many of the units that were similar to those of 1918. He spoke of the progress of transferring troops from Poland to the Western frontier that described mutinies in some units and recounted reports of drunken, undisciplined incidents by German troops at the front and on railways headed for the West.

Hitler continued to listen politely. His eyes were locked on Brauchitsch. The others noticed the red flash in his checks and the tightening of his lips. He followed every word Brauchitsch spoke. Hitler never moved, not a muscle, and though he seemed calm, everyone could feel the tension rising. And when Brauchitsch accused the German infantry of insubordination, Hitler exploded with rage that disarmed everyone present with its suddenness and fury. His voice was horse and laced with black anger and rose so shrill he could be heard by his secretaries sitting outside his study.

"Insubordination! In what units have there been any cases of lack of discipline?" he asked. "What happened? Where? How many? Can't you give me details?"

Brauchitsch's acquisitions of insubordination were false, or exaggerations at best. He hoped to deter Hitler with them, convince him that the army was not up to the task of unleashing an offensive against France and Britain, in the Spring of 1940. Instead, he caused Hitler to explode with indignation. Or so he thought. Hitler had earlier got wind of what Brauchitsch was up too, and his well-planned outburst of fury had the desired calculated effect that he planned. The Prussian general was not used to his mercurial temper and shrunk before Hitler's reaction.

Hitler long ago fine-tuned his outbursts, which were deliberate and contrived to quail anyone who opposed him. He appeared to lose control, but he never did. He was a master actor and perfected his performances. He instantly knew when to use them, and on whom they would be effective.

"What action has been taken by the army commanders?" Hitler demanded. "How many death sentences have been carried out? Details! I want details and names! Otherwise, don't waste my time with such nonsense!"

Hitler finally leaped from his chair and grabbed Brauchitsch's memorandum out of his hands, tore it up and then thundered at Brauchitsch. "Not one front line commander mentioned any lack of attacking spirit in the infantry to me. But now I have to listen to this, after the army has achieved a magnificent victory in Poland! I will not listen to you. It is not our soldiers who are afraid to fight, it's my generals. You have sabotaged our rearmament programs, ignored my orders and even conspired with the enemies of Germany." Hitler now stared directly a Brauchitsch. His eyes narrowed and burned with iron-cold resolve. He seemed suddenly under control once more as he looked at the Prussian general. "Do not make me remind you of Canaris' treason and the fate that awaits him and his collaborators." Hitler spun around and marched out of the room, slamming the door behind him.

Everyone sat silently and stunned until Keitel dismissed the meeting. Brauchitsch was in a state of shock and trembling when Keitel took him by the arm and pulled him over to one side, so that he could speak to him without anyone over hearing him.

"General, I would advise you to watch your step," Keitel said in a whisper. Brauchitsch looked at Keitel. He still had not recovered from Hitler's tantrum. "The Fuehrer seems to possess an uncanny intuition on sniffing out treason."

Brauchitsch stepped back, freeing himself from Keitel's grip.

"Herr Field Marshal, are you suggesting that I am…?" he didn't finish his statement.

"I am suggesting that you had better carry out the Fuehrer's orders and not try to sabotage his plans. Remember Canaris? The Fuehrer discovered his obstructionism. How he did, I still don't know, but I hope there is no obstructionism at Zossen to be discovered. If there is, weed it out, now!"

Brauchitsch nodded. "I understand."

"I hope you do, Herr Field Marshal," Keitel said.

Brauchitsch and Halder made their way back to the courtyard of the New Chancellory. The staff cars rolled out of the New Chancellory and down the *Welhelmstrasse*. Soon they had left Berlin by way of the *Berlinerstrasse*, passing through the industrial suburbs and then farmlands that surrounded the capital of the Greater German Reich. They were on their way back to army headquarters located outside the village of Zossen, about twenty miles from Berlin.

Neither Brauchitsch nor Halder said anything until they were well outside Berlin. Brauchitsch was thinking about what Keitel told him in Hitler's study, before he left. He was sure that Keitel was letting him know that Hitler suspected Halder's activities in trying to sabotage Hitler's plans. Halder had approached him on several occasions about his involvement in planning a coup, and sought his blessing. But Brauchitsch was always evasive. He never promised to involve himself in Halder's plans and refused to listen to what he planned, but at the same time, he never tried to discourage him. He would only say that though he would not support any attempt to remove Hitler from power, he would also do nothing if someone else did something.

"I think it prudent to terminate all plans you might have been working on and never speak of these matters again, not to me or to anyone else," Brauchitsch finally said without looking at Halder, who was sitting next to him.

Halder turned and looked at Brauchitsch, who was looking straight ahead. He swallowed and agreed.

"I will tolerate no further talk of treason," Brauchitsch said as he continued to stare straight ahead. He raised his left hand in anticipation of Halder's protest. "That is exactly what you have been engaged in. It's a disgrace for a Prussian officer to plot seedy little plots against our head of state while we are at war. The SS is rounding up conspirators. Their net is getting too close to the army. I do not want the stench of treason to blacken the army's reputation. In war, there is only one possibility for the soldier—to obey."

When Brauchitsch and Halder finally reached Zossen, Halder gave no signal for a coup to start, but instead, he sent orders to all his fellow conspirators to begin immediately destroying all incriminating papers, maps and code words.

Hitler arrived in Munich on the morning of November 8, to attend the annual reunion of the Old Fighters of the National Socialist German Workers' Party. He was scheduled to remain in Munich until November 9. The first order of business of the day after he arrived was a visit to the wife of the late Dr. Paul

Ludwig Troost, who was his favorite architect. He wanted to discuss his plans for the reconstruction of Munich with Frau Troost, who was an architect in her own right and was put in charge of Hitler's plans after her husband died. When he arrived at her studio with two bodyguards, she asked him why he was so lax about security? Why he didn't have more than two bodyguards?

Hitler laughed and assured her he had complete faith in Providence. He slapped his pocket and said, "See, I always carry a pistol, but even that would be useless. If my end is decided, only this will protect me." He put his hand over his heart. "One must listen to an inner voice and believe in one's fate. And I believe very deeply that destiny has selected me for the German nation. So long as I am needed by the people, so long as I am responsible for the life of the Reich, I will live. And when I am no longer needed, after my mission is accomplished, then I will be called away."

Frau Troost was spellbound. She never heard anyone speak with such faith in his own destiny. They spent the next hour talking about architecture and Hitler's plans for the reconstruction of Munich, transforming the city into the Mecca of the Nationalist Socialist movement. Without any warning, Hitler suddenly became nervous and distracted. "Excuse me, Frau Troost, but I must change my schedule for today." Hitler seemed confused for a few seconds and then resumed with his conversation with Frau Troost, as if nothing happened.

After he left Frau Troost, he visited Unity Mitford, an English woman who was a devoted follower of Hitler. She tried to commit suicide by shooting herself after the two countries she loved, England and Germany, went to war. She asked Hitler if she could return to her family in England, and Hitler promised to put her on the first train to Switzerland as soon as she was strong enough to travel. He promised her the war would be over in a year and then they could meet again under more favorable circumstances.

Hitler spent the afternoon in his Munich residence working on the speech he would give later that evening. It would be an attack on England. Hitler usually spoke for ninety minutes, but this speech was only about an hour long. Hitler didn't realize that his speech was thirty minutes shorter than his usual speeches. It was seven thirty in the evening when his escort arrived to take him to the Burgerbraukeller beer hall. The beer hall was huge and the site of his famous 1923 putsch. The main room of the beer hall was decorated with swastika banners and flags. The room was packed with people listening to music and drinking beer, waiting for their Fuehrer's arrival. Earlier that evening, before everyone arrived, a small, pale man with clear blue eyes and a receding forehead had slipped unnoticed into the hall. He worked in the beer hall, so no one noticed him when he entered, carrying a box. He was Georg Elser, a mechanic and cabinet maker. He was recently discharged from Dachau concentration camp where he was held as a Communist sympathizer. In the last few weeks he had built a secret compartment in one of the huge wooden pillars in the hall. He opened the panel and placed the box inside. Inside the box was a time bomb that he planned to use to kill Adolf Hitler. With no one noticing him, he quickly set the timer for the bomb to detonate at 11:20 PM. Hitler was scheduled to begin speaking at 10:00 PM.

Hitler arrived at the Burgerbraukeller at about 8:00 PM. Hitler usually arrived late for such meetings, but tonight he insisted on arriving on time. When he entered the cavernous hall, wild applause broke out. Hitler made his way to the podium located right next to the pillar where the bomb was located. Several people gave short speeches before Hitler. Then Christian Weber, who served as Hitler bodyguard in the early days of the movement, rose to the microphone and spoke for a few minutes, introducing Adolf Hitler. The audience jumped to their feet, applauding their Fuehrer for several minutes. These were men who had joined the Party in the 1920s. Hitler always held a special place in his heart for them. He always said that they, like him, could remember a time in Germany when it was hard to be a Nationalist Socialist. When the applause eventually died down, Hitler began speaking. It was ten minutes past ten. Hitler's speech began as they all did. He spoke softly and slow, as if he was trying to find the right words. He seemed to sniff the air, grasping the feel of the audience. Soon his words took on a new force and began to pour from his mouth with an energy that seemed to possess him. He became animated and swept away with the force of his speech. He was interrupted repeatedly with applause whenever he assailed the treachery of the English.

It was 11:07 when Hitler had the uncontrollable urge to leave. It was so compelling that he didn't question it. He abruptly concluded his speech and quickly departed as the audience continued to applaud. Unknown to him, just a few yards from where he was speaking the bomb was ticking away. Hitler didn't wait around shaking hands and chat with his old comrade as he usually did in the past. He rushed out of the building with Rudolf Hess and several adjutants right behind him, and piled into the staff cars waiting outside. Eight minutes after Hitler left his company thought they heard a distant explosion, but ignored it.

When Hitler finally arrived at his apartment, he received a telephone call from Joseph Goebbels in Berlin. Goebbels told Hitler of the bomb attempt, but at first Hitler refused to believe him, thinking it was a joke. But when Goebbels assured Hitler that he was serious, Hitler grew pale and grim. After he hung up and told everyone what happened, he called the Burgerbraukeller and spoke to Weber. He asked about the wounded and charged Weber with doing everything possible to help them. When he hung up, he stared at those present. He seemed stunned for a few minutes, but he quickly recovered and told everyone what happened. With eyes wide and brilliantly blue he spoke as if in a dream. "Now I am completely content. All day long I heard a voice warning me of some kind of danger. It spoke to me again while I was giving my speech, warning me to stop and leave immediately. I couldn't resist." He shook his head with disbelief. "I had the most uncontrollable urge to flee that I left the Burgerbraukeller earlier than usual. This can only be a corroboration of Providence's intention to let me reach my goal."

CHAPTER 3

▼

ONE HAND WASHES THE OTHER

Winter normally arrived in Moscow early, and 1939 was no exception. The first snow had turned the streets of Moscow white with a covering of snow. The Soviet's capital's gray atmosphere was turned white. People hurried along the streets of the Red capital, collars pulled up to protect themselves from the onslaught of Winter, and wearing fur hats to protect their heads from the icy winds that blew down out of the north. The Siberian winds whipped the snow about in dancing wind devils around the Kremlin. Inside, Stalin was conferring with his Foreign Minister, Vyacheslav Mikhailovich Molotov and the Andrei Zhdanov, the Communist Party boss of Leningrad. They were in Stalin's office. The room was twenty feet by fifty feet in size and Stalin rarely left it, except to go on his annual holidays. The walls were colored a dark green, the same color as the carpeting. The only decorating items were two large photographs: one of Karl Marx and the other of Lenin. On his desk was a battery of telephones, a holder for his pipe and another one that held a red and blue crayon, which he liked to doodle with. Stalin used his office as a conference room, and he held meetings sit-ting at one end of a long table that could seat ten people.

    Stalin sat motionlessly, with his left hand on his lap, hidden under the table. His left arm was three inches short than his right arm, and his left hand larger than his right hand. This deformity was the result of a boyhood injury, and it affected Stalin's sense of self-worth. It caused him to develop a heightened sense of inferiority. Added to his deformed arm was Stalin's shortness of stature, he was only five feet and four inches tall. He had a swarthy complexion, his face was very pockmarked and his second and third toes on his left foot were fused together. In his youth, he was ridiculed for his physical shortcomings, which scared his personality. He grew into a bitter and vindictive man. Added to this was his sense of intellectual incapacity that he developed while working with other Bolshevik leaders. Stalin was a peasant and lacked the formal education that such Communists as Lenin and Trotsky possessed. This sense of bitterness is probably the only human trait that his small, vicious Georgian devil from the Caucasus, possessed.

All his life Stalin wished to be tall and possess large hands. He was a product of the hard, wild life that peasants suffered in the Caucasus. He grew into a violence-prone man, giving up a career in the church for the life of a revolutionary. He might have lacked Lenin's ideological passion for violence, but he more than made up for it with his capacity to unleash unlimited violence on a massive scale whenever he felt it would further his goals. Sometimes he would inflict violence for no other reason then to terrorize people. His victims sometimes included his closest friends and comrades. His aptitude for cruelty and brute force was reflected in his personality. He was known to hold a grudge for years, for the slightest in fractures, and when he took his revenge, he took great pleasure in the pain he inflicted on his victims, delighting in their misfortunes. This half-gangster, and half-bureaucrat was driven by a lust for power that superceded all ideological motives. It manifested itself also in his crudeness in behavior and speech, which was laced with the most vile obscenities.

Molotov was reporting to Stalin on the satisfactory conclusion of their negotiations with the Finnish delegates on November 16, 1939. Molotov was a bookish little man who looked like a clerk in a civil service office. He never smiled and hid what he was really thinking behind his machine-like capacity to remain stoic. Behind his disarming, pudgy and pasty face was the mind of a bureaucrat, par excellence. His cold, calculating eyes displayed the warmth of a computer and his voice never deviated from its continuous, monotone quality. He was chosen by Stalin to replace Pavel Litvinov, who was Jewish and fiercely anti-Nazi. Stalin sent Molotov to negotiate the Nazi-Soviet Pact with Germany. Molotov did exactly as he was told despite that fact that he was married to a Jew.

"The Finns proved just as accommodating as the Estonians and the Latvians," Molotov said straight away. "All opposition to our proposal of October 12 crumbled. The borders of the Soviet Union, north of Leningrad will be moved twenty-five miles north of its present location. They will also surrender the

Rybacji Peninsula to us, as well as all islands in the Gulf of Finland and the port of Hanko, which we will lease as a navel base. This is a total of 1,066 square miles. In return for these concessions, the Soviet Union will turn over to Finland 2,134 square miles of territory along the central frontier that Finland shared with the Soviet Union."

Stalin nodded his approval, but Molotov didn't take notice. If he had been a different man, he might have expressed his relief at Stalin's approval, but one never knew how the Red dictator would react to any expression, so it was better to conceal one's true feelings around him.

"According to our reports," Molotov continued, "Marshal Carl Gustaf Mannerheim and Minister Paasikivi both approved our proposals, but the rest of the government, and the popular expression of the Finnish people objected. They were going to reject our offer, but finally decided to accept it."

Stalin smiled and leaned over to Zhdanov, who wanted to break off the negotiations and attack Finland. "You won't get the opportunity to play war now, Andrei. I suppose you'll have to go on playing with yourself?" Stalin laughed at the humiliating pun at Zhdanov's expense. Zhdanov simply smiled and tried to faint laughter, but he blushed and began to sweat. Stalin was pleased.

"Why then did they finally accept?" Stalin asked, turning back to his Foreign Minister. His eyes were squinted and locked on Molotov.

"Because of pressure brought on them by Hitler, personally," Molotov said.

Stalin's eyes opened wide. "Hitler? Really? You mean he intervened on our behalf?"

"According to our operatives, the Finns were begging Hitler to help them resist our generous proposal. They wanted to stand up to us, but Hitler not only refused to help, but threatened to support any attack made by our Red Army."

Stalin laughed and slapped both knees with his hands as he threw back his head. "I always said that I liked this Hitler. He's a ruthless opportunist. At first I was concern when he refused our proposal to change the conditions of our pact concerning the partitioning of Poland, refusing to accept additional Polish territory for Lithuania, but now, I'm sure he only wishes to abide by the letter of our original pact." Stalin pulled on his mustache with his right hand. His left hand disappeared under the table once more. "Yes. I like this Hitler. He is a brother. I can do business with him." Stalin then stopped dead and stared first at Molotov and then at Zhdanov. Neither man was reacting to the Red dictator's praise of Hitler. "But only until we're ready to attack Germany."

Molotov only closed his eyes, held then shut for a second and opened them once more. Zhdanov was less guarded and laughed approvingly. Stalin slapped the Leningrad party boss on the shoulder.

"And then, Comrade Piss-Pants, you can prove how warlike you really are by enlisting in the Red Army and take part in the attack on the Fascists, in the first wave."

Zhdanov almost relieved himself, at Stalin's insulting suggestion. Stalin could see his discomfort and it delighted him.

Stalin had been very clear about his aims when he agreed to the Nazi-Soviet Pact. He wanted two things. First, Stalin wanted to divert Germany's attention away from the Soviet Union and encourage German expansion westward. He hoped that Germany, France and Great Britain would exhaust themselves in a long and drawn out war of attrition. This could only help the Soviet Union, especially if she was sitting on the sidelines. "Let the capitalist fools butcher each other," he had said. He wanted the European powers to devour each other while he built up the Red Army, and when they were exhausted, after several years of bloodletting, he would launch his attack on all of Europe. In the meantime he sought territory in the Eastern Europe. This was his second objective. He hoped to annex the eastern half of Poland. He also wanted Finland, Estonia and Latvia. He did not ask for Lithuania, because he knew the Germans considered that country as part of their sphere of influence. He had hoped to convince Hitler to eventually hand it over to him, but Hitler refused. Lithuania was like an arrow aimed directly at the heart of the Soviet Union—Moscow. Stalin was furious when Hitler not only refused to surrender Lithuania, but insisted that the Red Army evacuate Vilnus. Vilnus was the ancient capital of Lithuania, and was lost to Poland in 1920. Hitler promised to return the city to the Lithuanians. Stalin did agree, but was incensed because Hitler had prevented him from getting everything he wanted.

In October 1939, the Soviet government approached both Latvia and Estonia. Stalin threatened them with invasion if they didn't give the Soviet Union permission to establish military bases on their soil. At first the Estonians and the Latvians appealed to Germany for help, but Hitler refused and suggested they agree to Stalin's demands. They quickly did so.

The Lithuanian government was concerned that Stalin would threaten them next. They decided to turn to Germany for help. Hitler immediately sent Ribbentrop to Lithuania and negotiated an alliance. Lithuania formally joined the Axis on October 27. Hitler had angered the Lithuanians when he forced them to surrender the German city of Memel earlier in the year, but after the defeat of Poland, Hitler lived up to his word and forced Stalin to withdraw from Vilnus on October 10. Stalin was angered at Hitler for siding with the Lithuanians, but when he heard that Hitler pressured the Estonians and the Latvians to give in to his demands, his angered dissipated. And now that Hitler had intervened again to help him get everything he wanted from the Finns without going to war, Stalin was beside himself with joy.

"First Hitler helps us get what we want from the Estonians and the Latvians, and now he helps us with the Finns. I'm sure we can do business with Hitler," Stalin said. "He is a man I can admire." Stalin was pleased with himself. Molotov only stared at his boss.

Stalin was pleased at Hitler's assistance in his acquisition of all his demands on Finland without resorting to war. He ordered that the Soviet Union live up to its part of the Nazi-Soviet Nonaggression Pact. The Soviets promised to ship Germany natural resources that included important minerals and especially oil. After Hitler refused to transfer Lithuania from Germany' sphere of influence to the Soviet's sphere, Stalin ordered that the resources promised to Germany in the Nazi-Soviet Pact be delayed. Stalin held up the shipping of most of these resources, but after he received Hitler's help with Finland, he gave the order to send the trains rolling into Germany with the promised resources. For the next six months the deliveries of trainloads of everything from coal, steel, oil and other precious resources flooded across the Soviet border into Germany. Stalin still hoped that after Germany and the Western allies devoured themselves in a war of attrition, the Soviet Union could attack from the east and overrun Poland and the Balkan, as well as Lithuania.

Stalin wanted a war between Germany and the West. When England and France approached him in the Spring of 1939 with an offer to form an alliance against Germany, Stalin refused. Instead, he sent Molotov to Germany with an offer of a nonaggression pact between Germany and the Soviet Union. He knew such a pact would give Germany a free hand to invade Poland. He also knew from England that the British would declare war on Germany, and this would drag France into the war as England's ally. This is exactly what Stalin wanted. When Germany invaded Poland, Stalin did not immediately attack Poland from the east. He waited until September 17, two weeks after the West declared war on Germany. When the Soviet Union finally invaded Poland, Stalin claimed it was only to prevent the Ukrainian and Byelorussian populations of eastern Poland from falling under German domination. This gave the English and the French an excuse not to declare war on the Soviet Union. In this way, Stalin got exactly what he was hoping for—the West and Germany at war with each other while the Soviet Union remained neutral, and yet the Soviets were still able to annex eastern Poland. This also provided Stalin with the opportunity to move against the three Baltic states, Finland, Estonia and Latvia. Stalin's formula for national security, rested on aggravating conflicts among the "imperialist" powers, and maintaining Soviet neutrality. The Soviet Union could buy the time necessary to build up their armed forces while the rest of Europe exhausted itself in a prolonged war of attrition.

In a speech given in Moscow on March 10, 1939, he told the Politburo, "Nonintervention represents the endeavor to allow all the warmongers to sink deeply into the mire of warfare, and for us to quietly urge them on. The result will be that they weaken and exhaust one another. Then we'll appear on the scene with fresh forces and step in naturally in the interest of peace and dictate terms to the weakened belligerents."

At a private meeting of the Politburo on August 23, 1939, he told Molotov, Keliment Voroshulov, Lavienti Beria and Nikita Khrushchev that he considered a war between the Soviet Union and Germany as unavoidable. He bragged that he momentarily tricked Hitler with the nonaggression pact to buy time for the Soviet Union. He wanted to build up the Soviet armed forces and be in a position to strike against Germany before Germany could attack them. "It must be our objective that Germany wage war long enough to exhaust England and France so much that they cannot defeat Germany alone. Should Germany win, it will itself be so weakened that it won't be able to wage war against us for ten years, it's paramount for us that this war continues as long as possible, until both sides are worn out."

It appeared to Stalin on November 16, 1939, that he was achieving all his objectives.

A group of physicists met in Washington in the first half of 1939. Two European scientists, Niels Bohr of Denmark and Enrico Fermi of Italy were discussing the success of German physicists in splitting a uranium atom. At Columbia University in New York City they confirmed the experiment by duplicating it. Fermi explained that each nucleus would shoot off two or three subatomic particles as it split. This could cause a chain reaction, Fermi claimed, which could result in an explosive chain reaction. When they were asked by a reporter if this process could be used to build an atomic bomb, both Bohr and Fermi lied and claimed that it would take another twenty-five to fifty years of research to produce such a weapon. The truth was Fermi and Bohr did not want it to become publically known that they were trying to develop just such a weapon. Fermi was already making plans to flee Mussolini's Italy and become an American citizen. He wanted to suppress all information on the development of nuclear fission for fear that he would be detained. Fermi planned to offer his research to the American government, and ask the United States would agree to support his work on developing an atomic bomb, as a weapon that could be used against National Socialist Germany and Fascist Italy. He even approached the United States Navel Department in hope of convincing the American government to support his research, on March 17, 1939. The Navy officials were not particularly interested, Fermi would not be put off.

Fermi was more determined than ever to get someone within the American government to listen to him. He knew that the German scientists were politically sophisticated enough to convince the German political leadership to understand what they were developing. Unfortunately, the native American scientists were not as accustomed to thinking in terms of applying their scientific discoveries in military terms. The same was true of their British counterparts. Fermi was convinced that only he could convince the United States government of the significance of his research. But he also knew that he needed help, and found it among a group of Jewish scientists who were all refugees from National Socialist Germany.

A meeting of five prominent scientists took place at Fermi's bequest. He was joined by Leo Szilard, Edward Teller, Eugene Wigner, and Victor Weisskopf. All, except Fermi, whose wife was Jewish, were Jewish and feared the possibility that Germany might build the first atomic bomb. They were all dedicated anti-Nazis and were determined to contribute to the defeat of Hitler and Germany, even though Germany was not yet at war with anyone. They liked to call themselves the "Fermi Five." Szilard decided that they needed help to reach the American government and considered their best hope was Albert Einstein.

Einstein was also a refugee from Germany. He was one of the world's greatest proponent of nonviolence, but he was also Jewish, a dedicated Zionist and hated the Nazis. He won world fame as a result of publishing his *Special Theory of Reality* in 1905, which it was rumored that he plagiarized most of it from the scientists, James Maxwell, Hendrik Antoon Lorentz, Albert Abraham Michaelson and Edward Williams Morley. His work on the photoelectric effect, for which he eventually won the Noble prize, was also reputed being stolen from Marx Karl Ernst Ludwig Planck. The same was true of his *General Theory of Relativity*, which was alleged to have been plagiarized from the work by the mathematician, David Hilbert. Despite being surrounded by rumors and accusations, Einstein soon became world famous. Einstein was never included in Fermi's small group of scientists. The Fermi Five did not consider Einstein capable of contributing to their work. But Szilard decided to turn to Einstein, because of his world-renown celebrity status.

The Fermi Five approached him in July, and easily convinced him that violence against Nazi Germany was not only justifiable, but necessary. Einstein agreed to put his signature on a letter addressed to President Roosevelt that the Fermi Five drafted. The problem now was to find someone who could reach the President and hand-deliver the letter to Roosevelt, personally. Szilard finally decided that a friend of his, Dr. Alexander Sachs, was just the man they were looking for. He was also Jewish and born in Russia. Sachs was educated in science, sociology, philosophy and jurisprudence, was known to be a brilliant economist and enjoyed international fame. But more important was the fact that he was a confidant of President Roosevelt, and was sure to obtain an audience with him.

On October 11, 1939, Roosevelt welcomed Dr. Sachs into the Oval Office.

"Come in, Alex. Come in," Roosevelt waved at Dr. Sachs. He was beaming a huge grin and holding his cigaret holder in his other hand. Sachs smiled and shook the President's hand, he sat in a chair opposite FDR, on the other side of his desk. "Please tell me how I can help you." Sachs continued to smile with an impish grin.

"I don't have much time to spare," Roosevelt said. "But, I can always find a few minutes for good friends like you."

Roosevelt liked to call anyone who was a supporter of his a good friend, even if they weren't.

"Mr. President," Sachs began with an apologetic tone. He recognized Roosevelt's style of letting important contributors sees him whenever they asked without ever really paying any attention to what they had to say. "I want you to know that I paid for my trip to Washington. I can't even deduct it from my income tax. I haven't come on my behalf. So won't you please pay attention?"

Roosevelt grinned and puffed on his cigaret holder. He then flicked the ashes into a tray on his desk. "Why, of course I will. You have my undivided attention. Please go on."

"Thank you, Mr. President," Sachs continued. "I have come on behalf of Professor Albert Einstein. He asked me to read a letter addressed to you." Sachs pulled out the letter and began reading it to the President.

The letter which was written by Szilard explained the process of nuclear fission and the progress made up to the present by physicists in Germany. The letter soon took on an ominous tone, warning the President of the possibility of Nazi

Germany developing the technology to built an atomic bomb that could destroy whole cities. It finally implored the President to import large quantities of uranium from the Belgium Congo, denying the mineral to the Germans, and suggested that the United States should begin developing its own bomb. Sachs finished the letter and the began reading one that he wrote warning the President of the international consequences of Hitler being the sole possessor of atomic weapons.

Roosevelt listened without interrupting Dr. Sachs. When the Doctor finished, Roosevelt flicked his cigaret once more. "What you are after is to see that the Nazis don't blow us all to kingdom-come?"

"Precisely, Mr. President," Dr. Sachs said.

FDR pressed a button on his desk. The door to the Oval Office opened and in stepped Brigadier General Edwin M. Watson, Roosevelt's military aid. He was affectionately referred to as "Pa" by the President for his grand fatherly appearance.

"Did you call, Mr. President?" the General asked as he stopped before the President's desk.

"Yes, I did, Pa," Roosevelt said as he smiled up at the General. "I have a task that requires your immediate attention."

Roosevelt gave the General the two letters and thanked Dr. Sachs for bringing this situation to his attention. After Dr. Sachs left the White House, the President ordered the General to set up an atomic bomb program, called the Advisory Committee on Uranium, under Dr. L. Briggs. In time, this committee would recommend that the United States government finance a project to procure four tons of graphite and fifty tins of uranium oxide, but no large sums of money were never made available for the project. In the next few months, Roosevelt's interest in the atomic bomb program would decline.

During the Winter of 1939–40 the western front remained quiet, except for several minor French incursions into the Saarland, which were repelled by the Germans in September and October 1939. There were no other incidents afterward. Both sides developed an attitude of live-and-let-live. The British and the French were reluctant to take any offensive actions. The French preferred to remain behind their Maginot Line, while the British argued about whether they should invade Norway or try and convince nations in the Balkans to declare war on Germany. Feelers were sent out to Romania, Yugoslavia, Greece and Turkey by the British government, trying to get them to join the Allies against Germany. The British air force restricted itself to dropping propaganda leaflets on Germany, much to the disgust of British Air Vice-Marshal Arthur Harris, a rabid proponent of massive strategic bombing on cities and other civilian communities. He complained that all the dropping of leaflets did was contribute to the continent's supply of toilet paper. Except for some minor battles on the high seas, in the Atlantic and the South Pacific between German and Allied ships, there was no fighting between the Germans and the Western Allies.

After Hitler's volatile meeting on November 5, he did not speak with Brauchitsch or Halder for weeks. On November 23, Hitler expressed his strong desire to replace Brauchitsch as Commander-in-Chief of the German Army, but he had not yet decided on a suitable replacement. The German General Staff was pleased at Hitler's order to postpone the attack in the West until Spring, 1940. During the months of November, December and January, the German economy soon began converting to a total war economy. Production of tanks, guns, airplanes, trucks, submarines and armaments all increased. Goebbels began a campaign to mobilize the German people for total war. He called on all Germans to tighten their belts and make sacrifices necessary to bring the war to a speedy, victorious conclusion by the end of 1940. Many Germans were concern about this move to total war. They still remembered the four long years of slaughter on the fronts, and the economic devastation at home during the Great War of 1914–18. But as 1939 passed into 1940, Germany was victorious in the east and there was still no fighting in the west. Germany was not faced with a two, or even a three front war as in 1914 (France, Russia and the Balkans).

Hitler was constantly requesting reports on the OKH's progress on formulating an invasion plan for the west. By November, he had still not spoken to Brauchitsch, but he had asked Lieutenant General Erich von Manstein, the Chief of Staff of Army Group A, to submit any ideas he might have for the future invasion of the West.

The German Army's plan for attacking France was a slight variation on the von Schlieffen Plan of 1914. It called for a massive sweep through Belgium and Luxembourg and then sweep down toward Paris. The German General Staff's Plan Yellow lacked sufficient motor transport. This would cause great difficulties in keeping the advancing armies supplied. The plan clearly pointed out that there was no chance of a complete victory over the fully mobilized French Army. The best the plan hoped for was capturing some of the Channel ports in Flanders for future operations. Hitler rejected the plan outright, accusing it of being infected with defeatism. Hitler was not pleased with the Army's plan and wanted to know why General Manstein had not submitted his proposed plan? Hitler rightfully suspected the Army of submitting a plan that had no hope of succeeding, because of Brauchitsch's and Halder's reluctance to attack. Both generals wanted to delay the attack until 1941. They were pleased that Hitler announced the postponement of the attack in the West until Spring, 1940, but they were not happy about Hitler asking Manstein to submit his plan for attack through the Ardennes. They hoped to do everything possible to further delay the attack.

With the mobilization of the economy for total war, Hitler ordered the German Army to be enlarged to 150 divisions and the number of armored divisions increased from 6 to 12. On October 10, Hitler had produced a 58-page memorandum describing in some detail the way armor divisions were to be organized for an attack. The principles of the Blitzkrieg were clearly laid out in the memorandum.

Manstein did as Hitler asked on September 29. He immediately returned to his operations headquarters at Koblenz and began working out the possibility of an attack in the West through the Ardennes. He was Chief of Staff of Army Group A in the West under Field Marshal Rundstedt. Manstein was able to obtain a copy of Plan Yellow and found it lacking. He could see that it would fail and cause the war to degenerate into trench warfare similar to that of the First World War. He even predicted that the front would stabilize along the Somme River. With Hitler's idea of an attack through the Ardennes in mind, Manstein suggested moving the weight of the attack from Bock's Army Group B in the north, through Holland and northern Belgium, to Rundstedt's forces east of the Ardennes. When Manstein completed his preliminary proposed plan, he made the mistake of not taking it to Hitler personally. Instead he submitted it through the OKH. Brauchitsch and Halder were not impressed, or they were, but did not want it to reach Hitler. They dismissed it out of hand. General Halder insisted that the plan should never reach Hitler, but Hitler would not be put off. On November 13 Hitler sent his chief military adjutant, Colonel Rudolf Schmundt to Koblenz to find out first hand what was happening. He was ordered to speak with Manstein and ask about the plan that Hitler requested. On November 19, Schmundt returned from his visit with Manstein, in a state of great excitement. He carried a copy of Manstein's plan for the campaign in the West. Manstein was smart enough to have made a copy of the plan he submitted to OKH, for himself. After Hitler looked over the plan, he ordered Manstein to come to Berlin immediately.

Major General Erich von Manstein was born in Berlin on November 24, 1887. His father was Eduard von Lewinski, a general in the Imperial German Army. He was descended from a Prussian military family that traced its roots back to the Teutonic Knights. Eduard's sister was childless, so he let her adopt his tenth child, Erich. Erich took the name of his stepfather, Manstein.

Manstein was not a National Socialist and in 1934 he locked horns with the National Socialist policy of expelling Jews from the armed forces. He had a reputation of being stubborn and intractable when he thought he was right. For these reasons, everyone was surprised when Hitler asked Manstein to submit his ideas on the future invasion of France, at the end of the Polish campaign. Not yet fifty-two years old, this hawked-faced, stern-looking Prussian possessed a unique intellect. General Guderian referred to him as "our finest operational brain." He had been given the responsibility by Rundstedt, his superior, to plan the invasion of Poland and the capture of the city of Warsaw.

On November 20, Manstein received the invitation from Hitler to join him for lunch in the Reich Chancellory on November 22, two days before his fifth-second birthday. Hitler liked to hold informal meetings with newly appointed generals. When Manstein arrived at the Chancellory, he was escorted to the dining room, where he discovered Hitler was not alone. With the Fuehrer were two other generals, Heinz Guderian and Erwin Rommel. Lunch was congenial and Hitler talked mostly of nonmilitary matters. When they finished their meal, Hitler invited the three generals to join him in his study to discuss Manstein's plans.

"I believe you have had some difficulties in submitting your plans, Herr General?" Hitler said to Manstein.

"Yes, my Fuehrer," Manstein said. "I found every effort to forward my plans to you blocked by the OKH."

"Yes. The OKH," Hitler nodded and shook his right hand before him as if he was shooing away a fly. "Brauchitsch and Halder. I could imagine their indignation over my selection of a junior officer, like you, to draw-up an invasion plan. The two of them have been procrastinating for weeks, though they were relieved when I postponed the invasion until next Spring. If they had their way, they would postpone the invasion indefinitely. They're like a couple of old ladies."

The three generals felt uncomfortable listening to Hitler degrade their superior officers, but they neither agreed nor disagreed.

"I wasn't at all pleased with the pathetic plan they submitted to me. All they could come up with was a watered-down version of the von Schlieffen Plan. This feeble plan is the best they can come up with. This proves my suspicions that the present High Command of the Army has grown old and senile. They lack the military tradition of the old Imperial Army."

Hitler motioned for the three generals to sit around a small coffee table in his study. Hitler took his seat. To his right sat Manstein. Rommel sat to Hitler's left, and Guderian sat directly across from the Fuehrer.

"I suppose you're wondering why I chose you, Herr General, to draw up the plan?" Hitler asked.

"Yes, My Fuehrer," Manstein said. "I am curious."

Hitler's eyes fixed on the General. "I was pleased with your plans for the invasion of Poland. You displayed a brilliant understanding of the principles of modern warfare, especially the roles played by the panzers and the air force. It was at the end of September when I had a brainwave about a possible plan for the invasion of France. It was like watching a film in the cinema. I saw it all clearly—columns of tanks streaming through the Ardennes toward Sedan, breaking through the French forces and racing across northern France to the Channel. I can't explain it, but the entire plan was laid out for me in my mind.

"Then, I remember hearing about a suggestion by General Rundstedt. He mentioned in passing that you talked about concentrating our panzers divisions along the frontier with the Ardennes and moving them through the wooded region. He thought the plan was audacious, but he was impressed, and so was I. That's why I asked you to draw up your ideas into a plan. I believe you have done so?"

"Yes, My Fuehrer," Manstein said. He sat erect and attentive, watching Hitler with amazement. Hitler had indeed impressed him and Manstein was not impressed easily. He reached into his leather briefcase and pulled out a folder filled with maps and papers. He placed them on the table before Hitler. Everyone leaned forward as Manstein began explaining his ideas.

"I had the same reaction to the OKH's plans for the invasion of the West, as you did, My Fuehrer. I realized that any tank formations moving through the Netherlands would quickly become bogged down in the water obstacles there. The Dutch will open their dikes and transform their entire country into one huge swamp. Our panzer divisions will become bogged down in the mud and will rapidly be rendered useless. Add to this the strung out urban regions with suburbs almost touching, forming a massive tank obstacle, we can conclude that it would be a foolish waste of our panzer divisions to send them through the Netherlands. We might just as well send them against the Maginot Line."

"Then, you think we should bypass the Netherlands, altogether?" Hitler asked.

"No, My Fuehrer," Manstein said. "We know from intelligence reports that the British and the French are expecting us to invade through the Netherlands and northern Belgium. They will send their armies deep into the northern regions of Belgium, to halt what they perceive is the most likely possible use of our panzer divisions, because they believe the heavily wooded, rough terrain of the Ardennes is too great an obstacle for them. But they are wrong."

"Our panzers suffered their greatest loses around Warsaw. Isn't that so, Herr General?" Hitler asked Guderian.

The General had commanded the German panzers that invaded Poland from East Prussia and surrounded Warsaw from the north.

"Yes, My Fuehrer," Guderian agreed. "Our panzers took heavy loses in the built-up suburbs around Warsaw. It's a waste of good armor to use them in assaulting urban areas."

Heinz Guderian was one year younger than Manstein, and one year older than Hitler. He was considered the architect of German armor tactics. His book, *Achtung! Panzer!* Clearly established Guderian as a supporter, not only of the modern principles of the Blitzkrieg, but of Hitler. Hitler had promoted him to Lieutenant General, and after meeting with the Guderian for the first time in February 1938, he appointed him commander of the world's first armored corp. Hitler promoted him over the heads of several officers, senior to Guderian. Hitler cultivated Guderian and pulled him into his inner circle by having him for dinner and sharing a box at the opera. Guderian considered Hitler a great man, the savior of Germany and another Napoleon. He supported the invasion of Poland because it meant the liberation of his family estate that was surrendered to the Poles after the first world war.

Manstein began sketching the new routes for the panzer divisions on the maps. "My idea is to reverse the importance of the roles of Army Group A and B. The weight of our panzers should be shifted from Army Group B in the north to Rundstedt's Army Group A in the south, facing the heavily forested region of the Ardennes, here." Manstein pointed to the location on the map. "Since the bulk of the French and British forces will be sent north to this area, from Antwerp to Namur, only a thin line of French forces should be manning the line from Dinant to Sedan."

Everyone watched as Manstein pointed to each place on the map that he was referring to.

"Do you mean to break through to the English Channel along the Meuse?" Hitler asked.

"Yes, My Fuehrer," Manstein said. "Our panzers can thread through the Ardennes unseen, under the cover of the forest. Instead of looking at the rough terrain as an obstacle, we should consider it a perfect means of concealing our panzer divisions. When they reach the Meuse, the French will be unprepared for the attack. Once across the Meuse, our panzers can race across the flat, open country which is ideal for armor, and reach the Channel here." Manstein pointed to the port of Noryelles-sur-Mer.

Hitler bent over to examine the sketches Manstein had made on the maps. Guderian and Rommel also stretched to get a better look at the red arrows representing the trek of the German panzer thrusts.

Manstein then placed another map before Hitler.

"From this point, our panzer divisions can shift north and rapidly take the Channel ports, including Boulogne, Calais, Gravelines, Mardich and finally, Dunkirk. The entire French, British and Belgium armies in Belgium will be encircled. The result will be the defeat and annihilation of all enemy forces fighting in Belgium, or north of the Somme River."

"If this is to work, the thrust will have to be quick and relentless," Guderian said. "The panzer divisions can't wait on the infantry. We must provide the means to make sure the infantry can keep up with the panzers."

Hitler turned to the third general present. "Have you checked on the production of trucks?" Hitler asked Rommel.

"Minister Albert Speer has assured me that truck production will double by February and triple by April."

"Very good," Hitler said.

Major General Rommel was three years junior to Guderian. All three generals were within two years of Hitler's own age of fifty. Rommel was everything that Hitler admired in a general. Though Rommel was not a member of the NSDAP, he represented a sharp contrast to the typical, stiff-neck Prussian officer that dominated the German Army, who were holdovers from the Imperial days. He was neither an aristocrat nor a Prussian. Hitler detested these old types and preferred younger generals like Rommel, Manstein and Guderian. But Rommel held a special place in Hitler's mind. Rommel rose through the ranks from common Swabian stock. He stood five feet, six inches tall, but he was strong and possessed an endless supply of energy. He had a nose like one belonging to a fighter, a firm chin and a good-natured mouth. He was known as a good listener, as even tempered and owning an agreeable, willing personality, and never smoked or drank.

Rommel admired Hitler and considered him to be a man of destiny. He disliked Himmler and admired Goebbels. During World War One he earned a reputation for being a courageous, dynamic and inspirational leader and won Imperial Germany's highest medal for bravery, the *Pour le merite*. It was his heroic nature that attracted him to Hitler. Hitler had appointed him as commander to his personal guard. When Germany occupied Czechoslovakia in

March 1939, Rommel accompanied Hitler into Prague. Hitler asked Rommel his opinion on how he should enter the city.

"What would you do if you were in my place?" Hitler asked Rommel.

"I should get into an open car," Rommel said, "and drive through the streets without an escort."

Hitler was mildly startled. He knew the Czechs did not exactly consider him their liberator, as the Austrians and the Sudeten Germans did. Yet, Hitler did exactly as Rommel suggested, and Rommel was enormously impressed by Hitler's courage.

Hitler was impressed by Rommel's book, *Infantry in the Attack*, which became a best seller throughout Germany, and was adopted as the training manual for the Swiss Army. But Rommel soon came to believe armor was the future of the German Army. When he asked Hitler for a command in the future invasion of the West, Hitler agreed and asked him what type of division he wanted. Rommel asked for a panzer division. Hitler agreed.

"We'll need a large amount of trucks and other transport vehicles to keep our panzers supplied," Rommel said, "and it will be just as important to provide mobility for the infantry to secure the extended flanks of our panzer penetration."

"I agree," Manstein said. "There is another dimension to the plan I want to point out. Our lightning thrust through northern France, will prevent the French army from redeploying in order to mount a counterattack. The route our panzers will take will be the precise location in the rear of the advancing French armies into Belgium. This will disrupt any attempt by the French trying to redeploying their armies. The entire French army will be cut in half. All enemy forces north of our thrust will be encircled and surrounded. The French in the south will not be able to mount a serious attempt to cut through and free them. I expect to capture and destroy over one million men, plus thousands of tanks and guns."

Hitler listened to Manstein with obvious approval. He was excited by the plan Manstein laid out before him. He leaned back in his chair and swept his brown forelock back across his forehead with a sweep of his left hand, and then ran both hands back over his head.

"This plan is just what we need to prevent the war from degenerating into a stagnated, struggle of trench warfare," Hitler said. "I will not let that fate be repeated. I suffered in the trenches and I don't want our soldiers to suffer through that type of warfare." Hitler's eyes darted from each of the generals' faces. All three generals fought in the first world war and understood all to well what Hitler was referring to, and they agreed.

"I want to end this war by the end of 1940," Hitler said. "If I am to accomplish this, I need to quickly knock France out of the war. This will require a bold and dynamic plan, and this plan is just such a plan. We will cut through the enemy's armies like a—what did you call it?" Hitler picked up Manstein's notes and looked for the word. "Ah! Like a sickle-cut. It's important to cut the British and French forces in Belgium off, and encircle them," Hitler continued to explain. "If we can prevent the trapped enemy forces in Belgium from either breaking out to the south, or escaping across the English Channel to England, as you say, Herr General, the rest of France can be overrun within several weeks. With France out of the war, and England left defenseless, England will have to agree to an armistice. But if they prove stubborn and refuse to end the war, then England will be forced to withdraw troops from the Mediterranean, North Africa and the Middle East to defend the British Isles from a possible invasion. Gentlemen, this will provide us with the opportunity to drive through the Mediterranean and overrun the Middle East. The Middle East oil will fall into our hands and the British will be crippled. They will have to agreed to an armistice. I intend to make sure this happens before the end of 1940."

"How can we do this with Italy neutral?" asked Rommel.

Hitler smiled. "Once France has fallen, I assure you, Mussolini will jump at the opportunity to end the war if I promise him enough French and British territories. Mussolini has a big appetite, but his problem is he doesn't have a big enough spoon." The three generals chuckled at Hitler's joke at Mussolini's expense.

Hitler stood up. The three generals did the same. "I had a reason for inviting all three of you here, gentlemen. You are probably the finest panzer officers I have. I am going to make sure that both Generals Guderian and Rommel command panzer divisions in the main thrust through the Ardennes. I also want to make sure that General Manstein here, is in command of the panzer thrust."

Manstein was taken back by Hitler's announcement.

"I understand General Ewald von Kleist has been put in command of those forces facing the Ardennes. General Kleist is a good officer, but he lacks experience and understanding of panzers. I want someone who understands the nature and objectives of the plan, and I can't think of anyone better than the man who originated it. But if you are to command, Herr General, you must have the rank. That is why I am promoting you to the rank of full General." Hitler shook Manstein's hand. "Congratulations."

Manstein was barely able to find the words to respond. "Thank you, My Fuehrer." He then snapped to attention and gave Hitler the straight arm salute. "Heil Hitler!"
Guderian and Rommel did the same.

When Germany invaded Poland on September 1, Britain gave Germany an ultimatum—cease hostilities and withdraw from all Polish territory or Britain would declare war at noon, on September 3. Immediately, Benito Mussolini, Il Duce and Prime Minister of Italy, rushed into the fry and offered to mediate a peaceful solution. Mussolini hoped to play the same role of peacemaker that he played during the Sudentenland crisis in 1938. Hitler informed Mussolini he was willing to a cease fire and a mediated solution between Germany and Poland. But when Mussolini conveyed Hitler's intentions, the British insisted on the withdrawal of all German troops from Polish soil. We will never know if Hitler would have accepted Britain's demand because Mussolini never passed it on the Hitler. On twelve o'clock noon of September 3, the British and French declared war on Germany.

Italy did not declare war on Britain and France, despite being a signatory of the Pact of Steel with Germany. Mussolini informed Hitler that the Italian armed forces had been depleted from years of fighting, first in Ethiopia (1935–36) and then in Spain (1936–39). The Italian Army was still using World War One rifles, and their tanks and airplanes were obsolete. Italy was not the industrial power that she would become in the second half of the Twentieth century. Mussolini never forced Italy to undergo the industrialization that Stalin conducted in the Soviet Union. In a letter sent by Mussolini to Hitler on September 3, he reminded him that in the Axis agreement, they had agreed not to go to war before 1944. Mussolini sent Hitler a grocery list of supplies and resources, as well as armaments that Italy would need to go to war. He knew that Germany could never deliver such an enormous list of goods and so Italy was able to remain neutral.

The Italian people were glad that Italy remained neutral, as did the Italian generals. Italy's foreign minister, Count Costanzo Ciano, who was also Mussolini's son-in-law, was anti-German and not only openly opposed Italy entering the war on Germany's side, but thought Italy should support the Britain and France against Germany. Ciano even read an anti-German speech before the Italian Parliament on December 16, 1939. He accused Hitler and Germany of breaking the spirit and letter of the Anti-Comintern Treaty that both Italy and Germany signed, by signing the non-aggression pact with the Soviet Union. He claimed that Germany also broke the agreement to maintain the peace of Europe that he and Ribbentrop had agreed too on May 22, 1939. Mussolini was conscious that he was considered a traitor by many Germans, and that his decision not to enter the war was being compared to Italy's refusal to honor her alliance with Germany and Austria in 1914. Il Duce liked to present himself as a war leader and felt neutrality was contrary to the spirit of Fascism. But Mussolini was also an opportunist and feared and admired the French Army. He believed it was superior to the German Army. He was not confident the Germans could defeat the French in an attack. Rather than joining Germany in its war with Britain and France, Mussolini played with the idea of declaring war on Yugoslavia and Greece, and abandoning Germany altogether. The thought of switching sides even appeared tempting. Throughout September and October Mussolini hoped for a negotiated peace. The truth is, Mussolini knew Italy was unprepared for war, and feared being drawn into the war on the losing side.

Hitler was not pleased by Count Ciano's speech, but he calmly swept it aside. He decided that the best course for Italy was to remain neutral, at least until after France was defeated. Hitler seemed to know that Mussolini was fearful of being forced to enter the war. His generals were amazed when Hitler changed his mind about Italy. Originally, Hitler was angry when Mussolini informed him that Italy could not declare war on England and France in the first week of September. Hitler's change of heart was actually welcomed by many of the German generals, who were aware of the inadequacy of the Italian Army to wage war. They felt Italy would be a drain on Germany's resources. Both the OKW and the OKH were relieved when Hitler informed them of his change of heart and preferred Italy remained neutral, at least for the time being. Hitler decided to reassure his ally. He was concern about Ciano's speech and sent Mussolini an offer to meet personally with him on the Brenner Pass on January 9, 1940.

Snow covered most of the purple slopes of the Alpine mountains in the Brenner Pass, in January. The winters in the Alps were colder than in the rest of Italy. The South Tyrol section of Italy was inhabited by Germans, about a quarter of a million people lived in this most northern region of the Fascist state. Hitler's train had arrived several hours earlier, and Hitler was already waiting for Mussolini when the Duce's train rolled into the border station. In the last several years, Hitler and Mussolini had met several times in the Brenner Pass. When the Italian train came to a halt, Mussolini found Hitler, Ribbentrop and Hitler's entourage waiting for him on the station platform. As the Italian leader stepped down from the train, he exchanged straight-arm salutes with Hitler and then they shook hands.

"I'm pleased you could break away from your busy schedule to meet with me," Hitler said as he smiled at his Italian counter-part. Mussolini knew that it was actually Hitler who had to interrupt his military conferences to meet with him, but Hitler knew how easily Mussolini succumbed to flattery, and his remark was orchestrated to do just that. Mussolini clasped Hitler's hand with both of his.

"No, Fuehrer. It is I who am grateful for your time," he said in his heavily accented German. Of the two leaders, Mussolini was the better educated. He was once employed as a teacher, a journalist and a newspaper editor in his youth. Mussolini spoke six languages; Italian, German, French, English, Spanish and Russian. "Our two countries march to a common destiny, of that I'm sure. I welcomed your invitation. It's important we have the opportunity to clear-up any misunderstandings that might have arisen from the present conflict that your great country is grappling with."

"Yes. I agree," Hitler said. "Won't you join me on my train?" Mussolini agreed. It was protocol for the meeting to take place on the train of the party that sent the invitation.

Hitler led Mussolini into his private car. The train was named, interesting enough, *Amerika*. Mussolini discovered the interior of the train car to be free of any military furnishings. There were no military documents, maps or even generals present. Hitler invited Mussolini to sit and then refreshments were brought in.

The Italian leader sat in a chair opposite from the one Hitler sat in. His dark eyes were passionate and expressive. He stood three inches shorter than Hitler at five feet and six inches tall, and always shaved his balding head. It lent an appearance of restless energy to his persona. He wore his grey uniform and black shirt, and his chess was decorated with an array of medals. Mussolini's ornate uniform contrasted with Hitler's plain uniform. The only medal Hitler wore was the Iron Cross that he was awarded to him for bravely when he served as a solider during World War One. Mussolini sat comfortably, leaning back into the large chair. His large hands, which were strong and callused from his youth as a laborer, grasped the handles of the chair. He raised his head sightly, so that his large, square chin stuck out, much as he did whenever he gave a speech. Hitler seemed oblivious to Mussolini's attempt to impress him, but Mussolini couldn't help having his ego inflated by Hitler's fawning praise. Mussolini was clearly the junior partner in the Rome-Berlin Axis alliance. Once he was considered Hitler's mentor, but after a string of bloodless victories by Hitler, from 1935 to 1939, their roles were now reversed.

"I was disappointed by the speech your Foreign Minister gave before the Italian Parliament last month," Hitler said. Mussolini was about to say something, but Hitler cut him off. "The anti-German tone was so apparent that many within my government, and the military, have expressed grave concerns about the reliability of your country's commitment to our alliance. The disappointment with Italy's performance so far has been very disconcerting."

Mussolini shifted nervously as Hitler's icy-blue eyes stared at him. He always felt uncomfortable with Hitler's eyes. Most people who have come into contact with the German Fuehrer have come away commending about the mysterious power that his eyes seem to possess. Mussolini tried to appear unmoved.

"Count Ciano spoke the truth," Mussolini said. "Your pack with the Soviet Union, though I understand its pragmatic diplomatic necessity, has caused painful repercussions, not only inside Italy, but in Spain and among anticommunist circles throughout the world. My government had to do something to reconfirm its commitment to the crusade against communism."

"I understand," Hitler said. "I did not want to sign that pack, but what could I do? Britain and France were trying to negotiate an alliance with Stalin against Germany. When Stalin asked for such a treaty, I had to jump at the chance of preventing such an anti-German coalition from forming. I didn't want war with the West. This war was started by the Jews and their allies in Britain and the United States. I made several attempts to bring this war with the English and the French to an end, but both governments have refused all my attempts. Why?" Hitler shrugged. "I'll tell you why. Britain and France would never have declared war on Germany if not for the Jews. We had every right to attack Poland. The Poles were persecuting thousands of Germans within their borders. We found evidence that as many as six thousand Germans have been killed. The situation was intolerable. God knows that I tried to avoid attacking Poland. I presented the Polish government with an alliance against the Soviet Union. But the Poles refused. The reason for their refusal was the prodding by Roosevelt and his Jewish wirepullers. We found documents that proved that the American government had encouraged the Poles to refuse our proposals with promises of support. The Roosevelt government was also promising support to Britain, and encouraged the English to declare war on Germany."

Mussolini nodded his agreement. He watched as Hitler grew more animated.

"If it wasn't for the Jews, there would be no war." Hitler waved his hand and then snapped it shut, as if he was trying to catch a fly. He slumped back into his chair and then brushed his unruly hair back over his head.

"I don't doubt that the Jew-ridden United States government was behind the Poles' stubbornness," Mussolini said. "The United States is giving moral support to the democracies, and I'm sure will eventually enter the war against Germany. This is why you must find a way to bring this war to an early end—either by a military victory or by a negotiated solution. Either way, I pledge Italy's support for Germany's war effort, but your pack with the Soviet Union has complicated things. The anti-Bolshevik unanimity among the Italian people is solid as a rock, but Germany is now viewed as an ally of communism. The Italian people and government, are divided. Italy is not ready to enter the war at this time, but you may consider Italy as Germany's reserve, to intervene militarily when the aid we need will not be a burden to Germany. It is my fondest wish for Germany to put an end to this war so that we might continue our crusade against communist."

"Yes. You're absolutely right," Hitler said. Mussolini was not expecting Hitler to agree with him so readily. He expected Hitler to pressure him to bring Italy into the war as soon as possible. "I also agree that Italy should remain as a reserve. I've placed Germany on a total war footing. The German economy is being fully mobilized with an unshakable determination to build up our military forces. The Wehrmarcht will soon be able to deliver a quick and decisive blow, knocking France out of the war. Once France has been rendered helpless, and forced to accept our peace terms, then and only then must Italy enter the war. But I repeat, only after France has been defeated."

Mussolini's eyes opened wide with surprise. He saw confidence in Hitler's eyes and felt it in his voice. He realized that Hitler was being careful not to give him any details about his plans. But that didn't matter, Mussolini was pleased. Hitler wanted Italy to remain neutral.

"Once France has been defeated," Hitler said. "Britain will be faced with the reality that she will stand alone against the might of the Wehrmarcht. Britain will have to decide whether they want to make peace with Germany or continue the war by herself.

"I can assure you, Duce, I will offer the hand of friendship to the English," Hitler said. "I will give them one last chance to end this conflict. The last thing I want is the destruction of the British Empire. Its destruction will benefit the Soviets, the Japanese and the Americans, but not Germany."

Mussolini thought that Italy also might benefit from the destruction of the British Empire, but he didn't voice his opinion.

"If Britain refuses to accept the hand of peace that I will extend," Hitler now said darkly, "then I will be forced to strike a blow that will shake her empire to its foundations. And that is when Italy must enter the war."

Mussolini wanted to ask about the details of Hitler's plans, but Hitler could not be stopped.

"I will shift the weight of Germany's might to the Mediterranean," Hitler continued. "We'll set up a joint German-Italian force that will sweep through the Mediterranean, North Africa and the Middle East. Once the English have been driven into the Persian Gulf, suffering the lost of the Suez Canal and the oil of the Middle East, they'll have to agree to end the war or risk losing what will be left of their empire. But to accomplish this, you will have to agree to a joint German-Italian command."

"I do not know if the Italian Supremo Commando will consent to subordinating itself to the OKW," Mussolini said. "The proud spirit of ancient Rome commands us to conduct our own war of conquest in the Mediterranean, when the time comes."

Hitler now leaned forward. His eyes were focused hard on Mussolini. Mussolini could feel the hypnotic pull of those blue orbs. "Duce. When you consented to the Anschluss between Germany and the land of my birth, Austria, I swore to you, I would never forget the debt I owe you for your support, and I meant it. And just as I swore then, I swear now that if you agree to Italian neutrality until after France is defeated, and then permit Germany to direct a war of quick and decisive conquest in the Mediterranean, your dream of constructing a new Roman Empire in the Mediterranean and Africa will be fulfilled."

Mussolini suddenly felt tears swelling in his eyes. He fought to contain the emotions that Hitler was able to solicit from him. Hitler's words acted like a drug, seducing Mussolini.

"I promise Italy will have an equal place at the peace table," Hitler said. "Nice, Savoy, Corsica, Tunisia, Egypt and more will become part of your new Roman Empire. All I ask is for you to join me when the time comes, and work with me as my partner."

"Of course, Fuehrer," Mussolini said. He heard the words coming out of his mouth, but it was as if someone else was speaking.

"Wonderful," Hitler said. He leaped to his feat, pulling Mussolini with him. "With Italy's assistance, victory will be assured, and then we can turn against the Russians."

When the meeting was over, Mussolini was led by Hitler to his train. Hitler continued to thank Mussolini over and over, assuring him of a glorious future. He made him feel as if the entire war depended on his assistance. Mussolini did actually believe that the outcome of the war would depend on what he agreed to do. The feeling was intoxicating, and Mussolini couldn't resist.

When Mussolini finally returned to his own train, and Hitler had taken his leave and departed for Berlin, the Italian leader was greeted by Count Ciano, who was waiting for his return.

"Well, Duce?" Ciano asked his father-in-law. Mussolini was standing, looking out of the window at the mountain slops in the distance. Ciano leaned forward in an attempt to get a better look at Mussolini. His face was beaming with joy. "How did the meeting go?"

Mussolini turned and looked straight at Ciano and then pinched his son-in-law's cheek. "It could not have gone better." He then plumped himself in one of the chairs, making himself comfortable, placing his hands behind his head, and planted his feet on an ottoman. "The Fuehrer wants Italy to remain neutral."

Ciano sat down slowly. He thought his father-in-law had lost him mind.

"Neutral?" he asked. "He *wants* us to remain neutral?"

Mussolini smiled once more and nodded. "Yes. The Fuehrer does not want Italy to enter the war until after France is defeated, and then, he promises to give us everything we want—the entire Mediterranean. He intends to drive the British out of 'Our Sea' and deliver it into our hands." Mussolini could see that Ciano was dumbfounded. He smiled and nodded again. "I still don't believe France can be defeated, but, we don't have to worry about being dragged into a war that we can't win. If Germany can't defeat France, I can always fall back on Hitler's insistence that Italy remains neutral until France is defeated. And if France is defeated, Italy will enter the war against Britain. There is no way the English can stand by herself against a victorious Germany and Italy. The Mediterranean will then fall into our lap."

Ciano was amazed. "You have just pulled off a major coup, Duce. This will solidify the love of the Italian people for their Duce."

"Yes," Mussolini said, as he once more looked out the window. The train was now picking up speed, heading south toward Rome. "This is going to be a good year for us."

Chapter 4

▼

TOTAL WAR

A large Mercedes sedan rode the whining steep mountain road the led up the side of the mountain, Obersalzburg. The man inside the sedan looked out the window and marveled at the transformation that took place over the last several years. Martin Borman had been responsible for the elaborate transformation. As assistant to the Secretary of the National Socialist German Workers' Party, Rudolf Hess, he made himself indispensable to Hitler over the years. From 1934 on Borman worked hard to remain in close proximity to Hitler's beck and call at all times. Never leaving Hitler's side, he was ready to fulfill the Fuehrer's every wish. He was able to win Hitler's trust by always appearing reliable, hard-working and dependable. A short, square-shaped man, Borman had a Stalin-like quality about him. A poor speaker and lacking all charisma he worked hard trying to win people over by appearing to be obliging to everyone. In this way, most people jumped at the chance of availing themselves of Borman's services. Even Rudolf Hess found it convenient to keep Borman close to Hitler. But Borman was a schemer, always working to undermine Hitler's opinion of anyone Borman felt stood in the way of his advancement, including his own immediate superior, Rudolf Hess.

Borman laid out a network of roads that cut through the magnificent countryside of the Obersalzburg mountain with little regard for the natural surroundings. There was always some project that was being constructed somewhere near Hitler's home, the Berghof. Barracks were built as well as a hotel for guest to Hitler's home. Every security measure was put into place so that the mountain side would become a fortress. Hitler never bothered himself about the construction details, and when he was asked about it he said he regretted all the construction but commented, "It's Borman's doing; I don't want to interfere, but when it's all finished I'll look for a quiet valley and build another small wooden house there like the first."

"Hitler first moved into his pleasant little wooden house on Obersalzburg in 1925. It had always provided a comfortable retreat for Hitler in an idyllic setting nestled away in the Alpine mountains around Berchtesgaden. Even after it had been asked to and rebuilt in 1935, Hitler stilled loved to escape to the lofty peaks of the Bavarian Alps.

When the Mercedes finally came to a halt at the foot of the flight of stairs that led to the main entrance to Hitler's home, a SS soldier dressed in black stepped up to the car and opened the door. The mountain air was cold and crisp in February and Dr. Albert Speer felt refreshed by its sensation on his face. He loved the mountains and was an ardent skier. Speer was sent by Hitler to visit him at the Berghof and report on his progress on converting the German economy to a total war footing. He was also in charge of overseeing the development of new weapons.

Speer proceeded to climb the long flight of stairs that led to the entrance of Hitler's mountain home. He glanced up, expecting to see Hitler walking down the stairs to greet him, as was Hitler's custom whenever quests arrived at the Berghof. Speer stopped dead in his tracks with one foot resting on the first step. He couldn't believe his eyes. Instead of seeing Hitler walking down the stairs to greet him, he saw Eva Braun, Hitler's mistress, standing at the top of the stairs. Momentarily surprised, Speer proceeded to climb rapidly until he reached Eva, who greeted him with a lovely smile and an outstretched hand.

Speer took her hand and gently shook it.

"It's good to see you again, Albert," Eva greeted him in the informal matter. She was enjoying Speer's obvious astonishment.

Eva was a simple Bavarian girl, attractive, with honey blond hair and possessing a shapely figure that she worked hard to keep in shape through a rigorous workout of calisthenics and gymnastics every day. She was impetuous, and her head was filled with dreams of love, fashion and movies. She often daydreamed of becoming a movie star. Totally devoted to Hitler, she lived a lonely life. Hitler never permitted her to be seen in public, and except for a small inner circle of acquaintances that Hitler surrounded himself with. Most people in Germany, including many of Hitler's most important supporters, did not even know of her existence. Hitler met her in the late Twenties, when she was working for his personal photographer, Heinrich Hoffman. A relationship soon developed between the thirty-nine year old politician and the seventeen year old assistant. At this time Hitler was involved with his half-niece, Geli Raubal. Eventually Geli committed suicide after she got wind of the growing relationship between Hitler an Eva. Eva earned her place at Hitler's side, but there was a price. She was expected to remain invisible. Hitler's Fuehrer image of being totally devoted to Germany could not include a love interest with any woman. Speer was a member of Hitler's inner circle, and it was his knowledge of her cloistered life that caused Speer's amazement when he saw Eva greeting him, as if she was the first lady of Germany.

"Dear Eva, what a delightful surprise," Speer said. He and his wife had become close friends with Eva over the years.

"I'm sure you never expected to be greeted by me," Eva said. "And by the look on your face, I thought you were going to have a heart attack." Eva giggled.

"I must say, I didn't," Speer said.

Eva and Speer began walking into the entrance of the Berghof.

"The Fuehrer asked me to greet you," Eva said. "He's busy with Field Marshall Goering and General Milch. They're discussing something about jets." Eva waved the subject off, revealing her disinterest in such matters.

Speer knew what she was referring to better than she did. In fact, one of the reasons for his being summoned to the Berghof was to report on the progress of the production of the jet fighter, the Heinkel He280. Hitler had ordered its production at the meeting on September 27 and charged Speer with overseeing its progress. Speer wasted no time. He immediately understood the significance of such a weapon. It was first test flown in August, 1939, but Hitler had not shown much interest in it. Hitler never expected Britain and France to declare war on Germany after he had concluded the non-aggression pact with the Soviet Union. But Hitler had a change of heart and was now very interested in its production. He was insistent that the first jet fighters be ready for operation by summer.

"I must confess, Eva, I never would have believed it if someone had told me they were greeted by you. It's so unlike the Fuehrer to ask you to greet anyone."

Eva smiled. She knew that Speer understood better than most what her life was like, and that he did not mean his observation as an insult.

"Six months ago I would not have believed it either," Eva said. "But ever since the war broke out, the Fuehrer has been acting different."

Speer's eyebrows rose on his forehead. He was not the only one who had noticed the change in Hitler. Others had mentioned it, but it was not something one openly discussed. The Reich government was a hive of ambitious men. Hitler had maintained an atmosphere built on the principles of Social Darwinism. He encouraged his subordinates to be ruthless in the advancement of their careers. It was one way Hitler maintained his own position of power. No one ever knew if a casual remark would be twisted or taken out of context and then repeated to Hitler. Speer was not afraid of disappearing into the night and whining up in a concentration camp. Such things were all too common in the Soviet Union, but it did not happen in the Reich. But such callousness could ruin one's career.

"How do you mean?" Speer asked. He deliberately lowered his voice, but Eva did not notice.

"He's no longer insistent that I remain out of sight," Eva said. "He insisted I join him when he welcomed Goering and Milch early today. I dear say, Goering was amazed to discover that I was more than just one of Hitler's secretaries."

"I could imagine," Speer said.

"You should have seen the look on Goering's face when Hitler called me his little Liebchen. He almost choked." Eve laughed.

"I wish I was there to see it," Speer said.

"The Fuehrer has always been affectionate to me in private, but always guarded his feeling toward me when other people were present."

"But, not anymore?"

"No," Eva said. "The servants were the first to notice the change." Eva stopped and looked at Speer. "Do you know what he told me last week?" Speer just shook his head. "He said he wanted to marry me."

Speer opened his mouth to speak, but no words came out.

"He told me, he expected the war to end soon, and he would achieve his objectives of gaining all the living space Germany would need in the next three or four years. Then, he told me we would marry and I would become the first lady of Germany. I still don't see him as much as I would like. He's always busy with the war, but when he's around, he's been especially tender and attentive."

Speer rubbed his hand across his chin as he thought about what Eva just told him. "I have also noticed a change in the Fuehrer in the last several months. It began at the end of September. I was worried at first, but after what you just told me, I must say, I am no longer concern." Speer smiled. He leaned closer to Eva, as if he was about to whisper a secret. "Any man who wanted to marry you, has to be quite sane."

Eva kissed Speer on the cheek and then, with both hand wrapped around his arm, she led him inside.

Hitler was waiting for Speer in his study. With him was Herman Goering and Erhard Milch. Milch was Armament Chief of the Luftwaffe, directly under Goering's authority. He was half Jewish, on his mother's side, but neither Goering, who never took the anti-Semitism of National Socialism seriously, or Hitler, held this against Milch, for Milch was a dedicated National Socialist and capable engineer. When Speer was ushered into Hitler's study, Hitler immediately stopped talking to the Reich Marshal and Colonel General.

"Ah! Herr Speer, you have arrived," Hitler said.

Speer saluted. "Heil Hitler," he said, but Hitler ignore his salute. "Come. I want to hear about your progress in transforming our economy onto a total war footing."

Speer shook Milch's hand. "Good to see you again, Albert," Milch said.

Milch and Speer had become good friends during the last several years. Speer had been commissioned to oversee the construction of many of the Luftwaffe's projects. Speer turned and greeted Goering, but Goering only nodded his greeting. Goering was still put off when Hitler awarded the young Speer with the position of Minister of Armaments and Munitions on September 27. Goering had hoped to firmly assert his authority over Speer as the leader of the economic Four Year Plan, which gave him authority over the entire economy. But when Hitler gave the position to Speer, he told Speer that he was to answer directly to him, and no one else. Hitler told Speer that if anyone tried to tie his hands, he was to refer that person directly to him. When Goering tried to exert his authority in November, Speer did just this and Goering backed down. He tried to claim that it was all a misunderstanding and blamed the attempt on incompetent subordinates.

When Speer was given the task of coordinating the production of weapons and munitions by Hitler, he lost no time in using Hitler's authority to establish for himself the extensive powers necessary to accomplish this mission. On October 12, 1939, Hitler publicly backed Speer's supremacy in armaments production in a speech to leaders of the armament industries. This enabled Hitler's youngest minister to do pretty much as he pleased within the widest limits. He displayed a ruthless drive to achieve his objectives that surprised most people. Equipped with Hitler's full authority and backing, and with Goering acquiesce to the reality of Speer's authority, Speer wasted no time in implementing his plan of industrial self-responsibility. Speer's plan called for entrusting eminent technicians from leading industrial firms with the management of separate areas of armament production. He did this through the formation of directive committees for different types of weapons and directive pools for the allocation of supplies. Almost immediately, armament production astonishingly skyrocketed. From October 1 to February 1, a mere four months, armament production had significantly increased by 21 percent for guns, 19 percent for tanks, and 80 percent for ammunition. Total production in all areas had increased by 46 percent.

Needless to say, Hitler was pleased, but Speer was astonished that Hitler did not seem surprise by Speer's performance. When he had asked Hitler about why he had chosen him for this position, Hitler fixed his icy blue eyes on him for a few second before finally saying, "A little voice told me that you were the right man for the job."

Hitler stood with his hands folded as Speer began making his report.

"First, let me report that I am pleased to announce that instead of our original estimation of ammunition production of 865,000 tons for 1940 has been changed to 2,000,000 tons. By December 1940, the Army will have enough equipment for a strength of 225 fully equipped infantry divisions and 45 armored divisions."

"How were you able to accomplish such a feat?" Goering asked.

"By reducing the size of the bureaucracy," Speer answered. "With the permission of the Fuehrer, I have begun the standardization of equipment and the consolidation of several research and development teams from different branches of the armed forces. This has eliminated a great deal of waste and redundancy. Production has increased because of the introduction of the assembly line in all plants. I have only begun making such reforms, and there still is more that has to be done, but the result so far speaks for itself."

Goering nodded reluctantly. Milch smiled his approval. Hitler displayed no reaction. Speer continued with his report.

Speer reported on the increase rate of production of cannons, tanks and ammunition in the last four months. "I estimate tank production for 1940 will be approximately 3,800 up from 247 for 1939. Truck production will reach 52,000, up from 32,558 in 1939 and aircraft production will increase to about 25,500 in 1940 up from 8,295 in 1939. This last figure, of course, will include the production of both the new four-engine, long range Ju89 bomber, or Ural Bomber, as well as the He280 jet fighter."

"How many of the Ural Bombers will be operational this year?" asked Milch.

"Only about a hundred, but production is expected to increase dramatically in 1941," Speer said. "The Fuehrer has stated that we won't need the bomber for operations against Britain or France, but it will be needed for a possible future war against the Soviet Union."

Hitler nodded once more without speaking as he continued to listen.

"But progress has been made by Ernst Heinkel on the He280 jet fighter," Speer continued. "He promised to have all the bugs out of the design that were discovered when it was first tested flown in August 1939, by June 1940. With the Fuehrer's decision to develop the jet fighter in September, resources have been allocated that is making it possible for Herr Heinkel to rapidly perfect his fighter. He has made remarkable progress in the last four months. Herr Heinkel conducted a second test flight on November 1 with remarkable success. Production of the He280 could begin by August."

Hitler finally spoke. "I want that jet fighter ready to deal with the British if they prove stubborn, in the summer. After we knock France out of the war, the only thing that will stand between our goal of acquiring living space in the east, at the expense of the Soviet Union, will be the British Empire. It will take at least eighteen months for Germany to develop the naval force to cross the English Channel assuming we reallocate enough resources. We don't have that luxury. Intelligence has reported that the Soviets have already begun to build-up their forces along their western borders with Europe. If our war with the Western Allies drags on into 1941, Stalin will not let the opportunity to attack Germany in the east, escape. I estimate the Soviets will attack Germany in the summer of 1941. That's why I need the He280 by the fall of this year. With it, we can drive the British out of the Mediterranean, Northeast Africa and the Middle East. With such loses, the British will not be able to continue resisting. They will have to come to terms with us. I only hope that the British are not so foolish as to let things get so far out of hand. It will only result in crippling the British Empire, and that will only benefit Japan, the Soviet Union and the Americans. How many can we expect to produce when production begins?"

"I have calculated that 200 could be produced in August, 400 in September and 1200 in October," Speer said.

"Very good," Hitler said. "Production will increase after we discontinue production of convention fighters. These jets will give Germany air supremacy in any future war with the Soviets. I want you to also investigate other research projects by Messerschmidt and Junker."

"I have already requested Messerschmidt and Junker, as well as Walter, Wolfram and Reimar Horten to submit plans for other jet planes, both fighters and possible bombers."

"Horton?" asked Hitler.

"Yes, my Fuehrer," Goering interrupted. He jumped at the opportunity of contributing to the good news and steeling some of the thunder from Speer.

"They have the most remarkable design for a jet fighter. It's shaped like a flying wing. I believe it has potential."

Hitler nodded and turned back to Speer, and ignoring Goering. "Very good, Herr Speer. But there is one more thing."

"Yes, my Fuehrer," Speer said as glanced for just a second at Goering.

"I want you to look into the development of a new type of tank," Hitler said. "I believe we must develop a new type of tank that is far superior to even our Mark III and IV. We will not need it for the attack in the west, but I want it for the invasion of the Soviet Union. It will have to be developed and ready for production by May 1941, at the latest."

"I understand," Speer said.

"Tomorrow, in Berlin, Reich Minister Goebbels is going to deliver a speech calling for total war," Hitler said. "When the British and the French declared war on Germany, I was apprehensive about putting the German economy on a total war footing. I remember the effect it had on the morale of the German people after four long years during the Great War. I do not want the people to suffer such privations once more, but I have come to believe that the German people are up to the task of making the necessary sacrifices needed to win this war in the shortest possible time. That's why I reversed my decision and ordered total war.

"Do you know that the SS has unearthed a treasonous nest in the Abwehr, after Admiral Canaris was arrested?" Hitler said, but he did not wait for anyone to answer. "I have always relied on my instincts, and they told me that treason existed within the Abwehr, but I had no idea how rotten to the core it was. I fear even our enigma code has been compromised."

"I doubt that very much, my Fuehrer," Goering said. "The enigma is impenetrable. There are over a trillion combinations. There is no way the Western allies could possibly break the enigma."

Hitler looked at the Reich Marshall. "But what if the British and French were able to get their hands on one of our machines? What if Canaris and his affiliates were able to pass on the secrets of the enigma to the British and the French? After reviewing the reports of the extent of the treason that Canaris and his cronies perpetuated, I would not be so sure as to dismiss the possibility. Anyway, if they have, we can use it to our advantage."

Hitler walked around to his desk and sat in the chair. He rubbed his hand across his mouth and looked out of the window at the majestic peaks in the distance. Speer, Goering and Milch watched him, waiting for him to speak once more.

"The destiny of the Reich will be determined in the next three years," Hitler said. "Britain and France must be dealt with in the next twelve months. Once we have put an end to this war, we can then begin the great crusade against Jew-ish-bolshevism, and acquire the living space Germany needs in the east. Only in the east can we find the needed territories for Germany to expand. I have written in Mein Kampf that the future lies with great land powers. Only a nation that controls a large, continuous expanse of land, inhabited with hundreds of millions of people of the same race, will remain a great power in the future. Three powers represent a threat to Germany and Europe in the future. They are the Soviet Union, the United States and China. But with living space in the east, I intend to create a Germany that will stretch from the Rhine to the Volga and contain two hundred and fifty million German speaking people by the end of this century. But the territory needed to lay down the foundation of this greater Germany has got to be acquired by 1943. If we fail to defeat Britain and France this year and the Soviet Union in the following two years, I fear the United States will enter the war against us. Roosevelt and his Jewish backers are itching for war, but the only thing standing in their way is the reluctance of the American people. But if we accomplish our objectives before 1943, the United States will never go to war against us, especially if the Japanese grow aggressive in the Far East."

Hitler stared up at the three men sitting on the other side of his desk. "We have much to do, and time is rapidly running out."

On February 15, at 8 PM, Dr. Goebbels was greeted by a thunderous explosion of *Heils!*, as he stepped onto the rostrum. He hobbled as he walked due to his deformed right leg. When he was seven, he suffered a medical disaster, probably osteomyelitis (a bone marrow inflammation) that caused him to be crippled for the rest of his life. His right foot was 3.5 centimeters shorter than his left. The heel was drawn up and the sole hooked inward. As a result, his right leg always hurt when he walked.

Even without his club foot, Goebbels was still short and thin in stature. His face was perceptibly flattened at each side. His nose was large and slightly hooked, and his upper teeth protruded. His head appeared too large for his body and his complexion was swarthy. His brooding, almond shaped eyes burned under his high, receding forehead. Goebbels was only half German—his mother was from the Netherlands. His diminutive appearance did not cause him to withdraw from the world, but instead it festered into a bitter resentment toward it. His enmity, plus his nimble mind, resulted in Goebbels turning toward radical politics. Even within the National Socialist Party, Goebbels inhabited the most radical wing. When the war broke out in September, he immediately advocated putting Germany on a total war footing, but Hitler vetoed his recommendation. But his disappointment did not last long and he was delighted when Hitler informed him in October that he wanted him to ready the German people for total war.

For the next four months Goebbels unleashed a propaganda campaign designed to mobilize the German people for total war. Every information and news media began exalting the need for sacrifices by the population. Goebbels' coined the slogan, *TOTAL WAR: SHORTEST WAR,* and it began appearing everywhere. Everything was done that could possibly be done to whip the German people into supporting the war effort. This speech was the culmination of Goebbels' efforts. He felt alive and excited. In the years before the war, Goebbels fell out of favor with Hitler. When Hitler ordered him to take charge of this effort, he felt reborn. This was the opportunity he waited for, dreamed about. It was a chance to redeem himself in the Fuehrer's eyes, and he was not going to disappoint him. The Sport Palace was packed to capacity with twenty thousand of his trusty Berliners. This was the most important mass rally of his career. He planned to deliver a white-hot speech. Every radio network in the Third Reich was geared to broadcast his speech worldwide. He had feared that the Fuehrer was not as radical as he was, but Hitler had shown the courage to order total war. He knew it all along that Hitler was as radical as he was. Was it not Goebbels who convinced Hitler to run against von Hindenburg for President in 1932? Though Hitler lost the election, it led directly to his being appointed Chancellor of Germany a few months later. The rest was history. Now Hitler had turned to him once more to take the most radical measures. No more moderation—no more compromise. The Fuehrer had decided to prosecute the war with total abandonment and ruthless determination.

Goebbels stood before the packed hall. Behind Goebbels was a huge poster that read: *TOTAL WAR: SHORTEST WAR.* He said nothing for several minutes, letting the suspense to build until it was almost intolerable. Goebbels was the greatest orator in National Socialist Germany, second only to Hitler himself. When he finally began to speak, he did so quietly and carefully. His words resonated throughout the enormous hall. "I want to speak to you from the depths of my heart, to the depths of your heart," he pleaded. "Some say that the German people have not the will and determination to seek it through this war, but I know the German people, and I know the German people with their discipline can persevere through this great endeavor. A savage, determined will lives in us to see this great conflict through to total victory."

He began his speech with a call for the community's eagerness to unite behind the Fuehrer, for total war and followed through with a warning that if the nation did not make a resolution to sacrifice for the war effort, Germany would be destroyed. He made them see that Germany's moment of destiny was at hand. "In the Great War Germany was surrounded and blockaded, fighting a war on two fronts. But not this time. There is no enemy in the east. We face an enemy only on one front. We are not handicapped as we were during the last war. We are not surrounded on all sides by enemies. If Germany loses this war it will be our fault. It will be the result of slackers and traitors who put their own, selfish interests before the good of the Fatherland."

The audience was on their feet, saluting and cheering. A chant began to fill the hall, "Fuehrer commands! We obey!" Goebbels pauses as he lets the applauding sweep through the hall. He stand's erect, with his hands on his hips, and his chin raised. His baritone voice continues to resonate once more. "If International Jewry and their British and the French allies are able to defeat us, the last bulwark against bolshevism will fall. Jewish capitalism will sweep across Europe. Is that what you want?"

The audience shouted, *No!* Over two hundred times the audience leaped to their feet and shouted their approval, interrupting the Minister of Propaganda as Goebbels harangued them with a call to arms and sacrifice.

Goebbels elaborated on the threat that Germany and Europe faced. "If we lose this war, not only Germany, but all of Europe and Western civilization itself will cease to exist. Only the Wehrmacht and the German people, and helped by their friends and allies, have the strength to save Europe and the white race from this mortal peril. If the Western Powers are triumphant, they will flood Europe with hordes of Africans and Asians from their colonial empires, to rule over us and defile our women. If the French have their way they will create a mulatto state stretching from the Congo River in Africa to the Oder River in Germany. Then nothing will halt the advancement of Jewish capitalism. This is the peril we face. We must act together, quickly and thoroughly lest it be too late."

Goebbels went on to enumerate the necessary measures that must be implemented for Germany to be victorious. He warned the people that it would be necessary to close cabarets, bars and nightclubs, lavish restaurants, opulent shops, fashion houses and hair dressing salons. People would have to cancel vacations and sojourns in spas and skiing resorts. Food, petroleum, and other necessities would have to be rationed. "The people are not afraid to accept this Spartan standard of living—in fact, they demand it!"

Goebbels went on to put forth ten questions. Each time Goebbels was interrupted with applause.

"My first question is: The English and French hope the German people lack the faith in victory. I ask you: Have you lost faith with our Fuehrer and the fatherland in the final victory of the German people?

"I ask you: Are you prepared to follow the Fuehrer in this struggle for victory, however hard the path may be, and however great you personal sacrifices?

"My second question is: The English and the French say the German people are spent.

"I ask you: Are you ready to plunge into this struggle with savage determination, impervious to whatever Fate may have in store, and until we are victorious and have wiped away the shame of 1918?

"My third question is: The English and the French say the German people are not willing to support the total mobilization of the German Reich.

"I ask you: Are you, the German people, prepared to work ten, twelve, if need be, fourteen and sixteen hours a day, if the Fuehrer orders you to do so, and give all you possess for victory?

"My fourth question is: The English and the French say the German people reject the government's measures for total war. They do not want total war but capitulation." I ask you: Do you want total war? Do you want war, if need be, even more total and more radical than we can imagine today?

"My fifth question is: The English and French say the German people are not united behind the Fuehrer.

"I ask you: Is your faith in the Fuehrer today greater, deeper, and even more unshakable than ever before? Are you absolutely and unconditionally prepared to follow him, and to do everything that is necessary to bring this war to a quick and victorious end?"

Each time Goebbels asked his question the audience leaped to their feet shouting their Approval with arms stretched out before them. With boundless enthusiasm they roared with one voice: "Fuehrer, order us and we shall obey!"

"My sixth question is: Are you prepared to give every ounce of your strength to supply our Wehrmacht with all the men and arms needed for a swift and victorious conclusion?

"My seventh question is: Do you give your solemn oath to be soldiers, that those at home will stand firmly behind them with an unshakable spirit and give them what they need for victory?

"My eighth question is: Do you, particularly you, our women, want the government to make arrangements enabling the our German women to put their whole strength behind the war effort? To fill the gap wherever possible, free men for the front, and thus help our soldiers at the front?

"My ninth question is: Do you approve that the most radical measures must be taken, if need be, against the small number of war shirkers and black marketeers, who, in the midst of war, play at peace, trying to exploit the people's needs for their personal advantage? Do you agree that whoever sins against the war should be put to death?

"My tenth and last question is: Do you want that in accordance with the National Socialist party program, all citizens should share rights and duties equally—particularly in the war-time—and that this burden should be distributed equally among the high and low, the rich and the poor?"

Each time Goebbels asked his questions, the Sport Palace erupted into thundering cheers of approval. The enthusiasm was contagious and euphoric, sweeping everyone up in its passion, drowning out Goebbels' words.

"We, the leaders of the party, the state, and the Wehrmacht, swear to you and to the Fuehrer that we shall weld the people at home into one united nation. Never again shall we fall into our old vice of indulging in too much objectivity, which has damaged us so much in the past.

"The nation is prepared for anything. The Fuehrer has given his orders and we shall obey. If ever in the past we believed in victory, loyalty and unity, we now believe in it more than ever. Just as proud as we are of the Fuehrer, he shall be proud of us. In times of crisis the truly strong show their mettle. Victory will be ours—we need only to unite and fight. We must only marshal the necessary will power to subordinate everything else to it. This is what the hour demands. Let, therefore, our motto be: 'Arise as one nation, and let the storm burst upon them!'"

For twenty minutes the applause continued the thunder throughout the Sport Palace.

Churchill was disappointed when the Finns capitulated to Stalin's demands in November. He was hoping that the Finnish-Soviet dispute would escalate into a full scale shooting war that would draw in the other Scandinavian countries. His predatory ambition was zeroed in on Scandinavia, and he was seeking an excuse for British intervention in northern Europe as early as October 1939. But when the Finns acquiesced to Stalin's demands, any plans by Churchill to draw the entire Scandinavian peninsula to the war with Germany died—at least for the time being. Churchill was a determined man, and after overcoming a life-time of disappointments and failure, he was not about to give up on a full scale war in Europe just because of the Finns' lacked a backbone.

Throughout the winter months Churchill was constantly pushing and badgering the British War Cabinet offering several different plans for British intervention in Scandinavia. Most of the plans involved British troops invading and occupying Norwegian ports, especially Narvik in the far north, and invading Sweden to occupy the Swedish iron ore mines at Gaellivare. Germany was receiving substantial iron ore from Sweden's mines in Gaelivare. During the winter months, when the Baltic Sea was frozen, Sweden's Baltic port of Lulea was icebound. The ore had to be freighted by train to the Norwegian port of Narvik. From this port in the far north of Norway, the ore was then shipped to Germany along the costal waters of Norway. So long as the ships remained in Norway's costal waters, any attempt by the British to sink the ships would be a violation of Norwegian neutrality. When it seemed that the Soviet Union and Finland would go to war, Churchill hoped to use the excuse of providing aid to the Finns through neutral Norwegian and Swedish territories as a pretext of denying the iron ore to Germany.

When the possibility of war breaking out in Scandinavia passed in November, Churchill had presented his new plan, entitle Wilfred, to mine Norway's costal waters. He hoped this would force the German ships into the open sea where the British could attack and sink them. He later advocated a bolder plan of simply occupying Narvik and other Norwegian ports, outright, but the British War Cabinet was not yet ready to violate Scandinavian neutrality.

When Churchill presented his plans in December 1939, Prime Minister Chamberlain replied, "Your plan is quiet illegal, Winston. I thought we were fighting for Law and Order."

Churchill smiled and then said, "I am willing to break the Law to protect the Order. If that means violating the neutrality of the Scandinavian countries, so much the better to entice Herr Hitler to send his Wehrmarcht divisions to the north. The more divisions that are tied down in Scandinavia, the less he will have at his disposal for the invasion of France and the Low Countries."

But Chamberlain would not listen.

Despite his failure to convince the British War Cabinet to invade Scandinavia, Churchill wasted no time during the winter months feeling out Britain's friends and allies on the possibility of such an invasion. In December he met with the American ambassador, Joseph Kennedy, before he returned to the United States for Christmas. He made Kennedy promise to present his plans for the invasion of Scandinavia to President Roosevelt. Kennedy, who feared American intervention in a war that he considered tragic, was more concern that Churchill's scheming would lead to an escalation of the war beyond Europe. Kennedy had several sons and the thought of one or more of his sons fighting and dying in a possible world war terrified him. He had plans for his sons. Especially his oldest, Joe Junior, who he was priming to run for the White House and someday become the first Irish-American, Catholic President of the United States. Kennedy was determined to warn President Roosevelt that First Lord of the Admiralty was willing to go to any lengths to bring the United States into the war. He was so concern about Churchill's scheming that before he left Lisbon for the United States on the ship, *The Manhattan*, he let it be publically known that not even if the ship he was traveling on was blown up in the Mid-Atlantic, would it serve as a pretext for the United States entering the war.

Churchill also met with Admiral Darlan from France in January 1940. Churchill was pleased to discover that Darlan was in favor of an Allied invasion of Scandinavia. Darlan agreed with Churchill and also felt that it would help to ward off a German invasion of France and the Low Countries, and offered to send several French divisions for the invasion. Two million German troops were stationed on Germany's western borders with France, Belgium, Luxembourg and the Netherlands. The French were anxious about a possible German attack through the Low Counties. When Britain and France both requested to plan a common defense of Belgium, the Belgian government refused. The Belgian refusal to cooperate with the Allies, and their determination to remain neutral induced Darlan and the French government to support any military adventure that would divert German attention elsewhere. If Germany got bogged down in a long and protracted campaign in Scandinavia, Hitler might be forced to postpone any plans for an offensive in Western Europe.

On January 11, a light German air force plane strayed across the Belgian frontier and crash-landed near the Belgian town of Mechelen-sur-Meuse. On broad was Major Helmet Reinberger, who was carrying plans for the invasion of Western Europe drawn up by the OKH. These plans called for a possible invasion to begin on January 17.

Major Reinberger tried to burn the plans before being captured by Belgian authorities, but enough of the plans survived. The plans were then forwarded to both the French and British military authorities. Both the Dutch and Belgian armies began to mobilize their troops on the German border. What they didn't know was that Hitler never seriously contemplated the invasion that was laid out in those plans. These were plans that Brauchitsch and Halder had drawn up on Hitler's orders. Their plan called for a modified version of the von Schlieffen Plan the Germans used in 1914. Hitler had not informed them that he that he had already commissioned von Manstein to draw-up plans for the invasion that would strike through the Ardennes. After discovering the nest of spies and traitors in the military intelligence bureau, the Abwehr, after Caranis' arrest, he did not want the army to know his exact plans. So when the German attack did not materialize in January, British and French military authorities assumed it was due to the capture of Major Reinberger.

Churchill was quick to jump on this incident as a pretext for pushing through his plans for the invasion of Scandinavia. He warned the British War Cabinet that it was by a mere chance of luck that the invasion was postponed and it was now imperative to invade Norway and Sweden. Only an invasion and occupation of Norwegian ports along the entire coast of Norway, and the occupation of the Swedish iron mines at Gaellevare, could force the Germans to abandon their plans for the invasion of Western Europe before the summer.

On February 5 the Supreme War Council, which was comprised or civilian representatives for both France and Britain, agreed to meet in Paris. Chamberlain invited Churchill, as well as Lord Halifax, Oliver Stanley and Kingsley Wood, to join him in Paris. They met with the French Prime Minister Edouard Daladier, Admiral Darlan, General Maurice Gamelin and Paul Reynaud. The purpose of the meeting was to discuss the strategic course of the war. Everyone was amused by Churchill's "strange, spurious naval costume," as Chamberlain referred to it behind Churchill's back. Like Goering, Churchill loved to dress-up in military uniforms. At the meeting Churchill insisted that the Allies adopt his plan for the invasion of both Norway and Sweden, which included the occupation of Narvik and other Norwegian seaports, and also the Swedish mining town of Gaellivare. The meeting only lasted three hours, but Churchill could not resist dominating the conversation. He constantly referred to the Scandinavian plan until finally, the French agreed to the idea.

Daladier accepted the plan in principle, but was reluctant to finalize it. Reynaud and Darlan were both more enthusiastic. Reynaud even suggested that the Allies bomb the oil fields in Baku, in the Soviet Union, to prevent the oil from being shipped to Germany. Churchill was pleased that the Supreme War Council terminated the meeting after agreeing to Churchill's plan to invade Scandinavia. Only two questions remained; when the invasion should take place, and what would be the reaction of both the Norwegian and Swedish governments?

Once back in London, Churchill grew frustrated as he discovered Chamberlain's delaying tactics. The Prime Minister never really warmed to the idea of a second world war. He found the entire affair horrifying and felt that he was dragged into it by his colleagues, especially Churchill. He wished he could find some honorable way to end it without ever fighting. For this reason he finally informed Churchill that before the Allies invaded Scandinavia, he wanted to obtain an invitation for the entry of British and French troops into Scandinavia, by the Norwegian and Swedish governments. When both governments answered with a resounding, no, he planned to hold a cabinet meeting vote to cancel the invasion.

Churchill was desperate and that's when luck intervened. He received word that British intelligence intercepted a German communication that revealed the Germans were planning to invade Scandinavia. Churchill immediately called for a meeting of the Supreme War Cabinet. If Churchill thought he was lucky to have intercept the German plans, Fortune was to smile once again on him. On March 21 Reynaud replaced Daladier as Prime Minister of France. It was agreed that a meeting between Reynaud and Chamberlain should take place on March 28, in London.

The Prime Minister of France was ushered into 10 Downing Street as soon as he arrived. Inside, Prime Minister Chamberlain, Churchill and Halifax were waiting for him. Reynaud was a tiny man, slightly under five feet tall. His eyes were slanted and his face seldom showed expressions, but when he talked his face usually was contorted "like a monkey" as Chamberlain described it, as his head moved in the most odd way. But despite Reynaud's physical shortcomings, he possessed a powerful will and self-confidence that bordered on arrogance.

"We are so very glad you could come to London for this meeting," Chamberlain said, expressing his appreciation. "I fully understand the delicate predicament that your government faces."

Reynaud stared at the Prime Minister of England from across the table. "Thank you, Mister Prime Minister. I also felt it was imperative that our two governments come to an agreement on what course of action our forces should take against the Germans. Now that I am in charge in France, there will no longer be any further procrastination on the part of France. I am anxious to commence with our plans for the invasion of Scandinavia. I hope it can commence within the next week."

"I still hope that we can obtain the consent of both Norway and Sweden for the occupation of their territories before we get the go ahead with our operations," Halifax said. "It would be criminal if our actions in Scandinavia were to be viewed by the world as those of the aggressor. It could hurt us in the eyes the world if our two governments are seen as invaders of neutral nations."

Churchill, who had been puffing on one of his cigars now leaned forward. "I wish to reiterate the fact that our course is one of international order and civility. If we must abrogate for a space of time some of the conventions of the very laws we seek to consolidate and reaffirm, we have the right to do so because it is our governments that have put our very existence on the line by taking up arms against the German aggressor. The small nations must not tie our hands when it is we who are fighting for their rights and freedom. Humanity, rather than legality, must be our guide."

"The First Lord of the Admiralty is perfectly correct in his assumptions," Reynaud said. He was on good terms with Churchill and the two had agreed to work together to motivate Chamberlain into consenting to the invasion of Scandinavia before the meeting. "We must ensure that Germany is denied the use of the Swedish iron ore mines. The lost of this most valuable supply of iron will cause a major disruption of the German economy that could cause Germany to lose the war. And to ensure that this is the case, my government feels that we must set a deadline on operations that will eliminate another source of dearly needed fuel. I am referring to the destruction of the oil fields in the Caucasus, especially those in and around Baku."

This was more than Halifax could take.

"To attack Baku could not be considered anything less than a declaration of war on the Soviet Union," Halifax said. "Presently, our two governments have more than we could deal with in facing the full strength of the German Reich. After Germany invaded Poland, Britain was forced to declare war on the Reich because of our treaty with the Poles. We all know that we would have not declared war if we could have found a way of saving face, but there was no way. But we did not see fit to declare war on the Soviet Union two weeks later then the Soviets attacked Poland. Stalin did not declare war on us, and I do not see why it is necessary to force Stalin's hand by giving him a perfect excuse to declare war on our two governments."

Churchill did not respond to Halifax's protest. He had no desire to declare war on the Soviet Union. It was Germany and National Socialism that he hated and his supporters wanted destroyed. But he was willing to use Reynaud's desire to expand the war even further to force Chamberlain's hand where Scandinavia was concern.

"Mister Prime Minister," Chamberlain began, "Let me be blunt. I know that the inclusion of the Soviet Union into this war as Germany's ally would help to consolidate your government by winning the support of the right-wing within

France, but I must agree with Mr. Halifax. The addition of Stalin as Hitler's ally would be a colossal mistake."

Reynaud sat still as he listened.

"Gentlemen," Churchill now said before the French Prime Minister could speak, "I think we should consider the French proposal of bombing Baku, but only after the operations in Scandinavia have been concluded. This should be done as soon as possible. That's why I suggest we agree on an invasion date of April 5. As our intelligence has confirmed, Hitler is planning his own invasion of the Nordic countries. We can't wait for the consent of the Scandinavian governments. After our armies have landed, they will protest, but once the Germans have invaded, they will then welcome us as the defenders of their liberties."

Everyone looked at Chamberlain. The Prime Minister realized that there was nothing he could do. He took a breath and then exhaled. "It would seem that there is nothing further to be said other than agreeing to the date for the invasion."

"Our military leaders have assured me that we can land two British and two French divisions on April 5," Churchill said. "That's two days before the Germans' plan to invade."

Chamberlain looked about the table. Only Halifax seemed disappointed. Reynaud still sat without expression. "Then it's agreed, but I want to give formal warning to both the Swedish and Norwegian governments of our occupation and the reasons for it." The Supreme War Cabinet agreed and Reynaud was on his way back to France before night fell. Churchill seemed exceptionally pleased, but Halifax was visibly despondent. Chamberlain wondered if he had made the right decision.

As early as December 1939, Hitler received a visitor from Norway. He was the former Minister of Defense of Norway, Vidkun Quisling. Quisling was sympatric to National Socialism and formed a small party of his own, the Nasjonal Samling (National Unification) Party. But because of his lack of talent as a politician, his party never received more than 5 percent of the vote. But Quisling still had contacts within the Norwegian military and he was informed that Norway's intelligence had information that the British were making plans to occupy Norway. Admiral Raeder was impressed by his claims and introduced him to Hitler. Quisling asked for money to build his movement in Norway. He claimed he had the support of many of the officers in the Norwegian armed forces, including Colonel Sundlo, the commander of Norway's defenses in Narvik. Hitler was anxious about the possibility of the Allies invading Scandinavia and promised support.

In the next few months Quisling proved unable to build his movement, but Hitler continued to worry about Scandinavia. The German vessel, *The Altmark*, was chased in Norwegian waters and boarded by the British ship, *The H.M.S. Cossack*. The Norwegians made a weak and unconvincing protest to the British government. Hitler was convinced that the Norwegians were in league with the British. Quisling sent to German intelligence, the SD, proof that the interception of *The Altmark* by *The H.M.S. Cossack* was prearranged by an agreement between Churchill and Carl Joachim Hambro, a Jew and the President of the Norwegian parliament (Storting).

On April 3, Hitler decided to inform both the Norwegian and Swedish governments with intelligence information that the Allies were planning to occupy their territories. Because of Germany's increased production, especially her expanded submarine force and the Luftwaffe, both governments were forced to give Germany guarantees that they would resist if their territories were violated by the British and the French. They also had to accept Hitler's offer of sending German forces to help resist any invasion of Norwegian and Swedish territories with German troops. Neither government knew that Hitler had given General von Falkenhorst instructions to prepare an expeditionary force for Scandinavia as early as January 20.

CHAPTER 5
▼

NORTHERN LIGHTS GO OUT

Churchill was as excited as a schoolgirl on her first date. His effort for the past seven months had finally paid off. "Germany," Churchill said to his Eden, "has made a major strategic mistake. By permitting us to step foot on the Scandinavian peninsula first, we have outfoxed the wolf in Berlin."

On April 5 four British divisions had landed at Narvik, Norway, under the command of General P. J. Mackesy. The landing was greeted by fire from the Norwegian troops stationed at Narvik. Colonel Sundlo, who was in command of the defending Norwegian forces, ordered his forces to resist the invading British army. He knew he could not hold Narvik with the forces under his command, especially with the British Navy offshore, but he would do everything in his power to resist. The Colonel was a supporter of Quisling and sympathetic to Germany. A small but influential circle of Norwegian officers in the Army had made preparations with the German Wehrmacht to coordinate their efforts to resist the British, until the Germans could come to their rescue. Colonel Sundlo planned on withdrawing from Narvik at the last possible moment, and then head north where he could continue to resist the Allies until he could received aid from Germany. But he was amazed at the weak performance of the British troops despite their superiority in numbers and firepower.

General Mackesy was not the right man to lead the invasion of Norway. He was a timid man and overcautious. He had complained that he did not have enough troops, and even requested permission to withdraw after the first twenty-four hours. Admiral Lord Cork ordered Mackesy to continue with the invasion, but it was only after the British Navy began bombing the Norwegian coastal defenses that Mackesy resumed the attack. By April 8 the Norwegians were finally forced to withdraw in land, and Narvik fell to the British. Mackesy's orders were clear. He was to regroup his forces and immediately move inland and cross the Swedish border. His objective was the capture of the Swedish iron ore mines at Gaellivare. With Narvik securely in their hands, the British now could use its invaluable port to reinforce their troops with men, material and supplies. They could use its airfield to build-up its forces, until they were strong enough to conquer all of northern Norway and Sweden. On the morning of April 7 the British forces crossed the Swedish border and advanced toward the iron ore mines at Gaellivare.

The government of Norway did not declare war on Britain and France, but King Karl Haakon announced a state of hostilities between Norway and the Allies. Haakon was sympathetic to the Allies, but he was confronted with an invasion of his country. Factions within the Norwegian government and armed forces were demanding that he declare war, and invite Germany to come to Norway's assistance. King Haakon was informed that if he did not call for German assistance he would be faced with a military coup d'état. Quisling had spoken to the people of Norway on the radio, calling on all Norwegians to resist the British and their allies. But he did not declare himself the head of a new government in Norway. He was notified by the German government that he would not be recognized if he did. On April 6 King Haakon reluctantly called the German ambassador to see him, and requested that the German Reich come to Norway's assistance.

With the call by the Norwegian government for German assistance, Hitler immediately stressed the peaceful intentions of the German government and occupation not only in Norway but also for Denmark. His directives were followed by General Falkenhorst's directives on the course of the invasion of Scandinavia. Throughout the winter, the Germans had been reading about a third of the British naval signals for months, and was fully aware of the British plans for the invasion of Scandinavia. Falkenhorst was able to prepare the German respond because he knew exactly where the British landings would take place along the Norwegian coast.

The situation in Sweden was different from that in Norway. Norway was on the western coast of the Scandinavian peninsula, and more vulnerable to Allied attacks. The Germans considered it imperative that Norway be occupied. The same was not true for Sweden. As soon as the British violated Swedish territory, the Swedish government also declared a state of hostilities with Britain and her allies, but the Swedes were determined not to fall under German occupation. Hitler knew this and his government did not demand Sweden permit the occupation of the entire country.

Hitler, however, did demand that Sweden permit the transport of a German force by rail to Gaellivare, to help defend the iron ore mines. The Swedish government consented. On April 7 Hitler gave the order to resist the Allied invasion of Scandinavia.

On April 8, German troops had already crossed the Danish border. The Allied invasion of Norway and the violation of Swedish territory, provided the perfect justification by the German government to demand the occupation of both Denmark and Norway. The German ambassadors in both Oslo and Copenhagen approached the governments of Norway and Denmark, demanding that Germany be allowed to send troops in the defense of these two Scandianian countries. Though both monarchs, King Haakon of Norway and his brother, King Christian of Denmark, were sympathetic to the Allies, they had no choice but to permit the German troops to occupy their countries without resistance. It was agreed that German troops would coordinate their activities with the Norwegian army against the Anglo-French forces, respecting the rights of the governments of both nations. Hitler desired not to conquer Scandinavia, but preferred to establish some form of Nordic confederation between Germany and the Scandinavian countries.

Denmark was quickly occupied with no resistance or loss of life, while the Norwegian army was now allied with the Germans in resisting the Allies. Many of the officers of the Norwegian army wanted to resist the Allied invasion and quickly accepted German assistance. If the Germans had invaded first, most of them would have just as quickly resisted the Germans. Hitler knew this and wanted the assistance of the Scandinavians. This is why he permitted the Allies to invade first.

Besides the landings at Narvik, the Allies also landed ten thousand troops above and below Trondheim. Maurice Force set down on the shores north of the Norwegian city of Namsos, while Sickle Force landed south of Trondheim at Andalsnes. These Allied forces consisted of British, French and Polish troops. Everywhere they landed, they were confronted with Norwegian resistance. The

Norwegians were no match for the Allies. British naval war ships supported the landing forces bombarding the defenders from sea. After the Norwegians put up token resistance they quickly withdrew inland. The Allied force immediately began moving on Trondheim from both the north and south. But things started to go badly for the Allies. The Allied landings ran into unexpected difficulties, most were due to incompetence and poor planning.

The German fleet sailed into Oslo with a diplomatic team. It arranged a meeting with the King of Norway and the Norwegian government. It was agreed that a new government would be formed that included Vidkun Quisling, and it would continue to run things internally without German interference.

The Germans also contacted the Swedish government. Hitler did not demand the occupation of Sweden, because Sweden's long coast was facing east, on the Baltic Sea, and was not exposed to Allied attacks, but Swedes gave the German the right to transport troops through Sweden to assist the Swedish army resisting the Allied invasion of Swedish territory from Narvik. Hitler was determined not to permit the Swedish iron ore mines to fall into Allied hands. The Swedish government consented to German demands permitting the transport of several divisions to Kiruna. These divisions moved immediately to assist the Swedes resisting the British forces that were moving on the iron mines at Gaelivare.

At Andalsnes, the Allied commanders did not land at the same site as their men, and confusion broke out. The British troops lacked ammunition because the carriages and mortar ammunition were mistakenly left behind in Britain. The British force tried to advance north despite the withdrawal of the Norwegian army, but failed because of the terrain. The British lacked the equipment necessary to cross the difficult Norwegian landscape, which was still covered with snow in early April. The Allies at Andaisnes then tried to move south toward Dombas but were stopped by a joint Norwegian-German force on April 29. The whole force was annihilated. Those British troops that surrendered were eventually flown to Berlin and marched through the city for the German public to see how easily Germany was able to defeat the British.

To the north of Trondheim, at Namsos, Maurice Force was in a state of confusion. The British antiaircraft guns did not arrive because they were loaded on the wrong ship, and were headed for Narvik. The French Chassers Alpins (elite mountain troops) could not strap their skies on their booths because they were issued the wrong straps. To make matters worst, the Allied supply ships were too large to enter the harbor there, and there were delays in unloading badly needed supplies. This prevented the Allied forces from moving south toward Trondheim. The delays lasted for weeks and soon the Luftwaffe began bombing the Allied forces and blasted Namsos to rubble. This gave the German troops that eventually came to the assistance of the Norwegians, time to launch a joint German-Norwegian offensive that eventually forced the surrender of the Allied forces.

At sea, the Allied naval forces found it difficult to maintain support for its landings along the extended Norwegian shores. There were now almost 50,000 Allied troops in Norway, but the Allies were finding it impossible to coordinate their invasion. The Norwegians were resisting and the Swedes also refused to permit the Allies to occupy their territory. The German navy was now moving along the entire Norwegian shore, as far north as Mosiden, while the German Army and Luftwaffe began intervening directly throughout Scandinavia.

As the British and Allied troops struggled to establish their bases along the coast of Norway and invade Swedish territory, the Germans were watching the events unfolding very carefully. When the German navy had set out for the North sea, its ships were flying the Union Jack. Their objective was to land German troops at the Norwegian ports, as far north as Trondheim. The Germans realized they were taking a major risk. The coast was swarming with British ships. All challenges to German ships were answered by the Germans, in English. The Germans were able to fool the British into thinking they were hunting German steamers along the Norwegian coast.

In Berlin Hitler, Keitel, Jodl and Raeder listened carefully to the reports on the progress of the German navy. They knew they were taking a great risk trying to transport thousands of German troops right under the nose of the British Royal Navy. By 5:15, on the morning of April 9, German troops began landing at the Norwegian ports of Arendal, Cristiansand, Egersund, Stavanger, Bergen, Alesund, and Trondheim. Hitler had coordinated his military and diplomatic force perfectly. He seem to have nerves of steel, and was convinced that they would succeed in outwitting the Allies. General Eduard Dietl was a tall and lean man and specialized in mountain and winter warfare. He was assigned by General von Falkenhorst with the mission of stopping the Allied advance on the Swedish iron ore mines in northern Sweden. Dietl's 10,000 German and Austrian mountain troops arrived at Kiruna, Sweden, on April 16. Once there, he quickly joined the Swedish troops, and together they launched an attack on the British. The British offensive was stalled while they waited for reinforcements. Ten thousand additional French and British troops had landed at Narvik on April 14, but not able to reach the front. The Norwegian Colonel Sundlo was launching his own attacks on British positions from northern Norway. This provided Deitl the perfect opportunity to ready his forces for a counteroffensive, which began on April

19. The German-Swedish forces struck before the Allied reinforcements could arrive. The Allies could not hold their positions, and were forced to retreat across the border into Norway. By May 1, the Allies were besieged in the port of Narvik. General Mackesy requested permission to evacuate his forces by the British Royal Navy. Churchill was not pleased with the request.

Churchill had received reports of the German intervention. German air attacks on the British Fleet was causing havoc for the British invasion forces. On May 1, Churchill had retired to bed just before midnight. He couldn't sleep and sat, propped up with several pillows, as he pawed over the reports and maps of Scandinavia. He was convinced that the Germans could not have anticipated their invasion and were not prepared to confront them in Norway and Sweden with the necessary forces needed to prevent them from achieving their objectives. Churchill had to prepare himself for an emergency meeting to be held at No.10 Downing Street the next day.

"Damn that fool!" Churchill thundered as he slammed his whisky glass on the table. He slumped into his chair and chewed on his cigar as he waited to be called into Chamberlain's office. He had rushed over to No.10 Downing Street for an emergency meeting with the French leaders. When he arrived, he found Eden also waiting. "I could have told the British High Command that Mackesy was not up to the task," Churchill said. "No steel in the belly. He's as soft as a baby's behind. I won't permit his forces to withdraw from Narvik. They must hold onto the port and fight to the last man."

"We can't permit that, Winston." Eden said. "Our forces at Andisnes and Namsos have both surrendered. The German and Norwegian navies have complete control of the Norwegian coast, as far north as Bodo. If we have the opportunity to withdraw our forces from Narvik, we should do it before they are completely destroyed. They will be needed if the Germans attack France and the Low Countries."

Churchill continued to pout as he crewed on his cigar. "We should send additional troops to Narvik and keep open this northern front," Churchill said. "So long as we can maintain a front in Scandinavia, the Germans won't attack in Western Europe."

Eden just shook his head. He could see that Churchill was despondent. The Scandinavian venture was his brainchild and it was turning into another Gallipoli. Twenty-five years ago, in the Great War, Churchill had pushed for an invasion of Turkey and the capture the Straits. If it had succeeded, Turkey would have been knocked out of the war and a supply lane to Russia would have been established. The Allies would than have controlled the Balkans, and Germany would have lost the war in 1916. But it did not turn out that way, and Churchill was forced to resign as First Lord of the Admiralty, after the defeat at Gallipoli. Now history was repeating itself. The invasion of Scandinavia was Churchill's idea, and it was turning out to be as great a defeat as Gallipoli. Eden believed that Churchill was worried that it could result in his disgrace once more, forcing him to resign once again. Before Churchill or Eden could say anything else, they were summoned into the Prime Minister's office, where the French leaders were waiting for them.

"It would seem that our operations in the Scandinavian peninsula are not going exactly as we hoped," Chamberlain said. He glanced over at Churchill, knowing full well that the Scandinavian adventure was Churchill's operation. Churchill ignored the Prime Minister as he continued to chew on his cigar, and stared at the top of the conference table. "We have to face the reality that we can't secure southern Norway, or even central Norway. If we hope to salvage anything from this operation, perhaps we should try and hold onto Narvik?"

"I don't believe we will be able to hold onto Narvik for long," Admiral Darlan said in his heavily French-accented English. "The Germans have reinforced the Swedes, and are now joined by the Norwegians. Narvik is being attacked from three sides. The Norwegian population in Narvik is hostile to us. Our troops are depressed. We should withdraw as soon as possible to prevent a total disaster."

Churchill now roused himself from his depression. "I disagree," he said. "The actual feat of supplying and maintaining our foothold at Narvik should not be difficult. We still maintain control of the sea, and the German's supply lines are overextended. As for the five thousand Norwegians who live in Narvik, we should begin shooting them and if necessary, use our ships to totally destroy all resistance through saturation naval bombardment."

"Really! Winston! We can't possibly do that," Halifax interrupted.

"Why not?" Churchill snorted. "If the Norwegians side with the Nazis, then they are the enemy. This is not the time for timidity. If we are forced to withdraw from Narvik, then we should see to it that the Germans can't use the port for their own purposes. In fact, We should do something possible to take the heat off our troops in Norway. I suggest the French army invade Belgium immediately, to forestall a German attack in the Low Countries."

Reynard, who had recently replace Daladier as Premier of the French government, now spoke up. "That would only antagonize the Belgians and perhaps cause them to invite the Germans into their country as allies, just as the Norwegians and Swedes have done. They have already moved their forces along their borders and with our borders. Besides, I thought the purpose of invading Scandinavia was to 'take the heat off' the Low Countries." Reynard smiled at Churchill.

"The Belgians have no stomach for war," Churchill said. "They are cowards. They have no desire to get into this war! But we can't concern ourselves about them. The Germans will soon launch their attack against western Europe in the next few weeks. It's better if we occupy Belgium before they do."

"If you're right," Reynard said, "then it would be better to end this campaign in Scandinavia, especially before Sweden and Norway formally declare war on us, and concentrate on preparing to meet this German attack in Western Europe."

"Mossier Reynard is correct," Chamberlain said. "The Scandinavian campaign has proven a failure. I will sent the order to General Mackesy to prepare for the withdrawal of his forces from Narvik."

The meeting was adjourned, but Churchill didn't protest. He appeared angry, but knew that he had to cushion the blow of the Scandinavian debacle. Everyone at Whitehall knew that Churchill was responsible for the disaster in Norway, but Churchill's public esteem was still too high for him to be publically rebuked. At the same time, Churchill knew that he had made too many enemies over the last month, and they would try and have him removed from the cabinet. His dominating personality caused many problems. He constantly interfered in affairs that were not part of his jurisdiction as First Lord of the Admiralty. As chairman of the coordination committee he often gave instructions without first consulting the chiefs of staffs or his political associates, which caused hard feelings and resentments. The chiefs of staffs felt ignored and bypassed by Churchill. Added to this was his erratic behavior and his constant contradicting of his own decisions. Churchill was able to avoid a full-scale revolt over his conduct of the campaign in Scandinavia, only by offering to resign his chairmanship of the committee. This would have caused problems for Chamberlain and split his government, causing it to fall. To prevent this, Chamberlain was forced to give Churchill additional powers to go along with the chairmanship and a small military staff. Churchill, in effect, had become a second Minister of Defense. This also created many enemies for Churchill, especially among those who were closest to Chamberlain, who felt Churchill had humiliated the Prime Minister. Many in the British government were now hoping to use the Norwegian fiasco to finally force Churchill to resign from the government. But Churchill had his own ideas about that. In the Great War, Prime Minister Herbert Asquith and Lloyd George forced him to resign after Gallipoli. But he knew that Chamberlain was not strong enough to force him to resign, and he did not have the support of the opposition parties.

General Mackesy's British infantry and snow-trained French mountain troops began withdrawing from Narvik by May 5. On Saturday afternoon, May 9, President Roosevelt had invited his Secretary of the Treasury, Henry Morgenthau, to met with him and his closet confident, Harry Hopkins, in the Oval Office of the White House. The day was bright and sunny. Hopkins was already present when Morgenthau arrived in the Oval Office at two in the afternoon. The President and Hopkins had just finished their lunch, and Roosevelt was in a jolly mood as he puffed on his cigarette holder.

"Ah! Henry has arrived," FDR said, interrupting Hopkins as Morgenthau was shown into the Oval Office by a White House aide. "Please, Henry, do sit down and join us."

"Thank you, Mr. President," Morgenthau said politely as he took a seat on the other side of the President's desk. "I hope I did not keep you waiting?"

"Not at all, old fellow," the President said as he flicked his cigar ashes into an ashtray. "You're punctual as always." The President quickly turned the conversation to the business at hand. "Harry and I were just talking about the situation in Europe. Damn well disappointing. Don't you agree?"

"If you're referring to the defeat and withdrawal of Allied forces in Scandinavia?—I do," Morgenthau said. "The Germans not only got the better of the Allies, but were able to transform a potential defeat into a major victory. Hitler was not only able to drive the Allies from Scandinavia, but he was able to neatly put the three Nordic countries into his back pocket."

"What do you think is going to happen next?" Roosevelt asked his Secretary of the Treasury.

"Now that northern Europe is secured by the Germans, it's just a matter of time, perhaps days, before they strike into Western Europe."

"Through the Low Countries?" asked FDR.

"Yes, Mr. President," Morgenthau said. "We can expect the Germans to strike through Belgium and Luxembourg, just as they did during the Great War."

"What about the Netherlands?" asked FDR.

"They might very well include the Netherlands in their invasion route this time," Morgenthau said as he adjusted his glasses on his face. "The air war is much more important today, and the Netherlands will afford the Germans an excellent site for airbases, to strike at England."

"Do you really think it will get that far?" the President asked. "I mean—the Germans overrunning the Low Countries."

"I don't know," Morgenthau confessed. "From the intelligence reports that I've read, I believe the British and French plan to move quickly into Belgium and confront any possible German invasion deep in that country, rather than on French territory, is a good plan. Whether they're able to keep the Germans out of the Netherlands, depends on what the Allies do. Will they try and move into the Netherlands or not is not known."

"What about the French and the British, Harry?" Roosevelt turned to Harry Hopkins. "Will the Allies be able to halt the Germans in the Low Countries?"

"Our intelligence services believe that they will," Hopkins said. "But the real question is—can they keep the Germans at bay, as they did in the Great War? The French army is the best in Europe, and has as many tanks as the Germans, if not more, and the British and French have almost as many aircraft, though the British are unwilling to send the bulk of their air force to the continent. I believe they'll be able to stop any German attack through the Low Countries, but they will need supplies and equipment from the United States. If we support them, they should be able to conduct a war of attrition for several years—perhaps to 1943."

"Good!" Roosevelt said as he slapped his palm on his desk. "By 1943 we should be able to bring the United States into the war against Germany. Germany will be exhausted by then. The U.S. will be able to send an army of five million to Europe, and crush the Germans, just we did in the Great War."

"Are you sure you'll still be President in 1943?" Morgenthau asked. "After all, no President has ever served a third term. Your cousin, Teddy, tried and failed. Will you be able to secure the Democratic nomination this summer?"

Roosevelt was annoyed by Morgenthau's question, but he refused to show his displeasure. His face stretched into the biggest smile he could summon. "Why Henry, dear fellow, do you really think that there is anyone else who could possibly unite the party?"

Roosevelt had not originally planned to run for a third term. His New Deal policies were a disaster for America. The depression returned with a vengeance in his second term, and the economic situation was worse than when he first was elected President in 1932. He had hoped to increase spending in his second term, to delay the effects of the worsening economy until he was out of office. He also intended to support his closest confidant and friend, Harry Hopkins, as his successor, as far back as 1938. Hopkins was the only person that Roosevelt could bear replacing him as President. He appointed Hopkins as Secretary of Commerce in an attempt to provide him with political visibility, and thus, help him secure the nomination in 1940, but his plans were dashed by Hopkins' poor health. Hopkins fell ill and was diagnosed with cancer in 1939. His doctors wrongly predicted he had only four weeks to live. But any hope of Hopkins running for the presidency in 1940 was impossible because of rumors about his ill health.

With the outbreak of war in Europe in September 1939, FDR decided that it was his destiny to lead the United States for the next five years. FDR hoped to use the war to put an end to the depression, and jump-started the U.S. economy through a program of rearmament. The stock prices on the New York Stock Exchange had actually jumped with anticipation of a U.S. program of arming the Allies. There were big interest groups within the Republican Party that saw the war as a means of turning the economy around. Many of the individuals and corporations that opposed FDR during much of his first two terms now supported him in his desire to enter the war against Germany. Roosevelt was sure he could win their support and form a coalition with those elements within the Democratic party, especially the New Deal socialists and Jews who saw National Socialism as the greatest evil on the face of the earth, in eventually bringing America into the war.

Roosevelt understood that most Americans did not want anything to do with this European war, but he hoped to eventually wean Americans into the war through a secret program of antagonizing Germany. He also knew that he could not begin such a program until after he was reelected in 1940. Until then, he had to present himself as someone who hated war and opposed America's entry into the war.

"Kennedy doesn't have much confidence in France's ability to hold out for long," Hopkins said.

"Kennedy is a secret Nazi-lover," Roosevelt said. "If I could dump that Irish bastard, I would, but I need him to win in November. So I'll keep him in England, where he can't do me much harm. But I wouldn't put much credence in what he reports."

"He'll denounced you, Mr. President, to the New York Daily News, in January," Morgenthau said.

"I know, Henry," Roosevelt said. "When I return to the White House in 1941, I'll exile Joe to political Siberia. In the meantime, I still need his support. He has a lot of influence in Boston. But what do you think are our chances of helping the Allies, Henry?"

"There's not much we can do until we convince Congress to increase spending on the military," Morgenthau said. "I have been meeting with General Marshall.

He has a list of what we'll need, especially planes. He advocates conscription for the army and increase plane production to 50,000 a year."

"I see," Roosevelt said as he rubbed his chin. "I had hoped to ask Congress to increase spending on the military later this year, but we might have to wait and see what develops in Europe first. I'm afraid that much of what Marshall wants, and what we need, will have to wait until after the election in November. I can't have the Republican candidate accusing me of wanting to go to war. The American people don't have the stomach to enter the war at this time. Do you think the French and British will hold out?"

"Yes, I do," Morgenthau said. "I think Harry will agree with me." Hopkins nodded. Morgenthau continued. "With the debacle in Scandinavia, it's just a matter of days before Chamberlain steps down and is replaced by Churchill, as Prime Minister. He's been inching for a war with Germany for years."

"Yes, he has," Roosevelt said.

"He's been a big supporter of the Zionist cause, a friend to the Jewish interests and a dedicated enemy of Nazism and Hitler," Morgenthau said.

"I remember Churchill in the Great War," Roosevelt said. "He was a piggish little man, always drunk and boorishly rude to everyone. But he is just the lout that England needs to continue the war against Hitler. Besides, with Churchill as Prime Minister, we'll be able to reduce the British to a willing lapdog that will jump head-over-heels for our financial assistance. What about the French?"

"Dalaider was replaced as premier in March, by Paul Reynard" Morgenthau said. "Reynard had been preaching that France should stand up to Hitler and Nazism for years. He's determined to fight."

"That's very encouraging," Roosevelt said. "With France and England holding Germany at bay, I should be able to convince Congress to provide aid and supplies to them in their struggle against Germany throughout the rest of the year. I can then concentrate on getting reelected in November. Who do you think the Republicans will put up against me, Harry?"

"Despite your promises to keep America out of the war, and your calls for peace and a negotiated end to the fighting, the Republicans will continue to paint the upcoming election as a contest between Democratic internationalism and Republican isolationism," Hopkins said. "In 1938, everyone, including the chairman of our party, Jim Farley, thought the Republican candidate in 1940 would be Senator Arthur Vandenberg, but after the Gallup Poll last year, it looks like the front runner for the isolationist camp is New York district attorney, Thomas E. Dewey, followed by a tied second place between Vandenberg and Senator Robert Taft of Ohio. Did you know that Joe Kennedy has made statements to columnist Drew Pearson that his favorite Republican candidate is Vandenberg? And that he would support Vandenberg against half the potential Democratic candidates?"

"Yes. Yes. I read that piece of crap by Joe," Roosevelt said. "Do you know, I think Joe has delusions about running for the White House? Can you image an Irishman as President? That's all we need. He'll turn the Oval Office into a saloon."

Hopkins and Morgenthau chuckled along with the President at his ethnic slander of Kennedy.

"So what do you think about Dewey?' Roosevelt asked. "Is he the one I'll have to face in November?"

"Well, he did beat Vandenberg in both Republican primaries in Wisconsin and Nebraska last month," Hopkins said. "And both states were considered Vandenberg country. Dewey's campaign is well financed, he's thirty-eight and presents an image of youthful vigor and confidence. His crusade against organized crime, as district attorney, has made him something of a hero, and he holds a commanding lead against Senator Taft. The Republicans would be wise to pick him as their candidate."

"But his isolationist views have alienated the internationalist-minded bankers, lawyers, and businessmen within the Republican Party on the east coast," Roosevelt said. "Did you know that crowd tried to stage a coup against me back in thirty-four, or was it thirty-five? But now they're on board with my interventionist and internationalist policies. I think we can work out a deal with them, to make sure the GOP puts up someone just as interventionist as I am. Don't you think so?"

Both Hopkins and Morgenthau smiled and agreed.

During the years between the Great War and the outbreak of the Second World War, the Conservative Party dominated British politics during most of the time. The Conservative Party continuously governed Great Britain from 1922, with the exception of two short-lived, minority Labor governments. The Conservative government remained popular, and if the Second World War had not broken out, it probably would easily have won reelecting in the elections due to be held in 1940.

When the war broke out, The Labor and Liberal Parties promised to support the war effort, but both parties refused to join a coalition government with the Conservative Party, so long as Chamberlain remained Prime Minister. Chamberlain knew this and hoped to win the war without fighting a war. His plan to defeat Germany was simple, but unrealistic. He believed that by avoiding all-out war, he could eventually topple Hitler through economic pressures. If his plan worked, he could ensure Conservative dominance, and his own future for a long time to come. But with the defeat in Scandinavia, this would now be impossible. To win the war would now require full-scale mobilization of the Empire's resources, and this would require a coalition government with the Labor and Liberal Parties. But there was no hope of this being achieved so long as Chamberlain remained Prime Minister. He knew he would have to resign.

The Conservative's 200 seat majority in the Parliament ensured that the only way Chamberlain could be toppled was through a revolt in his own party. There were no obvious successors to Chamberlain, except one. Anthony Eden, Sir Thomas Inskip and Sir Samuel Hoare had all missed their chances to replace Chamberlain before 1939. Lord Halifax was considered a possibility, but his peerage had excluded him in the past. The only obvious replacement was Winston Churchill, and Churchill knew it.

Before the outbreak of the war, it was the opinion by most in Britain that Churchill's political career was over. He was considered a loose canon, who had flipped back and forth among Britain's different parties. While he was a member of the Conservative party, he was considered a part of the far right. His anti-Bolshevik, pro-Mussolini, pro-Zionist views and his total opposition to any form of self-government in India, isolated him. His judgement was considered erratic and impulsive. People still remembered his debacle at Gallipoli campaign during the Great War. He was once described by the former Prime Minister Baldwin, as "a military adventurer who would sell his sword to anyone."

Chamberlain was forced to accept Churchill as part of his government in September 1939, because Churchill had been the primary critic of his appeasement policies, and an advocate for opposing Hitler, even if it meant war. Churchill knew that his appointment as First Lord of the Admiralty was his last chance to salvage his career and rise to the position of Prime Minister. He worked hard in the last six months to move himself into a position that made himself the obvious replacement to Chamberlain, if the latter was forced to resign. As First Lord of the Admiralty he was able to inflate his own imagine with the public, because the only real fighting took place at sea. And Churchill never missed a chance to personally report favorable news, and let others announce bad news. He was not above inflating figures, and announced in January 1940 that half of the German U-boat fleet had been destroyed. A month later he declared that two-thirds of German U-boats had been sunk. Both claims were false. When bad news was announced, he would spread rumors through his supporters that he was always against whatever decisions that had led to the debacle. The invasion of Scandinavia was Churchill's idea, but when things starting going against the Allies, he began to distance himself from the campaign. Though he was responsible for the debacle, he would claim that he was against the entire idea from the very beginning. Churchill new that the Scandinavian debacle was a golden opportunity for his advancement to the position of Prime Minister. Many criticized him for the failure of the invasion. General Ironside said the campaign proved that Churchill, was too unstable to become Prime Minister. Lord Beaverbrook, the press lord, said that Churchill was the man who let the Germans into Scandinavia.

Churchill skillfully used his contacts in the opposition parties to ensure that he was not made the scapegoat for failure of the Scandinavian campaign. While he feined loyalty to Chamberlain, his cronies in and out of Parliament spread rumors that blamed Chamberlain for the disaster in Scandinavia. His satellite, Duff Cooper and Leo Amery, were doing everything possible to create mischief for Chamberlain's government, and position Churchill as his obvious successor. Churchill had been busy in the last week of April, meeting with a pillar of the Conservative Party, Lord Salisbury, about forming a coalition government with both the Labor and Liberal Parties. He was also discussing with the leaders of both opposition parties of the possibility of his replacing Chamberlain.

Rising discontent within the government had come to a head in a two-day debate within the House of Common on May 7 and 8. The Scandinavian campaign had transformed the Parliament into a powder keg that threatened to explode in Chamberlain's face. Chamberlain gave a speech on the first day, but it was poorly delivered. Later, General Keyes, dressed in full uniform and a close friend of Churchill, gave a speech attacking the naval staff for the disaster in Scandinavia. Keyes went on to declare that Churchill was the genus that Britain should trust. His speech was received by thunderous applause. Keyes was followed by another Churchill crony, Leo Amery, who quoted Cromwell in referring to Chamberlain, "You have sat too long for any good you have been doing. Depart, I say, and let us have done with you. In the name of God, go!"

Even Lloyd George, who opposed the war and was an admirer of Hitler, spoke out against Chamberlain and in favor of Churchill. He blamed the debacle in Scandinavia on the admiral staff, but Churchill jumped to his feet and took full responsibility. Lloyd George defended Churchill by declaring that Churchill must not allow himself to be converted into an air-raid shelter to keep the splinters from hitting his colleagues. Churchill felt that Lloyd George's speech was devastating for Chamberlain.

On the second day of the debates, the Labor party decided to chance a vote of no confidence against Chamberlain, because of the rising tide of rebellion within the Conservative Party. Chamberlain was desperately trying to buy off his Conservative detractors. Churchill was last to deliver a speech in the House of Commons, in which he defended Chamberlain and invasion of Scandinavia. But his speech was so worded that he placed all the blame on Chamberlain and absolved himself completely. His speech brilliantly turned the tables. The vote was taken on May 8, and the government won by 266 votes to 215, with 50 votes abstaining. Chamberlain maintained a majority of one vote. He accepted that he could not continue to govern, and agreed to resign as Prime Minister. The only question left unanswered was—who was going to replace him?

With the progression of the war, Halifax's peerage was no longer an obstacle to his receiving the premiership. He was permitted to sit in the House of Commons, and his popularity among government officials had increased, especially since it was apparent that the only alternative to him was Churchill. Support for Halifax began to rapidly grow. It seemed just about everyone wanted him to become Prime Minister, all that is except Halifax.

At four-thirty PM, on May 9, Churchill walked across the Horse Guards Parade to see Chamberlain at No. 10 Downing Street. He was summoned by the Prime Minister to discuss who was going to replace him. All that morning Chamberlain had tried to convince Halifax to accept the office, but Halifax resisted. He would only take it if pressured. Both Anthony Eden and Kingsley Wood were present, and both of them were close friends of Churchill. They had lunch with Churchill and informed him he should not answer Chamberlain if he asked him to support Halifax as Prime Minister. If he remained non committal, it would convince Halifax not to accept and convince Chamberlain not to offer it.

Churchill arrived at No. 10 and was shown into Chamberlain's office. He found the Prime Minister and Halifax waiting for him.

"I rushed over as soon as I could, Mr. Prime Minister," Churchill said as he descended into one of the vacant chairs. "I hope I did not keep you waiting?"

"Not at all," Chamberlain said. The Prime Minister seem pale and drained. The events of the last two days had fatigued him.

"As you know," Chamberlain said, "the vote did not go well for us." Churchill thought to himself that the vote went very well—for himself. "A majority of one vote is not much of a majority. I will not try and form a new government, for it's clear to me that neither the Labor nor Liberal Parties would be agreeable to join a coalition government with such a slim majority of one vote. I therefore consider it necessary to accept the reality of the day and will submit my resignation as

Prime Minister. The question that is before us, is this—who will become Prime Minister after me?"

No one said a word as Chamberlain looked first at Halifax, then at Churchill and once again at Halifax.

"The situation demands that I place the national interests before my own, and I consider it vital that some form of national unity is maintained during the duration of this war. I called both of you here because I believe you two are the only possible choices to succeed me. I believe that Halifax is the more acceptable choice, where the House of Commons is concerned. That is why I am asking you," Chamberlain turned to Halifax, "to accept the position of Prime Minister and form a new government."

Halifax swallowed, but did not say anything. Churchill just stared at the Prime Minister.

"I believe you are the best choice, and will not find it difficult to form a national unity government," Chamberlain said to Halifax.

"I appreciate your confidence in me," Halifax said, "but I do not consider myself the best man for the position. If I tried to form a government, I would speedily be reduced to the position of honorary Prime Minister, and quickly lose control of the military operations." Halifax glanced at Churchill. He knew Churchill would have to remain in the government and would quickly usurp control of the military direction of the war. Churchill remained silent and took no notice of Halifax. "I think Winston would be the better choice."

Chamberlain looked at Churchill. He expected Churchill to demur and encourage Halifax to accept the position of Prime Minister. Even if Churchill wanted the position for himself, it was the gentlemanly thing to do, but Churchill remained stone-face, immobile and said nothing. Chamberlain swallowed hard and then turned back to Halifax. He leaned forward. "I truly believe you must try."

Halifax shook his head. "If I did, it would be a hopeless position. I should be a cipher, and I can't permit this to happen. I am not concerned about my own reputation. I am more concerned about the war effort."

"I must very reluctantly accept you final judgement," Chamberlain said. "If that is your final word on the subject, then I must ask Winston to accept the position of Prime Minister."

It was Halifax's turn to remain silent. "I will reluctantly accept," Churchill finally said, breaking his Sphinx-like silence.

Chamberlain swallowed once more and nodded. "I am going to meet with Attlee at 6:30 this evening, and ask him if the Labor Party will join in a national unity government under a Churchill premiership. If he does, it will be official."

The meeting broke up and Churchill hurried back to the admiralty. He chewed on his cigar and whirled his cane as he walked, almost skipping with joy. All his work for the last seven months had finally paid off. He had schemed and planned to undermine Chamberlain's government, and the failed Scandinavian campaign was the final nail in Chamberlain's coffin. If it had succeeded, Churchill would have taken credit for it. But it did not, and the fall of Scandinavia was blamed on Chamberlain and caused his downfall. The bloody fiasco was attributed to him and not to Churchill, who had given birth and nurtured the entire operation. Chamberlain could easily have blamed Churchill for the failure of the campaign, as happened in 1915, but Chamberlain choose not to do so. Fortune had smiled on Churchill.

Once back at the admiralty, Churchill wasted no time in organizing his government.

Attlee told Chamberlain that he could not speak for the Labor Party, but he believed a Churchill government would be acceptable. What Chamberlain did not know was that the leadership of the Labor Party had already assured Churchill that they thought he would be acceptable as Prime Minister.

At 4:45 PM on Thursday, May 9, 1940, Adolf Hitler and his special entourage boarded a special train that was code-named Amerika, in the Berlin-Finkenkrug station, just a few miles west of the Staaken airport. The train would travel on the Berlin-to-Hamburg line. It was announced that Hitler would travel to Scandinavia to review the German troops in Norway, but a few close members of his inner circle knew that Scandinavia was not his real destination.

Hitler had been driven to the station by plain-clothes members of the SD. Hitler was in a good mood when the train pulled out of the station and made its way to Hamburg. A long stop was made at Hagenow-Land, where telephone messages were taken. The train then pulled out once more but instead of going on to Hamburg, it detoured to Hanover.

Hitler sat in the buffet car, which was designed for comfort for him and his aides. The atmosphere was lively and optimistic. He had just finished reading a favorable report from his chief meteorologist, as the train pulled out of the station and headed south.

"It would seem that we are going to be blessed with perfect weather," Hitler said as he rubbed his hands together. "I have just forwarded the code word, Danzig, to Wehrmacht headquarters. Do you know what this means?" Hitler asked those with him. With Hitler was his Chief Military Adjutant, Colonel Rudolf Schmundt, Chief ADC adjutant, Wilhelm Bruckner, as well as Nicolaus von Below, his Luftwaffen adjutant, and Albert Borman, the younger brother of Martin Borman. No one answered, though they all had a very good idea of the meaning of the code word. "It's the order to begin our offensive against western Europe. The battle that will begin tomorrow will determine the fate of the German nation for the next thousand years. Our armed forces will attack tomorrow morning. My confidence in victory is unshakable. I'm sure that we will quickly knock France out of the war within the next six weeks. It's imperative that France is delivered a devastating blow, as quickly as possible, so that we can finish off the British before the end of the year. I'm sure that Chamberlain would be willing to come to some kind of negotiated conclusion with us, if France is soundly trounced, but I fear that he might not survive as Prime Minister. If he doesn't, and is replaced by someone who would prefer to fight, we will have to quickly begin operations to ensure the defeat of the British Empire. This, gentlemen, is something I wish to avoid. I have always wanted the British as our allies, but circumstances have made the British our enemy. This is due to the influence of the Jews and the Americans, especially Roosevelt. The American President is itching to bring the United States into this war against Germany, but he must wait until after the elections in November. Until then, he will have to play the role of pacemaker. But once he is reelected, he will do everything in his power to bring the United States into the war against us. This is why we have got to conclude this war before November."

"But can our forces truly deliver the necessary knock out blow against the French?" von Below asked.

Hitler smiled. "Yes. You'll see. Manstein's plan will achieve what it was designed to do. I'm sure of it, despite the objections of OKH. My generals objected to my promotion of Manstein and his appointment to commander of Army Group A's Panzer group. But it was necessary to ensure that he is in commander of the Panzer group. Once it has achieved a breakthrough, there mustn't be anything to obstruct its dash to the English Channel. It has to reach the English Channel as fast as possible. Once it has achieved this objective, the war will be won."

"Is there any possibility that the Allies will be ready for our offensive?" Schmundt asked.

Hitler shook his head. "Not since we have eliminated that nest of vipers in the Abwehr," Hitler said. "Once Caranis and his pack of traitors were eliminated, our intelligence service has improved dramatically. Caranis was leaking all our decisions to the British. If I had not put an end to his treachery, the Allies would probably be ready for our offensive. But that has all changed."

"How did you discover Caranis's treason, My Fuehrer?" Bruckner asked.

Hitler's eyes suddenly opened wide and a most wicked smile cross his face. "It was like a flash of lightning," Hitler said. "I was reviewing our intelligence reports during my return from Poland, in the last week of September. I had not noticed any irregularities in the reports, that is, until the next day. I don't know what it was, but suddenly, before the meeting that I held with my generals on September 27, I noticed certain details that led me to believe that Caranis was leaking vital information to the Allies. But it wasn't until I looked into his face during the meeting that the certainty of my suspicions was confirmed. Call it a little voice deep within my mind, if you will, but at that moment I was sure that he was a traitor, and that's when I confronted him. I stared at him and waited and see what his reaction would be. By all that was holy under the sun, he turned pale white and asked to be exhausted because he was feeling sick. I had given orders to Heydrich to station two of his best SD men outside the Chancellory, just in case Caranis tried to flee. They had orders not to stop him until he tried to leave the country. And that's exactly what he tried to do. But we caught him and arrested him. Do you know, he squealed like a pig? He confessed everything and turned in General Oster and the rest of traitors in the Abwehr. Well, that was the end of that and we quickly flushed out that cesspool. I know there are others who entertained treasonous notions, but I prefer not to act against them without proof."

"You should not permit any traitors to remain free and undermine our war effort, My Fuehrer," Albert Borman said. "Won't it be better to eliminate all traitors as soon as possible?"

Hitler shook his head. "I don't want to arrest anyone, unless they have truly acted in a treasonous way," Hitler said. "There'll always be those who object to our policies, but we can't go around arresting everyone who might entertain treason. Many of these individuals are the very best in what they do, and it's better to make an example of a few traitors. That will keep the others in line. If I start executing everyone who might object to our policies, there won't be anyone left to fight for the Fatherland. After all, we are not bolsheviks. Look what Stalin has done to his army. He has decimated his officers and thus, weakened the Red Army to the point that it might very well lead to his destruction and the destruction of the Soviet Union."

Hitler and his entourage were too excited to sleep and spent the entire night talking. The train finally pulled into the station, in the small town of Euskirchen, about twenty-five miles from Germany's border with Belgium. Three-axled Mercedes were waiting to convey Hitler and the others to a well-camouflaged Fuehrer headquarters, about twelve miles away. Albert Speer had originally prepared a castle at Bad Neuheim for Hitler's headquarters, but Hitler objected to this luxurious environment. He ordered Todt and Schmundt to construct a Spartan headquarters further north in the Eifel area, near Muenstereifel. He gave this bare field headquarters the Romantic name, *Felsennest* or Rocky Aerie. Hitler was to share this bunker with Field Marshal Keitel, Julius Schaub, one of his four adjutants, and a manservant. In a nearby bunker, Field Marshal Jodl, three military adjutants, Keitel's ADC and Dr. Heinz Brandt would take up quarters.

As the Mercedes pulled into the *Felsennest*, the sun had just come up. Hitler stood watching the breathtaking panorama view of the Rhine Valley that unfold before him, as the sun's morning light raced across the landscape. The weather was perfect and Hitler was exuberant. Overhead, wave after wave of German bombers, fighters and transports flew westward across the sparkling blue sky. Roads for miles in every direction were already jammed with traffic as trucks, tanks and other military vehicles clogged the avenues that led to the German borders with Luxembourg, Belgium and the Netherlands.

This was H-hour—5:35 a.m.—and for three hundreds miles, stretching north and south, the German Wehrmacht was waiting for the order to begin the assault on western Europe. The order would put an end to what the British called "the phoney war," and what the Germans called *Sitzkrieg*.

The British Ministers of Air and War, Hoare and Stanley, arrived at the Admiralty House at 6 a.m. (British time, which was one hour later than German time). They found Churchill already up, sitting at a table in his silken pyjamas, chomping on eggs and bacon, which occasionally puffing on his cigar, and downing everything with whisky.

"Winston, the Germans have invaded Holland," Standley said, excited and out of breath.

Churchill continued to eat without looking up. "I'm well aware of the situation in Holland," he said. "I have already spoken with the French ambassador, Monsieur Corbin. Did you know that the Germans have also invaded Belgium?"

"No. That's news we have not heard yet," Standley said. "I've already given the order for the British Expeditionary Force to cross into Belgium. Monsieur Corbin informed me that the French Army has done the same. Soon our forces will have taken up their pre-planned positions. I expect the Germans will be stopped in Belgium."

Churchill looked up for the first time. He raised the bottle of whisky. "Would you chaps like a drink?"

The Ministers were amazed at Churchill's composure. He acted as if nothing had happened.

Within an hour, Churchill had dressed and was conducting a meeting of the Military Co-ordination Committee. Churchill wasted no time. He issued orders like a well-oiled machine and then was off to an emergency meeting of the War Cabinet for 8 a.m., at No. 10, with the Prime Minister. Churchill was exhilarated. This is what he was waiting for, for the last twenty years. Everyone present seemed depressed at the joyless reports of German successes in Holland and Belgium. Churchill's report was the only hopeful news. He assured everyone that the planned Allied invasion of Belgium was well on its way. He reported that it looked as if the Germans were repeating the von Schlieffen Plan of 1914, just as they expected, and he was sure that they could stop the Germans in their tracks, deep in Belgium.

After hearing of the reports, Chamberlain began to play with the idea of not resigning, but he was pressured by his closest colleagues to go through with his resignation. He finally agreed, and submitted his resignation to the King later that afternoon.

The Royal Summons reached Churchill later in the evening. He immediately rushed to the Palace. The King stuttered his question to Churchill. "Do you know why you have been sent for?"

Churchill snickered and then answered. "Sir, I simply couldn't imagine why?" The whole affair took a few minutes. Churchill had already planned his new cabinet and simply handed his list to the King and then rushed back to the Admiralty. No sooner had he sat at his desk, did the telephone ring. It was the American ambassador, Joe Kennedy.

"Winston," Kennedy said, "I called to congratulate you on your success."

That's very gracious of you to call," Churchill sat. He wondered how Kennedy had learn so quickly that the King had asked him to take the position of Prime Minister. "Actually, I called to congratulate you on your chess game," Kennedy said, half laughing. Churchill seemed puzzled.

"Chess?" Churchill asked.

"Yes," Kennedy said. "It was well-played, but I have to give some of the credit to President Roosevelt for your success."

"Why's that?" Churchill asked. "You might have conceived the plan to invade Scandinavia, but I was the one to obtain Roosevelt's consent."

Churchill frowned in confusion. "Excuse me?" he said.

Kennedy chuckled. "Scandinavia," he said and laughed out loud. Churchill bit deep into his cigar. "Hence Prime Minister! Well done!"

Chapter 6

THE LOW LANDS LAID LOW

May 10, the first morning of the invasion, at 4 a.m., the Heinkel He111 bombers filled the skies over the Netherlands, Belgium and France. Their targets were Allied airbases. Their mission was to knock out as most of the Allied air forces as possible. As the Dutch and Belgian armed forces were knocked off balance, German Army Group B surged across the German border into the Netherlands and eastern Belgium under the command of General Fedor von Bock. As German troops rushed across the flat plains of the Netherlands and northern Belgium to draw the main body of the British and French armies into Belgium, the Luftwaffe unleash thousands of airborne troops in the Dutch skies. The airborne assaults were commanded by Major General Kurt Student. This fifty-year-old Prussian possessed a unique tactical imagination that impressed Hitler. Hitler ordered him to enlarge the airborne troops by fifty percent by the time of the invasion, and to double it for 1941. With the German economy on a total war footing, it was not difficult for General Student to fulfill his Fuehrer's orders.

The German airborne troops parachuted, glided and landed by transport planes behind the enemy lines, capturing key bridges, fortifications and communication centers. The Allied troops were taken completely by surprise by these revolutionary tactics—tactics that were tested and perfected a month earlier in Scandinavia.

Hitler had come up with the idea of dropping airborne troops behind enemy lines. He loved new and daring tactics and criticized the more conservative generals, referring to them as "too correct" and "lacking the imagination to think up such tricks."

Because of the total war-footing of the German economy, the German armed forces now held a superiority over the Allied forces that faced them. Including reserves, the Germans held a superiority of 147 divisions against a smaller total Allied force of 94 French, 10 British, 22 Belgian, and 10 Dutch divisions. The Allies held a slight superiority in artillery pieces (13,700 Allied to 10,300 German guns), while there was an parity in tanks (3,400 Allied tanks to 3,300 German tanks). But the Germans concentrated their tanks in Panzer divisions while the Allied forces spread them out as support for their infantry. The French had only four tanks divisions, while the German possessed thirteen. The German tanks also possessed radios, which the Allied tanks lacked. This would especially give the Germans the edge they needed on the battlefield. In the air, the Germans held a large superiority of 6,400 planes to only 3,100 Allied planes. The Germans also held a superiority in the quality of their planes. The Messerschmitt 109 was superior to anything that the Allies could put in the air.

The French General Gamelin commanded the Allied forces. He was very conservative in his thinking and thought in terms of the First World War. He imagined a repeat of the trench warfare of the previous war, and believed the fighting would soon result in a deadlock. His plan was to move his Anglo-French force as far into Belgium as possible, before the Germans could reach the French border. He was determined not to permit a repeat of the last war, where the bulk of the fighting took place on French soil. His plan was simply to stop the Germans in Belgium, before they reached France. Beyond that, he expected a long and bloody war of attrition. He was confident the Allies could win in two or three years. Little did the French general realize that his plan to move deep into Belgium was exactly what the Germans wanted him to do.

It was part of Manstein's plan that the Germans would rapidly move across the Netherlands and secure that country, preventing the Allies from using its territory as a forward base from which their air force could launch bombing attacks on German cities, deep in Germany. But the German invasion of the Netherlands also had the affect of encouraging the Anglo-French forces to move across Belgium and take up positions on the Belgian-Dutch border, far to the north of the Ardennes, where the main thrust of the German attack would take place.

Despite the fact that the German Eighteenth Army, which was the main thrust through the Netherlands, was out-numbered by the Dutch defenders, it had no difficulty in rapidly occupying most of the country. Screaming dive bombers dominated the battlefield throughout the Netherlands, attacking all strategic points. The small Dutch air force was quickly destroyed on the ground. German panzers roared across the level low lands, slicing the Dutch defenses into small islands of resistance which were quickly overcome by the advancing German infantry. The German Blitzkrieg rolled across the Dutch countryside. The Dutch tried to defend the Gelder Valley and the basin of the Eem and the Grift, but were easily overwhelmed. The Germans penetrated the valley and stormed the fortified positions around Holland itself. Both the Hague and Rotterdam were successfully occupied by the German airborne troops, but just barely.

General Student commented that if the Fuehrer did not have the foresight to order him to enlarge the airborne forces, he might not have been able to take both objectives in time. Even with the enlarged force, his causalities was great, but with both Rotterdam and the Hague securely in German hands, the 9th Panzer Division, the Eighteenth Army's vanguard, was able to cross the vital bridges south of Rotterdam intact. Though Student's forces were met by stiff resistance, they were successful in taking the Hague, the seat of the Dutch government and prevented the Queen of the Netherlands from escaping to Great Britain. Fifteen thousand infantry were dropped, securing the airfields around the Hague. Once the airports were secured, they converged on the capital, capturing the government, including Queen Whilhelmina. Hitler had planned the attack and was delighted when General Student reported the successful completion of the operation. The Dutch government was now in German custody.

By May 11 the Germans were in command of most of the Netherlands. While the Hague was captured and the Dutch government prevented from fleeing, Rotterdam was surrounded and would surrender within another twenty-four hours. With the bridges leading to the south now secured, the 9th Panzer Army was able to halt the French Seventh Army. The French were already racing north, in hope of supporting the failing Dutch defenses. This force had hurried 100 miles through Belgium, and was now racing through southern Holland. But the French Seventh Army was intercepted by the German panzers and forced to retreat toward Antwerp.

By 11 o'clock in the evening, the Dutch quickly declared Rotterdam an open city and surrendered to the Germans. The Dutch city was occupied by the Germans with almost no damage on May 13. In the early evening of May 14, the Dutch government formally declared its surrender. Another country had fallen to the German Reich's military might. General Henrik Winkelman, in command of the Dutch forces, declared a cease fire. The Dutch continued to resist for another twenty-fours in the Zeeland area until they received word of the cease fire. The Dutch army suffered a total of 100,000 casualties. Hitler quickly placed the Netherlands under the command of Arur von Seyess-Inquart.

The Dutch were overwhelmed before they could set their plans for the defense of their country in motion. There was no forewarning of the German attack. Hitler was pleased with the rapid and painless conquest of the Netherlands. Rotterdam and the Hague were captured before they could mobilize their defenses and the Dutch government, including the Queen was captured before they could flee to Britain. The bridges south of Rotterdam were captured intact and the Germans could now deal with the Belgian defenses.

From his bunker headquarters, Hitler scrutinized every detail of the operation. He demanded to be kept informed of the target set for each day and the plans for the attack, exercising close personal influence on every aspect of the invasion. He asked awkward questions that showed that he was well-informed about the terrain and obstacles that his armies had to face everyday. When news of the capture of the Dutch government and queen reached Hitler, the Fuehrer remarked that he hated to think what mischief Canaris could have caused them if he had not discovered his treason and removed him as head of the Abwhre months ago.

While the German Eighteenth Army was securing the Netherlands, the Germans were already engaged in capturing the fortresses at Eben Emael, Liege and Maastricht, as well as crossing the water barriers of the Albert Canal and the River Maas in Belgium. It was the mission of the German Sixteenth Army to move into northern Belgium, up to a line that ran between Antwerp and Namur. To achieve this goal, Student's airborne troops were once again given the task of securing the fortress that blocked the way of the Sixteenth Army. In the early hours of May 10, German paratroopers took off from Aachen and cross the Dutch Masstricht appendix that cut a fifteen mile stretch of territory between Germany and Belgium. Student's Fallschirmjaeger flew forty-two gliders, each carrying about a dozen men, heavily armored with machine guns and explosives. They had trained for months to carry out their special operations, to secure crossings over the Albert Canal and capture the Belgian fortresses at Eben Emael and Liege. The gliders were able to easily land on the tops of the fortresses. The soldiers quickly blew their explosive charges, and used flamethrowers to penetrate the fortresses. Flame and gas rapidly spread throughout the forts, killing the defenders inside. Within hours the Germans were able to capture the forts with the assistance of Stuka dive bombers, which helped to keep the Belgian troops from reinforcing the fortresses' defenses. The German commander suggested to the Belgian defenders that they might want to surrender before they completely destroyed the fortresses at Eben Eael. The Belgians agreed and surrendered. Shortly after the fall of the fortresses, the bridges across the Albert Canal were also quickly secured. Soon German infantry reached the forts to ensure their capture. The airborne assault was carried off swiftly and boldly and news of the amazing feats spread throughout Germany. The German panzers were able to cross the canal and race through the flat, open country of northern Belgium.

The German assault on the Netherlands and northern Belgium encouraged the French and British to rapidly move into northern Belgium. The clash of armor helped the Allies to secure positions along the Dyle River, a line from which the Allies planned to halt the advance of the Germans according to Gamelin's Plan D. Gamelin was exuberant at the success of his plan so far, but the tank battle at Hannut was a Pyrrhic victory. It permitted Gamelin to rush thirty Allied divisions east to meet the onslaught of German Army Group B. Along a sixty mile frontier in northern Belgium and southern Netherlands, the cream of the French Army and one division of the British Expeditionary Force joined the Belgian Army along a defensive line that ran from Antwerp in the north to Namur in the south. But Gamelin did not know that this is exactly what the Germans wanted the Allies to do. Gamelin and the French High Command were very pleased at the way the battle was unfolding, but what they did not know was that the Germans were equally as pleased.

The Allies were unaware that while the opposing armies faced each other in northern Belgium, the bulk of the German panzer force was stealthily moving through the heavily forested region of the Ardennes to the south of Namur.

When reports of the success of Manstein's plan reached Hitler, he was jubilant and said, "They are moving into our trap."

Reaction by the French High Command was similar to that of General Gamelin's, "This is the moment that we have waited for," he said. "The Germans are obliging us by doing exactly what we expected them to do. They have blundered by attacking through the Netherlands and northern Belgium. Our best troops will be waiting for them when they try and turn south into northern Belgium."

When the Germans first attacked in the west, the French First Army Group rushed across the Belgium border with over one hundred divisions that included the British Expeditionary Force. General Georges was in command of the front between the English Channel, south to Longwy, on the northern edge of the Maginot Line. All along this front the French Seventh, First, Ninth and Second Armies, along with the British, moved east to join with the Belgium troops desperately trying to form a defensive line to stop the Germans, somewhere along the Dyle River. This was know as the Dyle Plan, or Plan D.

The Dyle Plan assumed that the Netherlands and northern Belgium would be the principal battlegrounds. The opposing armies were evenly matched. But the Allies' plan was defensive, while the Germans' plan was offensive. This gave the Germans the advantage of deciding where the main battle would take place, but this depended on fooling the Allies into thinking it would take place in northern Belgium and the southern Netherlands. The French were planning on an extended war of attrition, similar to the First World War. The Germans wanted a quick knockout punch—a one-two. They would faint a blow in the north and then deliver the main blow in the south. If the French and British fell for the ploy, the best French troops would be in the wrong place, and the worst-prepared French troops would be guarding the route that the best German troops would attack. And it looked like the Germans were going to succeed in their deception.

By May 12, Gamelin was convinced the Germans were trying to conduct a Blitzkrieg through the Netherlands and northern Belgium. Though only one panzer division was taking part in the invasion of the Netherlands, the Germans were making good use of their elite airborne troops.

In Belgium, the size of the German attack was much larger. Belgian troops were successfully resisting the German advance, but the obstacle would only be temporary if the French did not arrive in time to join their Belgian allies. Gamelin was pleased with the first reports from the front. Though Belgian troops were pulling back, the French would be able to reach the Dyle Line in time. The Belgian forces would be able to withdraw behind the Dyle Line and together, Gamelin hoped, they would be strong enough to halt the German advance.

On May 12, French tanks met German tanks near the city of Hannut. It was the first large-scale tank-on-tank battle in the history of warfare. It was the first tank battle in history. Before the battle ended, both sides would lose about one hundred tanks, but the battle was a clear victory for the French. If this had been the main German offensive, then it would have been an indication of how the war would progress, and exactly how the French expected it to unfold. But Belgium was not the main battlefield. Unfortunately for the French, the Germans were preparing their main attack that would come through the Ardennes and strike exactly where the French were at their weakest.

Victor Schauberger was ushered into Himmler's office in Berlin by an attendant who pointed to a chair and requested that the Austrian engineer sit. The chair was comfortable and situated before Himmler's desk. Schauberger was a large man and possessed a most extraordinary intellect. He sported a large beard and handlebar mustache looking like a university professor.

The Reichfuehrer of the Schutzstaffel (SS) was seated at his desk, studying a folder. He did not look up as Schauberger, who was seated before him, and continued to read from the folder as the Austrian waited to be addressed by one of the most powerful men in Germany. Schauberger studied the man before him. He thought he looked like a Protestant minister or perhaps a simple clerk. He could be one of the countless, nondescript drones that fill some huge bureaucracy. And yet, Schauberger noticed something unique about the Reichfuehrer of the SS. He thought there was something calculating about him. This was not a man who took chances. He never did anything without first weighting every possibility. He was methodical, if nothing else. Finally, Himmler closed the folder and looked at Schauberger. His gray-blue eyes blinked behind his prince-nez. He folded his hands on the folder before him and slightly smiled, or at the least, only the tips of his mouth smiled. Schauberger suddenly felt as if he was a school boy once again, who was called into the principal's office for an indiscretion.

"It was good of you to answer my invitation, Herr Doctor," Himmler said, politely.

Schauberger suddenly felt a release, as if he understood that he was not called to the principal's office for an indiscretion after all. There was nothing diabolical in Himmler's appearance. He was actually affable.

"As you know, our forces have begun the attack in the West," Himmler said. "The Fuehrer is confident that victory will soon be our's and this war will be over by Christmas. Then we will begin our program of transforming Germany, and all of Europe, into a new and remarkable civilization. Our work will require the most ingenuous and original thinking. We will have to discover new forms of energy that will not destroy our world, but help to create a civilization in which the new Aryan man will live in harmony with nature. From what I understand, you also are thinking along these lines?"

"Yes, Herr Reichfuehrer," Schauberger said.

"I understand you had the opportunity to describe some of your theories to the Fuehrer?" Himmler asked.

"That's correct, Herr Reichfuehrer," Schauberger said. "That was in 1934. The Fuehrer requested a meeting. He asked me to explain my theories, regarding the process of implosion and bio-technology, and the possibility to generate endless, free energy through the process of the vortex."

"Yes. I believe you made claims that your process could be used as a conduit for the transmission of phenomenal levels of energy," Himmler said. "The Fuehrer did not forget the conversation. He has not contacted you because he was too preoccupied with other, more pressing matters. But he had filed your meeting away in his complex and extraordinary mind, until he deemed it was the right time to make good use of your theories. That time has come, Herr Doctor. So please, explain to me everything that you told the Fuehrer."

Schauberger was surprised and pleased. He suddenly became animated as he often did when he talked about his theories. "I explained to the Fuehrer that through the process of motion and temperature, the viable relations between soil, vegetation and water could be used to manufacture an endless and sustainable supply of energy that will help to ensure a viable society that was in harmony with nature. I warned the Fuehrer that the reliance on the present-day short-termism of Germany's economic strategy, would undermine everything that he hoped to accomplish—especially the biological foundations of the new Reich. I tried to make it clear that a new, Aryan science was necessary."

Himmler nodded his head as Schauberger continued to explain his theory of the "Impeller" which was a propeller that induced an inward flow of motion that drew water or air through a tube in a flowing pattern that he described as a "centripetal" force, as oppose to the usual centrifugal force.

"I told the Fuehrer that ten times the energy output could be produced through this process," Schauberger said. "It would make the conventual pressure turbine engine obsolete."

"So what you are claiming is that you have found a way to produce energy—free energy?" Himmler asked.

"Yes, Herr Reichfuehrer," Schauberger said excitedly. He moved to the edge of his chair with excitement. In fact, I can produce a radical form of aero-engine that will suck itself through the air, rather than push its way through the atmosphere. I have already submitted a patent with the Reich Patent Office describing the essential characteristics of my machine."

"Yes," Himmler said. "I have seen the patent."

"Yes, of course," Schauberger said, realizing that Himmler probably had access to all documents within Germany. "It's an entirely new process of propelling an aircraft through the air, or water."

"Then you are claiming that your process could also develop a new form of ship or submarine, maybe, as well as a totally radical form of aircraft?" Himmler asked.

"Yes, one that will travel beyond Mach 3," Schauberger said.

"Mach 3? Is that possible?" Himmler asked.

"Not for the type of aircraft my technology will produce," Schauberger said. "In time, we could even produce an aircraft that will fly by levitation, rising vertically and possessing the ability to change directions in an instant, without any hard or discomfort to the pilot."

"That is a most remarkable claim," Himmler said. "Is this what you're planning on developing in the company you have commissioned—what is it called?"Kaempfer," Schauberger said.

"Yes, that's it," Himmler said.

"I will build a prototype engine that I call the Repulsator, it can be used for submarine propulsion, or for use in a new, circular aircraft that I have designed."

"Circular?" Himmler said. "That is unusual."

"I have been using my own resources to develop this machine," Schauberger said. "It will rely on a turbine plate of waviform design that fits onto another molded plate of similar construction. There is a gap between the two plate which is whorl-shaped. It is this whorl-shape that will mimic the corkscrew action of a kudu's antler. The vortex motion will cause air to move through the waviform gap between the plates, generating a rapid cooling sensation. This will produce a massive reduction in volume. It is this reduction that will generate a vacuum of tremendous pressure by sucking additional air through the turbine." All that will be required to start the engine is a small among of energy to commence the process. But once it starts, it will literally whip the turbine up to 20,000 rpm. Once this has been accomplished, the motor will be turned off and its operations will be self-sustaining.

"We could use it to produce an endless supply of electricity—enough to power Berlin itself, all from one small machine, the size of a shoe box The aircraft that is powered by this engine will levitate, because of the vacuum created in the rarified zone immediately above the plates. The newly excited state of air molecules will cause the levitation."

"Herr Doctor, what you claiming is the discovery of anti-gravity," Himmler said.

"Yes, Herr Reichfuehrer. That's exactly what I am claiming," Schauberger said confidently.

Himmler continued to study Schauberger for a few seconds. The implications of what he was claiming went beyond creating a source of power that would make Germany a superpower. That is, if it was possible. But Himmler was a believer in the exotic, especially when it originated from a German mind.

"Herr Doctor, from this day forth, you will have the complete resources of the German Reich at your disposal," Himmler finally said. "I have been instructed by the Fuehrer to set you up in a base that we plan to build. It will located in the Sudeten Mountains, not far from Breslau. You will be permitted to assemble a team of your choosing. Everything you will need for the development of this new Aryan technology will be provided."

Schauberger was beside himself with joy. The most powerful country on the face of the earth was now going to give him the opportunity to prove his theories correct. It was more than he had dared hoped when he had first received Himmler's invitation. Now he believed that there was nothing he could not achieve.

Germany's total war footing permitted the Germans to increase tank production so that by May, 1940, the Wehrmacht was able to add two additional panzer divisions and increased motorized infantry divisions to their invasion force. The added divisions increased the possibility of success of Manstein's plan. The panzers were deployed in front of General Rundstedt's Army Group A in an unprecedented concentration of armor—nine of the Wehrmacht's armor divisions. They were deployed in three corps across a fifty mile front on Germany's border with Belgium and Luxembourg. There was a total of forty-seven divisions in Army Group A, and their aim was to pass through the heavily wooded and hilly region known as the Ardennes Forest, and break through the Allied lines between the city of Namur in the north and Sedan in the south.

The German right-wing, which included thirty divisions, drove into northern Belgium and the Netherlands, which convinced the Allies to move their forces north to stop a possible German drive into Belgium from the Netherlands. Manstein's plan was like that of a toreador waving his cape to distract the bull so that its side could be pieced with the sword as it lunged forward.

On either flank of the spear were two generals. Leading the northern flank was Major General Erwin Rommel. He was young, (only forty-eight) by German standards for a general and a dedicated supporter of Hitler, which made him unpopular with such ultraconservative generals like Rundstedt. His orders were to strike at Dinant with the 7th Panzer Division. He was given command of the division three months earlier as a favor by Hitler. He was not from the Junker class. His father was schoolmaster, but Rommel did win Germany's highest medal, the *Pou le merite*, in the First World War.

Erwin had a sharp mind and quickly learned the tactics of the Blitzkreig. When the attack began, he rode in the lead tank leading his division into battle. He was not one to waste time and his division quickly outran the rest of the XV Panzer Corps, under the command of General Hermann Hoth.

The other General that Hitler depended on was also young, only three years older than Rommel. He was General Heinz Guderian, who was in command of the four panzer divisions of the XIX Panzer Corps. His objective was to reach

Sedan on the left wing. Guderian was the architect of German armor tactics. He was able to prove his theories in the invasion of Poland, where his panzer divisions played a major role in Germany's victory. He hoped to once again prove his theory that mechanized warfare when "concentrated and applied with surprise on the decisive point, to thrust the arrowhead so deep that we need have no worry about the flank" was essential to a quick and decisive victory on the Western Front.

With a fanatical will to move forward, Guderian drove his corps straight ahead. He proved that he could get his panzers through the heaviest wooded region of the Ardennes with little difficulty. Overhead, Guderian saw only the Luftwaffe, so he was no longer afraid of being prematurely discovered by the French.

Everything was moving according to the plan. Guderian's 1st Panzer Division crossed Luxembourg without opposition and reached the Belgium border on the first day. An Airborne regiment was dropped behind the Belgium border to cause havoc, but it had little to do but wait for Guderian's tanks to reach them. On May 11 Guderian's panzers crossed the Belgium border and swiftly moved across the southern corner of Belgium toward Sedan. Manstein made sure nothing slowed down Guderian's advance.

The first German troops to reached the Meuse River belonged to the 7th Panzer Division under the commander of General Erwin Rommel. Rommel was under the commander of General Kluge of the 4th Army. Hitler also reinforced the 4th Army with an additional panzer division, the 11th Panzer Division. The mission of the 4th Army was to reach and cross the Meuse River between Dinant in the south and Namur in the north.

It was the 7th Panzer Division that reached the town of Houx, north of Dinant. Rommel's men discovered an old stone dam that linked both banks of the Meuse River with an island in the middle. Rommel waited until after nightfall and then sent a battalion of motorcyclists across. They found a break in the French defenses and soon established a bridgehead that Rommel wasted no time in reinforcing. By morning, several companies were on the west bank. Rommel then ordered infantry across the river after setting several houses on fire to create a smoke screen.

Rommel was a hands on type of commander. He never commanded a panzer division before and so he spent as much time as possible at the front. Rommel personally crossed the river at the head of the infantry in a rubber raft. Once on the other side, the German infantry was attacked by French tanks. Rommel rallied his troops and ordered them to attack the tanks with rifles. Fearing that the

Germans might have panzers across the river, the French retreated. Rommel's presence at the front helped to lift the spirit of his troops and win amazing victories.

Once he was able to enlarge the bridgehead, he sent his panzers across. By nightfall the bridgehead was two miles long and was being reinforced after German engineers created several pontoon bridges. On the morning of May 14, Rommel had some thirty tanks across the Meuse.

Rommel was a devoted follower of Hitler and his fellow generals, especially the older Prussian officer, distrusted him. He was considered a publicity hound and always wore a camera around his neck that was given to him as a gift by Joseph Goebbels. He never failed to have pictures of him taken and sent back to Germany. He also had his units carry cameras to document the progression of the Blitzkrieg.

By noon, Bouvignes was in German hands and his bridgehead was now three miles wide. Rommel was able to move up his artillery and especially his PzKw IV tanks, which sported 7.5 cm guns. The bridgehead stretched from Houx in the north to Dinant in the south.

General Guderian's XIX Panzer Corps moved across the southern edge of Belgium and Luxembourg and reached the Semois River on the morning of May 11. His 2nd and 12th Panzer Divisions crossed the river north of the Belgian town of Bouillon while his 1st and 10th Panzer Divisions crossed just south of the town. They were now racing toward the French city of Sedan. During the Franco-Prussian War the French made a stand at Sedan, and when the Germans defeated them there, they won the war. In the First World War, the French abandoned the city altogether. This time, the French had only lightly fortified the city with inexperienced and poorly trained troops because they believed the main thrust of the German attack would be through northern Belgium.

Guderian was pleased with the progress he was making. His commander-in-chief, General Manstein, who replaced General Ewald von Kleist as commander of the 12th Army by Hitler, was also pleased. The German Army High Command wanted the conservative Kleist to hold Guderian back, but with Manstein in command, Guderian was given a green light to strike as quickly as possible.

Guderian attacked the French at Sedan on the afternoon of May 12, while General Reinhardt's XLI Panzer Corp moved against the French city of Montherme to the north. Even though the city of Sedan was only lightly defended, it was the first major opposition that Guderian faced. The French had entrenched 150,000 troops on the western banks of the Meuse River stretching from Namur in the north, south to northern edge of the Maginot Line. These forces were divided into the French 9th Army under General Corap, and centered on the town of Dinant, and the French 2nd Army under the command of General Huntziger, and centered on the city of Sedan.

Guderian's Panzer Corp was reinforced with the addition of the 12th Panzer Division which was made possible by the increased mobilization due to Germany's total war footing. With four panzer divisions, Guderian was sure he could break through the French defenses and reach the English Channel, but first he had to cross the Meuse. To deal with this obstacle, he called in enormous firepower from both his artillery and the Luftwaffe. The main assault would be conducted by the 1st Panzer Division. To support the attack, he brought up his entire heavy-artillery, as well as his high-velocity 88-mm antiaircraft guns. He placed the latter at the water's edge and fired directly into the French fortifications on the other side of the river. Manstein approved of Guderian's plan to use the German Stuka dive-bombers to provide continuous support as his panzers crossed the river. The 200 Stukas of the 700 German bombers that bombarded the French positions with 500 pound bombs, delivered devastating strike that eventually demoralized the French soldiers.

The combined assault by the dive-bombers and artillery blasted an opening for the Germans. At exactly four o'clock in the afternoon, H-hour, the sixty yard expanse of the river was flooded with German infantry crossing in rubber rafts. Guderian was utilizing his elite Grossdeutschland Regiment and the 1st Rifle Regiment of the motorized infantry assigned to his XIX Panzer Corps. Once they established a bridgehead, they struck south under the hard-nose Lieutenant Colonel Hermann Balck. Balck attacked through the night, causing panic among the French defenders, and reached the village of Chimery, five miles behind the Meuse, by morning.

While the infantry attacked, pontoon bridges were being constructed across the river. In the morning, German panzers sped through the ranks of the panicking French 55th Division. When the Germans stopped to refuel near the village of Chimery, they were attacked by French armor and infantry. The panzers quickly regrouped and delivered a crushing counter blow by mid-morning.

The 12th and 2nd Panzer Divisions crossed the Meuse west of Sedan while the 1st and 10th Panzer Divisions cross to the east of the city. The two groups of panzers struck south to meet at the towns of Chehery and Bulson, which were already in the hands of the German infantry. The ferocity of the German assault kept the French off guard. By the morning of May 13, the infantry of the Grossdeutschland had taken the Marfee heights south of Sedan. They were there to welcome the approaching German panzers of the 10 Panzer Division. The Germans had pulled off a classic pincer attack. Sedan was surrounded and soon surrendered. Everything had worked out exactly as the Germans planned. Guderian was pleased and ready to continue the attack to the west, toward the English Channel.

Rommel was ruthless in the way he waged his attacks, and fierce in his position as commander of the 7th Panzer Division. He refused to remain in the rear and took command of the PzKw III. Mounting one of the tanks, he led about thirty panzers in the German advance on the town of Onhaye. His attack went far beyond Onhaye on Tuesday, and his almost reckless disregard in waiting for reinforcements convinced the French commanders that there really were thousands of German tanks on the western side of the Meuse River. This caused the French to abandon their defensive line along the Meuse. Further to the north the Germans occupied the Wasta plateau. This put them in a strategic advantage when the 7th Panzer Division began its assault on Morville, followed by the 5th Panzer Division. From north of the Wasta Plateau the 11th Panzer Division struck west toward Ermeton. By the end of the day the German panzer division had blasted a hole in the French defenses between the French 1st Army to the north and the French 9th Army to the south.

To the south of Rommel's 7th Panzer Division, General Reinhardt's XLI Panzer Corps was crossing the Meuse between Dinant and Montherme. His corps was the weakest, containing only two panzer divisions. The weight of his attack was nearer to Mohtherme. At 4 PM on May 13, the 6th Panzer Division was able to establish a bridgehead across the Meuse at Place de la Mairie. It was rough terrain and the Germans had difficulty crossing, but in time the 6th Panzer Division was across. Further to the north the 8th Panzer Division was able to reach the west bank of the Meuse at Nouzonville. Because of the deteriorating French positions to the north, facing Rommel's thrust, the French forces facing Reinhardt's forces were unable to contain him. They began to withdraw by the morning of May 15. Everything was going according to the timetable of the plan, and this pleased Guderian. By May 15 the Germans had established three bridgeheads across the Meuse River at Dinant, Montherme and Sedan. The two extra panzer divisions that were rushed into service because of the increased German production enabled the Wehrmacht to quickly pass through the Ardennes and cross the Meuse within five days. Now everything was in place for the Germans to begin their springboard maneuver across the wide open plains of northern France, and reach the English Channel.

The day before Guderian defeated the attempt by the French 3rd Armored Division to drive him back across the Meuse. The men of the 3rd Armored Division were in high spirits and fought heroically, but their division was formed only six weeks previously on May 10. It lacked antitank guns, radios, repair units and artillery. Its companies were below tank strength, though the French Hotchiss H39 tanks were able to deliver considerable fire power.

General Heinz Guderian was planning the next stage in the attack of his Panzer Corps. He hoped to cross the 150 miles between him and the English Channel without much delay, thus splitting the Allied forces in half. With the defeat of the French, he was ready to move west. He was waiting for confirmation for the attack when his field telephone rang.

"General Guderian, here," he said flatly and without airs.

"This is Manstein, Heinz," General von Manstein said, addressing Guderian by his first name, which was something the older, Prussian generals would never have done. "I wanted to personally call and convey to you the orders to attack."

"Then the word is go?" Guderian asked. His voice betrayed his joy.

"The word is go, Heinz," Manstein said. "I personally received the order from the Fuehrer to begin the attack in the morning. The Fuehrer wanted me to convey his congratulations on your victory today at Stonne. You must not let anything delay your attack. It's imperative that you reach the English Channel as quickly as possible."

"Nothing will stop me, I assure you, Manfred," Guderian said, also using Manstein's first name. He was pleased with Manstein's command of the 12th Army. He did not want to contemplate what delays could have developed if Hitler had not replaced Kleist as commander of the 12th Army with Manstein. It was true that General von Rundstedt was still the over all commander of Army Group A, but he was sandwiched between the Fuehrer and Manstein, both of whom thought alike on the nature and progression of the attack in the West. Rundstedt was of the old Prussian school, and an infantry man at heart. But he was also pliable and did not have the stomach to try and disrupt the plan. Hitler accepted his command of Army Group A to placate the German Army and its outmoded sense of priority and protocol. Manstein wished Guderian luck and then hung up so he could convey the orders to Generals Hoth and Reinhardt.

When the German Army planned the invasion of Poland, it called out of retirement General Gerd von Rundstedt. Tall, lean and erect, the sixty-four-year-old Prussian was at heart an infantryman, schooled in the old Reichwehr. He fell more comfortable with the tactics of the First World War, but he was flexible enough to adjust to the new tactics of Blitzkrieg. When the Army put him in charge of the all-important Army Group A, Hitler did not object because he had elevated von Manstein to commander of the crucial 12th Army. So when Manstein received orders from Rundstedt to postpone the advance by Guardian's XIX Panzer Corp, Manstein was able to appeal directly to Hitler.

Guderian was outraged at the order, but Manstein assured him not to worry and ignored the order. Manstein was able to make contact with Hitler, who counter-manned Rundstedt's orders to wait, and ordered Guderian to attack immediately.

Manstein was not concern with the stiffening French resistance south of Sedan because of the two extra panzer divisions and the increased mobility of the infantry, all of which was due to the total war production that was begun nine months earlier. As a result, Guderian was able to begin his sprint to the sea on May 15.

Farther to the north, Rommel was already moving forward on May 15. The French Ninth Army that was in front of him, was already in full retreat. It was commanded by General Andre-Georges Corap, who was a timid man, overweight and very unmilitary in appearance and mannerism. The retreat of the Ninth Army soon deteriorated into rampant chaos, and General Corap was unable to do anything to stop it.

Rommel ran into French tanks near the village of Flavions, but he quickly called up the Stuka dive bombers to deal with them. His own 7th Panzer Division wheeled around the French tanks and continued to move forward as the 5th Panzer Division, following close behind, dispatched what was left of the French tanks.

Rommel, who rode in the lead tank, zoomed ahead at forty miles an hour. His panzers fought on the move, swiveling their turrets to knock out any opponents they ran into. The greater maneuverability of the Germans were due to their superior radio communications among the panzers. Fifteen miles west of the Meuse, Rommel smashed through a new defensive line that the French Ninth Army tried to set-up. Rommel had to wait for the mobilized infantry to catch up and take prisoners before continuing his westward charge, but because of the increased truck and armored vehicle production in the last six months, it was not long before Rommel's panzers were on the move once more. His rapid advance to the west made the Allies fearful that Rommel might try and outflank the Dyle Line. This threat prompted them to finally decide to withdraw from the Dyle Line and take up new positions forty-five miles to the west, on the Schedt-Dender River line.

On May 16, Rommel's 7th Panzer Division crossed the French frontier and ran into a line of pillboxes designed as an anti-tank obstacle. Rommel called up his combat-engineers. They crawled up to the pillboxes and dispatched them with six-pound explosive charges. Within a few hours the road was once again clear for Rommel to continue his advance westward.

Even nightfall did not slow Rommels' advance. He ordered his panzers to "fire on the move, like the navy. Fire salvos to port and starboard." In the dark, the image of fleeing refugees and panic-stricken French infantry could be spotted trying to escape by the light of the moon. Rommel ordered his panzers not to harm civilians and let the German infantry that followed behind sweep up the prisoners.

The German attack by night took the French by surprise. The French were overwhelmed and were now retreating, abandoning tanks, guns and other heavy equipment in their mad rush to escape. Rommel was able to catch up to the remnants of the French 1st Armor Division at the town of Avesnes. He out maneuvered the French tanks and threatened to encircle them. They barely escaped. Rommel did not call a halt to his advance until 6:15 a.m. on May 17, on a hill east of the town of Le Cateau. His men complained of being exhausted, filthy and badly in need of a shave. But Rommel was not finished. He personally withdrew twenty miles in order to bring up units that had fallen behind, to his western most positions. He had to fight his way back through French soldiers that were trying to escape, personally capturing over 10,000 prisoners in twenty-four hours at the cost of 100 German casualties.

Churchill was waken out of his sleep by a telephone call from French Premier Paul Reynaud. Churchill stood in his skill bloomers as he listened to Reynaud. He could not believed what he was hearing.

"The war is lost," Reynaud said. "The Germans have broken through our lines at Sedan. Everything is finished. We've lost the war." Churchill tried to reassure Reynaud that things could not be that bad. He even promised to send four more air squadrons to the continent. The British had held back more than half of their air force for the defense of Britain, fearing that the Germans would launch an all-out bomber offensive against their cities. The air offensive never materialized, but the British war ministry thought that the next war would begin with massive waves of bombers devastating the combative's cities. The Germans had planned other uses for their air power. Unlike the Allies, they used the air force in conjunction with their ground forces.

"France is beaten, I tell you," Reynaud said as he sobbed. "Our troops are in full retreat. There is nothing we can do to stop the Germans."

Churchill pleaded with Reynaud not to lose hope and that he would arrive in Paris as quickly as possible.

After Churchill hung up he began shouting at his staff, while cursing the French, as he quickly got dress.

"Damn them!" he shouted. "I'll not let it happen again! I'll not let them deprive me of the opportunity to redeem my reputation. The Germans had broken through our lines in 1914, but we were able to stop them. Reserves were quickly raised and rushed to the front and we stopped those bloody Huns at the Marne. So what if they broke through our lines? All we have to do is use the reserves to cut them to pieces."

On May 16, Churchill flew from London and arrived in Paris to confer with the French leaders. During his trip rumors of the French army falling apart constantly plagued him. When he finally arrived at the Quay d'Orsay he met with Premier Reynaud and General Gamelin. He was shocked to discover a map on the wall of their conference room. It showed a sixty mile bungle in the front. The Germans had advanced that far west from the Meuse and there was nothing the French army could do to stop them.

"This is not possible," Churchill growled as he examined the map, while chewing on his cigar. "How could they have gotten so far?"

The French said nothing.

"Where are your reserves?" Churchill asked. "Why haven't you brought up your reserves to plunge-up this hole?"

"There are none," is all General Gamelin said.

Churchill almost snarled at the French general. His defeatism made him sick, but he held his tongue. He did not want to feed their depression.

"Why hasn't De Gaulle's 4th Armor Division attacked north, into the flanks of the advancing Germans from Reims?" Churchill asked.

Gamelin looked at Reynaud and then sighed.

"Colonel De Gaulle is preparing to attack the Germans near Marie," Gamelin said as he fought to hold back the tears. "He'll attack tomorrow, but our forces are being cut to pieces. It is hopeless. France is lost." Gamelin could not speak any more.

Churchill leered at the French general and then turned to the Premier. Reynaud looked away. He seemed helpless and embarrassed by the way Gamelin was reacting, but he could not find the strength to deal with him.

Churchill asked Reynaud if he could speak to him in private.

"You have to replace Gamelin," Churchill insisted. "I promise to send six air squadrons instead of four if you will replace him. We can stop the Huns, because we must. I'm sure De Gaulle's attack will work, trust me."

Reynaud listened as Churchill spoke. He nodded his agreement, but could only say that he would try. Churchill left the French leader and quickly returned to London. He had already made up his mind not to send any further air squadrons. With the French in their present state, he knew that France would fall. He was already thinking about evacuating the British Expeditionary Force fighting in Belgium before they were cut off and surrounded by the Germans. Let France fall, but he was determined that England would fight on, alone if necessary—at least until he could convince the United States to enter the war.

With orders from Hitler to continue his advance as quickly as possible, Guderian set out to the west with his 1st, 2nd and 12th Panzer Divisions, on May 16. He left his 10th Panzer Division, which was the southern most division to his rear, to cover his advance in case the French tried to attack from the south. He was elated to discover that General Halder, the army chief of staff, as well as Rundstedt were now enthusiastic advocates of keeping his panzers rushing forward toward the channel. This was the result of the combined support by Manstein and Hitler himself, as well as the success of the attacks.

As Guderian's forces rushed passed the town of Marie, the 10th Panzer Division had come under attack by the French 4th Armored Division, commanded by De Gaulle. De Gaulle was tall, forty-two years-old, sported a prominent nose and carried himself proudly and arrogantly. He had been the most adamant proponent of tank warfare within the French military establishment before the war. He had refused a very important political appointment within Reynaud's cabinet to command the newly created 4th Armored Division.

De Gaulle was appalled by the way the French soldiers were surrendering to the Germans. He was very proud of the French military tradition, and the sight of so many demoralized and dispirited French troops that simply surrendered without a fight, sickened him. He was outraged when he heard that the Germans did not even try to take the French as prisoners. They simply told them to lay down their arms and report to the nearest German infantry force that was following the panzer forces.

De Gaulle struck on May 17 from Laon. He commanded three tank battalions and was able to inflict some damage on the Germans near the hamlet of Lislet. But the Germans were able to bring up their flak guns and knock out the French tanks from the heights outside the town. The French were forced to turn around. They were low on machines, fuel and men and could not resist the fury of the German guns. As De Gaulle's tanks withdrew to their starting point at Laon, they were set up on German Stukas.

When Guderian learned of the failed French attack, he laughed and did not even bother to report the French attack until the following day. He did not consider it important enough to bother.

In the early hours of May 17, Guderian unleashed his panzers once again. The 2nd Panzer Division crashed through Saint-Quentin, which was twenty miles west of the Oise and made for the town of Perronne on the Somme River. Guderian was pleased that Manstein gave the green light to attack. He wondered what might have happened if Manstein was not placed in command by Hitler? The older generals were too concern about their flanks and probably would never have permitted him to dash so far out front of the rest of the German army. Guderian believed that open flanks are the best things Panzer troops could have; and the longer they are, the better. He felt that it would keep the enemy off balance. He told the Panzer commanders under him that, "So long as we ourselves remain in motion, so long must the enemy be in motion and is kept from getting into position to try and stop our advance." He knew that Manstein understood his concept of mobile Panzer warfare and was now going to carry out his theory to the fullest.

Guderian was amazed at the speed with which his panzers moved. It seemed that the French Army was no where to be found. The greatest impediment to his advance was the long columns of refugees that jammed the roads as they tried to flee south. Guderian did not even wait for his supply columns to catch up with his panzers. The panzers were able to fill up their gas tanks at civilian gas pumps.

With the start of the German attack in the west on May 10, millions of civilians fled their homes. Up to 8 millions French and about 2 million Belgian and Dutch abandoned their homes and farms to flee south. They heard so many stories about German atrocities during the First World War that they feared falling under German occupation. People took whatever they could carry with them. Some had automobiles, trucks and even more had horse-pulled wagons. But most could take only those possessions they could carry by hand or in baby carriages. They left believing that if and when they ever returned to their homes, they would find their possessions looted and their homes and farms burnt to the ground.

By the end of the 17th, both Peronne and Cambrai fell to the German. The way to the Channel was now open.

Thanks to Hitler's orders that the German economy be placed on a total war foot, not only did the German forces have two extra panzer divisions, but the infantry had a much larger arsenal of trucks and other vehicles at their command to ensure that a larger proportion of the infantry was mobilized. This freed the panzer divisions with regard to their flanks. The Germans were able to rapidly bring up enough infantry to secure the flanks of the advance panzer spearhead. This prevented delays in the German advance toward the Channel. By now the German Stuka dive bombers and heavy bombers had gained control of the skies over the battlefront. Support from the Luftwaffe rendered the German panzers invincible. Allied airfields were a major objective in the German advance. The capture of Allied air fields permitted the Luftwaffe to keep close to the front and provide maximum support for advancing panzers. The captured airfields also permitted the Germans to fly in spare parts and ammunition that were badly needed.

After the French 4th Armor Division's attack on the Germans from the south were repulsed, Guderian's panzers continued their to advance toward the Channel. They passed over the old battlefields of the last world war that an older generation of Germans had defended for four long and bloody years. Guderian was exhilarated as he left them far behind. This generation of German warriors would not make the same mistakes that their fathers did.

As the Germans crossed the Canal du Nord, the 14th Panzer Division was transferred from Bock's Army Group B to support the advance to the Channel. The English Channel was less than sixty miles away as the German panzers continued their advance from the canal on the morning of the 19th of May. General Gamelin wanted the French to attack the advancing German spearhead from the south. This would be Gameln's last order. Reynaud had wanted to replace Gamelin and now decided to act. He summoned General Weygand from Syria to Paris and then the French Premier ordered Weygand to the front. Reynaud announced on May 19 that Weygand had replaced Gamelin and that he would take over the Ministry of Defense. Working with the British to the north, the Allies planned to attack the Germans in the rear of their advancing panzer divisions. Elements of the British Expeditionary Force attacked south toward Arras and engaged Rommel's 7th Panzer Division. Rommel called in Stuka dive-bombers to halt the British advance, but the British fought on and continued their advance. The Germans began to lose their nerve but it was only after the personal intervention by Rommel that the Germans stiffen their backbones and were able to eventually repulse the British attack. The German 6th Panzer Division reacted to the British attack by turning north and attacked the BEF from the west. Pressed between the 7th and even the 5th Panzer Divisions from the east and the 6th Panzer Division from the west, the British could not continue their southern attack. With the

British withdrawing once again, Rommel's 7th Panzer Division resumed its advance before the afternoon was over, Rommel's 7th now began to move north. Guderian's 1st and 12 Panzer Divisions raced west along the northern banks of the Somme River. The French 4th Armor Division rushed west to join with elements of the BEF to try and stop the Germans from reaching the Channel. Before they could cross the Somme River, Guderian's panzers cleared the entire northern banks of the Somme and rushed in German mobilized infantry to fortify the river.

Guderian entered the city of Amiens, but did not remain long. He received word from Major General Rudolf Veiel of the 2nd Panzer Division that he had reached the town of Albert and was out of fuel. He requested permission to remain in Albert for twenty-four hours and wait for the fuel to be brought to him. Guderian reacted, and ordered Veiel to resume the attack immediately. "Whenever one of my commanders report that they are running low on fuel, it means they are tired and want to rest. If they become tired, they say they lack fuel." Veiel did as he was ordered and fuel was quickly brought to his panzers for their continued assault westward.

By Sunday afternoon, May 19, the 2nd Panzer Division reached Abbeville, twelve miles from the Channel. By the morning of May 20, a battalion of Austrians finally reached the coast near the town Noyelles-sur-Mer. In ten days Guderian did as he had promised his Fuehrer. He had reached the English Channel after crossing two hundred miles through Luxembourg, Belgium and France and cutting the Allied armies in half. A total of three French armies, (forty-five divisions) the entire Belgian Army and most of the British Expeditionary Forces (nine divisions), a total of one million Allied troops, were now trapped in a pocket north of the corridor that the Germans had carved out of France.

Hitler had moved to the headquarters of Army Group A set up at Bastogne, in Belgium. He was excited by the progress made by his armies and was sure that victory was only weeks away. "All the world hearkens as we redress the wrongs inflicted on Germany in the last war," Hitler told General Rundstedt. "Now is not the time to be cautious. We must drive toward the Channel." Rundstedt was still concerned about a possible counter attack by the Allies, but he refrained from expressing his concerns. A few hours after Hitler arrived, he received a telephone call from Brauchitsch.

"I congratulate you, My Fuehrer," Brauchitsch said. "Your plan has fulfilled its first objective. Our forces have reached the English Channel at the town of Abbeville."

Hitler was choked with emotion. He turned to General Jodl. "Victory is ours, General," Hitler said. Tears swelled up in his eyes as he clutched his hands together. "We have reached the Channel and cut the Allied armies in half. It's only a matter of weeks before France falls. I want a peace treaty drawn up. It will include the return of all German territory lost in the last 400 years. But we mustn't get ahead of ourselves. We will still have to deal with Britain. Once France surrenders, we will begin the second part of our strategic plan."

"But my Fuehrer," Jodl said. "The English can't possibly continue the war without France. Surely, the English will agree to an armistice?"

Hitler waved his hand before him as he shook his head. "No," he said. "If Chamberlain was still Prime Minister, the English would agree to put an end to this foolish war, but not that Churchill. He will insist that England continue to fight, even if it means the lost of her Empire. That is why I want our panzer divisions to continue their advance. Send orders to Manstein. He must now order his Panzer groups to turn north, without delay. It is imperative that we occupy all the Channel ports from Abbeville to here," Hitler ran his finger along the coast north to the small town of Dunkirk. "Our forces must advance to Dunkirk and cut off any possible escape by the British armies across the Channel to England. If we can bag the entire British Expeditionary Force on the continent, England will be left defenseless. Churchill will be forced to pull badly needed troops from North Africa and the Middle East to defend England from a possible invasion. Then we will have the English exactly where we want them. By the end of the year, our forces will be standing on the shores of the Persian Gulf, just as surely they now stand on the coast of the English Channel."

Chapter 7

▼

DISASTER AT DUNKIRK

The Panzer spearhead to the sea trapped a million Allied troops in a huge pocket north of the corridor that the Germans carved out of Low Lands. The Allied forces in the pocket included nine British divisions, forty-five French divisions and the entire Belgian army. Rundstedt, who was very conservative and trained as an infantry commander, was concerned about the possibility of the Allies cutting the corridor in half. Before sending the panzer divisions north, he wanted to bring up the infantry reserves to secure the bridgeheads over the Somme River. Rundstedt appealed to Hitler, requesting he order a delay of the advance north along the Channel coast for twenty-four hours. Hitler listened to Rundstedt out of respect, but he had already made-up his mind. That little voice deep in his mind told him to continue the advance. Hitler was sure that they had to continue to advance north and cut off any attempt by the Allies to try and withdraw across the Channel to Britain. He brushed aside Rundstedt's concerns and ordered the 12th Panzer Division to dispatch some of its forces, and hold the bridgeheads across the Sommes, while Guderian's and Reinhardt's Panzerkorps quickly moved north along the coast. The 2nd Panzer Division would move on Boulogne, the 1st Panzer Division would proceed to Calais while the 10th Panzer Division would race toward Dunkirk. Brauchitsch, Halder, Keital and Jodl all agreed with Hitler's decision.

On May 20th the 2nd Panzer Division moved north along the coast while the 1st Panzer Division raced toward Calais. Guderian was excited and sure that his 10th Panzer Division and part of the 12th Panzer Division would reach Dunkirk, completing the encirclement of the Allied forces before they could evacuate across the Channel to Britain. Reinhardt's XLI Panzerkorp was ordered to remain behind by Rundstedt, but his order was quickly countered by Hitler's order to continue north and hold the Allied forces back, so that Guderian's panzers could reach Dunkirk as quickly as possible. The British retreat to Dunkirk had actually begun as early as May 16th, when the British began withdrawing from the Dyle Line without informing their Belgian allies. When the French requested that the British join them in fighting on the Senne River on May 17th, the British commander, Lord Gort, ignored the offer and continued the withdrawal toward Dunkirk. The Belgian forces were forced to withdraw along with the British and surrender more of their country to the Germans. On May 19th, Lord Gort rejected another offer by the French 1st Army to join them in a counter-offensive and try to break out of the pocket. Instead, but the British continued their withdrawal, taking only 500 casualties and leaving most of the fighting to their Belgian and French allies. On May 20th, the War Cabinet finally ordered Gort to cease his withdrawal and join the French in an offensive near Arras.

At an emergency meeting in London of the British Cabinet, Churchill learned that Ironside had turned down Gort request for an evacuation of all British forces from the continent. Churchill agreed with Ironside and ordered him to inform Gort to attack, but the mood of the Cabinet was downcast. After the meeting broke-up, Eden murmured to Ironside, "This is the end of the British Empire." But Churchill was not ready to surrender. He made an impromptu radio broadcast to the British public, assuring them that a "scoop or raid of mechanized vehicles," could not possibly defeat four million French soldiers.

On May 21st the British Expeditionary Force under the command of Lord Gort ordered a strike at what he referred to as the neck of the German tortoise, south from Arras. The French would attack north and cut the German corridor in half near the town of Albert, while the British attacked south from Arras. Within hours the two British divisions had advanced eight miles before they collided with Rommel's motorized infantry attached to the 7th Panzer Division, near the village of Duisans. Rommel's motorized infantry was taken by surprise, and the British continued to advance south when they ran into elements of the Waffen-SS Totenkopf Division. The SS's 37-mm guns could not stop the British thirty-two ton Matilda tanks, but they did provide time for Rommel to bring-up his 88-mm flak guns, to use against the British. Rommel raced from gun to gun, assigning each gun what tanks to destroy. He seemed tireless and appeared to be everywhere at once, which raised his men's moral. All night Rommel kept up the assault until the British advance slowed and eventually was stopped. Despite the British lost of more than half of their tanks they were continuing to move south due to the casualties inflicted on the Germans. Rommel fought desperately to stop the British, and fear that the German silent might be cut in half. Despite the damage inflicted upon the British tanks, his own forces were quickly being depleted. If the British continued their attack, they could succeed in cutting the German salient in half. It would be the Germans who were then entrapped. But suddenly, Lord Gort, without reason, ordered a stop to the attack and being withdrawing his division. This order was made without first consulting the French.

By May 22nd Guderian had captured Boulogne and surrounded Calais, reaching the coastal town of Gravelines, which was located twenty miles southwest of Dunkirk. The British had agreed to join the French in defending Boulogne, but when the Germans advanced on the port, the British refused to disembark from their ships, while the French in the port, were destroyed by the attacking Germans. The Germans brought up their flak guns and forced the defenders of Calais to surrender by May 23rd. The British quickly withdrew from Calais and refused to assist the French, leaving them to their fate in German captivity. While elements of the 12th Panzer Division entered Calais, the 1st and 10th Panzer Divisions moved toward Dunkirk. By the May 23rd the Germans held a line that ran from Gravelines south along the Aa Canal. Guderians tanks had established a sixty mile wide front along the Aa Canal, from the coast all the way to Arras. They continued to press the British, French and Belgian forces trapped within an ever shrinking triangle. Guderian's tanks were now pressing from the southwest, pushing the Allied forces right into the advancing German forces of Army Group B, that was moving west through northern Belgium. Guderian knew that the anchor of the Allied pocket was Dunkirk, and so he concentrated his tanks of the 1st and 10 Panzer Divisions along an eight mile bridgehead across the Aa Canal, running from Gravelines inland. His divisions were less than a half-day from Dunkirk and only a division of French infantry blocked his way. All he had to do was strike at the port and bulk of the British and French armies would be hopelessly trapped deep within Flanders, concentrated around the city of Ypres. Kleist was concerned about the conditions of his panzer group and wanted to halt the advance so as to submit his panzers to a maintenance check. The commander of the Fourth Army, General Guenther von Kluge, was concerned about the fact that the panzers were too far out in front of the infantry.

Rundstedt agreed with him and brought their concerns to Hitler's attention once more. But Hitler was unmoved by their arguments. He immediately phoned Guderian and ordered him to begin the final attack on Dunkirk, as soon as he felt he was able. Guderian was pleased and begun the attack as soon as Hitler hung-up. On Friday morning of May 24th, Guderian's panzers struck across the flat lands of northern France, crushing the French infantry division, and surrounded Dunkirk. By the afternoon of the 25th, the bulk of the Allied forces were cut off from their escape route to Dunkirk, and effectively surrounded. The Allied forces defending Dunkirk could not hold out and had to evacuate the port. At 10 PM on May 25th, Dunkirk had fallen to the Germans.

The British had managed to evacuate 28,000 British troops, but the rest of the British forces were now surrounded along with their French and Belgian allies. The British were encouraging their Belgian and French allies to hold out against the Germans without informing them of their withdrawal. Lord Gort's chief of staff, General Pownall, remarked that they "did not care a bugger what happened to the Belgians," and considered the Belgian army rotten to the core. British Secretary of State for War gave permission for the British Expeditionary Force to withdraw from the continent, and not inform their Belgian and French allies of their intentions. But now it was too late. The British were trapped along with their allies.

The German forces, advancing from the east through northern Belgium, had broken through the Allies' northern front where the Belgian and British forces met. The Belgian port of Nieuport fell to the German Eighteenth Army at noon on May 26th. Upon hearing the news, King Leopold of Belgium was depressed and agreed to surrender to the Germans later that day. With the surrender of the Belgian army, a 217,000 British and 250,000 French troops. for a grand total of 417,000 Allied troops, were now encircled and trapped within, what was now referred to as, the Ypres Pocket. On May 29th, Lord Gort, realizing that there was no hope of escape, surrendered to the Germans.

Hitler was ecstatic at the news that Dunkirk had fallen, and the surrender of the surrounded Allies. His faced beamed with joy as Keitel, Brauchitsch, Halder and Jodl applauded the success of their army.

"I'll never question my instincts," Hitler said. "We've come this far because of my instincts. Let reasonable men rely only on their logical minds, but not me. I knew all along that victory would be our's if we did not delay. Everything depended on capturing the coastal ports, and cutting off the only escape route for the British. Now all of France is our's for the taking. We must turn our armies around and strike south as quickly as possible."

"What about invading England?" Brauchitsch asked. "With the surrender of the entire British Expeditionary Force, England is defenseless. We could drop our Airborne in England, and reinforce their numbers with gliders."

"No!" Hitler said abruptly. "If we did, we would never be able to establish a bridgehead because the British Fleet is still patrolling the Channel. White we tried to invade England, the French will be given time to regroup and attack us in our rear. We have got to move south and knock France out of this war. The invasion of the British Islands is too dangerous. We don't have the naval forces necessary to support such an operation. We'll stick to my original plan. I want the offensive against France to resume, but first, I want to withdraw Rommel and his 7th Panzer Division, along with the 12th Panzer Division, from France and transfer them to Italy."

"Do you think that's wise, My Fuehrer?" Halder asked.

"The Allies have lost 71 divisions, and have only 41 left to try and stop our 104 divisions," Hitler said. "Nothing can stop us from overrunning France. France will have to withdraw from this war before the end of June. But the British will not agree to an end to this war, even if we offer them generous terms."

"Why not, My Fuehrer?" asked Brauchitsch "Surely they realize that their island is defenseless. They'll be forced to withdraw most of their forces from North Africa and the Middle East to defend their island-nation. Surely they will sue for peace?"

"Not Churchill," Hitler said, as his face turned grim. "That drunken fool is consumed with his own reputation. He's known for the disaster of Gallipoli in the Great War, and after the defeat in Scandinavia, and now in the Low Lands, he won't agree to peace without at least one great victory to his name. He'll continue to pursue this war, even if it means the complete destruction of the British Empire. And if that's what it will take, so be it.

"We have to face the reality that the British won't surrender until the very existence of their Empire is at stake. Rommel and the two panzer divisions must be readied to leave for Libya. With Mussolini's 325,000 infantry stationed there, and an additional two panzer divisions that we'll transfer to North Africa after France surrenders, Rommel will sweep through Egypt and won't stop until he reaches the Persian Gulf. The British will be forced to withdraw as many of their troops in North Africa and the Middle East and transfer them to Britain, to defend their homeland from the threat of our invasion. I want the OKW to make arrangements to make it look like we're contemplating crossing the Channel after France is defeated. And I want our U-boats out in force, in the North Atlantic and the Channel, to hunt down the transport ships that will be bringing those troops to the British isles. With all of North Africa and the Middle East under our control, the British lifeline to India will be severed. The very existence of the British Empire will by teetering on the brink. The British will then be forced to accept our terms for peace."

Hitler turned to Jodl. "I want to communicate with Il Duce," Hitler said. "We must make arrangements to send Rommel to Libya as quickly as possible. Once his two panzer divisions are in place, he'll invade Egypt. We must put an en to this conflict with the Western Powers by October. If we don't we could find ourselves at war with both Britain and the Soviet Union."

"The Soviets?" asked Keitel. "Do you still believe Stalin will attack us?"

"Stalin hopes Germany and the Western Allies will become bogged down in a war of attrition in the West," Hitler said. "When we are exhausted, he will throw the full weight of his army against us. After he overruns Germany, he won't stop until his Mongolian hordes as washing their feet in the Atlantic Ocean."

"When do you think he will attack?" Halder asked.

"Probably sometime between the summer of 1041 and the summer of 1942," Hitler said. "That's why we have to end this war before the end of the year."

The British plan to withdraw from the Low Lands was cut short by Hitler's decision not to halt the advance of his panzer divisions, which resulted in the fall of the last of the coastal ports. With the fall of Dunkirk, Belgium surrendered and the British and French forces trapped in the Ypres Pocket surrendered. This was the greatest crisis that Britain faced in nine centuries of English history. The distrust in Churchill's government, lead by Halifax, now boiled to the surface. On May 26th, an emergency meeting of the War Cabinet was called by Churchill.

It was Halifax who felt that England's survival was at sake, and he led the faction that wanted to sue for peace. Lord Halifax was not a defeatist, nor was he intriguing behind Churchill's back. He was an acute observer of public opinion and instinctively knew which way the tide of events was turning. His only concern was for the survival of the British Empire. He had no interest in his own advancement, nor was he ambitious. If he was, he could have become Prime Minister when Chamberlain offered it to him. Halifax felt the time had come to confront Churchill, and let him and everyone in the War Cabinet know that he disagreed with him. And that's exactly what Halifax did.

The War Cabinet sat around the table as Churchill paced about the room, chewing on his cigar. He had been drinking, but was not drunk. He could consumed a great deal of liquor before becoming inebriated.

"There's no reason to assume that the surrender of the BEF in Flanders means that the French is finished," Churchill said. "The French army is still in tact, and Reynaud and Weygand have assured me that France will continue to fight. The Germans won't try and invade England, not so long as the French are in their rear, and our shores are protected by our Royal Navy and Royal Air Force. We were wise to hold back the bulk of our air force, rather than throw them away on the continent."

Halifax was not so confident in the French army as Churchill was. He never liked the French and never thought much of the French army. "The French army is at half its strength," Halifax said. "I seriously doubt if they'll be able to put up much resistance, if the Germans decide to strike south. And if France should surrender, there is very little chance that we'll be able to carry on this war alone. I believe the time has come to find out what terms the Germans will offer in return for a cessation of hostilities."

Churchill stopped pacing and stared at Halifax. He did not lose control or grow angry. "You can't serious believe that?" Churchill said. "Any attempt to accommodate Hitler now will mean the complete destruction of the Empire. Hitler is bent on nothing less than the domination of the entire world, and he'll build his new order of barbarism on the corpse of the British Empire."

"Really, Winston," Halifax said. "We're face with the reality that the French won't be able to hold out much longer, and that the possibility of imposing a complete defeat upon Germany is no longer possible. The primary issue is one of safeguarding our Empire. We should be willing to consider any proposals which might lead to this, provided our liberty and independence are assured. If the Germans agree to these terms, then we should be prepared to discuss terms for peace."

Churchill knew that he could not even consider Halifax's request. "No!" he said. "I would be willing to consider your proposal, if I thought it possible to get out of our present difficulties on such terms, provided we can retain the essentials and the elements of our vital strengths, even at the cost of some territory. I would like to remind you of the document the Chiefs of Staff had drew-up on May 17th. It was entitled British Strategy in a Certain Eventually. It detailed a course of strategy that was open for us in the eventually of France dropping out of the war. It clearly proved that we could continue to carry on the war for at least two year. In that time the Americans would enter the war against Germany. Roosevelt needs time to get re-elected in November. Once he has, he'll bring the United States into the war. In the meantime, Roosevelt will ensure us the financial assistance necessary for us to maintain naval and air superiority. Let me read it for you." Churchill said and then began reading the document in length.

For an entire hour Churchill read the document to Halifax's annoyance. Everyone present had already read the document, but Churchill continued to read despite several members trying to protest. Halifax was getting fed-up with Churchill's lengthily monologues and passionate arguments that he used effectively to wear down his opponents, but this time he held his temper. Finally, Churchill completed the document and looked over his glasses at those seated around the table.

"But how do we defend our Empire in the face of such a devastating defeat in Flanders?" Halifax asked. He remained composed and calm in the face of Churchill's adamant insistence of continuing the war. "We've not only been driven from the continent, but our entire expeditionary force has surrendered. If the Germans defeat France, they'll control all of Europe. We don't have the troops necessary to defend our home islands. And with the support of their Soviet allies, the Germans are invincible. They'll be able to sweep us from the Mediterranean and maybe even the Middle East. No one in Europe will lift a finger to support us."

"By letting the French know that we could count on financial support from the United States, we might convince them to continue the fight," Churchill said. "Reynaud will be able to maintain French morale and I am confident that he is willing to fight on."

"Reynaud is not as resolute as you think he might be," Halifax said. "He has suggested that we approach Mussolini and request that he mediate between us and Hitler. You could easily reason with Mussolini. We all know that you've maintained a cordial relationship with him over the last fifteen years. I do believe you should try."

Churchill shook his massive head. "We cannot trust that Italian," Churchill said. "It's better to hold out and resist."

"Even if France surrenders?" Halifax asked.

Churchill sniffed his contempt at the question. "If the French can't defend themselves, it might be better that they get out of the war, and out of our way, rather than they should drag us into a settlement which involved intolerable terms. I'm convinced that the terms the Germans would impose on us would be intolerable, especially if we went begging to Signor Mussolini and invite him to go to Herr Hitler and ask him to treat us nicely." Churchill's voice dripped with contempt. "I don't want to get entangled in a position of that kind before we have had the opportunity to really get involved in any serious fighting. If we have to ask for terms, it's better to do it from a position of strength."

"I agree with Halifax, and think let the French approach Mussolini and ask him to discover what terms Hitler would offer," Chamberlain now spoke up. "If Mussolini is prepared to collaborate with us in getting tolerable terms, then we should be prepared to discuss them with him. But Winston is also right. We must do it from a position of strength."

"And what would that mean?" Halifax asked.

It was Churchill who now spoke. "Even if the French sue for peace, the Germans will be faced with our islands guarded by our air force and navy. We should immediately begin withdrawing forces from Africa, the Middle East and even the Far East, if necessary, to reinforce the defenses of our home islands. Before we seek terms, we have got to show Herr Hitler that he cannot conquer our homeland."

"I think we should take into consideration what the entire Cabinet thinks about approaching Signor Mussolini?" Halifax said. He refused to let the issue of seeking peace terms drop.

Churchill's mouth was tightly shut and his jaw fixed as he stared out the window for a moment. He then turned and asked if the Cabinet thought Halifax was right about asking Mussolini's assistance in discovering Hitler's proposal? The majority of the Cabinet admitted that Halifax's idea should be considered. Churchill took a deep breath and then stared at Halifax. "I seriously doubt if such a deal is possible," Churchill said. "Approaching to Mussolini might be necessary, but only for the purpose of keeping the French in the fight, or delaying their withdrawal, but then we have to consider what it could have on British morale. If it got out that we were considering to give up British territory, the consequence will be terrible. I think it's better to make the French understand that we will fight on to the end, if need be, even without them. I admit that our prestige in Europe is low at the moment, but if we could show the world that Germany could not beat us, by resisting for another two or three months, our prestige would return. Then, if we have to seek terms, we would be in a better position to do so, but if we are beaten, we would be no better off than we are now."

The entire Cabinet thought Churchill's argument made sense.

Halifax nodded his surrender. "Then we'll hold out and prove that we are undefeated, but then, if we get to the point of discussing terms of a general settlement and find that we could obtain terms which do not postulate the destruction of our independence, we should not be so foolish as to reject them."

When the meeting broke-up, Halifax turned to his Assistant Foreign Secretary, Alexander Cadogan, who attended the meeting with him, and told him that he could not work with Churchill any longer. Cadogan calmed Halifax down and convinced him not to let Churchill vex him. "I know you're right," Halifax said. But Churchill speaks the most frightful rot, and I can't beared it for too long. I must confess to you that if Churchill leads the Empire down the path of certain destruction, I will not rest until he is destroyed."

In Rome Mussolini had been watching the progress of the German advance across the Low Lands with amazement. He had predicted the German drive to t he Channel would have gotten bogged down and stopped by the Allied armies, much in the same way that it did in 1914. He was pleased when Hitler told him that he did not want Italy to enter the war until after France had been defeated. Mussolini knew that the Italian armed forces had been depleted during the last ten years of intervention; first in Libya, then in Ethiopia, followed by three years of fighting in the Spanish Civil War and finally in Albania. Italy was not a great industrial power and in seventeen years of Fascist rule, Mussolini did little to encourage the expansion of its industrial base. There was no industrialization plan similar to what Stalin instituted in the Soviet Union. The Italian armed forces had almost no modern tanks, and what little armor they had were fifteen years obsolete. Even their rifles were of World War One vintage. Only the Italian Navy was considered modern, but it was no match for the combined Mediterranean fleets of Britain and France. Thus, Mussolini was relieved when Hitler insisted that Italy remain neutral until after France had been defeated.

With the news of the surrender of almost half-a-million Anglo-French forces in the Ypres Pocket and the withdrawal of Belgium from the war, Mussolini realized that it was just a matter of time before France surrendered. He had not believed Hitler when he told him that France would be defeated before the end of June, and then Germany and Italy would finish off the British during the summer and autumn of 1940. But now he was beginning to think that Hitler was a military genius. On May 29th, Mussolini called a meeting with the chiefs of staff of his armed forces. Present were General Badoglio, head of the Italian armed forces, Rodolfo Graziiani of the Army, Dominico Cavagriai of the Navy and Francesco Pricolo of the Air Force in his Roman office.

Mussolini was dressed in his gray uniform. Like Goering, he loved to wear elaborate uniforms and often had his tailors design new and flashy uniforms. "Gentlemen," Mussolini said in a enthusiastic voice, as he said behind his large desk. He was visibly excited at the German successes. "I've received a telegram from the Fuehrer. He has informed me that he is preparing to send General Erwin Rommel to Italy with two panzer divisions, in accordance with our plans to transport them to Libya. Two more panzer divisions, as well as a Luftwaffe detachment will follow after France is defeated. He has also assured me our troops in Libya will be fitted with the most up-to-date rifles and other equipment. If all goes well, Italy will declare war on Britain in July and our combined forces will drive through Egypt to the Suez."

Badoglio, who was not too fond of the Germans, objected. "I still don't like the idea of placing our troops under the command of the Germans," he said. "Our troops are not prepared to invade Egypt. If we permit our army in Libya, to be placed under the command of the Germans, they'll use them as cannon fodder."

Mussolini cut him off as his dark eyes flashed with anger. A month ago he would have agreed with Badoglio, but after the success of the German offensive, he was anxious to entire the war. Hitler had promised him not only a huge Mediterranean empire but also the French territories of Savoy, Nice and Corsica without having to declare war on France. "I can't agree," Mussolini said. "With the equipment that the Fuehrer promises, our soldiers will be able to fight just as well as the Germans. We have 325,000 infantry soldiers in Libya. With the two panzer divisions, our combined forces will sweep the British from the Mediterranean and the Middle East. The Fuehrer also assures me that with the capture of the British Expeditionary Force in Flanders, Churchill will be forced to withdraw most of his forces from North Africa and the Middle East, to defend the British Isles. We'll not only capture the entire Middle East, but we'll be able to drive down, through the Sudan, and link-up with our colonies in East Africa."

It was General Graziani who spoke up. "Duce, our army is unable to fight effectively without German equipment and assistance. I agree that there is opportunity for success in North Africa with the German panzer divisions and equipment for our infantry, but we must remain on the defensive everywhere else on land. You can expect nothing spectacular from the Army without German support."

"And the Navy must not engage both the British and French fleets," Admiral Cavagnari said. "Once France has withdrawn from the war, our fleet might have a chance of confronting the British, especially if the Germans begin conducting submarine operations in the North Atlantic around the British Isles."

Mussolini was annoyed at the conservative advice by both the army and navy. Only General Pricolo of the air force, was confident of success, but even he insisted that Italy had to agree to Hitler's plan and remain neutral until after

France surrenders. Then, Italy had a chance of preforming well in coordinated operations with the Germans.

"I will inform the Fuehrer that Italy will wait until France falls before declaring war on the British Empire, and agree to place our forces under the command of General Rommel, just as he requested" Mussolini said as he glared at Bagdoglio. "If the Germans can defeat France, then there is nothing standing in our way to establish our new Roman Empire. The British will not be able to stand against the combined might of both Italy and Germany."

It was raining in Washington, which did little to relieve the heat and humidity and was typical of this time of year. Roosevelt asked Harry Hopkins to join him in the Oval Office. "It's good of you to come at such short notice, Harry," Roosevelt said as he flicked his cigarette into the ashtray.

"I came as soon as I got your message, Mr. President," Hopkins said as he took a seat. He could see by the look on the President's face that he was in a dark mood. "It sounded urgent."

"I just received a communicate from Joe Kennedy, in London," Roosevelt said as he reached for a piece of paper and handed it to Hopkins. He continued to talk as Hopkins quickly read the communicate. "Joe informs us that the Allied forces have been surrounded and surrendered to the Germans. The entire British Expeditionary Force is no more. There are only two divisions of British infantry left in all of France, and the French only have about forty divisions left to defend the rest of France."

Hopkins finished reading the communicate and looked up at Roosevelt. "This is black news, indeed."

"Black news?" Roosevelt said as he slammed his hand on his desk. "This is damn devastating news!"

"Kennedy doesn't think Churchill's government will survive," Hopkins said. "He excepts Churchill to resign as Prime Minister and predicts that the Germans have won."

"Oh yes, he does," Roosevelt said. "Every word in that communicate drips with his 'I told you so.' Joe must have taken a sardonic delight in sending that communicate. Do you know, Harry, that I truly believe, Joe wants the Nazis to win? It's his damn Irish blood. He hates everything English. He told Drew Pearson that he favored the isolationist Vandenberg for President, calling him 'his favorite Republican candidate.' for the presidency and that he would 'back Vandenberg against half the Democratic candidates,' though he didn't mention if, I am probably included in that list of Democrats."

"If Kennedy is right, and Churchill does step down, then Halifax will most likely become Prime Minister, and he will most likely seek terms with a victorious Germany," Hopkins said. "That would make your chances of getting re-elected more difficult. The people would support you if the war continued, but if the war came to an end, most Americans would want America to remain out of any disputes that might arise from the peace process that would follow."

"Churchill won't step down," Roosevelt said. "He's craved power all his life, and now that he's Prime Minister, the only thing that will cause him to step down is a vote of no-confidence in Parliament."

"If he does, it'll change the entire international situation," Hopkins said.

"I'm more concern about how it'll affect the Republican nomination process," Roosevelt said. "Up to now, both Vandenberg and Taft were easily beaten by Dewey, but Dewey's support has been sliding as Willkie began stumping across the country. He's been gaining support, and it seems that he'll be the Republican candidate for President this year. He's a supporter of our policies of opposing the Nazis, but after the news of this defeat by the Allies gets out, I don't know if he can keep up the momentum. Dewey just might be able to pull off a victory at the Republican convention in Philadelphia, later this month." Roosevelt fixed his eyes on Hopkins. "If the Allies loose this war, I doubt if I can win re-election in November against Dewey."

Hopkins stared at his old friend. He could see tears in his eyes and wondered if they were for what a Nazi victory meant for the world, of if they were self-piety at the prospect of not winning a third term?

The spring of 1940 was a time when heads' of state came and went like a revolving door. In France, Daladier was replaced by Paul Reynaud as premier, while in England, Chamberlain had to resign and appoint Churchill as Prime Minister in May. The rapidly changing course of the war was even having an effect on the presidential races within the United States. The race for the Republican nomination was heated. Three candidates vied for the nomination; Senators Taft and Vandenberg, both isolationist. The third candidate was Thomas E. Dewey, an attractive prosecutor from New York. He had made a reputation for himself as a fierce opponent of organized crime. His thirty-eight years of age provided for an youthful alternative to the older candidates, whom appeared as caricatures of the old-fashion senators. Dewey was able to take the led in the race by winning both Wisconsin and Nebraska primaries in April 1940. He had a well-financed campaign, which was highly organized. He also was isolationist, but because he came from New York, and was young, he received support from the internationalist-minded east bankers, lawyers and businessmen that made-up the liberal wing of the GOP. But as they discovered that Dewey could not be so easily manipulated, they soon abandoned him and sought out a candidate that represented their desire to intervene in the war on the side of the Allies. That candidate was Wendell Willkie.

Willkie was forty-eight years old, an attorney from Indiana who made a name for himself in New York opposing Roosevelt's policies. Willkie was actually a Wilsonian Democratic turned Republican. It was Walter Lippman, backed by the eastern liberal establishment within the Republican Party, who led the charge to get Willkie the Republican nomination. Lippman, who previously supported Taft, turned to Willkie because of his willingness to bring America into the war against Germany.

Being Jewish, he hated the Nazis and began fiercely and tirelessly organizing support for Willkie campaign. By the first week of June, Willkie was the front-runner in all the polls. The justification for a Willkie candidacy was the need for a Republican President who could support the Allies in their war against Germany. Willkie claimed he could do a better job of this than Roosevelt, but now that the Allies suffered such a tremendous defeat in Flanders, most Republicans began to have second thoughts about Willkie. A poll taken on June 4 showed Dewey regaining his front-runner status. Willkie's rise to front-runner had been referred to as meteoric, but one must remember that a meteor is falling, not rising. It was beginning to look as if Willkie's campaign was running out of steam.

On May 31st, Hitler moved into his new headquarters at Bruly-la-Peche, *Wolfschanze* or Wolf's Redoubt, a name that Hitler chose instead of the original *Waldwiese* or Forest Clearing. After the fall of Dunkirk and the surrender of the British Expeditionary Force, Hitler was sure the war in the West would soon be over, but he was also not convinced that Britain would seek peace. He had come to trust his inner voice and it warned him the Churchill was determined to prosecute the war to the end—the end of the British Empire, not his end. Hitler was anxious to defeat France. On June 1st, the German forces were in place along the Somme. The German generals performed a miracle moving their forces into place while accepting the surrender of hundreds of thousands of Allied troops. At 4 a.m. Hitler gave the order for the final offensive in the West.

Chapter 8

THE FALL OF FRANCE

After the fall of Dunkirk and the surrender of the Allied forces trapped in Flanders, Rommel was summoned to Hitler's new headquarters, *Wolfschanze*. He had received orders that he was being transferred to Italy, along with his 7th Panzer Division and the 12th Panzer Division. Hitler had convinced Mussolini to permit Rommel to deploy four panzer divisions in Libya and prepare for the invasion of Egypt and the Middle East. Rommel knew that Hitler intended for him to command this operation, but he felt that it would be advisable to wait until after France had agreed to an armistice.

When Rommel's staff car finally stopped at Hitler's headquarters, he was quickly shown into the building, where Hitler was discussing the plans for Fall Roth, or Case Red—the final assault against France. Gathered around a table covered with maps was Keitel, Bruchitsch and Halder. Hitler was bent over with a magnifying glass, examining the deployment of the German armies when Rommel entered the room. Hitler, on seeing Rommel, cut off the discussion and rushed to welcome him to the annoyance of Halder. Halder disliked Rommel because he rose through the ranks with the help of Hitler. Halder considered Rommel an "Swabian upstart."

Rommel saluted Hitler, who returned his salute. "Ah! You have arrived, Herr General," Hitler said. He was obviously delighted to see Rommel.

"I came as soon as I received you summons," Rommel said.

"I assume you're prepared to leave for Italy?" Hitler asked.

"Yes, my Fuehrer, but, if I may speak?" Rommel asked.

Hitler nodded yes.

"I would suggest that we delay the redeployment of the two panzer divisions until France has fallen," Rommel said. "Every panzer division will be needed to assure France's speedy fall."

Hitler's icy-blue eyes were fixed on Rommel as he examined the short, stocky general. He then dismissed Rommel's suggest with a wave of his hand. "I understand your desire to be part of the drive through France," Hitler said, "but France is broken. The French will agree to an armistice before the end of the month. We must prepare for the final stage of this war—to bring Britain to her knees. And that can only be done either by invading the British Isles, or strike at the jugular of the British Empire. Since the former is impossible so long as the British Navy rules supreme in the North Sea and the English Channel, the only alternative is to attack through North Africa and the Middle east. Once our troops are standing on the shores of the Persian Gulf, the life-line of the British Empire will have been cut. There is no way that Churchill could possibly continue this war. His government will fall and cooler heads in the British government will agree to make peace with the Reich.

"My only regret is that this could reduce the British Empire to a second rate power. The decline of the British Empire is not in the Reich's interest. It will benefit the Americans, the Soviets and the Japanese. I truly did not want a war with the British. I even made the point that Germany and Britain should be allies in my book, *Mein Kampf*. I did not want this war, and I will give the British a chance to agree to end this war once France has been beaten, but I doubt if Churchill will agree. That's why it's imperative that you begin the preparations for the invasion of Egypt. I want you to begin operations by the middle of July. This war has got to be terminated before the end of the year.

"That will be your destiny, Herr General. To beat the British and end this war."

"Yes, my Fuhrer," Rommel said. He made no other protests. He could see that Hitler was serious by the tone of his voice. Though he still felt that it would be better to delay the deployment of the two division until after France fell, there was something about Hitler's self-confidence that convinced him not to make any further objections. Hitler seemed in possession of some kind of sixth sense. He had been right about every stage of the war so far, and Rommel felt that he was right, once again. He left the *Wulfschanche* with the determination to begin the preparations for the invasion of North Africa and the Middle East. As he left, he could see the hatred in Halder's eyes.

On May 27, Hitler approved the final version of the planned assault on France. The operation was named *Fall Roth*, or Case Red. The German forces were stretched out along a 225-mile front that began in the west on the English Channel, along the Somme and Aisne rivers to Montmedy at the northeastern edge of the Maginot Line. General Bock's Army Group B was stationed on the western most end of the front. To the east of Army Group B was General Rundstedt's Army Group A, which was deployed along the Aisne River. Opposite the Maginot Line, running from Luxembourg to the Switz border, was General Leeb's Army Group C. The attack would proceed in three waves, beginning in the west and moving east. Bock's group would attack first, south, on both sides Paris. Rundstedt's group would then attack, moving south and southeast to engulf the Maginot Line from the rear. Finally, Leeb's group would assault the Maginot Line directly.

General Weygand had deployed the French forces into a defense in depth, clustered around natural defensive positions that could be exploited. He referred to this plan as a *quadrillage*, or checkerboard.

While Weygand busied himself with patching together his defense, the Germans moved their panzer and infantry divisions into position to resume the offensive with skill and grueling speed.

On June 5, Army Group B struck south across the Somme River. Its 4th Army's panzers reached the Seine River, crossing it near Rouch. Further to the east, Manstein's 6th Army made rapid progress toward the Seine, but his panzer divisions met stiff resistance north of Paris. Manstein ordered his panzers to shift east so they could exploit a breakthrough along the Marne River. Four days later, Rundstedt's Army Group attacked across the Aisne River. Guderian's 12th Army broke through the French defenses near Junivile and moved south, west of the Maginot Line. The Germans broke through Weygand's defensive line at several points, and the French lacked the reserves to plug the gaps despite the heroic efforts of the French soldiers.

Guderian's 39th and 41st Panzer Corps broke through the front near Saint Dizier and plunged south toward the Switz border, effectively encircling the Maginot Line. On June 14, Army Group C assaulted the Maginot Line from the north and east, sealing the fate of the French nation. From the English Channel to the Argonne Forest, the French defensive line was crumbling before the onslaught of the German attack. German panzer and infantry swarmed south across France, eager to bring an end to the war in the West. The French desperately tried to construct a new line along the Seine and Marne Rivers, but they were swept aside by the advancing Germans.

In Paris, the French government fled to Tours. The citizens of the French capital accepted their fate, which became apparent to everyone on June 11 when Premier Paul Reynaud finally left the city to join his ministers in Tours. Despite the collapse of the front, Reynaud refused to accept an armistice. He was backed by his newly appointed undersecretary of war, General Charles de Gaulle. Both Vice Premier Philippe Petain and General Weygand had now come to accept the reality that there was no possibility of stopping the Germans from overrunning France. Marshal Philippe Petain had joined the government in May. He was eighty-four-years-old, and a retired World War One hero. Paris was declared an open city to prevent its destruction. Over one million Parisians fled the city to join the millions of French and Belgian refugees heading south in a vain attempt to escape the advancing Germans.

As the roads leading south from Paris were clogged with refugees, the German 18th Army entered the city early in the morning on June 12. Only two million of the city's population remained behind to greet the Germans when they arrived. The Germans entered the city from several routes. Uniformed squadrons of motorcyclists rode into the city, orderly regiments of marching soldiers in gray uniforms, cavalrymen pulling artillery, all smartly entered the city, as if on parade. The people of Paris offered no resistance. Few ventured outdoors to watch their city being occupied. Many feared a wave of rapes, murders and arrests. When none of these atrocities materialized, Parisians began to venture outdoors later in the day. They discovered a huge swastika flying from the Arc de Triomphe.

As many as ten million refugees flooded the roads and highways of France. Most were from Belgium and northern France. They deserted their homes, taking with them what little possessions they could carry. They blocked the road, making it difficult for both the advancing Germans and the retreating French armies to maneuver. In many sections of France and Belgium whole districts were devoid of people. Entire villages and hamlets were transformed into ghost towns. Most of the refugees never made it south of the Somme or the Seine Rivers. But about 1.5 million Belgians, about half of those that did flee, did make it to southern France. So many Belgian refugees reached Toulouse that it was referred to as little Belgium. By the end of June, the population of southern France had doubled. Only after the defeat of France did the refugees accept their fate and slowly returned home. Between July and October, most had return to discover that 98 percent of the Belgian homes and 80 percent of the French homes were untouched. They expected the Germans to looted their homes, only to discover that those few homes that were looted, were done so by their neighbors.

The fall of Paris was followed by the surrender of the Maginot Line. The advancing armies of Rundstedt and Leeb, led by the Guderian's panzers, entrapped the French defenders within the steel and concrete fortress that was now transformed into their prison. In the west, German panzers were racing toward Cherbourg and Brest and finally reached the Loire to the south. As Bock's divisions approached Tours, the French government was forced to flee once more, this time to Bordeaux in the southwest.

Churchill flew to France once again in a desperate attempt to stiffen the backs of his French allies. Premier Reynaud wanted to resist and played with the idea of moving the seat of the French government to North Africa, but too many members of the French government had enough of war and desired peace. When Churchill arrived, he found a black mood had infected the French government.

"I asked for assistance from President Roosevelt on June 10," Reynaud told Churchill. "The President replied by promising that he would do everything possible to support our continuation of the war, but he did not make any commitment about the United States entering the war."

Churchill chewed his cigar as he spoke. "It's inevitable that the United States will enter the war in a fortnight. Their response was just short of a declaration of war. That's why we have got to hold on."

Petain shook his head. The old soldier stared at Churchill with disdain. "The Americans won't enter the war. When we asked Roosevelt if we could publish his response, he refused to give us permission. Roosevelt won't enter the war because he can't. If he asks the Congress for a declaration of war, he'll lose his bid for reelection in November. Roosevelt pushed us into this war and has now abandoned us. We've got to face the reality that we are on our own."

Churchill hated Petain, but he hid his true opinion of him. "Then let me make a proposal," Churchill said. "I propose we form a union between Great Britain and France. There'll be one government, and every citizen of Great Britain will be a citizen of France and every citizen of France will be a citizen of Great Britain. Your fleet can sail for England and we can continue to resist Hitler in the British Isles and in North Africa."

The French were not impressed. Petain brushed Churchill's proposal aside. "You call for union, but what you are concerned with is the fate of the French fleet. What I want to know is, how many troops will you send to France?"

Churchill looked at Reynaud, who acquiesced to the old Marshal by diverting his eyes.

"We have none to spare," Churchill said. "With the failure to withdraw our forces from Flanders, we must cut the strength of our forces in North Africa, the Middle East and the Far East to defend Britain."

"In 1918, I gave you forty divisions to save the British army," Petain said. "Where are the forty British divisions that are needed to save ourselves today?"

Churchill's face turned red.

"It' clear to us that France is on its own," Petain said. "You can't help us and the Americans won't. We must think of preserving the French Empire. There are too many jackals across the Atlantic that seek to pick the bones of our empire while we are too busy fighting the wolf. I suggest you had better think of preserving your empire as well, before it falls victim to the jackals. We should try and seek the best possible deal with the Germans while we can." Most of the French delegates in the room agreed with Petain.

Churchill left France realizing that Britain now stood alone. He felt betrayed by the French and the Belgians. But the French also felt that the British had let them down by the limited assistance and Britain's continuously placing its own self-interest before the alliance and the defense of Western Europe. If the French felt that the British had let them down, they felt betrayed by the Americans. Roosevelt had consistently encouraged Britain, France and even Poland to resist Hitler with promises of assistance and the United States eventually entering the war as their ally. But now that France was on the verge of total defeat, everyone seemed ready to abandon them.

Premier Reynaud finally accepted the inevitable on June 16, and tendered his resignation. He rejected de Gaulle's proposal to move the French government to North Africa, and continue the war from the French colonies. Most of the government feared the fate of the French people by the Germans if they agreed to such a proposal, and Reynaud turned the government over to Petain. He promptly contacted the Germans and agreed to an armistice. Hitler jumped at Petain's request. He wanted the war in France concluded. He did not want the formation of a hostile government-in-exile that might turn the powerful French fleet over to the British. He was planning on a neutral France, which would secure Rommel's rear when he began his offensive against the British in Egypt.

While the French were seeking peace with the Germans, there were individuals within the British government, working with other prominent members of British society who were convinced that Britain could not win the war. They were working behind Churchill's back, trying to open channels with Germany through Italy, in the hope of ending the war.

With the German conquest of the Low Lands, the surrender of the Anglo-French forces in Flanders, and the imminent collapse of France, pressure from Britain's dominions to make peace with Germans was also growing. The Prime Ministers of both Australia and New Zealand urged London to end the war. Both countries feared what fate might await them if Britain was defeated by Germany. It could result in the collapse of the British Empire, which could leave both dominions at the mercy of the Japanese. The Australian Prime Minister, Robert Menzies, expressed his opinion that Churchill represented a menace to the existence of the British Empire. He feared that Churchill was prosecuting the war for his own egoistical reasons, and would continue to do so, even if it meant the destruction of the British Empire. He wrote the High Commissioner in London, Bruce, that he believed it was imperative that Britain seek peace. He felt that if they did not put an end to the war now, Europe would be dragged down and find itself at the mercy of its real enemy: Bolshevism.

After Churchill had returned from France, he met with the War Cabinet on June 17. His report was pessimistic. Not aware of France's offer of an armistice, he told the members of the War Cabinet that he believed France would make peace with Germany, and that Britain would have to stand alone. He did not believe the United States would enter the war before 1941, and with France defeated, Germany would turn the full force of its military might on the British Isles. But despite his gloomy report, Churchill insisted that Britain should continue with the war. It was suggested by Halifax that they should approach Mussolini, requesting he contact Berlin and ask what terms the Germans would accept to end the war.

Churchill rejected the idea. "We should at least continue to resist German aggression until we have dealt Hitler a defeat," Churchill said as he paced about the room. "Hitler will try and invade Britain, but to do so, he will have to effectively neutralize our air force and navy. I have deliberately held our air force in reserve for just such a possibility. If Hitler does try and invade our island, our air force and navy will foil his plans. Then, and only then, after we have demonstrated to Hitler that he cannot invade our island, should we seek terms to end the war."

The aristocracy and land-owning gentry of Britain were very conservative. They feared the spread of Communism more than they did Hitler and National Socialism. They were not pleased by the war, and feared that even if Britain did win, she would lose. They viewed Germany as a bulwark against the spread of

Communism in Europe, and if Germany was defeated, or even just weakened by a long, protracted war, it would be an invitation for the Soviet Union to invade Europe. Many of these upper class Englishmen fear the nightmare of Soviet troops on the English Channel.

Churchill was able to convince the War Cabinet to continue to resist, at lease for now. After he left, four members of the War Cabinet—Chamberlain, Halifax, Clement Attlee, the leader of the Labor Party, and Arthur Greenwood, the deputy leader of the Labor Party—reconvened to discuss what they should do if Churchill refused to listen to reason. With Churchill now busy writing a speech to address the British people, encouraging them to fight on, the meeting would be dominated by Halifax. "Now that Winston is busy else where, we should discuss among ourselves what should be done if the need to seek peace is presented to us," Halifax said. "Italy has not yet entered the war, and so, I believe we should explode the possibility of approaching Mussolini and soliciting him in discovering what peace terms the Germans would be satisfied with. We could play on Mussolini's and the Italians' fears of a German dominated Europe, to encourage them to suggest a general European settlement."

"But Mussolini will probably want territorial concessions from us, for his part," Greenwood said. "He could ask for Gibraltar, Malta and the Suez Canal. He might even demand Somaliland, Kenya and Uganda. This would be unacceptable, but we could offer certain French territories for Mussolini's support."

"I believe Hitler will accept our inquiry for peace terms," Attlee said. "I don't believe Hitler wants a long, protracted war. If he is reasonable, we could offer him the return of the former German colonies. He should be pleased if this war was concluded before the end of the year."

"Before we do rush into requesting terms, perhaps we should see what terms the Germans have offered the French?" Chamberlain said. "If the terms the Germans presented to the French seem reasonable, we could then seek terms to end this war. I doubt if the Germans would make the same demands against us as they would on the French. After all, we're still undefeated and possess our navy and air force."

"I agree," Halifax said. "I favor this approach. Let's see if there's the possibilities of creating a new European equilibrium from the armistice between Germany and France. In this way, it might be possible to save France from the wreck, and prevent the Germans from dominating all of Europe."

"If we do approach Italy, we must make it clear to the Italians that whatever terms the Germans offer us, they must not affect our independence," Chamberlain said. Everyone agreed.

"Then we agree that we should seek terms that do not result in the destruction of our independence and preserves the Empire," Halifax said. "If we succeed, we would be foolish not to accept them."

"But I believe we all know that Winston will never accept any terms from the Germans," Attlee said.

"That's why we have got to present him with a *fait accompli*," Halifax said.

The Foreign Office immediately contacted the Italian ambassador. Fortunately for Churchill, he had made sure that the Italian embassy was bugged. Churchill learned of the Foreign Office's inquiry and immediately vetoed the initiative at the next meeting of the War Cabinet, on June 18. He complained to Halifax, accusing him and comrades of their strong impression of defeatism. "I have said that I would be willing to accept an reasonable offer of peace from the Germans," Churchill said, "if it ensured our independence, even if it meant surrendering some territories, but I will reiterate that we must do it from a position of strength. We have the opportunity to deal the Germans a decisive blow. As we speak, our island is being reinforced by forces from other sections of the Empire. Everything is being done to ensure the successful repulsion of any attempt by the Germans to set foot on our shores. Once Hitler has been thrown back into the sea, we can then agree to sit down at the negotiation table with him, and arrive at a reasonable peace."

On the same day that the Germans accepted France's request for an armistice, Hitler was meeting with Mussolini and Ciano at the Fuehrerbau, in Munich. Mussolini was in an excited mood. He once again asked Hitler to permit him to declare war on Britain.

"No!" Hitler said adamantly, with a sweep of his hand. Both Italians were taken back by Hitler's forceful reaction. Before Mussolini could protest at being spoken to in such a way, Hitler's mood suddenly changed. His icy-blue eyes seemed to glow with an inner light as he focused them on Il Duce. "My dear friend, Duce," Hitler said as he smiled. "There is no hurry. France is beaten and Britain stands alone. I won't hide my regret at the stubbornness and obstinate determination of Churchill to drag the entire British Empire down to ruin and defeat. There are no limits to my reservations on the desirability of demolishing the British Empire, which could only disrupt the equilibrium of the international situation against both Germany and Italy. But I also recognize that so long as Churchill is Prime Minister, the war will continue. That's why we must stay the course, and make sure that our plans unfold on schedule. Within a month, Italy will enter the war. By then, Rommel and his panzer divisions will be in place, in

Lybia. Air detachments and airborne troops will be preparing for the assault on Malta, along with your navy and air force.

"I will make one more attempt at peace, but I doubt if Churchill will accept. I know there is a strong peace party in Britain, but they won't be able to stand up to Churchill. Before the English agree to peace, they will have to suffer a great defeat. This is why I made sure that the British Expeditionary Force could not escape from Flanders. The British Isles are defenseless. Churchill is already evacuating forces from North Africa and the Middle East to reinforce Britain. I'm ordering an air assault on the British Isles to begin in two weeks, but this will only be a diversion. I want to make Churchill think we're preparing to invade the British Isles. This will give us the opportunity to launch our offensive in Egypt on July 15."

Hitler leaned back and let himself melt into the comfort of his sofa chair. He wiped his hair back from his forehead with his left hand. Both Mussolini and Ciano could not believe Hitler's certainty of his plans, and they both seemed to be under his spell. They had heard his promises before, but this time, it all sounded new and exciting. Hitler nodded his head as he continued to speak, now looking at the ceiling, as if seeking the approval of a higher authority. "Before the year is out, our forces will overrun Egypt, and move south toward the Sudan. There, your forces in Italian East Africa will attack north. Then, across the Suez Canal Rommel will move, into Trans-Jordan. The French in Syria, will permit our planes to use their airfields, so that Rommel can continue his march across Iraq to the Persian Gulf. With the lost of North Africa and the Middle East, Britain will be forced to sue for peace, despite promises from Washington of additional assistance. Turkey, Iran and even the entire Balkans, will join the Axis."

Both Mussolini and Ciano was convinced. Hitler had preformed his magic once again. When the meeting concluded, the two Italian leaders spoke about their meeting on the train back to Italy. Mussolini seemed excited. He was still under Hitler's spell, and spoke in length of the formation of the new Roman Empire, but it was Ciano who understood that Mussolini's new Roman Empire would be just a shadow of the new Greater German Reich that Hitler was forging.

Hitler left his meeting with the Italians and hurried back to France. On June 20, the first day of summer, Hitler arrived at Compiegne, exactly at 3:15 in the afternoon. This was the same location where, in 1918, Germany's representatives had surrendered. The exact railroad car in which the Germans accepted the surrender terms had been brought to the location for the French surrender. Hitler quickly walked from his car. His face was chiseled in grave and solemn features that masked the excitement that bumbled like a mixed brew of vengeance and joy. He stopped before a granite block. On it were the words:

> HERE ON THE ELEVENTH OF NOVEMBER 1918 SUCCUMBED THE CRIMINAL PRIDE OF THE GERMAN EMPIRE—VANQUISHED BY THE FREE PEOPLE WHICH IT TRIED TO ENSLAVE.

The mask on Hitler's face melted before the hatred, anger, scorn and sense of triumph in setting a historical wrong right, as he read the words. Hitler stood with feet wide apart and hands on his waist. He could not hide his contempt for this place. He then turned to those who were standing with him. "Tomorrow we'll now begin the work of destroying everything that reminds us of the world that was born on that shameful day. I want this entire place razed to the ground."

The negotiations would begin on the morning of June 21, at 11 in the morning, but the French delegation was delayed, and the meeting did not begin until 3 in the afternoon. When the representatives entered the railroad coach, they took their seats on either side of a long plain table. Hitler's interpreter, Schmidt, sat so that he could hear both sides. Hitler sat next to Schmidt. The three heads of the German armed forces, Goering (air force), Reader (navy), and Brauchitsch (army) sat next to Hitler along with Ribbentrop (foreign minister), Hess (deputy Fuehrer) and Keitel. They sat on one side of the table. On the opposite side, the French delegates filed into the coach and took their seats. They were led by General Charles Huntziger, and included an admiral, an air force general, and a former ambassador.

The meeting began with Hitler rising. Both delegates bowed without speaking a word and sat down. Then, Keitel began reading the preamble which included the armistice conditions. It were written by Hitler. Both teams of delegates stared at each other with little reaction as Keitel continued to read. "Germany did not intend that the conditions should cast any aspersion on so courageous an enemy. The aim of the German demands is to prevent a resumption of hostilities, to give Germany security for the further conduct of the war against England which she has no choice but to continue, and also to create the conditions for a peace which will repair the injustice inflicted by force on the German Reich." Hitler wanted to offer the French a honorable peace, one which the British could also accept if they chose. He had hoped that the generous terms might still convince the British to end the conflict. The Germans would occupy the northwestern half of France, along with the Atlantic coast all the way south to Spain. The remainder of France would be under the jurisdiction of the government led by Petain. Its capital would be situated in the city of Vichy. The conditions made clear that Germany did no seek to challenge Britain's dominance of the sea by solemnly swearing not to claim the French war fleet for Germany. This stipulation was opposed by the German navy. But Hitler knew that if he did try and claim the French fleet for Germany, it could result in further French resistance, as well as hardening the English refusal to come to terms with Germany, when the time came.

After Keitel read the conditions, Schmidt had translated his words into French. Upon Schmidt's completion of the translation, Hitler rose and took his leave, along with the other German delegates. Keitel and Schmidt remained behind and were joined by Jodl and several other German officers. Before Hitler departed, he turned an stared at Keitel. The field marshal nodded, and Hitler left. Those who remained within the car could hear the military band playing first the German national anthem, which was followed by the Horst Wessel song.

Huntziger asked for time to re-examine the proposal, but Keitel refused. When Huntziger asked permission to transmit the conditions to his government at Bordeauz, Keitel grew inpatient. "Absolutely not!" said Keitel. "You must sign at once." When Huntziger insisted on telephoning General Weygand immediately from the coach, Keitel agreed. After speaking with Weygand for a few minutes, he then demanded the courtesy to discuss further the proposal overnight. "Impossible!" was Keitel's response.

"You can't expect us to sign without first discussing the proposal among ourselves," Huntziger said. "Though they are honorable, they are still merciless and far worse than what was forced on Germany in 1919."

Keitel's face grew hard. He leaned back in his seat. "It does not make any difference if you discuss the conditions or not," Keitel said. "The conditions will not change. You will either have to sign the agreement now, or the negotiations will be broken off, and the delegation will be conducted back to the French lines. If this seems hard, they are the same conditions that were forced upon the German delegation at Versailles."

Huntziger realized that there was nothing he could do. He swallowed hard and then sighed as he agreed to sign the armistice treaty. Huntziger then telephoned Weygand once more, informing him of the conclusion of the meeting. Before Huntziger left, Keitel asked him to remain for a moment. The two officers faced each other. Both were overcome by emotion. Each noticed tears in to other's eyes. Keitel finally congratulated Huntziger for representing France with dignity, and held out his hand. Huntziger stared at the hand extended before him for a moment and then shook it. Schmidt then translated Keitel's words.

166   THE LION IS HUMBLED

"You have saved your country from a far worst fate then you might realize by being reasonable," Keitel said. "You will see."

Huntziger fought to control his emotions. "I prayer to God that you are right," Huntziger said.

After Hitler received word of the French acceptance of the armistice treaty he began a tour of Paris. He was accompanied by an entourage that included two of his favorite architects—Speer and Giesler, as well as the sculptor Arno Breker. Hitler's plane set down in Paris on June 23, at 4 in the morning., at the airport located at Le Bourget, outside of Paris. It was a hot summer day when Hitler's group, which also included Leitel and Borman, climbed into their open cars and proceeded to begin their tour of the City of Light. Their first stop was the Paris Opera. They noticed how deserted the streets of Paris were as they drove through them.

"Paris has always fascinated me," Hitler said as they came to the Paris Opera House. "I've always wanted to visit the city. It's a true art metropolis, and that's why I insisted on taking along my trusted artists. I hope you'll be inspired by its beauty and grace when designing our cities." When they finally stepped out of their cars, Hitler stood before the Opera House. With his fists squarely resting on his waist, he looked over the building before him. "I've always thought this to be one of the most beautiful theaters in the world."

After leaving the Opera House, they made their way to the Eiffel Tower and then to Napoleon's Tomb. Hitler was moved by his visit to the tomb. He asked everyone to leave him alone. The others stood back to leave their Fuehrer alone with his thoughts. Standing with his cap over his heart, as if he was in a trance, he stood for a long time, gazing down into the deep round crypt where Napoleon's body was housed. When he finally looked up, he turned to Giesler and said, "You will build my tomb." He then turned to Borman and instructed him to transfer the bones of Napoleon's son from Vienna to France, so they could be interned by his father's side.

It was 10 a.m. when Hitler's tour of Paris finally came to an end. Hitler immediately flew back to his headquarters in Belgium. That evening, Hitler addressed his artists. He was deeply moved by his visit to the French capital. "Now the work on our cities can begin," Hitler said. "I thank Fate for permitting me to see this city and experience its magical atmosphere. I found it fascinating. I'm glad I gave the order for our troops to bypass Paris. It would have been a crime to damage it and its wonders. Paris is truly the most beautiful city in the world, but it must be eclipsed by our new Berlin." Hitler turned to Speer and told him he expected the reconstruction of Berlin to be completed by 1950.

Late in the evening of the next day, everyone sat around waiting for the armistice to go into effect at one hour and thirty-five minutes after midnight, on June 25. Champagne glasses were filled, and even Hitler, who hated champagne, had a filled glass. They watched their watches as the minutes ticked away. Silence filled the room until they heard a the blow of a bungle, which was the traditional signal for "Weapons at rest." Keitel rose and raised his glass, asking everyone for three *Hocks* for the Fuehrer, in honor of the great victory that he had delivered to the German Reich.

Everyone stood and raised their glasses and shouted *Hock* three times. Hitler remained seated. He felt uncomfortable with such displays, but he bowed to the Wehrmacht's tradition. He brought his glass to his mouth as a courtesy, but did not sip. He then set the glass down and stood before everyone. "France is defeated. Now we must dispatch England as soon as possible. It was a great responsibility. It is a great responsibility," Hitler said and then fled the room.

Hitler was not the only well-behaved tourist in Paris. He wanted to prove to the world, and especially to the British, that peace with Germany did not mean being dominated by the Germans. He was determined to present himself as a magnanimous victor who did not seek to punish his defeated enemies. Instead, he wanted the French, as well as the rest of Europe, including the British, to understand that he was offering them a partnership in a unified and prosperous Europe that would stand as a bulwark against the Communist threat from the east. One of his first orders in relation to the occupation of France, and the rest of the occupied territories, was a demand that his soldiers behave in their contacts with the native population. He wanted them to act as liberators, not as conquerors. Hitler said, he remembered how the French treated the Germans when they occupied the Rhineland after the Great War, and he did not want to repeat that mistake. He even ordered that any German caught looting be shot. He wanted to build a new understanding between Germany and France.

Fortunately, his orders were obeyed by his troops. German soldiers stationed in Paris did not behave as swaggering conquerors. They paid for every purchase and treated the local population with respect. The French had feared that the Germans would loot their shops, ransack homes, beat-up Frenchmen and rape their women. Slowly, the French came to realize their fears were unfounded and so lost their fear of the Germans, and eventually coming to accept their presence. They were soon welcomed in most shops as good customers, behaving as good neighbors, treating the women courteously and respecting the customs of the local population. The Wehrmarcht was even assisting those millions of French, who had fled their homes, to return.

President Roosevelt and Harry Hopkins decided to invite Democratic big-wigs, Edward Flynn of New York, Senator James F. Byrnes of South Carolina, Mayor Edward Kelly of Chicago and Frank Walter to an intimate dinner at the White House to discuss the political future of the Democratic Party on June 29. It was a beautiful, but hot Saturday evening in Washington. The Republicans had just concluded their national convention in Philadelphia.

"Well, I suppose you heard that the Republicans chose Dewey as their candidate?" Roosevelt said. "I was sure that the momentum that was being generated for Willkie, by our banker friends in the GOP, would have thrown the nomination to him."

"It would have, Mr. President," Hopkins said, "if the British had been able to salvage their Expeditionary Force from Flanders. The surrender of British Expeditionary Force and France's armistice with Germany caused the growing support for Willkie to collapse. That's why Dewey was able to win the nomination on the second vote. He was willing to make a promise to keep the United States out of the war, while Willkie kept talking about the need to support British."

"Let's face it," Byrnes said, "Dewey ran a well-financed campaign. He beat Vandenbreg and Taft in the primaries and made himself the front-runner among the isolationist wing of the GOP. If the British could have rescued their army from Flanders, maybe, Willkie could have stopped him. The effort to give him the nomination was led by Lippman, and he had the support of businesses and banks from across the country. Willkie clubs were popping up like mushrooms after a rain storm. But the double disasters of the surrender of the British Expeditionary Force and the surrender of France undermined the effort to hand the nomination to Willkie."

Byrnes was a born politician. He was born Catholic and Irish, but converted to the Episcopal faith to further his political career. Though he was born in New York City, he quickly endeared himself to the primarily anti-papist South.

"This is going to make it more difficult for the Democratic Party to maintain control of the White House," Ed Kelly said. "If Taft of Vandenberg had won the nomination, we could depict them as being too isolationist. And with Willkie, we would not have concerned ourselves with his stand on the issues, because he supported your New Deal and he advocated an interventionist foreign policy. But with Dewey, we could have trouble."

"If Dewey becomes President, I shuttered to think what could happen," Roosevelt said. "At the least, Vandenberg and Taft were isolationists, but they were not pro-German. But a Dewey administration could actually find it agreeable to work with Hitler. I'm referring to his advisers on foreign affairs, John Foster Dulles and his brother Allen. Both of them have connections with such companies as Solvay, International Nickel, Consolidated Silesian Coal and Steel that are partners with German companies in cartels. Do you know that John actually blamed the outbreak of the war on the British and French refusal to permit Germany to make peaceful changes in Eastern Europe?"

"You're right, Mr. President" Ed Flynn said. "Dewey could unite the two wings of the Republican Party and win the election in November. Then, Britain will find herself all alone facing a German-dominated Europe."

"I don't think internationalists within the GOP, who were backing Willkie, will support Dewey," Frank Walter said.

"That's true," Flynn said, "but enough of the rank-and-file who are internationalist could support him. That would mean we would be faced with an unified GOP, while our party is divided."

"You're referring to Farley and Gardner?" Roosevelt said.

"That's right, Mr. President," Flynn said. "The Vice President is going to run and Farley also hopes to seek the nomination. Both of them will unite the conservative, isolationist wing of the Democratic Party, especially in the South."

"And there's no one with the stature who supports the New Deal, who could oppose them." Byrnes said. Byrnes knew where the conversation was leading. He had heard the President say that he did not want to run for a third term in January, while agreeing that he would run if he had too. Others had told him that Roosevelt had been saying this to many within the Democratic Party, and it bothered Byrnes. But Byrnes was not the only one present who had heard Roosevelt recite his well-rehearsed denial.

Everyone suddenly fell silent. They all knew that Roosevelt desired to run for a third term, though he would often deny his intention to do so. Only Hopkins knew how much Roosevelt wanted to run. He originally wanted Hopkins to run, but because of his health he could not. Without Hopkins as a possible candidate, Roosevelt felt there was no one who could champion the cause of liberalism on the domestic front and lead a united America into a war against Germany.

"I believe that I have no choice but to seek a third term," Roosevelt said. "That's why I asked you to dine with me tonight." Everyone sat up at Roosevelt's announcement. "Now, let me say this first. I consider it critical that no one here repeat my decision. It's critical to keep the rest of the party in the dark about my intentions. In this way, those who might consider running, will be prevented from organizing a campaign properly in time to prevent me from taking the nomination. I can keep all potential candidates off balance right up to the convention. In the meantime, I'll publically state that I have no desire to serve a third term, on principle, all the while you continue to talk of the need to convince me to accept the nomination."

"A draft Roosevelt campaign?" Flynn asked.

"That's right, Ed," Roosevelt said. "Your part will be most important, especially at the convention, since it's going to be held in you city, Chicago. You'll have to engineer a popular demand for me to accept the nomination."

"That can be done," Flynn said.

Roosevelt flashed him one of his famous toothy smiles. "I knew I could rely on you, old fella."

"What about your running mate?" Hopkins asked.

"I was thinking of my Secretary of Agriculture," Roosevelt said.

"Henry Wallace?" Byrnes asked. "Are you sure? He's considered something of a wild-eyed mystic and ideologue."

"But he's young and dedicated to my New Deal," Roosevelt said. "You know that someone with my paralysis could suffer a breakdown at any moment. You all remember the slight heat attack I suffered in February?" Everyone nodded, but they all realized that the heart attack was much more serious than the President let on. "Well, I'll need someone as my vice President who is in good health, because there is no telling if I'll survive a third term."

Roosevelt suddenly unbuttoned his jacket and lifted his shirt, revealing a large lump under his left shoulder. Everyone reeled back in horror, except for Hopkins, who already knew of its existence. Roosevelt seemed to take great delight in shocking everyone. "I'm told by my doctors that it's flesh and muscle that wandered there because of my sedentary existence in this wheelchair. So you see why I need someone who will continue to fight for our programs and foreign policy if anything should happen to me. You can understand why its so important that I'm re-elected in November. If I'm not, all our New Deal reforms will disappear in the United States, and all my work in the realm of foreign affairs will be for nothing. The future of the world will either be dominated by Fascism of Socialism. If we fail, it'll most surely be the former."

CHAPTER 9

IL NOSTRA MARE

On July 1, Hitler held a conference at his headquarters in the Black Forest. Hitler wanted to review the details on the subject of their strategy for what was known as Operation Sphinx. Hitler asked the heads of the three branches of the Wehrmarcht, along with Brauschitsch, Keitel and Jodl, to attend the conference. Also present was Albert Speer. The conference was held because of the appearance of Mussolini. Hitler had asked Mussolini, and Ciano, to attend the conference so that Germany and Italy could coordinate Operation Sphinx.

Keitel immediately rose to his feat and thanked Mussolini for his attendance. "France has been defeated and now we must turn our attention to the matter of bringing the British to their knees," Keitel said. "For this reason, the Fuehrer has asked you to this conference so that we might begin the final operations of this war. It was Grand Admiral Raeder who has drawn-up Operation Sphrinx, and so I will ask him to explain the details of the plan."

Raeder rose and began to elaborate on Operation Sphinx. "There are only two means by which we could hope to defeat Great Britain: either by a direct invasion of the British Isles across the English Channel or by driving the British out of the Mediterranean and the Middle East. Since Germany cannot challenge the supremacy of the British Navy in the Channel or the North Sea, our only alternative is a drive across North Africa and the Middle East.

"This operation, code named, Sphinx, will begin on July 15, with the declaration of war by Italy on Great Britain. In the last four weeks, General Rommel, along with two panzer divisions, have been sent to Lybia. I understand that Rommel, along with the 7th and 12th Panzer Divisions are, already in place for the invasion of Egypt. Hopefully, Rommel will take Alexandria by August 1. Presently, we are in the process of arming the Italian infantry divisions, which consist of 250,000 men, with modern equipment, as well as providing enough motorized unites to ensure sufficient motor transport. The Italian artillery consisted of well-trained troops, but we are replacing them with German guns. Italian tanks are obsolete, and are being replaced with PzKw I and II. By August 1, the 5th and 1st Panzer Divisions will arrive in North Africa to reinforce Rommel's North Africa Army.

"On July 20, the assault on Malta will begin. This will be a joint German and Italian operation that will include German Airborne troops, contingents of the Luftwafte as well as the Italian Air Force and Navy. Then, on July 30, with the cooperation of Spain, we will begin the assault on Gibraltar. Once the western and central sectors of the Mediterranean Sea have been secured, Rommel will be able to continue his attack toward the Suez Canal. At least one Panzer division, along with sufficient infantry support, will then drive south, up the Nile River, and eventually make contact with Italian forces moving north from Italian East Africa. There are presently 200,000 Italian troops in East Africa, which will invade the Sudan and possibly occupy British Somaliland.

"Once this stage of the operation has been completed, Rommel will continue his assault by invading Palestine and making contact with French Vichy forces in Syria and Lebanon. At this point, we will have the use of airfield bases in Syria for the continuous drive east, through Iraq, to the Persian Gulf.

"At his point, let me also say that we are in contact with Egyptian military officers, as well as Iraqis, who are sympathetic to the Axis. There is also the possibility of Turkey entering the war on the side of the Axis once we have made contact with Syria.

"Our forces will face very little and weak resistance. The British have already begun depleting their forces in North Africa and the Middle East to reinforce the defense of the British Isles. The Fuehrer has suspected that the enemy has broken the Enigma code, and so we have been transmitting orders that have made it seem we are preparing for the invasion of the British Isles, across the English Channel. Because of the surrender of the British Expeditionary Force, the British are desperate, and have been cutting their troops throughout their Empire. This means Rommel will face only 20,000 British troops in Egypt, including the 7th Armored Division and the 4th Indian Division. The 6th Australian Division has arrived in Palestine, but we estimate there will be little more than 8,000 British troops in the Middle East.

"The major resistance will be from the British Royal Navy. The British presently have seven battleships, two aircraft carriers, eight cruisers, 37 destroyers, eight submarines and a small forces of gunboats in the Mediterranean. This force is divided between Force H, under the command of Admiral Sommerville, stationed at Gibraltar, and under Admiral Cunningham's Mediterranean Fleet, at Alexandria. To face this force is the Italian Navy, which consist of six battleships, 21 cruisers, 50 destroyers and 100 submarines. We'll quickly take control of the air with the addition of the two Luftwaffe contingents, that will be added to some 2000 Italian aircraft, which are station across the Central Mediterranean and the Dodecanese Islands." Raeder concluded his report and then Brauchitsch asked Goering to continue.

Field Marshal Goering reported that there was no way the British could maintain control of the air in the Mediterranean. "The British have only a few air squadrons that included obsolete Bombay medium bombers, Blenheim light bombers and Gladiator biplane fighters," he said. "Most of their better planes are being held in reserve to defend their home island. Our intelligence informs us that the British are cutting their forces across the Mediterranean because they believe that we'll try and invade England this summer. We're transferring two Air Fleets to the Mediterranean, that will part take in the attack on Malta and Gibraltar, and then support Rommel's attack on Egypt. Using bases in Sardinia, Italy, Sicily, Libya and eventually Spain and the Balearic Islands, the Luftwaffe and the Italian Air Force will ultimately dominate the skies from Gibraltar to Egypt.

"British production of new aircraft is rising at an alarming rate, but, they are keeping their new planes in England to defend their home island against the threat of invasion. If we make them believe that we're planning to invade, they'll keep most of their newer planes in England through October. After that, the threat of invasion will disappear because of worsening weather. Then, the British will reinforce their air force in the Middle East. If all goes according to plane, the British will be driven out of the Middle East by the end of the year."

"But, what if our schedule invasion comes up against unexpected delays?" Halder asked. "What if Rommel is unable to invade the Middle East before October? If the British are able to transfer their fighters to the Middle East, along with additional troops, they might be able to stop Rommel?"

Goering glared at Halder. He could see Hitler frowning. "But you are forgetting, Herr General, that production of the Heinkel's jet fighter. They'll in ready for operation by the end of September. Once they appear in the skies over

England, as well as the Mediterranean and the Middle East, no amount of British propeller-driven fighters will be able to stand up to our air force.

"But I would ask the Fuehrer for permission to unleash a force of 220 bombers against Southampton. For over a month now, the British have been bombing residential neighbors, killing women, children and the elderly. Let me give the order to strike back ten bombs for every bomb the British drop on our people."

"No!" Hitler said "I'll not be diverted from the task at hand. We won't be able to spare even one bomber. I'm transferring a portion of the Luftwaffe to the Mediterranean for operations against Malta, Gibralter and support for Rommel's push through Egypt and the Middle East. At the end of July, we'll begin our assault on the British Isle, but its purpose is to convince the British that we're going to invade. In fact, I want to increase coded communications giving validity to—what did I call it—oh yes, Operation Sea Lion. Oh, and use the Enigma machine."

"Are you still convinced the British have succeeded in breaking the Enigma?" Goering asked.

"Yes, I am," Hitler said. "But now, what about the assault on Malta?"

"The Italian Navy, along with help from both the German and Italian Air Forces, will prevent the British Navy from interfering with the invasion," Goering said. "The assault will begin with our airborne troops landing on the island. Their mission is to take control of the two airfields. Once their secured, and amphibious attack will begin. It'll include infantry, as well as amphibious versions of the Pzkw II and diving versions of the PzKw III and IV, which are fitted with floating air hoses and will be launched from landing craft. Remember, the British are stripping their forces throughout the Mediterranean, including Malta. Our forces will overpower the defenders of Malta. After all, the island are defended by what amounted to little more and two brigades. This force includes low-grade fortress troops and unemployed seamen. The British have only a few, out-dated tanks on the island."

Brauchitsch suggested that Major General Kurt Student's 7th Parachute Division should be used, but Goering insisted that the Luftwaffe could perform whatever tasks necessary to secure the island."

"Enough of this bickering," Hitler said. He turned to Keitel. "We'll use whatever forces necessary to take Malta. Make sure the OKW provides me with a report on the airborne attack." Keitel nodded and made a note of Hitler's request. "I want everyone to understand that the capture of Malta is of the utmost importance. Once it's in our hands, there will be nothing that the British can do to prevent us from supplying Rommel's troops. Supplying Rommel will be the key to his success in driving the British from North Africa and the Middle East. I'll let nothing interrupt the smooth operation of the assault on Malta. This includes inter-service rivalry, or rivalry between German and Italian armed forces. Don't you agree, Duce?" Hitler turned to Mussolini.

Mussolini was pleased to be included in the conference. His dark eyes flashed with delight. "Italy is cooperating completely with the preparations for operations in the Mediterranean," Mussolini said. "We've maintained the strictest secrecy. Rommel and his panzers have been ferried to Lybia aboard Italian merchant ships. My government has worked hard to maintain cordial relations with London, so that the British will not suspect our plans. I doubt if the British suspect that Rommel is now in Lybia. I've restrained my military, which was itching to declare war on France earlier this month, just as you request, Fuehrer, so that we can concentrate on ensuring complete surprise when we unleash our offensive against the British in Egypt."

Hitler was sure that the British did not realize where Rommel was, but did not speak his mind. His intuition had warned him that the Enigma was not reliable, and he had deliberately ordered messages sent that gave the impression he was planning to invade England, suspecting London would intercept them. Hitler knew that the Italian military had no wish to go to war. It was Mussolini who had to be restrain by Hitler. But Hitler knew how to convince Mussolini to cooperate. His greed was greater than his ego. He was jealous of Germany's successes so far and lust after military glory for Italy. But Italy's armed forces were not prepared for war. The Italian armed forces had depleted their forces in their war in Ethiopia and Spain. Germany had to rearm the Italians. Their tanks were outdated and their rifles were worse. The artillery had to be replaced with German guns, though the Italian soldiers manning them were well-trained. Only the Italian Navy could be considered modern, and though the Italian air force did not have the most up-to-day aircraft, their pilots were excellent and the Italians were even experimenting with jet technology that was almost as advance as the Germans. The problem the Italians faced was economic. Italy was not a great industrial power, and nothing like the industrialization programs that Stalin implemented in the Soviet Union took place under fifteen years of Fascism in Italy.

"The Italian Navy is ready to begin operations against the British naval forces in *Il Nostra Mare* (Our Sea)," Mussolini continued. "We'll make sure that the British Fleet does not interfere with our assault on Malta. What I want to know is, had Franco agreed to enter the war against Britain?"

"Franco had agreed to meet with me in two days," Hitler said. "I'm convinced that he'll bring Spain into the war. Franco owes us too much, for our assistance the Spanish Civil War. I understand from our ambassador in Madrid that Franco is anxious to enter the war. He is convinced that Britain is almost defeated. Without Canaris and his den of vipers, who were very close to Franco and had a very extensive network of agents in Spain, I should have not trouble convincing Franco that it will be to his advantage to enter the war."

Hitler then ordered Brauchitsch to elaborate on the plans for the attack on Gibraltar. "The necessary infantry needed for the operation will be provided by the Spanish army," Brauchitsch said. "But the real task will be reducing the fortress by artillery. General Karl Becker has informed me that his artillery will preform the operation with a concentration of super-heavy Bruno railway guns. They will fire across the bay from the region of Algeciras. Our engineers have already designed the necessary spurs that could be constructed within seven days. The caliber of the guns will be 238mm and 283mm. The weight of the shells that we'll hurled against the fortress will be between 9,400 and 15,000 kilograms. The range of the weapons is between 20,000 and 36,000 meters. The ammunition is especially designed for piercing heavily reinforced concrete fortifications. We expect Gibraltar to capitulate within three weeks."

"I'm pleased with the progress of Operation Sphinx," Hitler said. "I must say that I've come to believe that the God that created Germany is smiling on our efforts. My instincts have not failed me since this war erupted upon our continent. Everyone here must know that I never wanted a war with England and France. Our purpose in invading Poland was to right the wrong inflicted upon Germany after the Dictate of 1919. I even offered Poland a reasonable solution. I did not demand one acre of Polish territory. All Poland had to do was agree to the union of Danzig with the Reich and permit the construction of a modern railway and highway across the Corridor. In return, Poland and Germany would have been partners in an alliance against the Soviet Union. But we now know from documents discovered in Warsaw, the Polish leaders were receiving promises of support from Mr. Roosevelt and his Jew-ridden government in Washington. Roosevelt wanted this war. He wanted Germany, Britain and France to exhaust themselves in a war of attrition. Only after Europe bled itself to near exhaustion, would the United States enter the war and dominate all of Europe. Of course, Stalin hopes to do the same thing. That's the only reason why he signed the Non-Aggression Pact with us.

"My instincts tell me that Stalin means to betray us at the earliest possible opportunity. As you know, the Red Army has occupied both Estonia and Latvia.

From the reports of an increasing concentration of troops on the border with Romania, Stalin is also planning to invade that country. Fortunately, the Lithuanians have agreed to the occupation of their country by German troops. The Lithuanian government, which has moved to their new capital of Vilna, has signed a formal alliance with the Reich. Army intelligence reports have recorded the movement of heavy tanks massing across the frontier, and that Stalin might submit an ultimatum for us to withdraw from Lithuania next year. I'm sure our rapid defeat of France has shocked him. We received a communique from Molotov, informing us that the Soviet Union will brook no further delay, and might use force if Romania refuses to turn over Bessarabia and Bukovina. This is a violation of our agreement signed last August with Moscow. Bukovina, which has a large German population, and was part of the Austro-Hungarian Empire, was not included in the territories that would fall into the Soviet sphere of control. I predict that Stalin will grow increasingly aggressive in making demands in eastern Europe, especially in the Balkan."

"Do you expect the Soviets to attack us, my Fuehrer?" Goering asked.

"Yes, I do," Hitler said. "We can expect a Soviet attack on the Reich sometime in the summer of 1941. That's why we need to end this war with Britain. I have ordered an increase in mobilization from our present 165 divisions to 210 division by next spring. I have also scheduled a meeting with our panzer manufacturers, and will propose they design a new super tank that will be in operation by next June. Herr Speer," Hitler said as he turn to Albert Speer. How is the production of the Ural Bomber and the jet fighters progressing?"

"The first jet fighter, the *Volksjaeger,* He280, as it will be called because of modifications made to it, should be coming off the assembly line in September," Speer said. "We already have several of them being used for training. The first Ural Bombers will be operational by next March. The jet fighters will be available to deal with the British if they refuse to agree to an armistice, and the Ural Bombers will have the range to assault Soviet cities as far east as the Ural Mountains, from the present German-Soviet borders."

"Very good," Hitler said as he slapped his knee. "Once this war with Britain is concluded, we'll have to work to incorporate the Balkans, including Turkey, into the Axis alliance. The Soviet Union will be isolated and surrounded. Then we can devote all our efforts for the eventual destruction of Jewish-Bolshevism, once and for all. Once we have our empire in the east, we can begin the process of building the new Reich."

"But, my Fuehrer, what about the United States?" Keitel asked.

"Once Britain and the Soviet Union have been defeated, the United States will isolated," Hitler said. "I doubt if the Jews will be able to push the American people into war with us. We can then begin to reach out to the millions of Germans and other nationalities living within the United States, and win their friendship and support. They can be mobilized to work toward friendship with the United States and the new Europe.

"After Britain agrees to peace, we'll convene a peace conference in Munich. The borders of Europe will be redrawn. The western borders of both Germany and Italy will be moved westward. Germany will incorporate the Netherlands, Belgium and Luxemburg, annex Alsace, all of Lorraine, as well as the Flanders, east and south of a line running from the Somme estuary to Lake Geneva that includes the Franche Comte' and part of Burgundy. We'll restore the 1540 border between France and the Reich." Hitler turned to Jodl and ordered him to draft a contingency plan for the possible invasion of Switzerland. "If the Switz refuse our offer of incorporation, we'll have to invade it. Either way, it will be divided between the Reich and Italy.

"But, we must wait until after hostilities have ceased," Hitler insisted as he looked at Mussolini. "I don't want any of these proposals put down on paper. Nothing must be done that might cause Petain to transfer his fleet to the British. I have informed Admiral Raeder, as well as Reichsminister Ribbentrop and Reichsfuehrer Himmler that France will be expected to turn over Madagascar, which will be transformed into a new homeland for the Jews. All Jews, from Lisbon to the Volga, will be transported to Madagascar, where they'll be permitted to live impotently among themselves, unable to ever infect their neighboring nations with their vile contagion behavior."

Hitler's face was twisted with hate as he spoke about the Jews. Everyone watched as his facial muscles slowly relaxed and a frown soon replace the expression of revulsion. "I never wanted war with Britain," Hitler said once more. "The destruction of the British Empire will not be beneficial to Germany. It'll be detrimental to the White Race in Africa and Asia. But there is nothing that I can do. Britain must be defeated as soon as possible. But I will make one last effort. I'll deliver a peace speech before the Reichstag on July 14. In it, I'll extend the hand of peace one more time. If the British are too foolish not to accept, then we'll have to do everything within our power to bring the British Empire to its knees."

When the conference broke up, the Italian foreign minister, Ciano, who never felt much affection for Hitler, turned to Mussolini. "Hitler speaks today with a moderation and clear sightedness that I find very surprising, considering he has just won such a tremendous victory. I must admit, at this moment, I really admire him."

Mussolini looked at his son-in-law with eyes open wide. He swallow with jealousy and then nodded. "So do I," is all he said reluctantly.

When Churchill stepped out of his bathtub, it was 2 o'clock in the morning. He rapped himself in his terrycloth robe and then lit his cigar. There was a knock on the door and Churchill shouted for the guest to come in. When Eden entered Churchill's room, he stopped and examined the Prime Minister, who was standing before him in his bathrobe.

"So glad you could come at such a late hour," Churchill said. Churchill had made it a habit of staying up all night and holding meetings when most people were fast asleep.

"I assume it was urgent," Eden said, though he knew it probably was not. He was used to Churchill's unorthodox schedule, and behavior, and he had gotten used to Churchill holding meeting half naked.

"I've just the latest decoded messages from Ultra," Churchill said as he pointed to a stake of papers on a table. He had been reading them while bathing. "The best thing that ever happened was the breaking of the Enigma code. We can read every move the Germans make."

Churchill handed the stake of papers to Eden. "We haven't completely broken the code," Eden reminded Churchill. "Are you sure these reports are correct?"

"Correct enough to know that the Germans are planning to invade Britain," Churchill said as he sat. As he did, his robe opened, exposing his privates. He seemed not to notice or care. Eden ignored Churchill as he continued to read the reports.

"It looks as if the Germans are gathering their forces opposite the Channel," Eden said. "But there is something amiss."

"What is that?" Churchill asked.

"Rommel," Eden said. "The reports claim Rommel is in France, but our people in Madrid claim Rommel has been sighted in Italy."

Churchill looked at Eden. "That would mean Italy might come into the war on Germany's side?"

"That's what we think," Eden said.

"It wouldn't surprise me if Mussolini attacked us after giving us his assurance of his neutrality," Churchill said. "But even if he does attack, I doubt if his forces in North Africa are sufficient to invade Egypt."

"We are cutting our forces there," Eden reminded Churchill said.

"Yes, but Australians and New Zealanders will soon arrive in Egypt," Churchill said. "They should be there by September. That should be enough time to reinforce our forces in North Africa. The Italians, even if they are given support by the Germans, could not launch an invasion of Egypt until September. It's too damn hot in July and August. Hell! It reaches 130 degrees Fahrenheit. The real danger is from France. You will see. I'm sure the Germans are preparing to unleash their Luftwaffe against our home islands. Read on. You'll what I mean."

"It seems that the Germans will soon intensify their aerial attacks against our island," Eden said as he continued to read. "They're going to continue targeting our air defense installations, airfields, radar facilities and coastal defenses. They mention a two month period of bombing, which would mean they plan to invade some time in September. This would probably be during the high tide."

"Yes," Churchill said with a gruff.

Eden looked at Churchill. "You seemed displeased."

"I am," Churchill said. Eden thought he reminded him a pouting child. Churchill reached for a bottle of brandy and poured himself a large class and took a deep drink. "I was hoping Mr. Hitler would accommodate us with a little bombing of London."

"What?" Eden said. His mouth remained open.

Churchill took another gulp of brandy and then looked up at Eden. A mischievous smile crossed his lips. "There's been too much talk of peace," Churchill said. "The British people have no idea of the danger they're in—the seriousness of the situation. We have to do something to wake them up! If the Germans would only begin bombing London and other cities, the air raids would soon put an end to all this defeatist talk of peace, once and for all. We should have to do something to convince Hitler to begin the raids, and soon."

"What are you suggesting, Winston?" Eden asked.

"The R.A.F. began bombing Germany ever since the Germans invade the Low Lands," Churchill said. "It was one of my first orders as Prime Minister. I understand the Ruhr has been bombed into a mass or ruins." Eden frown. He knew that the reports that Arthur Greenwood had been feeding Churchill about the success of the bombing raids on the industrial region of Germany were false. "Somehow the German government has kept the full extent of the damage from the German public. I want to goat Hitler into attacking our cities, so that our people will be fortified in their determination to fight. I'm going to have to order the Air Ministry to plan raids on Berlin. That should push the Germans into sending their bombers against London.

"I won't be happy until there are round-the-clock raids. The Air Ministry predicts that the Germans could send 600 tons of bombs a day, inflicting 30,000 casualties. This ought to also wake up the Americans. The reports of Londoners suffering under the brutal and savage assault by the Huns should convince the Americans that they must enter this war as soon as possible."

"Winston, you're not serious?" Eden asked.

"Of course I am," Churchill said. "I'll do what ever it takes to bring the United States into this war. The Americans have soft hearts for the underdog. When they hear of the atrocities that the Huns are inflicting on every man, woman and child in England, they'll be demanding to enter the war."

"But what about the damage such raids will inflict on London?" Eden asked.

Churchill shift. "There are too many ugly buildings in London."

"Are there also too many ugly people in London?" Eden said with indignation.

Churchill's pink cheeks turned deep red. He stared at Eden and then smiled. I said I'll do what ever it takes to win this war," Churchill said.

"Would you even sell your soul to the devil?" Eden asked.

Churchill took another gulp of his brandy and slammed the glass down hard on the table. "Yes! Damn it! I would."

The French authorities in Oran, Algeria, were given an ultimatum by the commander of the British Fleet that had surrounded the naval port of Mers-el-Kehir. Most of the French Mediterranean Fleet had sought refuge at Mers-el-Kehir after France agreed to an armistice with Germany. The French Naval command feared the Germans would try and confiscate the French Fleet, but Hitler had no interest in the French Fleet. The last thing the French expected was a threat to the fleet from their former ally, Great Britain.

Churchill had ordered Operation Catapult drawn up and completed as soon as possible. He feared the Germans might try and confiscate the French Fleet. The ultimatum he sent the French demanded the surrender of all French ships to either British or American authorities. The French naturally refused, which was followed by an assault on the French ships. British planes took off from their aircraft carriers and drop bombs on the French ships. British battleships unleashed a hailstorm of deadly steel into the French hulks. The entire attack lasted only five minutes, but when it was over, more than 1250 French sailors were killed and the modern battle cruiser, *Dunkerque*, and the old battleships, *Provence* and *Bretagne* laid at the bottom of the harbor. But the French did not just sit by and let the British sink their ships. The battle cruiser, the *Strasbourg*, and the aircraft carrier, *Commandant Teste*, as well as five destroyers, managed to unleash a steam cloud as cover and escape through the encircling ships to cross the Mediterranean to dock at Tours.

At the same time as the attack on Mers-el-Kehir, all French ships still in British ports were boarded. Shock and anger spread throughout France. On July 5, the Vichy government of Marshal Petain broke off diplomatic relations with Great Britain. There was serious talk of declaring war, but Petain wanted to wait and see what course the war would take in the next six months. Churchill did not apologize for the attack. He justified it on the ground that the British Isles was defenseless and only the Royal Navy stood as an obstacle to the Germans invading Britain. He claimed he could not take the chance of the Germans utilizing the French Fleet in any attempt to invade Britain.

A modified He111 bomber flew over the Egyptian shore east of Sollum and moved inland across the arid desert until it finally crossed the border into Libya, and then proceeded north to the Libyan city of Bardia. The twin-engine bomber began to descend as it neared the Italian airfield outside of Bardia and taxed to a halt. German soldiers rushed to the plane with portable stairs, as the hatch opened. Out stepped a short, stocky officer. His blue-gray eyes adjusted to the desert sunlight before he descended the stairs. He was wearing the shoulder boards of a lieutenant general of the German army. He was Erwin Rommel, and he had just completed his latest reconnaissance flight over the Libyan-Egyptian border, which he took every few days.

His subordinates warned him against the flights, but Rommel wanted to see the situation on the border with Egypt for himself. The He 111 was modified and fitted with Italian markings to disguise it from the British. He had been making the reconnaissance flights ever since he arrived in Libya, four weeks ago. At first he wondered how he could possibly fight a modern war in the desert, but once he had become familiarized with North Africa, he discovered that the forbidding landscape of arid, flat desert and plains were perfectly suited for tank warfare. He visualized the vast deserts as a sea of sand and his tanks as ships that would sail across their burning surface. Except for the coastal regions, where both the Italians and British built a highway that rimmed the Mediterranean sea, where towns and farms sprain up, the landscape stretched endless to the south, devoid of any landmarks.

Rommel had been hesitant about leaving France before the French were completely defeated, but once he arrived in Libya he dived into the task of whipping the Italian army into a fighting force. There were almost 250,000 Italians in Lybia, but the Italian force was completely unprepared for war. His arrival was kept strictly secret and the British, and even after they suspected his presence in Libya, they had not discovered the introduction of German forces into Libya. Rommel took every precaution to disguise the presence of the 7th and 15th Panzer Divisions. Tons of equipment had to be shipped into the Italian colony on Italian ships. The Italians were still using rifles designed in 1898. Their tanks were too light and the engines underpowered. There was a shortage of anti-tank guns and the artillery was outdated, though the Italian soldiers manning them were well-trained. There was also a total lack of transport. One of the items that Hitler ordered into mass production at the start of the war was trucks. The German Wehrmarcht before the start of the war had never fully motorized itself, and the Italian armed forces was in worse shape. But the worse feature of the Italian forces that Rommel discovered, was the Italian officers.

Unlike the German officers, who had worked to build a comradery with their enlisted personnel by eating the same food and suffering under the same conditions, the Italian officers were usually from the upper classes of Italian society and looked down on their soldiers. They isolated themselves in luxury and privilege that their German counterparts had worked to eliminate under National Socialism.

Rommel was a fierce believer in winning the confidence of those who served under him. In the invasion of the Low Countries, he was always out front with his men, racing into the thickest of the fighting, taking risks alongside his men and sharing their discomforts. Rommel realized that he had to win the confidence of the Italian soldiers, who would make up 75 percent of his African army. With an endless supply of energy, Rommel was constantly on the move, visiting every unit of his new army. He mixed freely with both Italians and Germans, showing an interest in every aspect of their work. Soon he was winning the confidence and admiration of the Italian soldiers, but it caused him the scorn of the Italian officers, especially that of Marshal Rodolfo Graziani, the commander of Italian forces in Libya and technically, Rommel's superior officer.

Rommel was given orders by Hitler, that were backed up by Mussolini, to make whatever reforms that were needed.

Rommel's orders were to prepare for an invasion of Egypt by July 15. With the defeat of the Allied forces in Flanders, the British Isles were defenseless. Churchill was forced to make drastic reductions of British forces from other parts of the British Empire, so as to reinforce the defense of Britain. These cuts were also made in the British forces in North Africa and the Middle East, which were under the command of General Sir Archibald Wavell. British forces in Egypt were cut from 36,000 to 18,000, from 27,000 to 13,000 in Palestine, from 9,000 to 4,500 in the Sudan, from 8,500 to 4,500 in Kenya and from 1,500 to 1,000 in British Somaliland. Along with the reduction in soldiers, most of the Matilda tanks were sent to Britain. Churchill promised Wavell reinforcements from Australia, New Zealand and India, but they were delayed because of the need to transport troops to England.

Rommel was confident that he could sweep through Egypt with little difficulty, but he knew that the success of his invasion would depend on the fall of Gibralter and especially Malta. Attacks on both British bases were planned for the last two weeks of July. Their fall would ensure a continuous supply of equipment needed to power Rommel's invasion through Egypt and the Middle East. He was not concerned about his rear. With the news of the British attacks on the French Fleet, he was sure of French cooperation. With the support of Vichy Governments in Algeria and Tunisia, he could attack east without fear of an attack from the west. He was also expecting assistance from the Vichy French in Syria and Lebanon once he began his push through the Middle East to the Persian Gulf. Once Egypt fell and the Suez Canal was in German hands, he would send a small force south to link up with an Italian advance northward, through the Sudan, from Italian East Africa, under the command of the Duke of Aosta. The Duke would command a force of 200,000 Italian and native soldiers, many of the them veterans from the Ethiopian War and link-up with the Germans advancing south through Egypt. This this way, all of northeast Africa would in in Axis control.

After the fall of France, the Spanish leader, Francisco Franco, was excited about the possibilities for Spanish expansion and sent a congratulation to Hitler on his victory. He also suggested that Spain should enter the war as Germany's ally. Hitler immediately had Ribbentrop invite Spain's Minister of the Interior, Ramon Serrano Suner, who was married to the sister of Franco's wife, to schedule a meeting between Franco and Hitler on July 8. On June 12, Spain declared its new policy of non-belligerence in favor of Germany. On June 14, Spain occupied the international zone of Tangier in Morocco. Franco even sent General Juan Vigon, head of the Supreme General Staff to Berlin on June 19, to discuss the possibility of a joint German-Spanish attack on Gibraltar.

Franco had led a coalition of the Right during the Spanish Civil War that included the Spanish Fascists, known as the Falangists, but he was not one of them. His real allegiance was to the Catholic Church and the monarchists. Franco's brother-in-law was a dedicated Falangist and enthusiastic about Spain entering the war. He was glad that Canaris was arrested and sent to a concentration camp. Canaris had become close to Franco during the Spanish Civil War, and was very pessimistic about the future of National Socialist Germany. The former head of the German Abwehr had played an important role is establishing Hispanic-German relations during the late thirties. But what Franco had not known, and Hitler had discovered thanks to the data implants, was, how Canaris had transformed the Abwehr into the foremost ring of traitors within Germany. Ever since he had assumed the position as head of the Abwehr, he began recruiting other anti-Nazis until the entire organization was a den of anti-Nazis, right down to the secretaries. Canaris had become close to Vigon before the war, but with Canaris out of the picture, and unable to convince Franco, through Vigon, not to support Hitler, Suner was able to convince Franco that Spain should enter the war on Germany's side.

At 4 PM Hitler's train, *Amerika*, pulled into the platform of the railway station outside the small, French town of Hendaye, near the Atlantic coast. The region was more suited for a holiday, with its palm tress, than a meeting between the leaders of two nations. Franco's train was already waiting on the opposite side of the platform, where the larger railway-gauge track ended. When Hitler stepped out of his train car, he was greeted by the short Spanish Caudillo. Hitler was surprised at how short Franco was. Franco's olive face smiled up at the German Fuhrer, as he raised his hand in a salute. Hitler returned the salute and the two men shook hands.

"It's an honor to finally meet the great German leader who has defeated France," Franco said in Spanish. Hitler listened as his translator converted Franco's greeting into German.

Hitler continued to carefully examine Franco, noticing his large, dark but piercing eyes, his large nose and short plump frame, and wondered how such an uninspiring man could possibly become the leader of Spain?

Hitler thanked Franco for agreeing to the meeting and the two leaders inspected, first the Spanish guard of honor and then the German guard of honor. Hitler then invited Franco and Suner to join him in his drawing room car aboard his train.

Hitler began the discussion by suggesting that Spain agree to enter the war against Britain on July 30, with a joint Spanish-German attack on Gibraltar. German troops could begin secretly crossing the Spanish border within five days. Hitler began to explain his plans for the creation of a new Fascist Europe, united in a continental system. He wanted a Monroe Doctrine of his own, with Africa under the protection of the new Europe. "Spain should accept a greater role in policing the African continent," Hitler said. "Once Britain is defeated, there will be a general congress of all of Europe, and this will see a redistribution of territories, which will include the division of Africa. Though I cannot put it in writing at this time, Spain will receive additional territories that will include all of Morocco, Oran, territory adjoining Spanish Sahara, as well as territory around Spanish Guinea."

"Spain is already spiritually united with the German people, without reservations and in completely loyalty," Franco said. "Spain is glad to fight alongside Germany. The liberation of Gibraltar will correct a historical wrong forced on Spain by the British. General Vigon has explained your plan for an attack on Gibraltar. I believe the plan feasible. If you deliver the military hardware that you promise, Gibraltar should fall. My only concern involves the British resolve to fight on, even after losing Gibraltar. Churchill hopes to bring America into the war on her side. And then there is the situation in the Mediterranean. Even with Gibraltar in our hands, the British will still maintain a powerful naval presence in the Mediterranean Sea."

Hitler stared at Franco, fixing his hypnotic eyes on the little Spaniard from Galicia. "What I'm about to tell you must never be repeated outside this room," Hitler said. Suner leaned forward as Hitler spoke to Franco. "The British will be driven out of the Mediterranean before the year is out. More than this, I cannot say. But trust me, you'll know of our commitment to drive the British out of the Mediterranean Sea before the attack on Gibraltar begins."

Franco looked at Hitler. The look in his eyes was terrifying. He had never seen such eyes like his. It was almost as if Hitler believed he was looking into the future. His voice seemed to belong to some other worldly entity. Franco looked at Suner, who was transfixed and delighted.

"Germany will supply whatever military hardware is necessary for the assault on Gibraltar," Hitler said. "I have dedicated myself to ending this war before the year is out. And I will!"

Franco rose and shook Hitler's hand. "Then Spain will enter the war," he said. "The Spanish people are grateful for the assistance that Germany provided during our civil war."

That evening Franco was entertained by Hitler at a state dinner, in the dining car of Hitler's train. The event was warm and friendly. Franco was excited and Suner was charming. The two leaders agreed to begin preparations for the attack on July 30. Hitler promised that Spain would not have to enter the war before then, and would prove Germany's commitment to driving the British out of the Mediterranean before July 30. After the meeting broke up, Hitler told Keitel that, "If Canaris was still head of the Abwehr, I am sure I would never have been able to convince Franco into entering the war."

CHAPTER 10

RED STAR-BLACK SWASTIKA

During the months of Germany's victories in Western Europe, the Soviets were not asleep. Stalin had begun the incorporation of the two Baltic States, Estonia and Latvia, into the Soviet Union. Soviet troops were already station in the two countries. During May, Molotov began presenting the governments of the two countries with formal diplomatic complaints that Soviet troops were victims of "provocative acts." This was followed by a vigorous and xenophobic press campaign within the Soviet Union that whipped up anger toward the two Baltic States. Then, on June 15, the Soviet Union formerly invaded both countries. Neither country put up any resistance as Moscow referred to the invasions as "The liberation of the workers" in both countries. Stalin then "suggested" that the Estonian and Latvian workers set up new governments that could be described as "socialist" and "soviet." These new Soviet Socialist Governments of Estonia and Latvia then requested full incorporation into the Union of Soviet Socialist Republics on July 10.

Both countries became victims of Sovietization. All businesses were nationalized and all farms were collectivized. Thousands of Latvians and Estonians, who opposed Communism, were rounded up and arrested. Thousands more were shot immediately, while tens of thousands were sent to die in the concentration camps of Siberia. Only the *Volksdeutsche*, or Baltic Germans, escaped. They were deported to Germany, as was the agreement under the Non-aggression Pact signed between the Soviet Union and Germany in 1939. These Baltic Germans were eventually resettled in that region of Poland annexed by Germany.

The non-aggression pact also stipulated that the Romanian region of Bessarabia was included in the Soviet sphere of expansion. It also stipulated that the Germans would not object if the Soviets sought to annex the region. In May, Stalin began to build up the number of Soviet troops along the Romanian border. In response, the Romanians began mobilizing their armed forces in defense. It soon looked like the two countries would go to war, when King Carol of Romania, turned to Hitler for assistance. Hitler informed King Carol that the fate of Bessarabia was not Germany's concern and that Romania should accept Soviet demands. But after the Romanians accepted Soviet demands, Stalin began demanding all of Bukovina. This upset Hitler because it was not part of the agreement that was made between Germany and the Soviet Union in dividing eastern Europe.

Hitler had worked hard to forge better relations with the Balkan States, ever since he came to power. He liked to refer to them as the "great border colonies of the European East." As early as 1934, Hitler offered generous prices for their exports, making sure they were higher than what they could receive if they sold them on the world market. The payments would be stretched over a long period of time and paid only in German marks. This meant that the Balkan States could only use the marks to purchase certain types of goods manufactured in Germany, enabling Germany to sell antiquated weapons and other armaments to the Balkan States, while permitting German arms manufacturers to produce the newest and superior material for the Wehrmacht. In addition, Germany offered the Balkan States long-term investment credits that could be used for development of their industries. Once again, the stipulation was that the goods produced by these new plants would have to be sold in Germany, rendering the Balkan economy into an extension of the German economy.

Hitler decided that he would have to intervene, as he did with the Finns last year. Bukovina was never part of the old Russian Empire. It had belonged to the Austro-Hungarian Empire, and there was a substantial German population living there. King Carol was willing to turn over Bessarabia, but once Stalin began demanding all of Bukovina, the Romanians indicated they were willing to fight. Hitler feared that the Soviet Union would overrun all of Romania. Germany was receiving large sums of timber and food from Romania, as well as 1.2 million tons of oil a year. This was greater than the amount Germany was receiving from the Soviet Union. Hitler decided it was time to intervene.

The German ambassador in Moscow, Schulenburg, spoke with Molotov, who insisted that Bukovina was "the last missing remnant of a unified Ukraine, and had to be included in any deal concerning Bessarabia." When Schulenburg informed Hitler of Molotov's remark, Hitler was furious, but he maintained control of his anger. He thought about the problem and suddenly decided to offer just the northern half of Bukovina to the Soviet Union. He used the large German population, which was located in the southern section of the region, as an excuse for Romania to retain the region. The crisis passed when when Schulenburg informed him that Stalin had agreed to the compromise.

King Carol finally agreed, but only after Hitler promised to guarantee Romania from future Soviet expansion against Romanian territory. Hitler agreed and promised to station several German divisions on Romanian territory. The Romanians finally turned over a third of their territory, 286,000 miles and twenty million individuals.

Hitler returned to Berlin to prepare his speech he was to give to the Reichstag. But first he called a meeting with his military leaders, on July 8. Events were moving along as planned. Hitler was presented by intercepted conversations between Russian and British diplomats in Moscow from both his own Intelligence Service and the Italians. Hitler learned that Sir Stafford Cripps had been trying to convince the Soviets to declare war on Germany. Though the Soviets refused, Cripps did report of the extensive preparations that the Soviets were feverishly making for war. He believed that if the war between Britain and Germany last another year, the Soviet Union would eventually join Britain by attacking Germany. The reports even claimed that Churchill and Stalin were corresponding by personal letters.

"As you see from the reports," Hitler said, visibly upset, "Stalin is preparing to attack us. The British will not accept an honorable peace with us, so long as the hope of Soviet intervention exist. Therefore, we'll have to defeat the British on the field of battle. I wish there was another way, but there is none. A military defeat of the British will mean the collapse of the British Empire, or at best, seriously weakening the British as a world power, and that is not in Germany's interest. But it can't be helped. If we don't defeat the British, they will continue to hold out until the Soviet Union attacks us next summer. That's why I called this meeting."

Along with Keitel, Brauchitsch, Raeder, Goering, Jodl and Speer were present. Hitler continued. "The Soviets have been moving aggressively to extend their control over the Balkans. They have recently tried to instigate a war with the

Romanians. Only my timely intervention prevented the Soviets from overrunning Romania and denying us the use of the Ploesti oil fields, just as I prevented the Soviets from attacking Finland. Stalin has made suggestions that we turn Lithuania over the him, but I will not do so. Lithuania is like an arrow aimed at the head and heart of the Soviet Union—Moscow. It'll be our jumping off point for our invasion of the Soviet Union."

Hitler then turned to Jodl. His mood was turning stormy. "I want you to work with Manstein and Guderian in formulating a draft for an invasion," Hitler said. "The plan must make Moscow the primary target. We can achieve this with a panzer thrust deep into the Soviet Union and capturing the Red capital. With the fall of Moscow, the Soviet heartland, which is between the Don and Volga Rivers, will fall into our lap. This is not only the industrial center of the Soviet Union, but more importantly, it is the primary source of manpower for the Soviet army."

Brauchitsch was pleased. He and Halder had discussed a possible invasion, and both agreed that Moscow should be the primary objective. "Guderian has already voiced his opinion that an aggressive panzer offensive in the center of the Soviet Union, from Lithuania, aimed at Moscow, was the most effective way to capture the Red capital and crush the Soviets' ability to resist. This is why I've instructed Speer to increase truck production. Our armies must be mobile. Speed will be imperative if we are to defeat the Soviet Union before the arrival of winter. Communism is degenerate, and all we have to do is kick in the door for the entire rotting Soviet Union to collapse. The people under Soviet rule are praying for someone to liberate them. That is what our invading armies must be—liberators. Thus, it's imperative that we win the friendship and confidence of the Soviet people. Once we have, the entire Soviet Union will collapse like a house of cards." Jodl took notes as Hitler continued to present his plans.

"Secondary objectives will be Leningrad and Kiev," Hitler said. "With the help of the Finns, we'll take Leningrad. Then, our armies will turn south, moving between the Volga River on their left and the Don River on the right. The force of this pincer movement will slam down on Rostov, cutting off the huge Soviet forces that will be defending the Ukraine. Once this has been accomplished, we can then occupy the Caucasus, capture the oil fields there and then fortify a line that will run from Astrakhan in the south and Archangel in the north."

"It reminds me of a huge von Schlieffen Plan in reverse," Keitel said.

Hitler thought about it and then agreed. "Yes. But we'll also have an army in Iran. This will be Rommel's army. With the capture of the Middle East, both Iran and Turkey will be drawn into an alliance with us. We'll be able to count on the Turks, the Iranian and Finns, as well as the Romanians. But if we don't take the Middle East, the entire Balkans could be transformed into a base by the British against us. We found documents in Paris that clearly shows that Yugoslavia, Greece and Turkey are willing to support the British. The Greeks were even willing to permit the British and French to land troops in Salonika, and the Turks were willing to permit French aircraft to fly over Turkey, from Syria. Even the Romanians were will to help the Allies, but with the French defeated, the Romanians have turned to us for protection against the Soviets. I hope that the rest of the Balkan states will turn to us for protection and stability."

"What about the Hungarians?" asked Goering. "I understand they're itching for an excuse to attack Romania."

"The Balkans will have to be neutralized before the attack on the Soviet Union," Hitler said. "I suspect the Soviets will do everything possible to extend their influence into the Balkans. I'll have to deal with this problem over the next six months. And I will have to make sure Mussolini does not do something foolish, like attacking Yugoslavia or Greece. If he does, we'll most likely have to come to his rescue. We can't permit anything to happen that might stir up the Balkan hornet's nest. The Hungarians and Bulgarians are acting like a pact of wolves that smell blood after the Romanians agreed to surrender Bessarabia and the northern region Bukovina. They long to rip their own pieces of Romanian territories for their consumption. It only reconfirms my belief that only we Germans can unite Europe and lead it into the next century. But everything depends on our defeating the British. After we have driven the British out of the Mediterranean, the Balkan countries and Turkey, will gladly join our New Order. Then we'll have to prepare for the resumption of our march to the east.

"How soon can you have a draft of the invasion ready for me?" Hitler asked Jodl.

"Within two weeks, my Fuhrer," Jodl said confidently. Actually, he had already draft such a invasion plan. But he would have to incorporate Hitler suggestions. Of all Hitler's officers, Jodl was probably closest to Hitler. The Fuhrer had come to rely on Jodl's daily briefings in all OKW theaters of operations. They often discussed plans, and so Jodl already knew most of what Hitler had said. He was the brightest of Hitler's generals and served Hitler in the capacity of a military tutor. Hitler seemed to trust this reserve and quiet officer, and had relied on him during the Scandinavian operation earlier in the year. Jodl always sat next to Hitler during their meals and he considered Hitler a genius.

Hitler nodded his approval. "Very good," he said. "Now I will make one last offer of peace to the British, and God help them if they refuse."

Zhukov smartly marched into Stalin's office after being searched twice by the NKVD men that guarded Stalin. He hated the Soviet secret police, but had to submit to their searches. He remembered what had happened to Molotov. The foreign minister had returned in a hurry from London, to speak with Stalin, and forgot to stop to be searched. When it was discovered that he was carrying a gun, he was bodily thrown to the ground by the NKVD guards. When he complained to Stalin, Stalin merely reminded him that he was lucky to have gotten away with his life. The short, stocky Russian general was among the lucky few who had survived Stalin's purges of the Red Army, and he was not going to throw his life away now.

Zhukov had become one of Stalin's favorite officers. This was due to his victory over the Japanese in at Khalkin-Gol. By using his infantry, artillery, tanks and air force in a highly coordinated double pincer movement, and with a total disregard for casualties, he was able to deliver a crushing defeat upon Japan in 1939, causing the Japanese to abandon their plans of expansion into Siberia and seek peace with the Soviet Union. Of course, this could not have pleased Stalin more. It freed Stalin from a threatened invasion from the east if he should invade Europe. Stalin had transferred Zhukov to Kiev shortly after his victory over the Japanese. Now he was summoning the ruthless Russian general to the Kremlin to discuss plans for a future invasion of Europe.

When he finally entered Stalin's office, he found the Soviet leader sitting behind his desk. In a chair before the desk, was sitting the stoic foreign minister, Molotov. Stalin was puffing on a cigarette when Zhukov came to a stop before the desk.

"Comrade General," Stalin said through a big smile, "please sit and make yourself comfortable. We have much to discuss."

Zhukov sat in a chair facing Molotov. "Thank you Comrade Stalin," he said. He glanced at Molotov and then turned to face Stalin. He did not like Molotov, who said nothing, but simply nodded to the general. He considered the foreign minister Stalin's lapdog. Stalin had replaced Liptinov with Molotov as foreign minister in 1939, because the former was a Jew, and Stalin wanted a non-aggression pact with National Socialist Germany.

"You know why I called you?" Stalin asked. Stalin rarely spoke, and preferred to listen, or half-listen. He never looked anyone in the eyes, but he had a unique ability to detect the alterations of rhythms in one's voice. Like a good policeman, he had trained himself to detect whether someone was lying by the way the spoke.

"Yes, Comrade Chairman," Zhukov said. "To discuss plans for the future and inevitable war with the Fascists." Zhukov was very careful about what he said to Stalin. He knew that the Georgian was deeply suspicious of everyone, and considered everyone, even his closest and most loyal confidants possible enemies. He saw conspiracies everywhere, and his pathological paranoia had resulted in the extermination of 90 percent of the officers of the Red Army. If Zhukov believed in God, he would have considered it a miracle that he survived the purges. He knew that Stalin did not necessarily mean what he said, which made it difficult for people to deal with him. It was better to let Stalin speak first and then make sure you didn't contradict him.

"That's correct, Comrade General," Stalin said. "I signed the Non-Aggression Pact with Germany to prevent the Western capitalists from trying to drag the Soviet Union into a war with the Fascists," Stalin said proudly. "I outfoxed the capitalists, and they found themselves in a war with the German Fascists. But this Hitler surprised me. He was able to defeat the French, and it now looks like he'll do the same with the British. The war could be over by next year. Do you know what that means, Comrade?" Stalin leaned over and stared at Zhukov, who remained stone-face and said nothing. "It means that the capitalists won't beat each others' f__king heads to death. I was counting on the Fascists and the capitalists finding themselves locked into a long and bloody war. After several years, they would have so exhausted themselves that our glorious Red Army could have walked over their rotting corpses and liberate the workers of Europe. But now we're going to have to speed up our plans. I want you to draft a plan to attack Germany, and I want it as soon as possible."

I understand, Comrade Chairman," Zhukov said. "I can have a draft for the invasion of Europe within a month."

"Very good, Comrade," Stalin said. "We must be ready to act by next summer. The British have already tried to trick us into entering the war to pull their arses our of the fire. Even the United States has tried to convince me to declare war on Germany. But I won't! Not yet! I believe Hitler will not attack us before 1942. Even if he beats the British next year, he'll have his hands full trying to pacify the territories under his domain. I'm sending Comrade Molotov to Berlin to talk with Hitler." Stalin looked at Molotov as if sending him a mental message that it was now his turn to speak.

With his usual stony expression, Molotov began explaining the situation to Zhukov. "The German Fascists are trying to extend their power into the Balkans, and eventually, in the Eastern Mediterranean and the Middle East. This is unacceptable to the Soviet Union. If the Fascists are successful, they'll have the Soviet

Union surrounded, and could attack us from the north, where German troops have already entered Finland, the east and then the south, through Turkey and Iran. As we speak, German troops are pouring into Romania. If we don't stop them, they'll eventually occupy all of the Balkans, right down to Athens."

"This is why we have got to be ready to attack by next summer," Stalin spoke once more. "Tell him, Comrade Molotov."

"Yes," Molotov continued to speak, taking no offense at Stalin's interruption. "We must do whatever possible to ensure that the Balkans become Hitler's Spain." Zhukov understood the analogy that Molotov was making, referring to Napoleon's fatal attempt to conquer Spain. "We should be able to convince the Yugoslavs and Bulgarians to resist Fascist encroachment. If we can tide down Hitler's army in the Balkans, we'll have time to prepare for our war of liberation."

"If Hitler had not interfered in Finland and Romania, we could have overrun both countries," Stalin said.

Zhukov doubted that the Red Army could have defeated either country with the easy that Stalin claimed, but he was to much of a fox to voice his opinion, especially when it contradicted Stalin's.

"The new British ambassador, Stafford Cripps, I believe is his name," Stalin said as he tried to recall the name, "claims that the Germans are going to invade Britain, but I know he's full of s__t. I have it on the highest authority that Hitler has no such plans. I know everything that Hitler says and plans. I even know when he takes a crap."

Zhukov had heard that Stalin had a spy who occupied a position high in the government of Germany.

"So you see, Comrade General," Stalin continued, "I'm giving you the glorious task of preparing the invasion that will liberate Europe from the Fascist yoke."

"I understand, Comrade Chairman," Zhukov said, "and thank you for the honor."

When Zhukov finally left Stalin's office, he was determined to present a plan that would force Stalin to think about making badly needed reforms in the structure of the Red Army. Before the purges of the 1930s, the Red Army had 1.2 million paratroops and the largest strategic bomber force in the world. Tanks were organized into armor divisions, much like the Germans panzer divisions. Marshal Mikhail Nikolayevich Tukhachevsky had built the Red Army into one of the most powerful armed forces in the world before he was executed in Stalin's purge of the Red Army. Tukhachevsky had studied the way the Germans were organizing their ground forces into armor divisions and this immediately made him a suspected spy in Stalin's eyes. Unknown to Stalin or Zhukov, the German SS had planted false incriminating evidence about Tukhachevsky that sealed his fate. Once Tukhachevsky was executed, almost the entire officer class of the Red Army followed him to the grave. Stalin immediately began undoing all his reforms and return the Red Army to the ponderous and outdated force it was before Tukhachevsky. The strategic bomber forces was reduced, the paratroopers were eliminated, and tanks were once again dispersed among the infantry divisions. Zhukov hoped he could devise a plan that would require the re-institution Tukhachevsky's reforms. He had hoped for a war with either Finland or Romania, but was disappointed when the Soviet Union did not attack either country. He believed that any offensive against either country would have gone very badly for the Red Army. He was confident that ultimately, the Red Army would have won, but he would have been able to point out the horrendous conditions that had descended over the Red Army. He only hoped that he could still point out these conditions to Stalin without a war, and thought he knew how he could do so.

Churchill had a fetish for uniforms, much like Goering, and he liked to especially wear air force uniforms, when he wasn't walking about in his bathrobe. The British Prime Minister excepted the Germans to unleash a massive air assault against London when the war broke out, but it never materialized. Almost a year later, Churchill was still waiting for the assault. In fact, he was hoping it would materialize. Beginning in May there were small skirmishes which grew in frequency, but the skies over Britain were mostly free of enemy planes trying to bomb Britain into the stone age. Hitler had discussed the possibility of bombing Britain with his generals and concluded that sufficient forces were not available. Hitler had ordered Goering to conduct modest sorties across the Channel. Even when July dawned there were no great armada of German bombers crossing the Channel intended on reducing British cities to rubble. The truth was, the Germans did not have the capacity to conduct such raids.

From its conception, the Luftwaffe was designed to support the German Army and not to fight a separate air offensive. Its organization consisted of units attached to army groups. The Germans never divided the Luftwaffe into separate Bomber Command and Fight Commander as the British did with the Royal Air Force. In 1940, no air force anywhere in the world possessed a long range bomber with four engines. Even the Soviet Union had abandoned their long range bomber fleet under Stalin's purge of the Red Army. The Luftwaffe had two designs in 1936, the Ju89 and the Do19, but they were abandoned. After the fall of Poland, Hitler did order the resurrection of the four engine bomber. After extensive research and development, it was decided that the Ju89 design would go into production, and be ready for operations in 1941, but they were for the war that Hitler was planning against the Soviet Union.

Churchill turned to speak with Anthony Eden. "We need to convince Mr. Hitler to send some of his bombers over our cities," Churchill said. "We'll never convince the Americans to enter this war unless we can convince them that Britain is on the verge of collapse."

"Are you saying you want the Germans to bomb our cities?" Eden asked.

Churchill looked at Eden and smile. "I'm saying we need the Germans to bomb our cities. It's the only way we can get the United States into the war."

"I don't believe I'm hearing this," Eden said.

Churchill shifted and then took a deep gulp of whiskey. "Don't act so innocent," Churchill said. "People die in war, and victory doesn't come cheap. If our cities were exposed to the full force of the Luftwaffe, you'd see the British people unite as never before in their determination to resist Mr. Hitler and his Nazi thugs. You would also see the hearts of the American people break for the suffering our people would have to endure. You'll see support for the United States entering the war grow in America. Yes. I must do something to convince Mr. Hitler to begin bombing our cities."

Eden did not like what he was hearing and wondered if Churchill was mentally unbalanced. He shared Churchill's hatred of the Germans, and especially of the Nazis, but Churchill's talk about trying to convince the enemy to bomb British women and children was something else.

Churchill suddenly turned and faced Eden. Eden could clearly see between the mostly closed eyelids that his eyes were red from drinking too much. "I want the RAF to begin bombing German cities," he said.

"The RAF is already bombing German cities," Eden reminded Churchill.

"I'm not talking about bombing factories and plants," Churchill said. "We've got to bomb residential neighborhoods."

"Good Lord!" Eden said. "You're talking about killing women and children."

Churchill swirled around, almost knocking the bottle of whiskey off his desk. "I'm talking about winning the war!" Churchill's fist pounded a stack of books on his desk. "Our Empire lies prostrate before the Hun. I've had to order the transfer of half of our troops from North Africa and the Middle East to build up the defenses of our home islands. I want to convince Hitler to try and invade our island. We have at least 1475 first-rate planes to defend the islands. And with our new radar network, we'll be able to detect and intercept German planes as they are still crossing the Channel. We'll send the entire Luftwaffe to the bottom of the English Channel. Hitler has got to be convinced to try and invade our homeland. I've received reports from General Wavell in Cairo. He claims that our reconnaissance flights have detected heavy activity in the Libyan port of Tobruk. It seems that the Germans are sending the Italians enormous amounts of military hardware. That could only mean the Italians are planning to entire the war. If Hitler should strike in the Mediterranean, he could overrun all of the Middle East. Do you realize how that will affect our Empire?

"Hell! We won't have an empire! We've got to convince Hitler not to strike in the Mediterranean and try instead to invade the British Isles. I'm confident that our navy will prevent the Hun from reaching British soil. I must speak with the Air Ministry and make plans for the assault on German cities."

On July 10, Hitler was invited to the Roggenthien airfield outside of Rechlin, where the Luftwaffe was about to conduct a demonstration of Ernst Heinkel's latest manifestation of his jet fighter. With Hitler was Goering, Milch and Speer. Heinkel almost ran to greet Hitler, as he stepped out of his Mercedes. "Heil Hitler!" he shouted as he gave the open palm salute.

"Heil!" Hitler said as he return the salute and then shook Heinkel's hand. "Well, Herr Heinkel, what have you got to show us today?"

"Something that will revolutionize air warfare, my Fuehrer," Heinkel said. Heinkel was a year older than Hitler, short and stocky, and possessed an eternal optimism that fed his jovial disposition. "Heil Hitler!" Heinkel said to Goering, Milch and Speer. "Please, gentlemen, come with me. We're already to conduct a test flight of the He280. Dr. Ohain is performing a last minute check, to make sure everything is in order."

Heinkel led everyone through a door that opened into a huge hanger. Within the hanger was the He280. It was a double engine jet fighter. Several engineers were finishing servicing the aircraft. A tall, solemn man wearing a long, white coat saw them and immediately approached.

"Heil Hitler!" Dr. Ohain said, as Hitler and the others returned his greeting and salute. Hans-Joachim Pabst von Ohain had joined Heinkel's company because Heinkel was a visionary who was willing to listen to new and radical ideas.

"Is everything ready?" Heinkel asked.

"Yes, Herr Heinkel," Dr. Ohain said. "The crew has completed its inspection. Everything checks out, and we can begin the demonstration at once."

"Very good," Heinkel said. "But before we do, let me inform you of the modifications that we've made."

"Please, do, Herr Heinkel," Hitler said.

Heinkel immediately began explaining how they had to remodel the entire aircraft. "You can see we've removed the turbojet from the fuselage, and replaced it with two turbojet engines placed under the wings. The engine has also undergone major improvements. Dr. Ohain has worked hard to make improvements to the Hes3D engines. Thanks to the generous resources that Herr Speer has provided for the research and development, we were able speed up the timetable and complete our modifications in time for this demonstration. Let me point out an important improvement over the He178. If will you note that the wings are swept back. This is very important for obtaining the higher speeds."

"How fast can it fly?" Hitler asked as he carefully examined the engines and wings.

"Maximum speed is 560 mph at 19,000 feet," Heinkel said. "It has a range of 404 miles and possesses a 3x30mm MG151 cannon."

Hitler seemed pleased. "What about production? When can we begin manufacturing it?"

"Right away, my Fuehrer," Speer said. "If everything goes well today, the first jet fighters will be operational at the beginning of September."

"Very good," Hitler said as he continued to examine the aircraft. "Well, Herr Heinkel, perhaps we should proceed with the demonstration?"

"Yes, my Fuehrer," Heinkel said happily. "Please, if everyone will follow me to the viewing stands, Dr. Ohain will have the He280 taxied to the runway."

Everyone took their positions in the viewing stands, as the He280 took its position for take off. The sky was sparkling blue and cloudless, perfect for a test flight. Heinkel made sure everyone had a pair of binoculars to watch the flight of the jet. The pilot took his seat in the cockpit as the ground crew departed. Soon the roar of the jet engines could be heard, and the aircraft began to race down the runway. Within seconds the He280 was rising into the air and ascending with accelerating speed. Heinkel was excited and pleased with the way the jet was preforming so far. Everyone watched as it disappeared into the distance, only to turn and then race pass the viewing stand at 500 mph.

Hitler remained stone-faced as everyone smiled and congratulated each other at the remarkable speed of the aircraft. "The pilot will now take the aircraft to a height of 19,000 feet," Heinkel said as everyone watched the jet shrink into the distance and begin to ascend into the blue heights. The He280 rose higher and higher and then began to turn to the right and then to the left until it finally began diving straight down only to rise once more. It turned and raced back at a low altitude and finally raced by, as it made a corkscrew maneuver. The jet finally began to slow as it descended and finally set down on the runway once more.

Heinkel led everyone out to the runway to ask the pilot how the aircraft preformed.

"It was hard to control the craft in the turns, but not impossible," the pilot explained. "Any experienced pilot should have no difficulty. It was also difficult to accelerate speed once more, after I began to land the jet. Otherwise, the jet handled well."

These are minor problems that can be worked on," Heinkel said.

"What do you think?" Hitler asked Milch.

"There's no reason why it can't go into operations right away, my Fuehrer," Milch said confidently.

"Herr Reichmarshal?" Hitler turned to Goering.

"I concur, my Fuehrer," Goering said as he beamed with joy. "With a fleet of these jets, the Luftwaffe will sweep the skies of the enemy."

Hitler nodded as he thought for a moment. "I agree," he finally said. "Herr Speer."

"Yes, my Fuehrer?" Speer said.

"Begin production immediately," Hitler ordered. "We will cease production of all propelled, turbo piston-driven fighters. I want the first jets sent to Mediterranean as soon as possible. Others will be sent over Britain to terrify the English, but the main task for these jets will be to ensure that the British are driven out of the Middle East before the end of the year."

"Can it be used as a drive bomber?" Goering asked.

"With modifications," Heinkel said.

"We'll need a jet-powered aircraft that can replace the Stuka as a drive bombers," Goering said.

"Our present supply of Stukas will suffice for any operations in the near future," Hitler said. "But we'll have to find a replacement for the Stuka in the future."

"There are other jet-powered designs that the Junkers, Messerschmitt and Dornier are presently working on," Milch said. The RLM has been reviewing all these new designs during the last nine months."

"Then we'll have to look into them as soon as possible," Hitler said.

"I have other designs, my Fuehrer," Heinkel said. "They're just in the planning stage, but they can be developed and tested."

"Do so, Herr Heinkel," Hitler said. "In the meantime, I understand Willy Messerschmitt is working on a jet fighter."

"We can send out a call for new designs to the manufacturers and see what develops?" Speer said. "With the He280 a reality, I think rival designs will rush to provide new and exciting variations on the jet plane."

"I agree," Hitler said. "I want the Luftwaffe to begin providing specifications on what is needed in new jet-powered aircraft for future warfare."

"It'll be done, my Fuehrer," Goering said.

"There are two brothers, Walter and Reimer Horten, who have been working on a radically new type of aircraft," Speer said.

"Yes, I'm aware of them," Hitler said. "They base their designs on a flying wing. Has the Luftwaffe provided them with funds to develop their new aircraft?" Hitler turned to Goering.

"We have, my Fuehrer," Goering said, "just as you ordered. But their progress is slow."

"Perhaps we should increase the funding for their projects?" Hitler said. "I'll have to look into it, but first we must get the He280 into production. We don't have the luxury of exploring new designs until this war with the British is done and finish."

The next day, Hitler met with several manufacturers in Berlin. He wanted them to come up with a new and powerful tank. Hitler was unhappy with the quality of his panzers, and he voiced his dissatisfaction to his generals over the last year, despite the tremendous victories in Poland and in Western Europe. Guderian and Manstein had agreed with Hitler and encouraged the planning of a much more powerful tank. Brauchitsch and Halder both felt confident that the Panzer II and Panzer III were more than sufficient for the needs of the German Army.

"Our panzers have performed wonderfully against the French and British in Western Europe," Halder insisted. "There's no reason we should detour important resources to the development of a new tank this late in the war. The British will be driven out of the Mediterranean and the Middle East, just as you plan, my Fuehrer. The war will be over before a new tank will be designed."

"I am thinking of the future, Herr General," Hitler said. "There will be war with the Soviet Union. It's my unshakable belief that Stalin is planning an attack on Germany and all of Europe by next summer. Don't ask me how I know, for instinct along dictates to me that we need a tank that is far superior to our present panzers. I'm sure the Soviet are developing a tank that will be superior to our Panzer IIs and Panzer IIIs."

"Even if we did detour resources to the development of a new tank," Brauchitsch interrupted, "it would not be ready for production by next spring, when we would have to attack before the Soviets attacked us. There's no reason our Panzer II and III tanks, which are fast-moving, capable of operating on most kinds of terrain and were impervious to most infantry weapons, could not do as well in an invasion of the Soviet Union, if we strike fast and deep, straight at Moscow, just as you have ordered."

Hitler shook his head. I'm telling you that our panzers will not measure up to the ordeal they will face in the east. Russia is not France. The deeper we move into Russia, the wider the battlefield will become. We'll need a tank that will smash through anything the Soviet will be able to throw at us. No! We need a new type of tank, and I'm confident that our economy will be able to begin mass production my the end of next June. Is that right, Herr Speer?"

"If we can come up with a finished design by next March, production should begin by June. The first new tanks will be ready for combat by the end of June 1941," Speer said. "With our economy on a total war footing, this will not present a problem once we have the specifications. But there is one precondition that is necessary, whatever the design, we must be capable of mass producing it on an assembly line. If we don't reorganize our production methods, we won't be able to me a deadline of July 1941."

"How do you mean?" Hitler asked.

"Our heavy industries are too slow in producing heavy equipment," Speer said. "I've been studying the American method of mass production of automobiles that was invented by Henry Ford. If we apply this method to tank production, we could triple our output of tanks."

Hitler listened carefully to Speer. He was especially pleased with the mention of Henry Ford. Hitler considered Ford, who had supported Hitler in the early years of the struggle with fund, and supported National Socialism in Germany, a genus. "You have already developed such a plan for conversion?" Hitler asked.

"Yes, my Fuehrer," Speer said.

"Then begin putting into operation," Hitler said. "If you receive any resistance, let me know. I'll pass a Fuehrer Directive, if you need it." Hitler then turned to Guderian. "What do you think, Herr General?" Hitler asked Guderian.

"Our Panzer IIs and IIIs will perform well, but the deeper we move into the Soviet Union, the more difficult will their tasks become," Guderian said. "If the Soviets are designing a new and more powerful tank, they will not come to dominate the battlefield during the summer months, or in autumn, at the latest. And even if we achieve all our objectives before the onslaught of winter, we'll find ourselves still fighting the Soviet into 1942. Then, it will be imperative that we have a tank that is far superior to anything we possess today."

Hitler kept nodding as Guderian talked. "Exactly what I mean," Hitler said. "Gentlemen, we will be forced to attack the Soviet Union before the summer of 1941. If we don't, Stalin will order the Red Army to attack us. Therefore, if we must invade the Soviet Union, we'll have to cut deep into the vastness of the Russian space and capture Moscow. Once Moscow is ours, we can then proceed to destroy the Soviet forces east of the Volga. This must be achieved before winter. It is my unshakable belief that we can do it. The Red Army has been reduced to a rotting corpse of its former self after the purges that Stalin submitted it to, but I fear Stalin will eventually agree to reforms. This is why I did everything I could to prevent the Soviets from fighting the Finns or the Romanians. If the Soviets did fight these two small nations, the Red Army would have performed badly, and Stalin would have been convinced to make major reforms that would have been completed by 1942. But now, hopefully, Stalin will not make such reforms, and the Red Army will be in such a state that our Wehrmacht will possess such an advantage that it will be able to crush the Red Army before it can retreat into the hinterland of the Soviet Union.

"But even if we do achieve the necessary objective of occupying all Russia up to a line running from Archangel in the north to Astrakhan in the south, we'll still be faced with a vast Siberia controlled by the Bolsheviks. This is why I ordered the development of a Ural Bomber, as well as jet aircraft. And this is why we will need a new and superior tank."

There were no augments from those listening to Hitler. Hitler's icy blue eyes jumped from face to face. Discovering no opposition, he spoke once more. "Very well, we should speak to the manufacturers," He said as he rose. The others did the same and marched into the conference room where representatives from several firms that accepted Hitler's call for the development of a new tank, were waiting. After the introductions, Hitler began describing the type of tank that he needed.

"The tank that will be needed must be more powerful than any other tank in existence today," Hitler said. "The weight should be at least twice that of the Panzer III's twenty-three tons. The armor plating must also be able to take whatever punishment that the enemy will be able to administer. I would expect somewhere between three to five inches of armor plating in the front, at the least. But you must take in consideration of speed. Don't sacrifice speed for armor. There must be a balance. Our panzers will need speed when operating on the vastness of the Russian landscape. As for firepower, the old 37mm or even 50mm cannons won't be acceptable. I want the 88mm cannons mounted on the new tank. But most of all, the new tank not be too complicated in its construction. If it is, it'll slow down production."

Hitler then asked a young SS adjutant to pass out folders, bound in leather with a swastika and eagle embroidered on them. "You'll find all the particulars I mentioned and more, as well as design suggestion in these folders," Hitler said. "But I must stress one more factor—we will need your designs as quickly as possible. I expect production to begin my next spring."

Everyone was amazed at what Hitler was asking. Of the dozen representatives, only two rose to the challenge—the Henschel and Porsche companies.

It was announced that Hitler would make a major speech to the Reichstag that evening. The day was declared one of celebration for Germany's victory over France. All over Germany the people turned out to express their joy at the prospect of an early and victorious conclusion to the war. Unlike 1914, when the First World War began and thousands of people in every city, not just in Germany but in every country that had declared war, there was no massive expression of support or celebration when war was declared in 1939. People remembered the suffering and destruction, not only at the front, but at home, and they feared what they might have to suffer in this new war. Everyone expected and feared that the conflict between Germany and the Western Allies would degenerate into another war of attrition, where millions of men would be butchered in another war of stalemate and trenches.

But with the quick and painless defeat of France, the people of Germany could not help but believe that they had all but won this second war. Early in the day, the streets of Berlin were filled with tens of thousands of enthusiastic citizens lining the streets. Thousands had also gathered before the Chancellory Building, shouting *We want our Fuehrer!* until finally, Hitler appeared on the balcony. Arms rose into the air to the shouts of *Sieg Heil!*

At noon, Hitler took his position in his huge, black Mercedes and drove down the *Whilhelmstrasse*. Right behind Hitler's car were several other vehicles with Goering, Keitel, Brauchitsch, and Raeder. In another Mercedes sat Joseph and Magda Goebbels, Albert Speer and Eva Bruam. Hitler now permitted Eva to accompany him on most public events, and soon the public began to notice the pretty, young blond woman with their Fuehrer. Goebbels had been ordered to slowly introduce her to the German public as Hitler's "girlfriend." Hitler had promised to marry her as soon as he had completed his expansionist policies, which included the conquest of the Soviet Union. She understood that might take several more years. She was now twenty-nine-years-old and maturing into a serious young woman who suddenly realized that she would have to eventually play the role of Germany's first lady.

As the motorcade slowly made its way down Berlin's fashionable avenue an intoxicating rush of victory spread throughout the crowds that lined the street in hop of getting a glimpse of their Fuehrer. Red, white and black Swastika flags hung from every window and millions of smaller flags were waved by men, women and children as they cheered in the rising excitement. Flowers were thrown from the buildings and flew on the air currents like a winter snowstorm. Most of the people were women, children dressed in the Hitler Youth and Young Maidens uniforms, elderly people, as well as soldiers back from the front. The military marched up the avenue. The *Liebstandarte-SS Adolf Hitler* marched in the parade. Goebbels played up the role of the Waffen SS in the fighting in Western Europe. Hitler wanted the German people to learn about the ne fighting SS units.

"I still can't believe that we've defeated the French," Magda Goebbels said as she watched the massive expression of exhilaration all around them as they rode down the avenue. "It's like a dream."

"The French are defeated, my dear," Goebbels said, "and we owe it all to our Fuehrer. And soon we'll be celebrating the defeat of Great Britain. Truly God has sent him to us to restore Germany's greatness."

"Oh, I hope so," Eva said. "I can't wait until all this fighting has passed."

"You should, my dear," Magda said as she smiled and held Eva's hand. "You'll soon be the luckiest woman in the Reich."

"And the most envied," Speer said. "You'll soon be known as Frau Hitler."

Eva blushed with joy. "I still can't believe the way Adi has changed ever since this war began," Eva said as flowers floated down all around her. "He's changed so much, I hardly recognize him."

"And I can't help but notice the change in you," Speer said. "You've never seemed more happy."

"I've never been happier," Eva said. "I only hope that I can do justice as the wife of the Fuehrer. I never realized it before, but it'll be such a grave responsibility."

"It certainly will," Goebbel said without sarcasms. "But we'll make sure that we do everything possible to help you in your new responsibilities, though I fear that there'll be some who will do everything possible to make your life a living Hell."

Everyone stared at Goebbels for a moment.

"You're referring to that lout, Borman," Eva said.

"Yes, I am, my dear," Goebbels said.

"I don't trust him," Speer said. "He's like a spider, hiding and waiting for the right time to spring a trap that he has set. I don't know why the Fuehrer keeps him around?"

"Because he's made himself indispensable," Goebbels said. "If his boss, Hess, was not so busy examining astrological charts and meditating, Borman would never have worked his way up to such an exalted position. And Hess is the only thing standing between Borman and real power. So we must make sure that Hess remains in his position as Secretary of the Party and Deputy Fuehrer. I would not like to think what could happen if Borman ever replaced Hess in both positions."

"Borman! Deputy Fuehrer! Good Lord, the Fuehrer would never bestow that position on that bastard," Madga said.

"I hope not," Speer said.

"Don't worry about Borman," Goebbels said. "I don't."

The others were taken back at the certainty of Goebbels' remark. They looked at the little Minister of Propaganda and Information, who just smiled like the cat who had swallowed the canary.

It was announced in advance that Hitler would deliver a speech of grave importance to the Reichstag on July 14. The Reichstag was convened at the Kroll Opera House, which had been used for meetings of the Reichstag ever since the Reichstag Building had been torched in 1934. The speech was scheduled for 7 PM and Hitler was expected to make a proposal to Britain to end the war. Besides the delegates to the Reichstag, the heads of all three branches of the military were present, along with their senior staff members and the senior staff members of the OKW. All branches of the government and NSDAP leaders and all auxiliary staffs were also in attendance.

Hitler entered on time. He usually appeared late for most speeches, but he knew the entire world would be listening. Hitler took his place at the podium before the assembled members. Sitting behind him was Goering, who was also leader of the Reichstag. Behind him was a huge, metallic eagle with wings spread wide, and in its talons was clutched a swastika.

Hitler spoke for several hours. He explained how he never wanted a war with Britain and France, and how they declared war on Germany. The many attempts to end the war after Poland was crushed and right up to the invasion of Western Europe were retold in detail. Hitler then reminded the world of how he had offered peace once more to Great Britain after France had been defeated, offering an alliance to defend the British Empire.

"It almost causes me pain to think that I should have been selected by Fate to deal with the final blow to the structure which these men have already set tottering. It never has been my intention to wage wars, but rather to build up a state with a new social order and the finest possible standard of culture. Every year that this war drags on is keeping me away from this work, and those who are responsible are men who are but ridiculous nonentities.

"It was Mr. Churchill who has declared his intention to wage war. It was Mr. Churchill who has reiterated his declaration that he wants the war to continue. Mr. Churchill ought to believe me when I predict that unless he listens to reason, a great empire will be destroyed—an empire which it was never my intention to destroy or even to harm. I do, however, realize that this struggle, if it continues, can end only with the complete annihilation of one or the other of the two adversaries. Mr. Churchill may believe that this will be Germany, but I know it will be England.

"This is why I make this final offer of peace to the British people and their leaders. "Let us put an end to this war. Germany seeks no territories from the British Empire, only the return of its former colonies. Germany wants nothing in the way of financial compensation from England. We ask only that England respect the new order of things on the European continent, and in return, Germany will guarantee the preservation of the British Empire.

"But I must say this for the last time—if this offer is refused, then Germany will prosecute this war with all the resources at its disposal, to end this conflict as quickly as possible. Germany will do whatever is necessary to achieve victory over an enemy that refuses to see wisdom and accept the hand of peace. But if that hand is clasped, then both the British nation and the German people may live together in peace, as the defenders of civilization against the forces of destruction."

The entire Reichstag rose in a thunderous applause that evolved into an explosion of continuous shouts of *Sieg Heil!* Goebbels, who was sitting next to Speer, whispered, "The next twelve hours will decide the fate of England."

What Goebbels meant was that Churchill and the War Cabinet had twelve hours on whether or not to accept Hitler's offer of peace. It they fail to do so, Rommel would unleash his Offensive to crush the British Empire.

Earlier in the day, Hitler had made sure a message was passed to Churchill's War Cabinet in London through their *charge d'affaires* in Washington. The message was simple—a full transcript of the German peace terms were available if Britain desired to review them before Hitler delivered his speech. When this message was passed on to London, Churchill ordered Halifax to reject the offer. But Halifax ignored the Prime Minister's orders and asked for the transcript. He passed them on to the entire War Cabinet before Hitler delivered his speech, for its consideration, much to Churchill's anger.

Most of the War Cabinet thought the terms were satisfactory and pressed Churchill to accept them.

"Never!" Churchill growled. "I'll never extend the hand of peace to that—Hitler!"

"You must listen to reason, Winston," Halifax implored Churchill. "Our military situation is growing worst every day. We have reports that Italy and Spain are considering entering the war on Germany's side. Whitehall is sure that Rommel is in Lybia and Wavell is certain the Italians are planning to attack Egypt. Preparations for the invasion of our homeland are being speeded up across the Channel. Stalin has refused to enter the war on our side, and the United States is unable."

"I won't listen to any discussions of peace until after we have dealt the Huns a military defeat," Churchill insisted. "We must crush any attempt by the Germans to invade our home islands. Once their invasion force is rotting at the bottom of the Channel, then we'll seek peace from a position of strength. Survival is now at the top of the agenda, gentlemen. In the next few weeks we must prove that Britain can stand. Once we have made this point, we can expect the Americans to entire the war, and then we can push that scoundrel out of Europe. That will be our peace term."

Halifax knew there was nothing the cabinet could do short of declaring a non-confidence vote, which would only cause the government to collapse. But this was unsatisfactory at this point in time. It would only plunge the British government into a crisis.

CHAPTER 11

▼

PANZER ROLLEN IN AFRIKA VOR!

Lieutenant-General Archibald Percival Wavell was the son of a general and considered one of the most cultured soldiers in the British Empire. He was commander of North Africa and the entire Middle East, and ruled more like a potentate than a commander. A stocky built man with a face as wrinkled as the leather gaiters he liked to wear, he was the opposite of Churchill in every way. While Churchill was exuberant and aggressive, Wavell was reticent, reserved and enjoyed meditation. By nature he was humble and cautious and preferred not to underestimate his opponents. He found it difficult dealing with Churchill, who deeply distrusted generals just as much as Wavell dislike politicians.

Wavell had served in Egypt and Palestine during the First World War and was assigned Commander of North Africa and the Middle East in 1937. He disliked most Arabs, but was careful to respect their customs so as not to provoke them to armed rebellion, while Churchill was a dedicated Zionist. Wavell was not pleased when Churchill began withdrawing men and arms from his command to reinforce the British Isles, but there was nothing he could do about it. Though he agreed that the British Isles had to be defended, he felt that the Germans would attack Egypt, sooner or later. As reports began to reach his desk in Cairo of the build up of forces in Lybia, he began warning London of an impending attack. But like Churchill, he agreed that it was too hot to begin an offensive in July and

August, and if Egypt was attacked, it would probably take place in September or even October. He hoped there was time for the replacements that Churchill promised from Australia and New Zealand, to reach Egypt.

Wavell had called Major-General R. N. O'Connor from Palestine to take command of the Western Desert Force, as the forces facing the Libyan frontier was called. O'Connor was a modest man and a poor dresser, who detest publicity and never laughed, but he was very popular with his men and a soldier of the old school. There were only 18,000 British troops in Egypt, which was technically neutral. The heart of this force were the excellent 4th Indian Division and the 7th Armored Division, but the latter was stripped of a third of its tanks to defend Britain. The 6th Australian and 1st New Zealand Division would arrive somewhere between October and December. Though they were facing nine regular Italian divisions, two Blackshirt divisions and two native divisions, he knew that the Italians possessed antiquated equipment and outdated tanks and artillery. But O'Connor, like Wavell, was concerned about the reports of the arrival of the Germans in Libya.

At 9 o'clock in the morning of July 15, London time, the Italian ambassador in London delivered the Italian declaration of war on Great Britain. Fifteen minutes later in Rome, which was 10:15 in the morning because of the hour difference in time, Mussolini had gathered a huge crowd of Blackshirts and Fascists in the plaza outside his office, where he announced his declaration of war on Great Britain. He announced the birth of a new Roman Empire. As Mussolini spoke, the armored cars of the Stahnsdorf 3rd Reconnaissance unit crossed the frontier with Egypt and led the invasion. The 7th and 12th Panzer Divisions raced across the yellow landscape of the Egyptian desert one hundred miles south of the coast, while the Italians marched across the frontier between Sidi Omar and Bir Wair. Stuka dive-bombers began assaulting British oppositions all along the frontier. Rommel's 8.8-cm duel-purpose guns began cewing up British tanks all along the frontier. The British quickly abandoned Sollum and began withdrawing along the coastal road and railroad to Sidi Barrani.

Rommel had organized his force into three corps. Along the coast was the XXI Italian Corp which included four Italian infantry divisions: *Bologna, Pavia, Trento* and *Genoa*. South of the XXI Corp was the XX Italian Corp which included the *Ariete* and *Trieste* Armored Divisions, both supplied with German Panzer IIs and IIIs. Also included was the Italian infantry division, *Savona*. Farthest to the south was Rommel's Afrika Korp which included the 12th and 7th Panzer Divisions, as well as the Italian infantry *Brescia* Division.

Most of the fighting was taking place along the coast. Rommel considered the desert a tactician's paradise and a quartermaster's hell. The coastal region is higher than the desert to the south. The British, led by O'Connor, considered the interior to sandy for modern, mobile warfare and feared the sandy landscape. But Rommel considered the desert an opportunity to obtain the maximum effect for his tanks in the assault on Egypt. He realized that his forces could not pass the Qatara Depression, which ran west to northeast until it formed a narrow gap between its eastern edge and the Mediterranean coast. El Alamein was situated there, and Rommel knew that the British would try and make a stand at this sixty mile bottleneck. At this narrow point, the British could use their smaller force more effectively, just as the Greeks did with the Persians at Themopolie. He predicted the British would try and make a strategic withdraw to El Alamein, and so he planned to counter this withdrawal much in the way the Germans struck through the Ardennes and cut off the British and French before they could withdraw. His two panzer divisions were placed on the far right of his flank and attacked inland, moving rapidly east along the northern edge of the Qarata Depression. The Libyan Plateau, which ran east into Egypt offered a perfect landscape for his panzers. Their objective was to reach coast between the retreating British forces and El Alamein.

Rommel constantly sent out the Luftwaffe as reconnaissance, keeping an eye on what the British were doing. Ariel photographs revealed what he suspected—the British were in full retreat. He only hoped his panzers could reach the coast before the British had a chance to reach El Alamein.

The British headquarters in Cairo was thrown into confusion with the news of Rommel's attack. They could not believe the reports, thinking they were mistaking simple reconnaissance units for a full-blown invasion. The very idea that Rommel would attack in the blistering heat of July was too incredible to believe, if not impossible. Despite the confusion that was whirling around him, Wavell remained calm and he was sure that if Rommel was actually conducting a full-scale offensive, it would eventually falter and come to a halt long before it reached its objective. He could not believe that Rommel had enough trucks to transport the needed water and fuel for an invasion to reach El Alamein. Wavell decided that the best course of action was to retreat and make a stand at El Alamein. He immediately called O'Connor and ordered him to keep his forces together and move along the coast road and railroad back to El Alamein. O'Connor objected and wanted to send out his tanks to the south, to protect his flank as he retreated, but Wavell vetoed his suggestion. He did not believe Rommel's tanks could travel through the arid landscape and the hot, burning sands of the

Libyan Plateau, and would instead concentrate his tanks along the coast. Wavell was soon to learn just how wrong he was.

Rommel was leading the charge of his panzer divisions. He was not the typical office who liked to remain fifty or sixty miles in the rear of the offensive. He took his place in a tank with the 7th Panzer Division, which was known as the Ghost Division, because of its ability to appear where it was not expected to be, in France. Around his neck he wore the Knight's Cross with oak leaves, which was personally awarded to him by Hitler himself, for his feats in France. Rommel had out-foxed the Allies in France and was once again out-thinking the British at every turn. Some of his troops began referring to him as the Desert Fox.

He had instructed his air force to concentrate on destroying the British supply lines, as well as ordering his Stukas to seek out and destroy all British tanks. They swooped down on the enemy tanks as they raced east along the coastal road. O'Connor was cursing Wavell's orders to stick as close to the coast as possible. The British army was falling apart. Their troops began to panic and burned petrol and other stores that they could not take with them as they retreated, to keep them from falling into German and Italian hands. Rommel was aggressive and ambitious. He knew that Hitler wanted him to take Egypt as quickly as possible. He hoped to destroy the bulk of the British forces in Egypt while the British were still weak. If he could trap the bulk of the 7th Armored Division and the 4th Indian Division east of El Alamein, Egypt would fall. He could then refit the port of Alexandra as a supply center for his eventual advance through the Middle East, to the Persian Gulf.

The Afrika Korp raced along the Libyan Palteau in a wide maneuver. Rommel was heading for Mersa Matruh. To his north, the XX Italian Corp was racing toward the town of Habata, which was a railroad center situated about twelve miles south of the coast.

On July 19, Rommel finally reached the coast between Mersa Matruh and Fuka, to the east. He had successfully cut the railroad line and coastal road that the British needed for their retreat. Stretched out before him were the blue waters of the Mediterranean Sea. His men shouted with joy. Rommel called his reconnaissance team to determine whether the bulk of the British forces were east or west of his location. To his surprise and joy, he was informed that the British were just twenty miles west of Mersa Matruh. The Italians had been successful in capturing Habata, which caused havoc among the retreating British. Rommel ordered his forces to dig in and prepare a welcome for the retreating British. Along with his tanks he had 8.8cm Flak guns which served effectively as anti-tank artillery.

THE LION IS HUMBLED

The British forces were desperate to escape the German and Italian forces advancing along the coast. They were constantly harassed by dive-bombing Stukas. O'Connor was doing everything possible to keep his forces from disintegrating into a rabble. The British were able to stay ahead of the Italian XXI Corp advancing along the coast, and O'Connor felt he had just escaped the trap when he discovered that Habata fell to enemy armored units. Most of his forces, though scattered, were east of Sidi Barrani and heading for Mersa Matruth. He was beginning to think he was going to successfully reach El Alamein and the prepared defensive positions that blocked the path to Alexandra. If he could reach it, he felt he still had a chance to stop Rommel, at least long enough for Wavell to bring forth reserves out of Palestine. But on July 20, he ran straight into the trap that Rommel had prepared for him.

With several brigades of German and Italian tanks on his heels, O'Connor's army ran right into Rommels 8.8cm guns. Then, from the south, the Panzer IIs and IIIs rushed out of the wilderness, right into the right flank of the British forces that were stretched out along the coastal road. Most of the British were moving through Mersa Matruth when Rommel struck, and so, were unable to form an effective defensive line. The battle that took place lasted only two hours, but within that short time, the entire British army was destroyed. The British fought heroically, but they were outnumbered and outgunned. Thousands of British officers, including O'Connor, was taken prisoner by Rommel.

"Let me say that you fought heroically," Rommel said to O'Connor, "considering you were so outnumbered."

O'Connor saluted the German general. "It's very kind of you to say so," O'Connor said. He was suspicious of Rommel, but the short German general soon won his confidence.

"Your men will be treated well," Rommel said. "Even the Indian troops. They fought fiercely."

"Most of them are Sikhs," O'Connor said. "Bloody courageous, they are. The finest soldiers in all of India. They're loyal as well as bloody good fighters."

"I hope so," Rommel said. "You'll need their loyalty too keep control of India."

"Do you think you're going to reach India?" O'Connor said.

"No, Herr General," Rommel said. "We won't have to get that far. Your Empire will agree to peace long before that will happen. I only hope it will be before its collapse. The destruction of your Empire would be a crime against the White Race. The British Empire is a cornerstone of stability in the world, and it will not be in Germany's interest for it to disappear. That's not only my opinion, but that of the Fuehrer."

Rommel impressed the British general by his sincere admiration. "It's a piety we had to be enemies. Our two armies should be fighting side-by-side. What a formidable force we would have made."

O'Connor was amazed to hear Rommel speak with admiration toward the British. He was under the impression that all Germans, especially the officers, were arrogant, goose-stepping Huns who thought everyone else was inferior, and at best, destined to serve as their cannon fodder. "It was not our fault that we find ourselves on opposite sides of the battlefield," O'Connor said. "Germany invaded Poland."

"But Great Britain declared war on Germany," Rommel said.

"To honor our promise to the Poles," O'Connor said.

Rommel looked at the British general. "I think, when this war is over, you'll discover that it was less to honor your promise to the Poles, as it was to honor you pledge to the Americans."

O'Connor looked at Rommel and frown. "What do the Americans have to do with this bloody war?"

Rommel snickered. "You really don't know, do you?" Rommel did not wait for an answer. "When this war is over, and it will be very shortly, all the dirty laundry will be laid bare, but now, Herr General, you must excuse me. I have to conquer Egypt." He saluted O'Connor. The other British officer returned his salute and Rommel left. He did not walk far before he noticed something in the wreckage of a British jeep. It was a pair of oversize goggles. He picked them up and examined them and then placed them on the gold-braided rim of his own peaked cap. He turned to an adjutant. "How do I look, Herr Colonel?"

The Colonel nodded. "I like it, Herr General. They make you look dashing."

"Dashing, eh?" Rommel smiled. "I think I'll keep them."

Within twenty-four hours Rommel had reorganized his forces for the final assault on El Alamein. He had received word that the combined German and Italian assault on the island Malta had begun. He was not concerned that the OKW would divert forces and goods from his own force. Italian merchant seamen were performing heroically under the aerial assaults from British planes stationed on Malta, making sure the flow badly needed supplies reached the ports of Tobruk and Tripoli.

"The time has come for the complete destruction of the British army in Egypt," he declared to his men on the morning of June 21. He went on to congratulate his men on their success, but reminded them that their offensive had just begun. "I vow that we will reach, not only the Suez Canal, but before this operation is over, we'll be standing on the shores of the Persian Gulf. Only once in a lifetime does the Goddess of Victory smiles, and she is smiling on us today."

Rommel knew that speed was the most important element right now. It assured him that the enemy would be taken by surprise and would not have time to prepare for his arrival. Wavell had sent every last man he could spare to El Alamein to man the defensive line that had been constructed, but he knew it would not be enough. He placed Lieutenant General Sir Philip Neame in command of the defense of El Alamein. Churchill had cut the British army in Egypt and Palestine to the bone. Rommel also knew this and did not want to stop or delay his advance, which might give the British time to reinforce their forces in the Middle East and Egypt.

Rommel attacked later that morning. He found El Daba unoccupied by the British and continued his advance east. When he reached the British position before El Alamein, he sent his panzer divisions south, striking the British line on its flanks. The 7th and 12th Panzer Divisions advanced in the south, attacking British positions stretched out across the Ruweisat Ridge. Further to the north, the Italian *Ariete* and *Trieste* Armored Divisions and Italian infantry, supported by Germans armed with the 8.8cm guns, assaulted the defensive perimeter around El Alamein. The British put up stiff resistance and both the Germans and Italians suffered heavy causalities, but their superior numbers and firepower, backed up by air superiority, was too much for the British. Wavell had transferred every soldier he could from Palestine to reinforce El Alamein, but it was not enough. With Wavell's permission. Neame decided to evacuate El Alamein and retreat eastward. He knew that they would need every soldier available to try and hold the Suez Canal. His retreat was a bonanza for Rommel, who quickly sought to exploit it.

Without delay, he decided to divide his forces and take both Alexandria and Cairo. The road to both cities were undefended. If he could take Alexandria, he would have the important port for the reinforcement of his army for the eventual invasion of the Middle East. And, if he took Cairo, he could then send a force south to relieve the Italians in Italian East Africa and drive the British completely out of northeast Africa. What Rommel did not know was that Wavell had already ordered the British Fleet to withdraw through the Suez Canal and the abandonment of Alexandria.

The British ruled the small island of Malta, located sixty miles off the southern coast of Sicily, since the defeat of Napoleon. From this island, 122 square miles, the British could dominate the central part of the Mediterranean by stationing there airplanes, submarines and warships, that could intercept Italian convoys to North Africa. Churchill hoped to reinforce the island in September. On July 20, there were only 15,000 soldiers garrisoned on Malta when the joint German-Italian assault on the island began early in the morning. It was one of the few colonies that Churchill did not draw soldiers from to defend Britain.

Since the defeat of France, Hitler sent two Luftwaffe groups, Luftflotte I and II to the Mediterranean. They included 350 planes that included the German medium range bombers, the Ju88, Stukas, Me110s and Me109fs. Part of this force had been active supporting Rommel's invasion of Egypt, but most of it remained stationed in Sicily, in preparation for the assault on Malta.

Over command of the Luftwaffe force in the Mediterranean was Field Marshal Kesselring, who was known as the smiling general because of his good-natured optimistic personality. The island was submitted to heavy area bombing by massed formations of Ju88s. The targets included the Grand Harbor, where most of the naval installations were located, as well as the three principal airfields located at Hal Far, Luq and Takali. The damage inflicted in just five days was enormous. All ships were forced to evacuate the island, submarines had to remain submerged, work on the docks were brought to a halt and the airfields were unusable. The bombing raids continued around the clock, both day and night. The situation on Malta rapidly became critical as a shortage of food and water soon caused rationing to be instituted.

The assault began with Kurt Student's XI Airborne Corp, which counted 20,000 elite parachute and glider *fallshirmjager*. Along with the Germans was the 10,000 Italian paratrooper of the *Fologore* division. Italy, like Germany and the Soviet Union, took an early interest in airborne warfare. The Italian parachute battalions were well-trained and possessed a high *esprit de corps*. The total invasion force included 30,000 airborne and another 70,000 to land by sea. Four hundred Ju88s and Savoia82s took off from Sicily along with five hundred gliders. Six Italian infantry division would assault the coast, protected by the Italian Fleet, which now ruled the Mediterranean, as a result of the British Fleet's withdrawing through the Suez Canal to the Red Sea.

The assault began with 5000 German and Italian paratroopers dropping on Hal Far in the southeast corner of the island. They were supported by Stukas, giving them the opportunity to establish a bridgehead. In the second drop zone, near Birzebbugia, the Axis losses were heavier, but the drop was well organized and the highly professional German and Italian airborne troops worked well together. Soon, the Axis invaders had established a bridgehead that stretched five miles, from Zeitun in the northeast to Sijuwi in the west. Seaborne reinforcements, consisting of one German and two Italian divisions, were ferried into the port of Kalafrana. The Italian battleships began bombarding the British defenders from the sea. Fighting continued throughout the day and into the night as the Axis forces began moving across the island. The British fought bravely, but they could not halt the advance as additional Axis forces continued to land on the island. By noon of July 21, 25,000 Axis troops were on the island. The British had to retreat to Valletta on the northern coast of the island.

Lacking sufficient air cover or armor, the British authority in Valletta reported to London that they could not hold out and would surrender. Churchill wanted to send ships stationed in Gibraltar to evacuate British troops from Malta, but decided against it for fear that Axis forces would inflict heavy losses on the ships. They would be needed to defend Gibraltar against any attempt by the Axis to take the fortress. The British forces finally surrendered at midnight. There were still sporadic resistance throughout the island that lasted for several more days, but by July 25, the island had effectively been occupied by the Axis.

Student was promoted to Colonel-General by a pleased Hitler. The casualties were acceptable and Hitler was pleased with the performance of the airborne and decided to expand their numbers. With Malta now secured, Hitler was ready for the next step in his plan—the attack on Gibraltar.

Anthony Eden entered the bomb-roof bunker that Churchill had constructed for his use in an abandoned subway station under Downy Street, near Knights-bridge. It was late and Churchill invited Eden to dine with him.

"Please come in," Churchill said, sitting in his bathrobe while gulping down oysters and champagne. "The oysters are excellent. Do have some."

Eden sat at the table and filled his plate with oysters. The aristocracy of England had not deprived itself of the pleasures of the rich, even as millions of working class English suffered from food rationing. Eden noticed that Churchill was in black mood. He refilled his glass with the sparkling wine and washed down another mouthful of oysters, and then fixed his bloodshot eyes on Eden.

"The island has fallen," Churchill said with a finality that could have been heard on the streets above. "Malta is now in the hands of the Germans and the Italians."

"That is bad news," Eden said.

"Worst still, Rommel has taken Alexandria and is headed for Cairo," Churchill said. "Wavell has informed us that he is evacuating Cairo and planning to make a stand at the Suez Canal."

"Have you informed the War Cabinet?" Eden asked.

"Yes," Churchill said, letting his bathrobe fall open, not caring that Eden could see his nakedness beneath. Eden was used to Churchill's behavior and ignored it. Churchill did not seem to notice either. "We've got to do something to cause Hitler to turn his attention back to the British Isles. If we don't, the entire Middle East could fall into his bloody hands."

"What about the reinforcements from Australia and New Zealand?" Eden.

"They won't be ready until September," Churchill said. "But if we don't do something to slow Rommel down, he'll drive us out of the Middle East before they arrive."

"What do you propose?" Eden asked.

"I want the Royal Air Force to step up its bombing of German cities," Churchill said. "We've got to turn Germany's cities into piles of rubble. General Harris believes we could crush the Germany economy and destroy the morale of the German people by a massive campaign designed to flatten German cities, residential neighborhoods as well as industrial centers."

"Good Lord, Winston!" Eden said. "That would mean mass murder of civilians."

Churchill look at Eden with indignation. "This is war!" Churchill insisted. "Besides, why are you so concerned about the Germans? You hate them."

"I hate the Nazis," Eden said, "not the German people."

"Is there a difference?" Churchill asked.

"Halifax and Chamberlain won't accept this," Eden said.

"Chamberlain is in hospital with cancer," Churchill said. "The doctors doubt he'll survive the year. History will deal severely with Chamberlain after this war is over. I know—because I shall write it. And as for Halifax—well, he doesn't have much support."

"I don't know about that," Eden said. "Once the news about Malta and Egypt gets out, it'll strengthen the hand of the peace crowd."

"They're a pack of defeatists," Churchill snarled. "I don't intend to surrender the interest of the Empire—not to those cowards or for anyone."

"But unless we can reverse the present course of events, we might loose the Empire?" Eden said.

"Nonsense!" Churchill said. "I have faith in the tenacity of the British people. They'll hold. Even if the Middle East is lost, we can still holdout. You might have forgotten that I have already told the War Cabinet that I am prepared to surrender the Middle East and the Mediterranean. I made this point in June, after the Prime Ministers of Australia and New Zealand wanted assurances that we would protect them from any possibility of Japan entering the war. I am still prepared to make such sacrifices, even if the Japanese don't enter the war. We'll continue to resist Fascism, as long as our island remains free. So long as our navy is intact, the Germans won't be able to invade our island. And so long as this island remains free, the Empire will stand—at lease, long enough for the United States to entire the war."

"And how long will that be?" Eden asked.

"A year, at the most," Churchill said. "In the meantime, we'll crush Germany's cities, and the will of the Germans to resist."

Eden said nothing more. He took a glass of champagne and emptied the entire contend of the glass. He let the effects of the wine course through him and wondered if Churchill was right. He spoke with such conviction, but was it based on reality or false hope? He wondered.

After Roosevelt's meeting with his political strategists in June, he relied on his personal dexterity of talent, mixing his famous chasm with ambiguity over his goals and outright lying to anyone and everyone he thought it was necessary to fool about his true intentions. In this way, he was able to manipulate, like a master politician, the Democratic figures, like pawns on the political chessboard of American politics. This enabled him to keep the entire Democratic Party in a state of confusion about his through intentions, thus preventing any powerful potential candidate to set forward that might stand in his way of being nominated for a run at a third term as President.

The Democratic convention was held in Chicago, in the middle of July. Roosevelt's men set into motion a well thought-out plan to capture the convention. By the time the convention opened, the delegates were still bewildered. No one seemed to know what was going to happen. Roosevelt still had not declared his intentions, and other than Vice President Garner and James Farley, the Postmaster General and chairman of the Democratic National Committee, there were no other declared candidates for the party's nomination. Both men opposed Roosevelt, and the many delegates that supported the President and his New Deal seemed leaderless. They had no idea if he was going to declare his candidacy, even at this late date. Roosevelt deliberately kept them in state of confusion by constantly declaring that he did not desire a third term, while refusing to support or even suggest that there was anyone that he favored, or thought was qualified to replace him. When anyone asked him what they should do, he simply told them to ask Jimmy Byrnes. Though Byrnes was officially in charge of the convention, he was only the front man for Happy Hopkins, who was directing events from a toilet. He used the public phone to keep a direct line to the White House open, reporting everything that happened at the convention and taking orders on what to do like a well thought-out script.

Roosevelt sent a message which he had read to the convention. In it he once again cleverly insisted that he did not wish to run for a third term, without actually saying that he would refuse the nomination of the convention if it was offered to him. The reaction was a stunned audience. The delegates seemed even more confused than ever, not knowing how to react. Then, suddenly, without warning or introduction, a voice began booming over the loudspeakers: "We want Roosevelt! Everybody wants Roosevelt!"

The voice belonged to Chicago's superintendent of sewers. He was in his quarters underneath the stadium, broadcasting over a microphone especially installed for this purpose by the party organization. As the booming voice filled the hall, operatives belonging to Chicago's Mayor Kelly's political machine, who had been deliberately planted throughout the convention hall, and began to pick up the chant of "Roosevelt! Roosevelt!" until just about everyone joined in, calling for Roosevelt to accept the nomination for a run at a third term. It continued for fifty-three minutes and when the voting finally took place, a huge majority of the delegates voted for Roosevelt as their candidate.

Hopkins informed a delighted Roosevelt, who broadcasted an acceptance speech over the radio at 12:25 a.m. to the convention. The hall fell silent as the Roosevelt's voice pledged to arm the nation in defense against any possible aggression by the worst tyranny the world had ever witnessed. He warned them against turning the country over to "untried hands" and attacked what he referred to as "the appeaser fifth columnists who charged him with hysteria and warmongering." Roosevelt then went on to say that he could not resist the call to serve. "Lying awake, as I have, on many nights, I have asked myself whether I have the right, as Commander in Chief of the Army and Navy, to call on men and women to serve their country and, at the same time, decline to serve my country in my own personal capacity, if I am called upon to do so by the people of my country."

Then, to the dismay of the convention, Roosevelt instructed them to vote for Secretary Of Agriculture Henry Wallace as his choice for Vice President. Most of the delegates did not like being instructed on how to vote, and even more disliked the wild-eyed mystic Wallace, but they could not resist Roosevelt's charm and dutifully, in locked step, they did as they were instructed, like good little Democrats.

On July 29, the Spanish ambassador in London delivered a ultimatum, demanding the surrender of Gibraltar and the withdrawal of all British forces from "Spanish territory." London, of course, reject the ultimatum, and Madrid declared war on Great Britain, one minute after midnight on July 30.

Admiral Sommerville had been forewarned that Gibraltar could be the target of a German assault after Malta was attacked. He ordered his ships to withdraw from Gibraltar and escape into the Atlantic. Churchill decided, after the Admiralty warned him, that it was impossible to stop the Germans from taking Gibraltar if Spain cooperated with Germany. Several hours after the last of the British fleet had escape, at 0600, German guns opened fired on Gibraltar from across Algeciras Bay. From positions further south, Spanish medium artillery joined in the assault. The Germans had moved through Spain and took up their positions in secrecy. The airstrip was destroy, transformed into a cratered wasteland. The town was in flames and the British garrison, which was small, retreated into a series of bunkers and galleries dug into the Rock. After two days of bombing, Gibraltar was overrun by Spanish infantry, supported by German artillery, airborne troops and the Luftwaffe. The 600 British garrison in the Rock held out heroically for a week, but their positions were cracked open by heavy German artillery.

The British struck back when the aircraft carrier, the Royal Ark, sent a sortie of swordfish bombers over the Spanish naval port in Cadiz. Three Spanish Cruisers and five destroyers were sunk. Afterward, the British Force H sailed for the British Isles.

The news that Gibraltar had been liberated reached Madrid. The Spanish people flowed out into the streets of the Spanish capital. The Flangists organized huge rallies celebrating the unification of Spain. Franco knew that he ruled a divided country. The memory of the Spanish Civil War was still fresh, and the scars of the conflict had not heal. Franco hoped that this quick and decisive victory would help to unite his people. He stood before the multitudes in Madrid, waving as they cheered. He turned to Serrano Suner and General Vigon. "This is a great victory," Franco said as he continued to salute and smile. "The Germans and Italians are overrunning Egypt and Malta has fallen. Once the British have been driven out of the Middle East, they will make peace. And then we'll have an empire with almost no bloodshed."

"I hope the British will be reasonable and agree to make peace," General Vigon said.

"They will," Suner said. "With the lost of the Middle East and North Africa, the British Empire will be vulnerable in the Far East. If they don't agree to end the war, the Japanese will take over their possessions in the Far East. This war is virtually at an end."

Churchill's pleas for assistance from the United States were now becoming shrill. Roosevelt was sending as much guns and ammunition to the British as possible, but he insisted that the British pay for everything they received. He knew that the British Empire was no longer the largest, greatest and wealthiest of the world's powers, as it was before the First World War, and he also understood the grave financial situation that Britain found itself in as it tried to fight all of Europe united under Germany, all alone. Roosevelt represented powerful financial interests in the United States that sought to transform the United States into the dominate economic force in the world. They wanted to break open the closed markets of Europe's empires, and knew that the war in Europe would provide the opportunity to take control of these markets. Both the Republican and Democratic Parties possessed such internationalist wings, and they were now untied in the goal of making their form of predatory capitalism the dominate force in the global economy. Roosevelt, representing this internationalist force, sought to bankrupt the British Empire, and all of Europe. Once Europe was exhausted, they hoped to bring the United States into the war. With its economic infrastructure untouched by the war, the United States would dominate the world economy, once the war was over.

When Churchill pleaded for the United States to give Britain fifty outdated destroyers, Roosevelt, with the assistance of a group know as the Century Association, did everything they could to marshal support for aid to Britain. The Century Association's membership included most of the most powerful people in the United States. It was an elitist organization that counted among its members, lawyers, politicians, judges, publishers of the most important newspapers and magazines, the clergy, university presidents and retired admirals and generals. They marshaled their collective influence to find a way that the President could give fifty destroyers to Britain by executive order, thus circumventing the Senate with its filibuster roadblocks. In return for the outdated ships, Roosevelt insisted that Britain turn over its bases in the Carribean and in the Atlantic to the United States. Churchill agreed.

The British were unpopular in Egypt, which was technically independent, but it was under the military protection of the British Empire. The British acted as if Egypt was still a colony of the British Empire, which it was for a short time before the First World War, and the Egyptians resented their presence. The nominal ruler of Egypt was King Farouk, who appointed as Prime Minister, the pro-Axis Ali Maher-pasha. When London requested that Egypt declare war on Germany and Italy, he refused, even after Egypt was invaded. Churchill could not take any chances and had Wavell remove Maher as Prime Minister.

Though Ali Maher was no longer the Prime Minister, he still remained close to King Farouk, and convinced the king to maintain friendly relations with the Axis. The king's father-in-law, Zuhicar-pasha, who was the Egyptian ambassador in Teheran, in Persia, informed the Germans there that the king hoped the Germans and Italians were victorious, and he welcomed their liberation of his country.

The chief of staff of the Egyptian military was General Aziz Ali el-Masri-pasha before he was also removed along with Ali Maher. He was also pro-Axis, and the British tried to arrest him, but he was able to escape Egypt with the help of the SS and the Free Officers Group. This group was a pro-Axis group of young Egyptian military officers, mostly lieutenants, captains and majors. Among their members were two prominent officers, Major Gamel Abdul Nasser and Major Anwar as-Sadat. These two majors kept in contact with General el-Masri, who had made it to Libya, via Italy.

When the new of the British defeat at El Alamein reached Cairo, university students began holding demonstrations. Within a few days, the demonstrations grew into huge crowds demanding the return of Ali Maher. Sensing that the British were about to withdraw from Cairo, King Farouk asked Ali Maher to return as Prime Minister. As soon as he did, Ali Maher, with the support of the Free Officers Group began arresting all British personnel still in Cairo.

There were actually very few British subjects arrested. The Egyptians wanted the British to leave and the British were willing to accommodate them. General Wavell had ordered the evacuation of Egypt. When he left Cairo, the city's streets were filled with people waiting for the arrival of Rommel. Wavell had also ordered his forces to abandon Alexandria and sent in demolition teams to destroy every port facility there, to prevent their use by the Germans and Italians. Wavell hoped to make a step-by-step withdrawal through Egypt to the Suez Canal. Everything that could be used by the advancing Axis forces was destroyed by the retreating British. British forces further south withdrew into the Sudan, where they would withdraw from Port Safaga, on the Red Sea by the British Fleet. Wavell received news that reinforcements from Australia and New Zealand, promised for Egypt, would be diverted to the Persian Gulf. They would arrive in September and then cross Iraq to join him in Palestine and Jordan. But Wavell wondered if he could holdout in Palestine until the reinforcements arrived?

In Rome, Mussolini was overjoyed at the success of the invasion of Egypt, as well as the fall of Malta and Gibraltar. He appeared before a jubilant crowd in the plaza, before his palace, and eagerly announced to the Italian people that the Mediterranean was once again a Roman lake. "Romans once again dominate the Mediterranean Sea," he declared to the cheers of *Duce! Duce!* Behind the scene, Count Ciano was working out the details for Mussolini's triumphant entry into Cairo. Word was sent to Berlin that Mussolini wanted to be the first to enter Cairo, but the OKW informed Mussolini that he would have to leave immediately if he wanted to be the first to enter Cairo. Rommel intended to occupy the city as quickly as possible. He did not want anything to delay the resumption of his offensive into the Middle East. Right after Mussolini completed his speech before the cheering crowds in Rome, he left for Egypt aboard a German transport plane.

There was now nothing to oppose Rommel west of the Suez Canal. The planning that took place throughout the last six months on Hitler's orders was now paying off, as the supply network that was organized to make sure water and fuel would continue to reach Rommel, as he continued his advance eastward. With the fall of Malta and Gibraltar, and the withdrawal of the British fleet to the Atlantic Ocean and Red Sea, the Mediterranean Sea was now an Axis lake. German and Italian armored brigades were racing for Alexandria along the coast, south toward Cairo and due east, capturing the bridge that crossed the Nile at Kafr el Zaiyat, in tact. With an ample supply of trucks, the infantry was able to keep up with the rapid advance of the armor units. By August 7, the last of the British had crossed the Suez Canal and Rommel was approaching the outskirts of Cairo.

Rommel had to wait for the arrival of Mussolini before he entered the Egyptian capital. Hitler wanted to reward Mussolini for containing his impatience, and not attacking France early in June. Mussolini had followed Hitler's plan, and as his reward, he would enter Cairo alongside Rommel. But Rommel did not waste the time. He sent panzer units east to capture the town of Suez located on the southern tip of the canal, as well as south, up the Nile and north into the Nile Delta. By August 8, German and Italian troops had occupied Ismaliliya and Port Said on the western side of the Suez Canal.

Rommel needed time to reorganize his forces before he could continue the offensive. He was informed that the 15th and 5th Panzer Divisions had arrived in Tobruk and were on their way to join with him in Egypt. At the same time, Mussolini flew to Egypt, to join Rommel when he entered Cairo on August 12. Il Duce was excited about his entry into Cairo. He was given a place of honor, riding a white horse, surrounded by a honor guard of armed Blackshirts. Right behind Mussolini rode Rommel in his staff card, followed by the 7th Panzer Division.

The streets of Cairo were filled with Egyptians waving German and Italian flags. Thousands of people turned out to welcome the Axis forces as liberators from British rule. The Egyptian military, led by General Aziz Ali el-Masri-pasha, was waiting to welcome them. With the military was Prime Minister Ali Maher-pasha. Mussolini gave the Fascist salute as he rode through the streets filled with cheering people, but after a short time, his enthusiasm subsided as he began to realize that the name that was most shouted was that of Rommel. When the military procession finally reached the Egyptian welcoming party, it was Mussolini who represented the Axis forces as the head of state for Italy, but most of the Arabs fawned over Rommel. Mussolini and Rommel were taken by Ali Maher to King Farouk, who thanked Mussolini and Hitler, through Rommel, for liberating Egypt. He promised Egyptian cooperation with the Axis and declared the two nations as the protectors of Islam. King Farouk also called for all Arabs to rise up and drive the British from their countries, and welcome the Axis forces as friends and liberators.

The ceremony was short, as least for Rommel. He left Mussolini to bask in the glory, as he addressed the Egyptian people, standing next to the king, promising Italy's friendship to the Arab people and Islam in general. Rommel returned to his headquarters in Cairo and quickly began making plans for the resumption of the offensive. Fuel and water was now available in plenty. Alexandria was quickly restored as a port by Italian and German engineers. Axis forces took up positions on the Suez Canal, and quickly forced the British forces to retreat across the Sinai Desert. Rommel agreed to send the newly arrived 5th Panzer Division, along with the Italian infantry division, *Genoa*, now known as Afrika Korp III, south. Their objective was to move up the Nile and link up with the Italian forces that had invaded the Sudan from Italian East Africa. The 15th Panzer Division would be assigned to Afrika Korp II, along with the Italian armored *Ariete* and the Italian infantry division, *Savona*. The 7th and 12 Panzer Divisions and the Italian infantry division, *Brescia*, would make up Afrika Korp I. Rommel was anxious to resume the offensive on August 15.

Chapter 12

THE SUN NEVER SETS ON THE BRITISH EMPIRE?

As Rommel prepared to resume the offensive in Egypt, the situation in the Balkans began to heat up once more. After the Soviets occupied Bessarabia and Northern Bokavina, the Hungarians began making demands that Romania return Transylvania. This mountainous region was transferred from Hungary to Romania after the First World War. The region had a mixed population of Romanians, Hungarians, Germans, Turks, Slavs and Jews. The Romanians made up about 50 percent of the population and the entire region was annexed to Romania. Now, the Hungarians wanted Transylvania returned, and their demands threaten to explode into a war between the two Balkan countries.

Hitler decided to intervene. After the Romanians submitted to Soviet demands, King Carol asked Germany for protection and settle the dispute. Hitler was more than pleased to oblige because of the valuable Romanian oil wells, and he did so without consulting Stalin, which he was suppose to do under the Nazi-Soviet Pact. Hitler sent two divisions to Romania, but as tensions grew with Hungary, Hitler decided to act to ensure German domination over the entire Balkan peninsula. Hitler sent Ribbenstrop, with the assistance of the Italian, Ciano, to mediate between the two countries. It was agreed that the northern half of Transylvania should return to Hungary. The settlement caused political convulsions in Romania, forcing King Carol to abdicate. Through the SS, Hitler supported the rise of General Ion Antonescu as dictator of Romania. To back him up, Hitler sent additional German troops, ten divisions, to Romania, and agreed to train the Romanian army, bringing it up to German standards.

On August 13, the Luftwaffe began its assault on England's airfields, airplane factories and radar stations, in force. Up till now the air raids on Britain were small, but now the Luftwaffe began a serious effort to win control of the skies over the British Isles, or so that was what was being reported by the Germans through their coded messages. The German OKW was confused when Hitler insisted that he knew that the British had broke their Enigma coding machine. His generals insisted that it was impossible to break the code, but Hitler said that his instincts warned him that the British had do ss—enough to learn much about their true intentions. So he began sending orders that made it seem as if Germany was preparing to invade England before the end of September. After all, it seemed the next logical step after the fall of France.

Acting according to Hitler's orders, the German Navy began gathering thousands of barges and other boats that could be used to ferry large numbers of troops across the English Channel in the ports of northern France and the Low Countries. At the same time, the German Army began constructing fake barracks, building phony tanks and doing everything possible to convince British reconnaissance flights that everything was being done to gather a huge invasion force to invade within the next six weeks.

During the second half of August and into September the melees between German and British aircraft increased and grew more intense. The destruction of planes continued to increase on both sides, but the British loses outnumbered German loses. British pilots were being killed at twice the number of German pilots, and the British were having a difficult time training replacements. British airfields were being destroyed faster than they could be repaid and the destruction of British radar stations were making it difficult for the Royal Air Force to predict where they attacks were going to take place.

Churchill was becoming desperate. He had ordered British bombers to begin dropping bombs on German cities, targeting civilians, in hope that the Germans would divert their attacks from the air force to British cities. Many in Germany, including Goering, began calling for retaliation for the attacks on such Germany cities as Berlin, Hamburg, Bremen and those within the industrial Rhur district. But Hitler refused to take the bate. He refused to change the Luftwaffe's orders and continued with the assault on the British Air Force and airfields. He knew that so long as he did, Churchill could not release troops, tanks and aircraft necessary to defend Britain from the threat of a cross-channel invasion and reinforce British forces in North Africa and the Middle East. He insisted that the war could only be won by breaking the spine of the British Empire.

In the water surrounding the British Isles, German U-boats were busy sinking British merchant ships. With the introduction of a total war economy in October 1939, the German U-boat fleet had rapidly grown into a force that was sending 70 percent of goods headed for the British Isles to the bottom of the ocean. By the middle of August, the situation in Britain was becoming critical. Vital goods necessary for maintaining the war effort was become scarce. Rationing had to be introduced and people were beginning to starve. Many wondered if there would be enough fuel and food to get them through the winter?

In the skies over England, the RAF's 600 single-seat Hurricane and Spitfire planes were meeting the challenge of Germany's Luftwaffe with heroic bravery, but they numbers were decreasing. Although German loses were also high, German factories were now producing twice as many aircraft as the British, and very soon the British were about to be introduced to a new and terrifying threat that would appear in the skies over England. The first of the Luftwaffe's new jet fighters were ready to take to the skies in September.

After Mussolini had spent several days as the guest of King Farouk, he returned to Italy to celebrate the creation of his New Roman Empire. For several days Rome was the site of parades and huge crowds, but back in Egypt, Rommel set about preparing for the resumption of the offensive into the Middle East. Rommel was anxious to put an end to the war. He realized that eventually both Germany and Italy would have trouble dealing with the Arabs. He knew that the Middle East was going to be a hotbed of ethnic and religious conflicts, and desired to conclude the war before these disputes exploded. Though he did not think much of Mussolini's grandstanding, he did agree with the Italians that King Farouk and the Egyptians could not be trusted. Despite his misgivings about the reliability of the Arabs as allies, he was becoming a German Lawrence of Arabia. Egypt was placed under Italian jurisdiction, and an Italian Civil Commissioner was appointed, while a German officer would be appointed to support the Italian commissioner.

On September 7, Rommel crossed the Suez Canal and then occupied the Sinai, which the British had abandoned. Wavell was forced to withdraw and defend Palestine, because of the growing unrest. There Hostilities between Jews and Arabs escalated as Zionist groups began to arm themselves in anticipation of the arrival of the Germans. The Zionists were divided between the Irgun Gang, which had suspended hostilities against the British after the Germans invaded Poland, and the Stern Gang, led by Avaraham Stern, who considered the British a greater evil than the Arabs. Stern felt the Germans were destined to win the war and wanted to work with Germany in resettling Europe's Jews to Palestine.

In anticipation of the British being driven out of Palestine, the Grand Mufti of Jerusalem, Amin Muhammed el-Husseini, called for all Arabs in Palestine to rise up against the British and the Jews and welcome Rommel's army as a liberating force. He spoke to Rommel, trying to convince him to organize an Arab Legion to fight alongside his troops. Rommel was polite and thanked him, but informed him that there would not be enough time.

Rommel kept the XXI Italian Corp in Egypt along with a small German detachment, while Afrika Korp III moved south, up the Nile into the Sudan. Afrika Korp I was station between Port Said and Ismailiya and crossed the Sinai along the Mediterranean coast, while Afrika Korp II would cross the canal near the port of Suez. Rommel sent out his Luftwaffe reconnaissance to discover if the British had tried to fortify the Sinai. The reports informed him that the British had withdrawn to Palestine. The Italian Fleet had sailed to the Palestinian coast and began bombarding the British forces, while the Luftwaffe struck up and down Palestine, providing cover as Rommel's two corps raced across the Sinai desert.

Wavell set up his new headquarters in Ammam, in Jordan. His supply line ran along the desert road from Jerusalem, through Amman to Rutbeh in western Iraq, to Baghdad and down to Basra on the Persian Gulf. He withdrew all British forces from the island of Cyprus to reinforce the defensive line that he established in Palestine. It ran from El Arish on the coast to El Quseima and then to the east. It actually was a series of forts connected by minefields. Wavell would make a last stand here in hope of holding out until reinforcements reached Basra. If he was lucky, he could gain enough time force his reinforcements to establish a base of operations in Iraq and continue to struggle from there.

When Rommel's two panzer corps reached the British positions they were greeted by heavy fighting. The British forces fought with heroic determination. The minefields knocked out many of Rommel's tanks, but they could only slow his panzers down. After heavy fighting, the 7th Panzer Division was able to break through British lines after Rommel's 88mm guns, combined with Stuka dive bombers, blasted a path through the line just south of Abu Aweigila. The 7th Panzer Division raced north toward Kafr Shan and Rafah on the coast, cutting off

British forces near El Arish, while the 12th Panzer Division passed El Quseuma on the north, and took El Auja. The fighting continued for the rest of the day, but by the evening of September 18, the British could no longer stop the German panzers from racing north, into Palestine.

Further to the south, the 15th Panzer Division and the Italian armored *Ariete* division met tough resistance by the Indian Division, but after twenty-four hours of vicious fighting, the German and Italian tanks broke through and made for the Dead Sea. The British were now withdrawing throughout Palestine, trying to make for Jerusalem before they were surrounded and cut off from escaping into Jordan, by way of the Allenby Bridge across the Jordan River. On September 20, Rommel entered the holy city of Jerusalem.

News that Rommel had entered Jerusalem spread throughout the Middle East, causing crowds to fill the streets of most cities. In Beirut, Damascus, Ammam, Hafia, Baghdad, Basra, Tehran and many other cities, Swastikas appeared on walls and waved from windows. Rebels rose up calling for a holy war against Great Britain. I had become apparent to Wavell that he could no longer remain in Ammam. The threat of Arab rebellion could easily transform British territories into quicksand which could engulf all his forces everywhere. Wavell informed London that he intended to withdraw to Iraq as quickly as possible.

Churchill was furious. He sent word to Wavell to remain and fight on the Jordan River, but even if Wavell wanted to obey his order, he did not have the forces necessary to make a stand with a hostile Arab population in Jordan. On September 21, the last of the British forces were retreating east along the desert road toward Rutbah in Iraq.

On September 20th, Marshal Petain, as President of Vichy France, declared that France was in a state of war with Great Britain. German and Italian aircraft began landing at airfields in French Syria, by way of Italian aircraft carriers, where they began attacking British forces in the Middle East. In Palestine a guerilla war broke out between Arabs and Jews. Thousands of Jews were attacked throughout the region and hundreds were killed. In places like Tel Aviv, where Jews outnumbered Arabs, Zionist groups took retribution on the Arab minority. The Germans had to step in and restore order.

While the Germans were trying to establish order in Palestine, the British were withdrawing to Baghdad. Wavell hoped to establish his headquarters in the city, but Iraq was already in a state of rebellion. This landlocked country, except for a small coast on the Persian Gulf, was centered on the fertile river valley centered on the Tigris and Euphrates Rivers. Two principles pipelines pumped oil from the oil across the Middle East to the Mediterranean. One of the pipelines crossed into Vichy France, while the other crossed Transjordan to its outlet at Haifa. Both pipelines had been shut off by the British. Wavell had given the order to destroy both pipelines as he retreated.

The Germans had maintained an extensive espionage network in the Middle East. They were able to make allies with Arab nationalists through the Iraqi leader Rashid Ali el Gailani. Rashid Ali was a plump, little, bespectacled man of middle age, with a large Semitic nose who was a Nazi sympathizer. With the support of Iraqi military officers known as the Golden Square Society, and support from the Germans through Syria, he led a rebellion on September 25, driving out the pro-British regent Emir Abdullah Illah, who ruled in the name of the young King Faisal II. The British Ambassador, Sir Kinahan Cornwallis was placed under house arrest in his embassy. Rashid Ali threaten to kill every member of the embassy if the British tried to oppose his putsch, which was a devastating blow to the British. Iraq produced 15 million tons of mineral oil, as opposed to the 6.5 million tons produced in Romania, which was Germany's main source of oil. All of northern Iraq was quickly secured by Rashid Ali. From French Syria, German He111 bombers and twin-engine Messerschmidt fighters began attacking the British posts in Iraq. During July and August, the French fleet had transported additional troops to Syria, which invaded northern Iraq on September 27, occupying Mosul and Kirkuk with the help of the 22nd German Airborne Division.

Rommel was informed of the developments taking place in Iraq, and considered it a blessing. He learned that the 287th and 288th Brandenburg companies, commanded by Rommel's old friend, Colonel Menton, had arrived in Syria and was moving through northern Iraq, where he would link up with 40,000 Iraqi soldiers loyal to Rashid Ali. Rommel wrote Hitler immediately. "We will defeat and destroy the British Army now in the Middle East and sweep through Jordan and Iraq. With the entire Mediterranean coastline, from Gibraltar to Haifa, in our hands, supplies are arriving in North Africa and Palestine unmolested. There is nothing standing in our way of driving east into Persia and Iraq and take possession of the oil fields, creating a base for future operations in central Asia and India."

Wavell finally reached Habbaniya on September 26. The airfields there were already under assault from German aircraft stationed in Syria. With Baghdad in a state of rebellion, Wavell realized he could not hold Habbaniya and decided to withdraw south to Basra and Abadan, where he would dig in and wait for the long promised reinforcements. British aircraft provided air cover and Wavell still had about fifty tanks that could break through any obstacles that the Iraqis might tried to put into place and stop his retreat. Reports of events in Persia were already reaching Wavell. He learned that a stream of German armaments had begun to flow into Persia, by way of Turkey. With German success in North Africa and the Middle East, the Turks began to move closer to Berlin. The SS quickly began organizing a fifth column among the 4,000 Germans active in the commercial life of Persia. They helped to reinforce the Persian army, which now included ninety German tanks. Wavell realized that his situation was hopeless, and now doubted that the reinforcements would ever arrive in time. The best he could hope for was preventing another disaster like the one in Flanders.

On the afternoon of September 7, Goering and Milch stood on a cliff near the English Channel, as they watch the armada of Luftwaffe aircraft flighting overhead, on their way to England. There were over 1,000 aircraft in all, with fighters outnumbering bombers by two to one. On the sides of the fighters, the pilots had painted lightning bolts, Thor's hammers, shark teeth and eagle's heads, but on one fighter was painted a Mickey Mouse crewing a cigar. It belonged to Germany's top ace, and the plane he was piloting was revolutionary. His name was Major Adolf Galland and he was leading a group of sixty He280A-2a jet fighters that were part of the armada. They were the first of their kind off the assembly line and ready for operations. Within two weeks, another 150 jet fighters would join them in the attack over England. Galland was twenty-eight-years-old and had flown almost 500 missions in Spain, Poland and Western Europe. Also piloting a He280A-2a was Werner Moelders, Germany's number two ace. Galland had 57 kills to his credit, two more than Moelders.

When the fleet of aircraft reached the British Isles, they were greeted by British Hurricanes and Spitfires. Britain had lost almost 1,000 fighters and was having trouble replacing those shot down. The Germans were able to outproduce the British in aircraft production, and thus keep the pressure on the RAF. The total mobilization of Germany's economy caused aircraft production to triple in the last nine months. The RAF had lost 230 of its original 1,000 pilots, and was finding it impossible to replace them fast enough. And now, with the introduction of the new jet fighters, it seemed that Britain was about to face a threat that they could not withstand, even with all their guts and courage.

Britain had just passed through five days of continuous, around the clock assaults by the Luftwaffe. The RAF command tracked the approach of the armada which began dispersing and head off toward their designated targets of airbases and radar stations that stretched from Ventnor on the Isle of Wight in the west, to Dover in the east and as far north as Duxford and Dunwich. The skies over the southeast region of England were alive with dogfights, as British fighters rose into the sky to intercept the German flying armada. At first, everything went according to the usual routine. Spitfires and Hurricanes began diving and whirling about in an aerial ballet with German Me110 medium range fighters and the Bf109 long range fighters, as German bombers unleashed their deadly cargo on British airbases and radar installations. The British were doing exceptionally well, considering they were exhausting both their manpower and machines, and it seemed as if the Germans were doing more dodging than fighting and trying to lull them into higher altitudes. Then it happened. As the British fighters rose ever higher they were set upon by flying machines that raced by them with speeds so fast that the British pilots were unable to identify them. The German jets began flying at the British fighters so fast that at first the British had no idea what was happening. Panic set in at first until the British pilots were finally able to get a good look at the new German fighters. They reported the appearance of the German jets back to command headquarters. In most cases, it was the last thing they did.

The Jets raced about the sky at speed reaching 560 miles per hour. By the time the raid was completed, the British lost 135 fighters while the Germans loses included 15 Messerschmitts and no jets. The results were devastating for the RAF. Goering was jubilant at the news of the success of the new He280A-2a fighters. Throughout the next week the British continued to suffer loses almost as higher. News of the devastation of the RAF was reaching the British public, even with the restrictions on the news media that Churchill had imposed. It was becoming apparent to everyone within the British government that they could not continue to takes such loses for much longer. Even Churchill was beginning to face the reality that with the new jet fighters, the Luftwaffe was now methodically exterminating, not only the radar stations and airbases, but the entire Royal Air Force. He seemed baffled that Hitler had not turned to the destruction of British cities, even after the assault on German cities that he had ordered.

Dewey ran an effective campaign comparing Roosevelt to Wilson, reminding the voters how Wilson, like Roosevelt, promised to keep America out of the First World War, and then, as soon as he was swore in, the United States entered the war. His strategy was to transform the election into a plebiscite on America's entry into the war. Though most people were more sympathetic to Britain than Germany, the majority of Americans harbored resentment and suspicion regarding Britain's motivation. Dewey attacked Roosevelt as a warmonger who served British interests before America's. He was able to tap into a large number of disillusioned, anti-Roosevelt Democrats. Dewey also attacked FDR for thinking he was better than Washington, who refused to run for a third term. He even hinted that Roosevelt entertained illusions about being President for life. He reminded people that the New Deal was a failure and that now FDR was restoring to militarism to rebuild the economy. "The program of building up the Armed Force as a means of rebuilding the economy was successfully tried by Adolf Hitler and the Nazis," Dewey said. "This program took Germany into war. Will Roosevelt's program take America into war?" He then asked, "Do we have to have a war to get jobs?"

As Britain continued to loose the war, Dewey warned the voters that Roosevelt was taking America down a very dangerous road. The anti-war sentiment was growing as Britain continued to loose battles in North Africa and the Middle East. Most of Roosevelt's campaign was conducted by his supporters because of his health. He tried explain that he wanted to remain above the campaigning.

Dewey's hard-hitting campaign finally forced Roosevelt to abandon his strategy of "remaining about the fight" and begin actively campaigning. Roosevelt was forced to repeat a promise over and over. He would say in almost every speech, "While I am talking to you mothers and fathers, I give you one more assurance. I have said this before, but I shall say it again and again and again: Your boys are not going to be sent into any foreign wars." Roosevelt reminded people that he kept them out of war, but also that he pledge to keep the United States strong, as the only means of preventing the Axis from attacking America. He then charged that Dewey's campaign was supported by what he referred to as "appeaser fifth columnists," by which he meant Nazis. Without saying it outright, he was saying that Dewey was a Nazi.

Throughout October the campaign grew intense. Dewey's support continued to climb. The Republican Party had been split at the beginning of the campaign. What was referred to as the Eastern Internationalist wing of the GOP had opposed Dewey and refused to support him after he picked the isolationist Senator Arthur H. Vandenberg as his running mate. But as Britain continued to loose the war, this wing of the GOP began reconsidering its opposition to Dewey. Polls showed Dewey moving up in the polls until finally, by the end of October, the race was neck-and-neck.

As the Battle of Britain continued to go badly for the British, and Wavell was retreating into Iraq, Churchill's War Cabinet was beginning to collapse. The Labor Party leaders in Parliament began calling for Churchill's resignation. The leader of the Labor Party, Attlee, was telling everyone of his dissatisfaction with the way the war was progressing, and that Labor was blaming Churchill for it. Within the Conservative Party, the anti-Churchill faction was gaining strength. The peace faction was openly demanding that Churchill resign and began looking toward Lloyd George as his replacement. George, who opposed the war and admired Hitler, was now telling everyone who would listen that he was willing to take the post of Prime Minister if he was called to do so, for the good of Great Britain. He said that he could obtain such a peace with Germany that would ensure the survival of the British Empire.

On October 7, Joseph Kennedy met privately with Halifax, and his assistant, Alexander Cadogan. The two men had become the *de facto* leaders of the opposition to Churchill. They met at Cadogan's private residence. The meeting was held in the greatest secrecy.

"Thank you for coming," Halifax said to Kennedy. "I'm sure I don't have to worry about anyone learning of your presence here tonight?"

"You needn't worry," Kennedy said. "I made sure that Churchill's men were not following me."

"You can be assured that no one within a five block radius saw the Ambassador arrive here," Cadogan said. "I have our people stationed everywhere. If he was followed, they would have noticed and intercepted the good Ambassador three blocks away."

Kennedy looked from Halifax to Cadogan and then back the Halifax. He recognized the graven look of desperate men. "I expected this meeting to be a matter of the upmost importance when I received you call, asking me to meet and make sure no one knew of it, not even the President," Kennedy said. "But all this cloak and dagger business?"

"I'm truly sorry for it," Halifax said, "but it could not be helped. We're faced with the complete collapse of the British Empire. Britain is facing total and utter defeat. It has fallen on our shoulders to see to it that the British Empire survives."

Kennedy swallowed hard. The Foreign Minister's word had the impact of one of the many bombs that the Germans were dropping on Britain. "I understand," Kennedy said. "But why did you ask me here?"

Halifax looked at the American and shook his head. "I doubt that you do," he said. "I do know that you have opposed this war from the beginning. The truth is, Mr. Ambassador, we would not be in this fix if it had not been for the prodding of your government. Chamberlain never wanted this war, but your President applied certain pressure that caused Chamberlain to declare war last September. Britain is not the great power it once was. It survived the Great War much reduced in strength. Your United States came through that war much greater in power and influence. It was do to the pressure of your government that Great Britain was forced to permit our alliance with Japan to elapse without renewal in 1922. The Japanese wanted to renew it, but your government opposed it. And, because Britain was in such financial debt to the United States, we could not refuse. It has been like that for the last twenty years. Our Mr. Churchill, who is half American, by the way, has piggishly pushed his way into becoming the Prime Minister, and he has refused to consider peace offers made by the Germans, even at this late day—peace offers that are, if I might say, quit generous. We have just receive another offer by the German government, through a third channel, that has made it clear that Germany does not desire the destruction of the British Empire."

"Really?" Kennedy said. "What are the terms?"

"Simply that Germany dominate Europe and Britain maintain control of her empire."

"Why hasn't Churchill accepted?" Kennedy asked. "Surely he must realize that Britain will be crushed in the next three or four months?"

"Because of his bullheadedness!" Halifax said as he slammed his fist on the table. "He's locked himself into a course of action that he cannot detach himself from. His belief that Britain could hold out until the United States enters the war has brought our Empire to the brink. If the Germans had not begun their offensive in the Mediterranean, perhaps Great Britain could have held out alone against Germany and her allies, until the United States enters the war, but that is an impossibility now. We have got to make peace, but Churchill still refuses to consider this possibility, so long as your Mr. Roosevelt remains in the White House. He has bet everything on the eventuality that Roosevelt will get reelected to the third term and then bring the United States into the war early next year."

Kennedy listened carefully to what Halifax was saying, and was amazed at his frankness. Someone of Halifax standing and experience in foreign affairs and diplomacy never spoke so open and frank. He began to understand just how desperate was Britain's situation. "So Britain's survival as a great power depends on Roosevelt being defeat?" Kennedy asked.

"The very existence of the British Empire depends Roosevelt being defeated," Halifax said.

"Then you're asking me to compromise my country for the sake of Britain?" Kennedy asked.

Halifax looked at Kennedy and knew that the question was probing. "If Roosevelt is reelected, your country will go to war. Do you want your country to go to war?"

Kennedy lowered his head and scratched his forehead. "I have sons," Kennedy said. "I do not want them to go to war."

"Then take these," Halifax said as he nodded to Cadogan.

Cadogan pulled a bunch of papers from a leather bag and handed them to Kennedy. Kennedy began examining them for a few minutes. He then looked up at Halifax and then at Cadogan. Both wore somber masks. "This is political dynamite," Kennedy said. "Are they real?"

"Oh yes," Halifax said. "They are telegrams that our Mr. Churchill and your Mr. Roosevelt have been passing between themselves for over a year now. They prove that Roosevelt and Churchill have been working together to plunge all of Europe into war, and that Roosevelt has been promising to bring the United States into the war after he his reelected."

"What do you expect me to do with these telegrams?" Kennedy asked.

"I believe there are people in the United States who will publish them before election day," Halifax said. "I leave it to your judgement and wisdom to see to it that they are made public. If you love your country as much as I love mine, you will do what is right, just as I have done so today."

CHAPTER 13

VICTORY!

Wavell tore up Churchill's orders to hold Basra and Abadan. His men was exhausted and he was running low on supplies and armament. The reinforcements that Churchill promised had not arrived, and Rommel's forces were moving south toward the Persian Gulf. All of Iraq was now under the control of Rashid Ali and Persia had joined the Axis. The entire Middle East was lost and Wavell knew that India was threatened. On October 7 the Luftwaffe began bombing the ring of fortresses that he had constructed. He knew that it was just a matter of time before Rommel attacked. His only hope was to withdraw to Kuwait. It might buy him time until the reinforcements arrived.

Rommel was inspecting his troops, talking to his men and making his presence felt where ever he could. He liked mixing with his men and sharing in their hardships. He took his meals with them and ate the same rations as they did. He had just finished lunch when Colonel Menton arrived.

"Ah! Colonel, I'm glad to see you," Rommel said as Menton saluted him.

"I came as soon as I received your orders," Menton said. "My men are moving into place as we speak."

"I understand they performed with excellence in the north," Rommel said.

"The 287th and 288th are among the best companies in the Wehrmacht," Menton said with pride.

"That's why I recommended them to the Fuehrer for this operation," Rommel said. "They did excellent work in northern Iraq, securing the region before the

British could or the Soviet intervened. And now they will have to preform once more. Let me explain."

Rommel pulled out his map and explained to Menton the British situation and where his companies would attack. "It all comes down to one last push and the British will find themselves swimming for their lives in the Persian Gulf," Rommel said. "They're in a desperate situation, dug in along this line with the Gulf to their backs. It's Flanders all over again."

"Could they withdraw to Kuwait?" Menton asked.

"Yes, but then we'll simply pursue them, if they do," Rommel. "But I doubt if they can hold out. The attack will begin tomorrow morning. Are you men ready?"

"They haven't had time to rest, but they don't need to," Menton said. "We'll be ready when you give the order."

"I thought you would," Rommel said and smiled. "Now Colonel, you had better return to your companies."

"Yes, General," Menton said as he saluted and then departed.

The next day the assault on the British began when the Luftwaffe began bombing their positions. Stukas flew low over British positions, as German artillery began lobbing shells at the British dug in around Basra. Next, Rommel's panzers began the assault, supported by his flak guns. The British fought bravely, but Wavell realized that they could not hold out for long. They were outnumbered and outgunned four to one. He thought about retreating to Kuwait, but decided against it. All around him his men were being butchered. No one even entertained surrendering, but he knew that they could never stop the Germans. His only hope was a withdrawal. Finally, he gave the order to withdraw, not to Kuwait, but to Abadan, where boats were waiting to ferry his men away, but it was too late. He received word that the German panzers had surrounded him. Basra was cut off. He decided to surrender and save as many of his men as possible.

At noon, on October 9, Rommel accepted the surrender of the British forces in Iraq. He made sure the British troops were treated well. They had performed heroically and deserved to be treated as soldiers. Once the surrender terms were completed, Rommel drove south until he reached the Persian Gulf. He stepped out of his vehicle and looked out at the blue waters that stretched south before him. The sun was bright and almost blinded him. He turned to his adjutant.

"We've done it," he said. "We've carried out the Fuehrer's orders."

"What does this mean, sir?" the adjutant asked.

Rommel turned to him and smiled. "Why, this means the war is over."

News of Wavell's surrender caused the British Parliament to explode with calls for Churchill's resignation. Both the Labor and Liberal Parties threatened to withdraw from the war coalition. News of a new German peace offer, and Churchill's refusal, had been leaked. Clement Attlee, the head of the Labor Party, rose in Parliament and demanded that Churchill step down.

"The Prime Minister promised to keep the Empire intact," Attlee said. "He promised that the United States would come to our aid. He asked for three or four months. Well, three or four months have passed and Great Britain still stands alone, and our Empire is being overrun by the Germans and Italians. All of Europe is allied against us and now Iraq, Iran and perhaps even Turkey will enter the war on the side of the Axis. Our military strength is wavering and at its lowest point. We have been driven from Europe, from North Africa and now the Middle East. The entire Mediterranean is lost. Egypt and the Sudan are lost and our troops were driven out of Somililand. The Italians have invaded Kenya and all of French Africa has joined the Axis. The Axis is poised to attack India, while the British Isles is on the brink of starvation. Our ships are being sunk and the Germans dominate the skies over our island homeland. Only by the grace of God have the Germans not bombed our cities to rubble. In the East, Australia and New Zealand are now at the mercy of any power that might decided to enter the war against us, and there are rumors that we might loose all our possessions in the Far East. And now, we face financial ruin. All this could have been avoided if only we had accepted the peace offers extended to us by the enemy in June and again in July. But our Prime Minister told us not to worry. He told us that we could preserve—that we could hold out until the Americans came to our aid. But now we are telling Mr. Churchill that he must go! That he must resign! Now!"

The vote taken was overwhelming. Churchill's war government had collapsed. "You must be reasonable, Winston," Halifax said. "The war is lost. If we don't try and make peace now, the Empire will disintegrate."

Churchill was sitting, dressed in his flowered Chinese dressing gown. He looked dejected. In one hand he held a glass of whiskey and in the other, the telegram informing him that his government had collapsed. He raised the glass of whiskey to his lips and swallowed the entire content and then sighed as the telegram escaped from his numbed fingers and floated to the floor. Halifax could not help but feel pity for Churchill, though he hated him and thought he would enjoy delivering the telegram and the news. But he did not feel like gloating. Perhaps it was the reality facing his country—the future that awaited the British people. They could have accepted a honorable peace anytime in the last four months.

The Empire was still in tact, but now, Britain laid prostrated before a victorious Germany.

Churchill finally looked up at Halifax. "You must be enjoying this?" he asked.

"No, Winston, I'm not," Halifax said. "How could you think that I would have time to gloat over your predicament when our Empire and nation have suffered just a devastating defeat?"

"The fools!" Churchill said. "They're all cowards. They betrayed me. I could still have won this war. I could still win this war. I won't resign."

Halifax now felt nothing but contempt. "Always you, Winston," he said. "You think it's always about you. But it isn't. It was your egomania that brought our Empire to it knees. All because you had to feed that tremendous ego of your's. The truth is—you're not important. You're nothing. So why don't you go? Go to America. You should, you know. You won't be very popular in Britain after today."

Churchill rose to his feet with clinched fists, but Halifax almost laughed at seeing Churchill standing before him dressed only in his flowering grown. "They'll get what they deserve. The British lion has become a pussycat. A nation of pussies," Churchill said.

Halifax shook his head and turned to leave.

"I could have won!" Churchill shouted one last time.

It was Halifax who suggested that Lloyd George become the new Prime Minister and charged with the mission to seek peace terms from Berlin. The elderly statesman accepted. George was a friend of Hitler's and opposed the war. Like Petain, he belonged to the generation of the First World War, and like Petain, he agreed to try and save his country in its most darkest hour.

Halifax convinced Parliament to permit Churchill to flee England, though many called for his arrest. Churchill was able to convince Roosevelt to permit him and his family to sail to the United States on board an American ship. He pleaded that he was, after all, half American. Besides, Halifax argued, it would be better for the country. The Germans might want Britain to turn him over to them for war crimes. Both Roosevelt and Churchill were lucky that Kennedy had already left Britain to return to the United States. At first Roosevelt refused to consider Churchill's request, but when Churchill threatened to reveal everything about his communications with Roosevelt, the President agreed to his request. On October 24, Churchill, his wife and children sailed into exile.

News of Churchill's fall and Britain's request for an armistice with Germany had the effect of a bomb going off in the White House. Roosevelt spoke in Dayton, Ohio on October 12. "Our course is clear, he told the audience. "Our decision is made. Despite the surrender of Great Britain, we will continue to pile up our defense and our armaments. We will continue to help those who resist aggression, and make sure that the aggressors do not violate the territory of the Western Hemisphere. The United States is the last hope for freedom and democracy in the world, and we must remain secured against all possible aggression. We must not surrender to fifth columnists within the United States who would make deals with the devil for the sake of compromise." Roosevelt continued to make the suggestion that Dewey and the Republican Party were in league with Germany and were supporters of Hitler.

Hull, Morgenthau, Welles, and Hopkins were all gravely concern about how the news would affect the outcome of the election on November 4, but not as concern as Roosevelt was about what Kennedy would do or say once he returned to the United States. He cabled Kennedy while he was in route to Boston that he wished to meet with him as soon as he arrived, and asked him to say nothing until they had a chance to talk. Roosevelt knew that Kennedy was angry and feared he was going to turn against him and confirm Dewey's charges. He hoped to bribe him with promises of support for his son's intended run for governor of Massachusetts, or even agreeing to support Kennedy if he decided to run for the presidency in 1944. Roosevelt even offered to make Kennedy the chairman of the Democratic National Committee, at Byrnes' suggestion.

Kennedy announced that he wanted to take a vacation as the reason for his return to the United States. He debarked for the United States on October 5 and received the news of Churchill's resignation and Britain's request for peace terms while en route. When he received Roosevelt's cable for a meeting, he tore it up. He had no intension of seeing the President. When his ship docked in Boston, he immediately met with William Randolph Hearst, the powerful owner of a national chain of publications and newspapers, along with Hearst was General Robert E. Wood, head of the newly formed America First Committee. Wood had sent Kennedy a letter begging him to reveal the truth about Roosevelt's secret commitments to Great Britain. Kennedy had hesitated about betraying Roosevelt, but as Britain's fortunes declined, he became convinced that he had to stop Roosevelt from winning a third term. Also present was Henry Luce, editor-in-chief of Time magazine, and his wife Clare Booth. Henry Luce and his wife had urged Kennedy to return to the United States and speak out against Roosevelt. It was Luce who had set up the meeting.

Kennedy turned over the telegrams that Halifax gave him to Hearst and Henry Luce, along with his own documentation of Roosevelt's duplicity and involvement in encouraging Britain, France and Poland to confront Germany, as well as promises of American support, which included the eventual entry of the United States into the war on the side of the anti-German coalition. Wood was excited and Hearst was grateful.

"This information is too important to remain the property of just one, or even a few newspapers," Hearst said. "I believe it should be passed on to every publication that is willing to give it maximum coverage."

"I agree," Henry Luce said. "We should send copies to Robert McCormick and Joe Patterson."

"At the least," Hearst agreed. "You have done your country a tremendous service, Joe," Hearst said to Kennedy. "We won't forget it, and we'll make sure that the American people understand just how great a service you are rendering to your country."

Kennedy was pleased. He knew that if his oldest son, Joe Kennedy Jr., was ever to have a chance to be elected President, he would need the assistance of such powerful leaders within the news media.

Roosevelt kept asking Byrnes if he heard from Kennedy.

"He wired us today, thanking you for the invitation to dine at the White House," Byrnes said, "but he didn't say anything about accepting your invitation. His ship should dock today. I don't like it. The telegram seem vague. I don't trust him."

"Did you state that I wanted to seem him immediately and that he should not speak before I had a chance to talk to him?" Roosevelt asked.

"Yes, Mr. President," Byrnes said. "All he sent was he was thanks."

"He deliberately waited to answer until the day he docked," Roosevelt said. "I don't like it. If he tells the press what he knows, it'll destroy us at the polls."

"The defeat of Britain has already caused the public to question our policies," Byrnes said. "Dewey is gaining in the polls."

Roosevelt thought for a moment. "See if you can reach Kennedy at once," Roosevelt said. "Tell him I'm prepared to announce my support for his son for governor. Tell him I'll appoint him to a cabinet post. Hell! Tell him I'll make him the King of England, if it'll get him to come here at once."

"Yes, Mr. President," Byrnes said as he left the Oval Office. "I'll do my best."

"I only hope it'll be enough," Roosevelt said.

The headlines of the *Herald American* of New York read, *FDR PROMISES TO GO TO WAR!* The story explained in detail how Roosevelt promised aid to Poland if they resisted German demands in 1939, and the promises of aid to Britain and France if they came to Poland's defense. It went on to explain how Roosevelt promised to bring the United States into the war against Germany if he is elected to a third term. Similar headlines appeared in Robert McCormick's *Chicago Tribune,* Joe Patterson's *New York Daily News* and his sister's paper, the *Washington Times-Herald.* The sensation shook the entire country, and Roosevelt's standing in the polls took a beating. Overnight the entire political landscape of the United States was transformed. Huge America First rallies were held protesting Roosevelt's treasonous activity. Charles Lindbergh, the famous pilot who flew over the Atlantic solo, and was sympathetic to Germany, joined the America First Committee and called for Congress to open an investigation into Roosevelt's foreign policy. He charged that three groups, the Roosevelt administration, the pro-British business interests within America, and the Jews were engaged in a conspiracy to bring America into the war in Europe. There were even calls for the arrest of Winston Churchill, who had just arrived in the United States, but calmer heads reminded people that Churchill broke no American laws.

Though Lloyd George had not held office for almost twenty years he was willing to accept the call for him to become Prime Minister. He had been waiting for the call that he believed was inevitable for almost a year. As a member of the once powerful Liberal Party. He was considered the obvious choice to lead Great Britain in her darkest hour. His role was similar to that of Marshal Petain in France, but unlike Petain, he possessed an advantage that the aged French marshal lacked. Lloyd George was an acquittance of Adolf Hitler. He had visited the German Fuehrer at the Berghof before the war, and considered himself an admirer of Hitler. Hitler, in turn, had come to respect and admire the elderly British statesman.

Lloyd George had reflected on the First World War and had come to consider the struggle a terrible catastrophe for all of Europe—for the victors as well as the vanquished. He feared that this war would be even worst and expressed his fears to the *Daily Mirror's* Cecil King at the beginning of the year. He referred to the war with Germany as "this damn crazy war." Churchill feared George and wanted to bring him into his War Cabinet as a way of neutralizing him, but George refused all of Churchill's offers. He believed that Churchill's leadership was leading Britain to the edge of the abyss, and as the victor of the Great War he believed he would be asked to accept the responsibility to seek the best possible peace terms with a victorious Germany.

Lloyd George was asked to come to Berlin and speak with Hitler. Hitler had no desire to humiliate Britain as he did with France. All of Berlin was excited at the prospect of Lloyd George's arrival in Berlin. He arrived at the Chancellory building and was ushered through the long corridors and hallway that was designed to impress all visitors with the grandeur of the new Germany. Hitler was waiting for George in the courtyard of the Chancellory. When he arrived, he was welcomed by Hitler and then the national anthems of Germany and Great Britain were played before the two leaders entered the conference room. Once inside, the mood had suddenly become less formal.

"I regret that we should meet again under such conditions," Hitler said. "I remember fondly your previous visit to Germany."

"So do I," George said as he sat across from Hitler. "But as one who understands the new Germany, and who considered this war a terrible mistake, I'm glad that I could be the one who now represents my country at this hour."

Hitler nodded as the translator explained what George had just said. "I too am glad that Great Britain still have men of vision among their ranks who could step forward to represent the English people. That's why I requested that we meet in private before any official signing of terms." Hitler fixed his blue eyes on the old gentleman. He knew he had won him over when they had first met and he hoped that he could continue to exert a similar influence over him now. "I never wanted this war, especially with your country. I have always felt that the German and English were two nations that should be working together to secure the supremacy of the White Race. I have stated this many times and have even written of the hope that our two countries could have been allies, in my book, *Mein Kampf*. And now that this war is concluded, I hope that we can salvage my dream of an Anglo-German alliance."

Lloyd George was moved. Hitler was not speaking to him as the leader of a victorious country that had just defeat his country. He was offering a way out for Britain. Suddenly, George was moved by his own sense of destiny. "Yes. I agree," he said with obvious relief.

Hitler continued. "The peace that I'm offering includes the following terms. First, Great Britain will have to surrender Egypt, Palestine, Jordan, Cyprus, Malta, Gibraltar, the Sudan, Somililand, Kuwait and return those former German colonies under the trusteeship of the British Empire. Other modifications to Britain's colonies in Africa might be made via-vie French colonies, but Britain will be compensated for territories lost with the Dutch East Indies and Belgian territories in Africa. Secondly, Britain must accept the supremacy of Germany on the continent of Europe. Third, the British government must permit the return of the Duke of Windsor, the former King Edward VIII, to the throne as Edward IX. Fourth, Winston Churchill must be turned over to Germany. We do not intend to prosecute him for war crimes. After all, I understand that Churchill is an artist—a painter. I too am an artist and painter. I can identify with him. He will be permitted to live comfortably in Germany, but under our direction, he won't be able to cause any more mischief. Next, Britain must release those individuals who were arrested at the outbreak of the war because of their sympathies toward National Socialism and Fascism. Britain should not only maintain possession of her navy, but it is imperative that she does. The British Navy is vital for the security of the White Race throughout the world. Lastly, Great Britain and Germany will sign a military alliance guaranteeing the integrity of each other's country and possessions."

Lloyd George listened very carefully to Hitler's offer and when the German leader had finished, George did not hesitate to agree to the terms. "Considering everything that has happened, I believe these terms are very generous," George said. "I don't foresee any problems by my government accepting the terms. There is only one problem."

Hitler frowned. "What might that be?"

"Churchill had already fled to America," George said.

"He wasted no time in fleeing," Hitler said.

"I'm sure there will be no problems regarding the rest of the terms," George reassured Hitler.

Hitler was pleased. "Then we can consider the first week of December as agreeable for a peace conference?"

"That would be acceptable," George said.

"And the location will be Berlin," Hitler said.

"Also agreeable," George said. He really had no choice, but he was amazed at Hitler's generosity. "Then it's agreed," Hitler said. "We'll convene a Congress of Berlin, which will he held in the first week of December. In the meantime, representatives of your government will be sent to Berlin in three days to begin the planning of the Congress. Italy, Spain, Sweden, Slovakia, Lithuania, Egypt, Iraq, Persia, Finland, France, Denmark, Norway, Hungary, Romania and Turkey will also be present. All issues regarding the New Order in Europe and the Mediterranean will be discussed and peace treaty will be signed at its conclusion."

Hitler then stood up. Everyone else in the room, including Lloyd George, did the same. Hitler looked deep into the old man's face. His eyes seem to glow, not with the same vengeance that filled them when he had signed the armistice with France. George was moved as Hitler fixed his gaze on him. He thought he saw tears in Hitler's eyes. Hitler extended his right hand to the British leader. George took his hand, but before he could shake it, Hitler grasped his hand with both his hands and held it.

"What we have agreed to here, today, will lay the foundation for a new order in Europe that will ensure the survival of our civilization and race's survival for centuries to come," Hitler said with deep emotion. "Don't ask me how I know this, but I do. I know this as surely as I know that the sun rises every morning. You will go down in history as the savior of your nation."

George was moved beyond words. His voiced failed him. He nodded in agreement as tears rolled down his face. Afterward, he dined with Hitler, who treated him as if they had been allies instead of enemies. When George left Berlin the next morning, he was confident that he had achieved what Chamberlain failed to achieve in 1938. He had achieved peace in his time.

All across Germany people celebrated the end of the war. Huge rallies and parades were planned for November 9. That date was usually reserved for the remembrance of the failed *putsch* of 1923, but this year all of Germany would celebrate Germany's greatest victory. On that day all Berlin was out in celebration. It was declared the most glorious day in the history of the German armed forces. The three branches of the Wehrmacht were out in force along the parade route with units of the Waffen SS. Troops carried battle flags and rode in tanks and armored vehicles. People threw flowers as infantry soldiers marched along the route. People lined the parade route, waving and cheering. Arms were extended in the Fascist salute. Nazi flags were everywhere and huge banners hung from every building. SA and SS troops desperately tried to restrain the throng of enthusiastic people celebrating the victory.

Hitler rode in the front seat of his staff car. He stood up as the car slowly made its way along the parade route. Even with thousands of people lining the route, he needed little protection. He had made it a habit throughout his long career of traveling through Germany's cities, towns and villages in an open car with no protection. People often surrounded his car as they desperately tried to shake his hand. Today was no different. He made a very easy target for anyone who wanted to take a shot at him, but in all Germany there was no one who desired to try. Even those Germans who opposed Hitler considered him the greatest German in German history this day.

Similar celebrations took place in Italy. The ancient city of Rome was filled with cheering people shouting for Mussolini with cries of *Duce! Duce!* Mussolini appeared before the Roman people and declared the rebirth of the Roman

Empire. Black Shirts were everywhere celebrating. Other countries also witnessed masses of people celebrating the end of the war. In Spain, Franco's popularity also rose. The Spanish people were concerned about their leader bringing Spain into the war against Britain after Spain had suffered such a terrible civil war just a few years before. But the war was short and victorious, and Franco was able to use this victory to help heal the wounds that scared the Spanish people during their terrible civil war.

There was subdued celebrations in other countries that were allies of Germany. In Sweden the people celebrated more that was war was over than its victorious conclusion. In Denmark, Norway, Romania and even in France, people were celebrating the end of the war. There were even thousands of Germans and Italians in the United States that began celebrating the victorious Axis powers. In New York City huge crowds filled the streets of German and Italian neighborhoods cheering Hitler and Mussolini. Similar demonstrations of support for Germany and Italy took place in other American cities where there were large German and Italian populations. Even many Irish-Americans celebrated the defeat of Great Britain in hope that Ireland would now be unified and free of British domination.

The revelations of Roosevelt's diplomatic intrigue by Joseph Kennedy had tipped the scales in the American Presidential election. Up to then, a large percentage of the American people had remained undecided who to vote for. With the defeat of Great Britain, many people were concerned about the relations of the United States with the new, German-dominated Europe. Everyone knew that Roosevelt was hostile to National Socialist Germany, but they had believed him when he promised never to send "American boys to war." He had often told them that he wanted peace, but now the revelation that Roosevelt wanted to take the United States into the war shocked millions of Americans. The American people had always believed that their government represented their views, and more than 80 percent of the American people felt that the United States should not become involved in Europe's war. They had believed Roosevelt when he told them that he agreed with them, but now they felt betrayed by Roosevelt. Support for Roosevelt evaporated quickly and on November 6, Roosevelt only received 19 million votes to Dewey's 31 million.

Dewey's amazing victory also translated into Republican victories in both the House of Representatives and the Senate. The Republicans once more controlled the government and many Democrats, especially those in the South who hated Roosevelt, were willing to work with Dewey. People felt that Dewey could ensure America's place in the new order that had descended over Europe. "I can't believe how many people are cheering the victory of Germany," Dewey said as he paced his office in New York City. The little man from the Mid West who had made a name for himself fighting crime in New York was meticulously dressed.

"Most of them are of German and Italian descent," said John Foster Dulles. "They feared and opposed the United States entering the war against the countries of their ancestry."

"But they're American first," Dewey said. "Or, their suppose to be Americans first."

"I'm sure they are," Allen Dulles said. He was John Foster's brother. "But they hated the idea of having to send their sons to kill their relatives living in Germany and Italy. And they remember how Germans, even those who were good Americans, were persecuted in the Great War."

Dewey stopped in his tracts and stared at the Dulles brothers. His lips pressed together as he nodded. "I can understand that," Dewey said.

"There are many others, especially Irish-Americans, who're celebrating Britain's defeat," John Foster Dulles said. "I understand Northern Ireland might be returned to Ireland."

"And there are many other people in this country who are pleased with the end of this war," Allen said. "Their not necessarily pleased with Germany's victory, but they are relieved that the United States won't be dragged into another war in Europe."

"I understand that," Dewey said. "I also understand that I must unite the American people under my leadership if I'm to find the proper place for the United States in this new world order. That's why I have asked you both to join my administration."

The Dulles brothers nodded their understanding.

"John, I want you to be my Secretary of States," Dewey said. "Your contact with Sweden will be most advantageous in the months ahead. After all, Sweden was Germany's ally. Your contacts in Sweden can help us negotiate a new understanding and accommodation with the new Europe."

John Foster Dulles had been in the employment as the corporate attorney to Wallenberg Holding Company, which was owned by the Swedish banking brothers Jacob and Marcus Wallenberg, who ran the powerful Swedish, Enskilda Bank. Their corporation owned American Bosch, which was a subsidiary of a powerful German concern in Frankfurt. Through their financial dealings, the Dulles brothers had made many contacts and friends in both Sweden and Germany. They had advocated that a Dewey administrations should seek accommodations with National Socialist Germany.

I'll do everything in my power to fulfill this objective," John Foster Dulles said.

"Please understand that I don't like these Nazis any more than Roosevelt did," Dewey said. "But I hate the idea of going to war even more."

"There is the matter of Japan," Allen Dulles said. "Roosevelt had slapped several embargoes on certain items that Japan desperately needs for their economy. His intentions were clear—he hoped to provoke Japan into attacking the United States."

"I know," Dewey said. "I want you, Allen to look into this matter once we take office. I don't want to go to war with Japan any more than I do with Europe. I believe my new direction will help to united, first the Republican Party's Eastern wing of international financiers and the more traditionalist populists in the heartland. With control of the Congress, I hope to unite all America once more, and use that unity to once and for all put an end to the economic depression that the American people have suffered under."

Dewey sat behind his desk. "Gentlemen, we have a brand new world to learn to live in. I surely hope that we can forge a new place for the United States in this world."

Winter had come to Moscow early in November 1940. Snow was falling from the gray canopy of storm clouds that covered central Russia. The mood within Stalin's office was just as cold and gray.

Stalin had watched the growing power of Germany and dread the consequences of this development for the future. He was not pleased with Hitler's interference in Finland and Romania. German troops were pouring into Hungary, Lithuania and Romania at an increasing pace. He was receiving unpleasant reports of increased concentrations of German forces all along the Soviet frontier. And now, German troops stood in Iran and the Middle East and threatened the Soviet Union from the south. Stalin sat behind at the end of a long table, doodling with his red crayons as, Zhukov and Molotov sat on either side of the table. He was drawing pictures of the new German jet fighters. Stalin did not look at either man. His pock-marked face remained fixed on his drawings, as he spoke. "We have nothing like these jet fighters," Stalin said. "The German jets purged the British RAF from the skies over England. If the Germans attack the Soviet Union, will their jets purge our skies of our air force?"

Stalin's crafty eyes now looked at first Zhukov and then Molotov, as he stopped doodling. Neither the foreign minister or general spoke.

"Why don't we have jets?" Stalin asked. "Why did we not know of their existence?"

Zhukov now spoke up. "We did know that the Germans were working on jet technology," he said. "Our informer within Berlin had transferred intelligence that they were developing jet technology, but we had no idea that they had succeeded in actually building a operational jet."

Stalin took a puff on his cigarette and leaned back as he examined Zhukov. He never trusted his generals, and had killed thousands of them just a few years ago. He wondered if he should have killed Zhukov. But most of the generals who were killed had fought in the civil war and knew that the official propaganda that Stalin manufactured, declaring that he played a role in the Bolshevik Revolution and the Russian Civil War, and was an equal to that of Lenin in leadership, was a lie. He killed them and raised a younger generation of officers who did not take part in the revolution and civil war, to the leadership of the Red Army. Zhukov was one of those officers. Stalin smashed the cigarette in the ashtray.

"Comrade General," he said. "I made the non-aggression treaty with Germany to buy us time. I did not expect the Germans to defeat the British and French so soon. I had hoped that the capitalist and Fascist powers would rip each other apart for several years, much like what happened in the Great War. I had hopped to use that time to build up our armed forces so that we would be ready to attack after both the capitalists and fascists had exhausted themselves. Our Red Army would have over run all of Europe. But now we are confronted with the reality of a Europe dominated by the Fascist Germans. The Fascists also dominate all of the Mediterranean, the Middle East and Africa. And now, even the British Empire is at their disposal. The Germans are more powerful than we could have imagined just one year ago. And with the victory of the Republican Dewey as President, in the United States, we could expect a possible alliance of the capitalist United States and Fascist Europe against the Soviet Union."

"I doubt if the capitalists in the United States will form an alliance with Fascist Europe," Molotov said.

"I doubt if you have a brain in your head," Stalin said contemptuously. He had very little respect for Molotov. He had only elevated him to foreign minister to replace the Jew, Litinov, so that he could negotiate with the anti-Semitic Nazis. "We have succeeded in placing over two hundred Communist agents within the Roosevelt administration. I doubt if we'll be able to accomplish this with the new administration in Washington."

"The new American President owes his victory to American isolationists," Molotov said. "The new American President will not enter into an alliance with Germany."

"Perhaps not," Stalin said. "But, without the capitalists in Western Europe confronting the Germans, Germany is free to attack us. And this means that we'll have to stand alone, against the united forces of Europe. We need allies."

"We could find allies in Belgrade," Molotov said. "Perhaps even the Japanese will agree to an alliance, or at best, a non-aggression treaty. There will eventually be war between Japan and the United States. It's only a matter of time."

"The Foreign Minister speaks true," Zhukov said. "It would be to our advantage to seek some kind of accommodation with the Japanese. The Fascists in Europe will attack us. So we must attack them first. It'll be better if we don't have to worry about a two-front war."

Stalin agreed. "We should try and sign an alliance with Yugoslavia, and perhaps even Turkey," Stalin said. "And we must face the reality that war is only a matter of time. How soon could we be ready to attack the Fascists?"

"If we begin an extensive program of mobilization, we could be ready to attack the Germans in either June or July of next year," Zhukov said. "I have already begun preparing a plan of attack."

Stalin nodded. "Very good, Comrade General," he said. "I want to see this plan as soon as possible."

"I can have a first draft for you to examine in January," Zhukov said.

Stalin was pleased. "In the meantime, I want you to contact Berlin and arrange a meeting," Stalin said to Molotov. "You should go to Berlin and meet with Hitler. Try and discover his plans and buy us more time. Perhaps we could even set up a meeting between myself and Hitler. If I could win his confidence, perhaps we could prevent the Fascists from attacking us before we're ready to attack them?"

"I will send the request at once," Molotov said.

"I would like to meet this Hitler," Stalin said. "I do admire him, though he must be destroyed. What a piety he's not a communist."

Hitler left Berlin for the Berhof shortly after the victory celebrations to meet with his military leaders. He understood the need to begin planning for the invasion of the Soviet Union. Hitler knew that he had to be ready for the invasion by next spring and wanted nothing to interfere with his plans. He had already ordered Jodl to draw up such plans, and now he wanted all the branches of the Wehrmacht to be informed of his plans. Jodl had returned a few days later with plans for Hitler to review and make alterations. Now Hitler was prepared to present the plans to his staff.

The huge Great Hall at the Berhof was transformed into a war conference room. Keitel and Jodl of the OKW were present, as were Brauchitsch and Halder from the army, Reader and Doenitz from the navy and Goering and Milch from the Luftwaffe. Others were also present. They included Ribbentrop, Speer and Borman, as well as Himmler and Heydrich of the SS. Everyone was present and waiting for Hitler to arrive. The Fuehrer's reputation as a military leader had rose considerably in the last fourteen months. Most of the generals considered Hitler lucky when it came to political matters when the War in the West had begun, but most felt he lacked a true understanding of military affairs. But with the continuous string of victories over the last fourteen months, he was considered a Twentieth century Napoleon. It seemed he possessed some kind of instinct that never failed. Some, like Himmler, like to speculate that the old Germanic gods of war were whispering advice in the Fuehrer's ear. Hitler often spoke of hearing an inner voice, speaking to him whenever he had to make difficult decisions. And now that the War in the West was over, Hitler refused to demobilize the Wehrmacht. Everyone knew Hitler planned to invade the Soviet Union. He often spoke of his desire to destroy Jewish-Bolshevism, as he referred to the Soviet Union. Now, they would learn of his future plans.

Hitler finally arrived with his Deputy Fuehrer, Rudolf Hess. Hess took a seat with the others as Hitler stepped up to a podium that was erected, facing those seated in the Great Hall. From where Hitler was standing, he could look over the heads of those assembled and view the great purple and white peeks of the Alps that loomed in the distance. Hitler felt as if he and the others were Olympian gods assembled upon their noble mountain domain, planning the future of course of humanity.

"Gentlemen, I welcome you today to discuss plans that will ensure that the Greater German Reich that we have created in the last fourteen months, will never again fear attack from any continental enemy," Hitler said as his blue eyes roamed from face to face. He wanted to look into the eyes of each and everyone present. He no longer saw doubt, even in those eyes belonging to Brauchitsch and Halder. When Hitler first spoke of attacking the Soviet Union, many felt it was a terrible idea. Even Keitel had his doubts, but now no one questioned Hitler's wisdom. "Now that the War in the West is over, we have already set about the task of reorganizing all of Europe, the Mediterranean, Africa and the Middle East, as well as assisting the English in restoring control over their Empire. All the resources at our command must be mobilized for the eventual conflict with Russia. And conflict with Russia is inevitable. There is no way Europe could continue half-National Socialist and half Jewish-Bolshevik.

"When we entered into an alliance with Stalin, we did so to prevent the Western powers from bringing Russia into their planned war against us. And they did plan that war, for we have discovered documents in Paris that clearly show that Britain, with the backing Roosevelt, planned to partition the German Reich if they were victorious. Stalin had refused to enter the war on their side because they would not permit him to annex eastern Poland as well the Baltic States and territory in the Balkans. Stalin entered the alliance with us so that he could buy time to build up his armed forces and make preparations to attack us and overrun all of Europe. Stalin hoped that the war between the Western Powers and the German Reich would degenerate into a war of attrition that lasted years, much as happened in the Great War. But that's not how the war turned out. We had other plans."

Hitler smiled and waved his hands as those assembled applauded and laughed.

"Well," Hitler continued, "how disappointed and shocked Stalin and his Jews must be when our victorious forces overran the decadent Western forces and eventually went on to swept them clean from the Mediterranean and the Middle East. But this had the negative affect of causing the Bolsheviks to speed up their rearmament. According to the SD's intelligence reports a gigantic rearmament effort has been instituted since last summer. With total victory over the West, we can expect the effort of rebuilding the Red Army to continue to accelerate. Plus, reports that the Bolsheviks are using Soviet trade missions, which were permitted under our Non-aggression Pact, to spread Communist propaganda and organize Soviet cells, in our plants and factories. We have seen how quickly Stalin occupied the Baltic States and tried to pressure Romania and Finland into surrendering territory. Only our intervention prevented Stalin from invading both countries and annexing them to the Soviet Union. But these two regions, Finland and the Balkan, might still offer Stalin excuses to attack us in the future. This is especially true now that we have control of the Middle East and its inexhaustible supply of oil. This is way I have begun talk with Turkey, Yugoslavia, Bulgaria and Greece, to pull them into our New Order. And now that England is our ally, and we are responsible for assisting them in securing their control over India, Stalin feels encircled. He has no place to expand. It's just a matter of time before Stalin sends his Red Army steam rolling over Europe. For this very reason we are secretly sending troops to Finland.

"I have been asked, why I have not begun to demobilize our forces. The answer is simple: we are going invade the Soviet Union in the spring. Sometime between May 15 to June 10 our forces will roll into the Soviet Union and knock down the whole rotting Jewish-Bolshevik structure. But to do this, we must first make every preparation necessary to invade. This is why I ordered the design of a new tank, which I hope will be ready by the time we invade. And it's well that I did. We've learned from our Japanese friends that the Soviets have a new tank, the T-34, which the Japanese encountered in their brief war in Mongolia, with Russia in 1939. We have also developed out new jet fighters, and a long range bomber, the Ural Bomber, is presently under construction. With the bomber we will be able to devastate industrial centers deep within the Soviet Union. With the jet fighters, our Luftwaffe will sweep the skies over Russia clean of the Red Air Force. We should have at least 250 divisions, of which 180 will be German and the rest will be contributed by our allies.

"But if we are to defeat Russia, with its vast territory, population and resources, we must do it quickly. Three objectives must be achieved. First, we have to penetrate deep into Russia's European heartland. This includes a vast triangle between Leningrad in the north, the Crimea in the south and Kazan in the east, on the Volga. Within this triangle lies most of Russia's heavy industry, but even more importantly the majority of the Russian population. So long as this region remains in Soviet control, Stalin will be able to raise countless new divisions from its huge manpower potential. Secondly, we must win the hearts and minds of the vast Soviet population. I have no love for the Slavs. Most are subhuman Asian-mongrels, but if we come as liberators, the entire Soviet monstrosity will cave in as millions of Soviet citizens rebel against their Bolshevik masters. Once we have established out mastery over the Soviet Union up to the Volga, we can then proceed with our colonization program. Millions of colonists from Europe, and perhaps from North and South America, will settle in European Russia. We will sift through the native population and choose those whom we deem racially suitable for Germanization, and give this vast region a new German character. Third, we must convince the Japanese to attack the Soviet Union in the Far East. Stalin won't be able to mange fighting on two fronts."

Once Hitler had completed his introduction, he order Jodl to explain the plan that the OKW had devised for the invasion of the Soviet Union. Everyone rose and gather around a large table located before the huge window overlooking the view of the Alps. Maps had been spread across the top of the table and everyone jostled to get a good position. Jodl began to explain the plan.

"As you can see from the frontier with the Soviet Union," Jodl said, "the Lithuanian salient acts like a dagger aimed at the heart of the Soviet Union—Moscow. The Red capital is only 650 Kilometers (424 miles) from our forward position in Lithuania. The OKW's plan divides our main invasion force into three fronts: Army Group North, Army Group Center and Army Group South, with two secondly fronts, Army Group East in Turkey and Iran and the Finnish Front. AGN will contain 23 infantry division, 4 panzer divisions and 5 reserve divisions. It will be stationed in northern Lithuania and will strike north, through the Baltic States and south of Lake Peipus and Lake Ilmen. Its aim is to link up with the Finns moving south toward Leningrad and between Lake Lagoda and Lake Onega.

"AGC will be stationed along a stretch of frontier beginning in Lithuania, and terminating south of Warsaw. It will contain 66 infantry divisions, of which 20 will be French and 15 panzer divisions, which will be divided into four panzer armies. It will also have 12 reserve divisions. Two of its panzer armies will be located just north and south of Vilna. The third will be in East Prussia and the fourth just south of Warsaw. AGC will attack due east, toward Moscow, using its panzer armies to entrap the Soviet forces in great encirclements along the way. The third group, AGS, will include 68 infantry divisions, of which 32 will be drawn from our allies, and 8 panzer divisions, broken into two panzer armies. It will have 15 reserve divisions. Additional German troops will be stationed in Finland. They will move through Lappland. In AGE, Rommel will strike north from Iran with 3 panzer divisions, and reinforced with additional infantry. Turkey will also attack across its border into Georgia.

"In support of the ground offensive will be over a thousand jet fighters, as well as the four engine, long range Ural Bombers that will strike deep into the Soviet heartland. Moscow, Kursk, Kharkov, Stalingrad, Gorki and other cities on the Volga, as well as those industrial centers in the Ural mountains and beyond, once we have advanced deep into Russia, will all fall under the smashing terror of our new Ural Bombers."

Jodl stopped for a moment and looked about the table. His eyes finally fell on Hitler, who seemed to be nodding in agreement with everything he had said.

"Can we raise such a large force?" General Halder asked. His bristly mustache seem to wiggle as he spoke. The perpetual frown he usually wore after the previous year of victories, was no longer present.

"Herr Reich Minister Speer, why don't you answer that question?" Hitler interrupted.

Speer appeared cool and calm with the professionalism of his architectural background.

"Our economy has been on a total war footing for twelve months now," Speer explained. "Our production has surpassed that of England and France combined.

There in no reason why we cannot field an army of 250 to 300 divisions. And with the integration and mobilization of all of Europe's industrial output combined, we could even field an army of 400 divisions in the next two years."

"But that won't be necessary, gentlemen," Hitler interrupted. "The campaign to conquer the Soviet Union won't last that long. By playing on the hatred of the oppressed peoples of the Soviet Union, we will be viewed as liberators. They will rise against their Jew-Bolshevik slave master. All we'll have to do is kick in the front door and the whole rotting edifice will collapse." Hitler looked up at the window, toward the sun-baked mountain peaks that loomed across the valley. "The world will hold its breath!"

Several black Mercedes were making their way through the winding forest road that led high into the remote Sudeten Mountains in Lower Silesia, about thirty miles from Breslau. The road led them up, into a valley tucked away deep within the looming mountains. A heavy mist clung to the tree tops that lined both sides of the valley, like a huge canvas. The valley was unusually active with thousands of men working. Railway tracks ran through the valley, and seated on the top of a hill was a nineteenth century type building with arched windows overlooking the valley.

When the automobiles came to a halt, an SS guard rushed up to the one with banners belonging to the Reichfuehrer of the SS, and opened the door. Out stepped Himmler in his black uniform. With him was Victor Schauberger. Schauberger immediately looked about, amazed at the activity in this isolated part of the world. He felt he had been transported to another realm, belonging to another world.

"As you can see, Herr Doctor, we are making excellent progress," Himmler said as his eyes examined Schauberger through his round glasses.

"Yes, I can see that," Schauberger said. "Very impressive."

"Did you expect anything less?" Himmler asked. He did not wait for an answer. "The facility will be completed in three months. Everything is being constructed according to you specifications, right down to the tiniest detail."

"I'm sure it is, Herr Reichfuehrer," Schauberger said, still overwhelmed by the gigantic magnitude of the project.

"Let me show you some of the features," Himmler said and then led him to a mine shaft next to the building. Men were moving in and out, carrying equipment. Most of them were slave labor from Poland, made up of mostly Jews. They were guarded by SS guards. Schauberger chose to ignore it all, overwhelmed as he was by the scope of the project. This was the old Wenceslas Mines that the SS had coveted, because of its isolation and self-sufficiency. At the far end was a huge power plant that could consume thousands of tons of coal each day, providing enough electricity for all of Schauberger's experiments.

The mine shaft took them deep below the Earth's surface and opened into a gigantic subterranean chamber, 30 square meters, and possessing walls covered with ceramic. Hundreds of people were working, but most were technicians and scientists. Dozens of smaller chambers were being filled with equipment of every imaginable type.

"When this is completed, you will be able to conduct your research and experiments at your leisure," Himmler said.

"You did order the rubber for the walls?" Schauberger asked.

"It will arrive later," Himmler said. "You needn't concern yourself about the supplies. Everything you have requested will be provided, and anything you might need once you begin your research will also be procured for you. You have *carte blanc*, Herr Doctor. I'm most excited about the prospects of your research."

"So am I, Herr Reishfuehrer," Schauberger said. "There is no way I could possibly fail to prove my theories with such generous accommodations."

"If you succeed in breaking the secret of anti-gravity and providing unlimited free energy, the German Reich will be invincible," Himmler said.

"I'm glad to be of service," Schauberger said.

"The Fuehrer is pleased, very pleased," Himmler said.

"I'm pleased to serve the Fuehrer," Schaugberger said.

"Your work is extremely important for the future of the German people," Himmler said. "In fact, if you succeed, it will have revolutionary implications that will transform civilization as we know it today. We will have made a technological leap of a hundred years into the future, maybe even thousands of years. Any attempt by the Jew-capitalists and Jew-Bolsheviks to threaten the Reich in the future will by futile. The future will belong to us!"

To be continued.

0-595-32651-X

Printed in the United Kingdom
by Lightning Source UK Ltd.
106211UKS00002B/72